HERO

OUT OF THE BOX
BOOK 22

Robert J. Crane

HERO
OUT OF THE BOX: BOOK 22

Robert J. Crane

1st Edition

2.

Passerini
Situation Room
The White House
Washington, DC

"They came over the border in the night," Secretary of Defense Bruno "Hammer" Passerini said, using a laser pointer to draw the red dot across the map projected onto the biggest screen in the Situation Room. "On trains, for the most part, though trucks brought in some of the smaller components—"

"What am I even looking at here?" President Richard Gondry asked, his glasses catching the glare of the projection and making his eyes look like puddles of white light. "I don't need a geography lesson. You said this was important—sum it up."

"I'm trying to explain, sir," Passerini said. Five nights of this, of watching and waiting as the nation of Revelen did their thing with Russia. Now this, and he was lecturing to a college professor who was maybe the biggest idiot he'd ever met. Proving once again that education didn't equal intelligence. "Last night, Russia trans-shipped their SH-08 Gazelle missiles over the border—"

"I don't know what the hell any of that means," Gondry thumped a sheaf of briefing papers onto the table in front of him. "Do you even realize what troubles we have domestically at the moment? Wildfires in California. A hurricane churning toward the east coast. And this—this—Minnesota prison nonsense—" The president gritted his teeth together at the last.

Passerini didn't want to touch that one. He'd heard the rumors that Sienna Nealon, the metahuman criminal and apparent full-time bee in Gondry's bonnet, had somehow escaped the metahuman prison complex outside Minneapolis last night. "Sir," Passerini said, trying to manage up, "I assure you, I wouldn't be wasting your very valuable time if this weren't incredibly important and urgent. Revelen has installed missile batteries to protect against—"

"This is an allied country, yes?" Gondry asked, pushing his glasses down the bridge of his nose. In the semi-dark, Passerini could see the president's eyes. They looked like beads of black.

"Sir," Secretary of State Lisa Ngo spoke up from down the table, "we have a few nominal treaties with Revelen—the usual boilerplate—but that's all. They're not what we would consider an ally. And as Secretary Passerini is trying to inform you, they're presently making moves, along with Russia, that suggest that they are anything but friendly."

"We've been at peace with Russia for years," Gondry said. "The Cold War is over, people." He chortled. "I swear, the military is always looking to fight the last war again."

Passerini suppressed the urge to sigh through long practice. "Sir, I wasn't in the Cold War for the most part. I joined up in the last decade of it, and my experience is mostly in fighting the War on Terror. So while you think that I'm just looking to pick a fight that I understand … believe me when I tell you, sir, this is not a fight I would go looking for. Russia possesses more nuclear weapons than any other country on the planet. Getting into any sort of conflict with them is not on my priority list on any given day—"

"Now that's just blatantly false." Gondry chuckled. "You're the military. Of course you're looking for a war to fight. It's the reason for your existence."

Passerini's blood ran surprisingly cool. Normally in moments of insult, it tended hot, the Italian in him rising to the surface along with the desire to throw a choice expletive at top volume, the way his father did at times of stress and challenge. He didn't do that now, though, because he was standing in front of his boss, the Commander in Chief.

And the man had just told him, in the midst of what looked like a terrible geopolitical conflict on the rise, that he thought Passerini's job and disposition was to *make war.*

"Sir," Passerini said, voice falling to a low register that it seldom hit, "my job is not to make war. I'm the Secretary of Defense. My job is to defend the United States. If that means prosecuting a war, so be it. But I'd be a lot happier if I could do my job and never fire a shot."

"Sure you would," Gondry snorted. Good God, the man was an arrogant prick.

Passerini gathered himself and turned the laser pointer back on the new emplacements around Revelen's capital, Bredoccia. "They've also taken these Russian anti-missile systems, which normally take months or years to install, and they've emplaced them overnight."

Gondry might have been looking at him, or he might not have been. His glasses were back up, the glare preventing Passerini from gauging where the president's attention was.

"How did they do that?" National Security Advisor Bethany Cantrell asked. Passerini had seldom had contact with the National Security Advisor, which was a pretty decent indicator of how importantly Gondry viewed that role. Cantrell was a cheerleader for the administration, her national security bona fides about as serious as Passerini's interest in gardening, i.e., not remotely.

"They appear to have used metahumans to move the earth and lift the emplacements," SecState Ngo answered for him. He gave her a nod, and she nodded back. In his opinion, she was the only competent one at the table.

"Good for them," the president said. "Using metahuman labor to simplify things is the wave of the future. Too long these people have stood in the shadows, afraid to show their faces—"

"Sir—" Passerini knew full well he was risking incurring the wrath of this former academic, who, he knew by experience, hated to be interrupted mid-lecture, "they may be slave labor, for all we know."

"Don't be ridiculous," Gondry said, eyes flaring to life as the glasses slipped down his nose again. "This is Eastern Europe. There's no slavery remaining there."

The fragment of some old quote about trying to be the coolest head in the room floated through Passerini's mind, somewhat dousing the heat of his rising temper. "The point remains, sir, that in one night, Revelen has emplaced anti-ballistic missile defenses. They are now prepared in the event that someone launches on them." He debated whether to whack Gondry over the head with the facts, then realized if ever there was a person who needed whacking with facts, it was the academic Gondry, with his massive, arrogance-driven blind spots. "Sir … they're preparing for war with us."

"And with you in charge of our military, I don't see why they wouldn't," Gondry said, pulling his glasses off and handing them to his aide. "Normally, I would do this in private, but I find after the last day, I'm past the point of caring. Secretary Passerini, if I could fire you right now for your intransigence and warmongering, be assured I would."

"Sir," Passerini said, strangling off the rising alarm crawling up his throat.

"You came highly recommended to me by what is apparent to me now, *not* the best and brightest of my cabinet," Gondry said. "It took me a while to get a handle on everything once President Harmon … was assassinated, but now I know the score. I realize what's happening here, and all the little fiefdoms that each of you are trying to protect. I recognize," he wagged his finger at Passerini, "this military-industrial complex that feels the need to rear its ugly head and feed the perpetual war machine—"

"Sir—"

"Don't interrupt me," Gondry said, voice rising. "It's plain as the nose on your face that you want a war with this Revelen, one you can expand to Russia. Your saber has been at rest too long, is that it?" He shook his head. "I will not oblige you. As soon as I can muster the support in Congress to pass through a new SecDef, I'm going to replace you. Until then … do try not to burn the place down with your … impetuousness, will you?"

And Gondry left, secret service detail flowing out behind him. One of them shot Passerini a sympathetic look before closing the door. Half the room left with the president, the light flooding in from the hallway until they were gone, then the door closed to leave the Secretary of Defense alone with the Secretary of State and a few others in utter silence.

"Oh, hell," Ngo said, putting her face in her hands. Her jet-black hair flooded over her fingers. "Did that just …" She looked up at him, an expression of horror on her face. "I didn't just have a nightmare prompted by lack of sleep, did I? Did the president just—"

"Tell his Secretary of Defense he was fired, right as it looks like we're heading into a war?" Passerini asked. He sounded surprisingly calm, considering what had just happened. "Yeah. Yeah, you didn't dream it." His scalp was chilly under the thin threads of hair that remained after a lifetime of service for his country. "You didn't dream it at all."

3.

Sienna

"Welcome to Bredoccia, capital city of Revelen," "Sophie" said as she unfastened my bonds with a gentle clink, undoing a lock or something beneath the stretcher. Light streamed in through the plane windows, bright and cheerful and totally at odds with my present mood.

"Thanks," I said, sitting up as the tight metal bindings fell away. I felt a little like Frankenstein's monster sitting up for the first time. An apt metaphor, since I was apparently in the nation of Dracula now. "I'd say it's good to be here, but … well, you'd know I was lying."

"But it beats the hell out of prison, right?" "Owens" asked. Between Vlad, Sophie, and Owens, I realized I knew absolutely no one here's real name. Which was good, in a way, because it was a firm reminder not to trust a damned soul in this country.

"For the moment," I said. "Sophie" smiled. And I'm sick of using scare quotes, so … Sophie.

The plane came to a stop and the cockpit door opened to reveal a woman in a trench coat with a strange, oblong bulge at her sleeve. Her wavy brown hair partially covered her eyes; it looked like she'd been out in the rain and hadn't had a chance to style it. When she spoke, it was in the same voice I'd heard on the overhead speakers, and when her dark eyes found me, she smiled, though her expression had a little edge to it. "Last stop. Everyone off."

"Did we make a stop in the middle while I was sleeping?" I popped to my feet, causing Sophie and Owens both to take a step back out of an abundance of caution. I didn't come at either of them, though, so they didn't retreat farther.

"For fuel in New York, yes," the pilot said. "Like old times, eh, Sienna?"

I stared back at her. "Well … sure. I guess we did sort of cross paths at the Javits Center that one time."

ArcheGrey1819. That was the only name I knew her by. She was a hacker with skills so prodigious she could command fortunes for her work. I'd run across her when Jamal and I fought against a guy who had it in mind to expose the entire world's cyber secrets. Which would be bad if for no other reason than it would be like the Fappening writ large, with every person who'd ever taken a nude selfie exposed for all the world to see. I couldn't be the only person concerned that a Michael Moore nude would someday make the rounds. Jamal, Arche, and I had banded together to prevent that calamity from coming to pass. And won.

The world was, thus far, safely Michael Moore nude free. Yay us. And freedom from blindness.

Still, Arche had been in it for her own reasons, and I'd known at the time she was tied to Revelen somehow. It wasn't surprising she was involved. Just a surprise that she'd be here and flying me out of America.

"Do we have a greeting party?" Sophie asked, cool as ever.

"They're driving out now," Arche said, putting down the ramp. The plane looked like a new model Gulfstream. I rubbed at my wrists where the bonds had been tightest.

"So … I know you two have worked together before," I nodded at Arche and Owens, "on that New York job, destroying the evidence against Nadine Griffin—"

Arche and Owens exchanged a look. "We didn't work *together* on that," Owens said. "We were contracted independently."

"But you're working together now?" I asked. "For Vlad?"

Arche answered. "Yes." So succinct. She almost put Sophie to shame.

"And how do you fit into this puzzle?" I asked, turning to Sophie. "You a contractor, too?"

"I pursue my own interests," Sophie said, walking past without so much as a look.

"You're interested in me?" I asked. "I'm flattered, but you're not really my type. No offense. I know I'm coming off a long stretch in prison—"

"You were in three days." Owens rolled her eyes.

"Well, it felt long," I said. "Plus, did you catch that part at trial where they tried to blame me for what you and Arche did in New York? How much were you laughing your ass off at that moment, scale of one to ten?"

"At least a twelve," Owens said, deadpan. She headed for the ramp behind Sophie, leaving me standing in the passenger space by my lonesome. "The irony was especially delicious, me standing right behind you as they pinned my crime on you."

I made a sour face. "I can't blame you for not stepping up and saying something, really, but still … shitty."

Owens shrugged. "I dropped a building on people. Letting you take the blame is hardly the worst thing I've done."

Not even lately, in fact, since she'd killed Clara in prison. I forced a smile. "Right you are." Another reminder: these were not people I could trust.

Sophie was waiting at the exit, looking back at me. "Come on. We're leaving."

"What if I don't want to go?" I asked, planting my feet. "What if I don't want to meet Vlad the Impaler? Who thus far seems a lot more like Vlad the Spender on lots of metahuman help?"

"Then enjoy your stay in the plane, and when you decide you're hungry or wish to leave, our people outside will escort you to the castle," Sophie said, and she just walked out.

"Dammit," I muttered and hurried down the aisle. Because what was I going to do? Beat the hell out of their guards and escape over the border so I could return to the US and probable captivity without even meeting the guy responsible for—conservatively—60% of the shit that had come my way in the last year or two?

Hell-to-the-no. I was going to look Vlad in the eyes and beat the ever-loving hell out of him first chance I got. Which might not be right away given that he was surrounded by Arche and Owens, whose powers I knew, and Sophie, whose powers I didn't. Plus whatever else he had at hand. I had suspicions on that score, having tangled with a couple vampires before.

"Change your mind about hanging out?" Owens asked, smiling at me with a tiny hint of amusement or malice. Tough to tell which.

"I didn't see a minibar on the plane anywhere so, yeah," I said.

"Plus, you're a recovering alcoholic," Sophie called back to me from outside. "It'd be a shame to break your sobriety now. You've been doing so well."

"It annoys me that you all know so much about me," I said, "but I know so little about you." I stared at Owens. "Like your real names, for instance."

Another spark of snarky amusement lit Owens's eyes. "My real name? It's Yvonne."

"And your real last name?" Every little bit helped when it came to info about your potential enemies.

She shrugged. "I don't even remember anymore." And headed down the stairs built into the door.

Another lie. I had a feeling I'd be getting a lot of those here.

Leaving the stale confines of the Gulfstream behind me, I stepped out into the open air and found myself staring up at a grey sky. Mountains waited on the horizon to the east, and the city of Bredoccia stood before me, a single mighty skyscraper rising up out of a downtown that reminded me of a mid-sized US city, or maybe Glasgow … a little bit, if you ignored the mountains.

The castle I'd heard about from Uncle Friday was perched atop a mountainous rock that overlooked the city. It reminded me a little bit of Edinburgh Castle, save for the mountains that rose up behind it, framing it as though it were a foothill of the range beyond. It was only a couple miles away, maybe less. The airport, along with the city itself, was on the flatter ground beneath it.

"Huh," I muttered under my breath. Sophie, Arche, and Owens—Yvonne, I mean—were all waiting at the base of the ramp with a man in a grey suit. I took a moment to survey everything before me rather than rush down to meet them. They showed no sign of leaving, after all. Why accommodate them when I could make them accommodate me?

It was daylight, and I had a good view of the castle's details. It had old-school ramparts and towers, the kind constructed to protect against assault in the Middle Ages and before. I'd been in more modern castles, and they were like country estates, lacking defenses against siege. This one had been planned with siege in mind, for sure. The walls followed the edges of the rock it sat upon; if someone wanted to try and lay siege to it from below, they were going to have a hell of a climb to cope with if they didn't go through the front gate. A thousand feet straight up, at least.

"So that's Dracula's castle?" I asked, taking my sweet time as I descended the ramp. Nobody seemed to be impatient with me, but I hoped that was an act, because I was trying to infuriate them. Sophie's uninterested gaze may have suggested I was having little effect on her, but I figured that was just window dressing. There was no way she could spend as much time as she had with me, me at full intransigence, without getting a little pissed off. She was just really good at hiding it.

Still … something about her manner was aggravatingly familiar. I was sure she was telling the truth, that we had met before.

I just wished I could remember it.

"Sienna, this is the steward of the castle," Sophie said, nodding to the man in the suit standing at the base of the ramp, waiting. He had black hair with grey streaks, slicked back, a widow's peak making its way a good half inch down his forehead. He wore a kind of pained, long-suffering smile.

Heh. And he'd just met me.

"My name is Ian," he said, with a thick accent that reeked of old Europe, offering a hand up the ramp to me. I eyed it, shook it as I descended, and walked past his smiling face onto the tarmac, where Sophie, Yvonne/Owens, and Arche all stepped back to make way for me. Ian was already out of the way, standing well to the side of the ramp in a classic display of deference to me, the guest.

"This city looks almost modern," I said, looking at downtown Bredoccia. I was trying to count the number of buildings over ten stories. There weren't many, save for that tall one under construction. It didn't look like it'd be Burj Dubai height when finished, but it was clearly aiming to be the crown jewel in their growing city. Cranes scattered across the city hinted at a construction boom, the skeletons of other new buildings rising to take part in the burgeoning skyline.

"It's only polite to give your name when someone is introduced to you," Sophie said, and now the irritation bled through. I turned to find her standing at Ian's shoulder, looking put out for the first time since we'd left the prison.

"It's only polite to give your *real* name when you're being introduced," I said. "None of you, except possibly Yvonne here," I nodded at her, "have given me a real name, so …" I shrugged. "You really wanna lecture me on etiquette? Try not lying to your guest."

This had a definite chilling effect among my welcome party. Ian's smile was perhaps the only thing that didn't freeze, and that was because it faded, becoming just a faint curl of his bloodless lips at the corners. "Your Uncle Friday described me to you?"

"Yeah, he did," I said, staring at "Ian"—these people and their lying names and me having to overuse scare quotes—what assholes. "And I'd say it's nice to meet you, Vlad, but given all the hell you've tossed my way this last couple years …" Any trace of smile vanished from my lips, as well, "… why don't we just get down to it and start kicking each other's asses?"

4.

Dave Kory
Brooklyn
New York

"Don't you need another source before you can run this story?" Mike Darnell asked. He had wrinkles and lines stretched on top of wrinkles and lines, a face that was leathery and suntanned, like he'd really seen it, man, walked the miles of shoe leather that it took back in the pre-internet days to break stories and do real reporting.

Dave Kory didn't really go in for that kind of thing, but he respected it. And Mike. Because Mike was really the only old-school investigative reporter on flashforce.net's payroll, and so it was at least worth nodding along when he said something. Like this, for instance.

"Yeah, I know, normally," Dave said, nodding along. "Normally I'd be all over the two-source thing, but … come on." Dave could feel the glow in his eyes. "This is huge. Bigger than—I mean, it's huge-normous. And no one has reported on it yet."

The sun was breaking over the horizon in New York, and flashforce.net's offices in Brooklyn. Dave had, as per his habit, worked late into the night. Normally he wouldn't be at the office for several hours yet, but this was one of those all-nighters. He'd left the office just before midnight to get a drink at his favorite bar in Williamsburg, got the text, and now he'd been back all night. Three Red Bulls later, he was not remotely interested in going home.

Not with this story cooking, ready to hit publish on.

"If you publish this without a second source to confirm, you're setting yourself up to get burned," Mike said, shading his eyes as he scanned the page.

"I didn't graduate J-school yesterday, okay?" Dave snapped. In fact, he hadn't graduated journalism school at all. His focus had always been on the tech side of things. Writing articles was easy. Implementing a website with an interface that didn't suck? Way harder.

Flashforce.net had quickly become one of the top news sites on the internet, according to Alexa.com. Fifty million unique visitors per month. They'd displaced Buzzfeed and HuffPo in the first twenty-four months, and now Dave was looking to displace the *New York Times.*

Better yet, they made *money*. Which was more than he could say for a lot of these stupid startup sites.

"Look, I know you've got your way of doing things," Mike said, tearing his eyes from the copy and looking straight into Dave's. This was the conflict at the heart of everything, Mike, the old, versus Dave, the new. The young, maybe? That was probably better. "But if you run with this, you're asking to have your credibility shredded."

Dave plastered a stupid smile on his face. It probably looked condescending. He certainly meant it to. "Look, man, I know you've been at this for just short of forever, but lemme apprise you of how shit has changed—it's not about getting one story right anymore, okay? Even though this is, for sure, right. As rain."

"Oh?" Mike settled back, leaning against the desk. He was really listening, so Dave laid it on. It was good to teach an old dog a new trick or two. Maybe he really could learn. "How so?"

"See," Dave said, "you're right. Maybe, without the second source, this doesn't hold up to the old-school model of reporting, the two sources thing—"

"And we usually like people to go on the record, too," Mike

said.

Dave tried not to roll his eyes. He failed. "Yeah, whatever. So let's say that everything I've written here is wrong." He broke into a wide smile. "So what? Our users? They're going to keep coming back because who else are they going to go to for quick news? They're loyal. They've got nowhere else to turn, really, not for this format. As long as it's not news that's going to seriously piss them off, they don't care if we make a mistake. They know we're human. And we still get the clicks to the story while it's up, which means the advertisers still pay us, which means *you*," he pointed at Mike, "get paid. While other reporters continue to get fired and laid off from these local papers and dime store blogs because they don't drive enough traffic." He folded his arms in front of him. "Simplicity itself. See?"

"So that's it, huh?" Mike asked. There was a little flicker behind his weathered eyes. He'd only been on staff for a few weeks. Learning the ropes of the new media reality, that was how Dave viewed him.

"Yep," Dave said, looking around. There were only a few people here. Night shift/early morning shift was shit duty. Everyone who had some seniority preferred to work noon to eight. He glanced at his story one last time and clicked the mouse button to publish it. "Clicks and views, my friend. Traffic to the site. These are the holy grails that we have discovered, the tools that allow us to thrive in a world where most of the dinosaurs are going or have already gone extinct."

"That's called a mixed metaphor," Mike said. "It's sloppy writing."

"Yeah, whatever," Dave said. The story was published, and he flicked his browser to the main page of flashforce.net.

There it was, in all its glory, top of the page.

SIENNA NEALON ESCAPES FROM PRISON

"What about the truth?" Mike asked as Dave brought up the TIMES VIEWED counter. He always liked to watch once something went up on the main page. How many times his article was viewed determined whether he wrote a follow-up or moved on to something more interesting to their audience.

Sienna Nealon? She was always good for clicks.

Clicks meant traffic to the site.

Traffic to the sight meant eyeballs on the ads.

Ads meant money.

"Yeah, yeah, the truth," Dave said. The counter was climbing. A thousand clicks in less than a minute! Hell yes, this story had legs. He was going to have to write a follow-up for sure. Even without anything fresh … no new sources … where could he take the story? "Top Five Places Sienna Nealon might have fled," he muttered under his breath.

"You don't even know for sure she's escaped," Mike said, "and you're already speculating about where she might have fled?"

"Gotta feed the beast, bud," Dave said, spinning around in his chair and grinning at Mike. This guy was going to be a project. Maybe you really couldn't teach an old dog new tricks. "You'll get it," Dave said anyway. Better to avoid conflict. He had a follow-up story to write anyway.

"Thanks for the tips," Mike said, nodding. He folded his arms in front of him and off he went. He'd showed up about an hour ago. Early shift, and he hadn't even been asked to cover this morning. Wow. Crazy that anyone would voluntarily be up at this hour.

Dave turned his gaze back to the counter. Five thousand clicks already! Boom. Yeah, this was going to be a good day. And he needed to get that follow-up going NOW NOW NOW. He'd make it a listicle, a slideshow, making each possible destination into its own page with a little background coverage, come up a reason she'd go there. Each page of the listicle was good for a click each. That'd really drive the page traffic numbers up … and if he could make it ten locations … hell, fifteen? She'd been enough places in her storied career—yeah, that'd really rack up the page counts.

He started making his list, keeping one eye on the counter as he began to compose the follow-up. Damn, this was going to be great.

5.

Sienna

Vlad smiled at me, a toothy grin that didn't show the abnormally long canines you might have expected from the inspiration for Dracula. "Well, I must say, it is a pleasure to meet you after all these years. As you might imagine, I have heard so much about you. From the news … from my spies …"

"I bet almost 12% was true," I said, staring into his sky-blue eyes. There were flecks of grey in there, and they were quite striking. I was assessing him for danger, from the top of his pointed widow's peak down to his tasteful black shoes. His hands were neatly clasped behind him, and he didn't exude the aura of menace that Friday had described. When Friday had met Vlad, he'd experienced something so horrifying that he was left catatonic for two weeks afterward.

There was none of that present. In fact, Vlad was almost … chipper.

"It is interesting how reputation works, is it not?" His accent sounded like it had been dragged through Europe until it had picked up stray sounds from every language on the continent. "I hear about you, you hear about me, but neither of us truly knows the other. We only know what we have been told, in some cases by … less than reputable sources, yes? Why, I am impressed you even recognized me, based solely on your uncle's description."

"I've also seen you with my own eyes, once before." I tossed that out there, and it prompted Vlad to raise his dark brows. I didn't explain it, because that would end the torture.

"Interesting," Vlad said, trading a look with Sophie. "Because I have not been in your presence before, and you have never been here before."

"It is interesting, isn't it?" I walked past, nodding at the city of Bredoccia beyond him. "So … why here? Of all the gin joints in all the world?" I came up alongside his shoulder, but faced in the opposite direction, like we were passing one another and stopped for a little chat.

He smiled, either because my question had tickled him or he liked that I'd rebuffed his inquiry about how I'd seen him when we'd never met. He didn't need to know that it had been in a time-travel vision when I'd clashed with Akiyama a few months prior.

"It was a quiet place in an unquiet world," Vlad said, doing a fine job of controlling his curiosity. Old school.

"Translation: there was no one here with enough power to oppose you," I said, looking at the skyline. "How long have you had this place in your stranglehold?"

"It is hardly being strangled," Vlad said, and Sophie shifted behind him. She was offended; he was not. Interesting. "Revelen is in the middle of a renaissance of power. Last year, we peacefully annexed Canta Morgana, a jewel of the Baltic Sea. This year we have concluded a pact with the Russian Federation that will allow us unprecedented access to their resources, military and economy." He stretched a hand around, encompassing the city. "Talk to the citizens. You will find they are pleased with their fortunes of late."

"Yeah, I'll get right on those man-on-the-street interviews," I said, "right after I learn to speak … uh … whatever the local language is."

"Almost everyone here speaks English," Sophie said. "It's taught in schools alongside the native language."

"Smart," I said, letting my gaze drift over Arche and Yvonne. "Were you two educated locally?"

Arche didn't even bother to answer. Yvonne shook her head.

"I'm not from here."

"Why didn't you ask me that?" Sophie focused her attention on me. The sun was making her squint.

"You predate public education systems," I said. "By a considerable margin, I'd guess."

Vlad looked at her. "She's calling you old."

Sophie's face showed a flicker of something, but it was too quick to register. "I got that."

"Look, I'm kinda … I was gonna say tired, but even well-rested, my tolerance for bullshit is really low—" I started.

"That, I have heard," Vlad said, nodding.

"Because I told you," Sophie said.

"—but standing here, surrounded by liars, fresh off a prison sentence and breakout?" I looked at each of them in turn. "My patience is ultra-thin. Like the level of thin that condom manufacturers only wish they could get to without totally losing structural integrity."

Vlad looked at Sophie. "Was that subtext about her boyfriend and their struggles with intimacy, do you think?"

"She's standing right there. Ask her yourself," Sophie said.

"I am not—my boyfriend has nothing to do with this," I said, my face burning. "And I don't have one anymore." Vlad's left eyebrow rose. "Don't get any ideas there, old guy. I'm not interested in becoming someone's child bride, especially not to some terror legend of the Carpathian Mountains, Vigo."

"That … oh, that was excellent," Vlad said, nodding at Sophie. "See, she tied in both *Ghostbusters*—Sigourney Weaver, see?— and my reputation." He actually clapped. "Well done."

"Oh, you get me, you really get me," I said dryly. "Still not marrying you, if that's what you've got in mind. Sovereign tried that, he ended up—"

"Yes, we are all aware of the fearsome way in which you handled him," Vlad said, nodding. "Far be it from me to become your new nemesis. This is not why I have brought you here."

"Oh, yeah?" I eyed Vlad. The fact that he hadn't delivered a coup de grâce from afar suggested that maybe this was the truth. But he'd still sent an awful lot of trouble my way that had no explanation—thus far—and required one. "Then why did you bring me here?"

"That … is the question, isn't it?" Vlad smiled again. It wasn't reassuring, by any means, but it also wasn't sinister. "And I am prepared to explain, in great detail, should you choose to come further." He pointed to the castle in the distance. "Come with me and I will tell you … everything."

6.

Reed

"We've got three views on the video so far," Jamal said as I stepped out of the Concorde and into the sunlit day, suddenly embiggened by Greg Vansen to full size. Jamal was holding up his phone, brandishing it with its blank screen as though I could read the free passage of electrons the way he did. "Three whole views."

I frowned. This was the surveillance video proving Sienna's innocence we were talking about. "Okay. How do we get it out to more people?"

Our office building was just a step away. I reached for the door as Angel popped into full-size view a step behind me, returned to her usual stature by Vansen after our epically fast trip in the Concorde. His travel system beat the hell out of using private jets or dealing with the TSA. It involved him firing up his plane in miniature, then stepping in and out a half dozen times to bring everyone onboard, which took less than a minute, then bringing us up into the sky at gradually increasing size, then throttling up to supersonic speeds and growing the plane to full size. All told, it took less than ten minutes to be up and flying and maybe three hours to cross the entire country. Faster if he deigned to use his SR-71 Blackbird.

"You make it go viral," Augustus Coleman said as he popped into existence with Greg. Vansen disappeared again immediately after letting go of him.

"You cannot *make* a video go viral any more than you can just walk into Mordor, okay?" Jamal stared him down. "There are mountains in the way."

"Come on," I said, pulling us into the door as Greg reappeared outside with our prisoner. His name was Andy Custis, and he was lacking shackles for transport, much to my thinly veiled annoyance. "You too, Andy."

"Okay," Andy said, walking like an automaton, following my orders only with a little resistance. That made sense, though, since he was compelled to do so against his will. Doubtful he would have listened to me if he had any say about it.

Eilish popped into view behind him. "Is he listening like a good boy?" she asked, strawberry blond hair gleaming in the light, Irish accent in full force.

"Well enough," I said. "Come on. Let's brief the others."

Our office building was not ours alone, but it was quiet at this time of day. The sun was barely up, and the crew seemed to be keeping to themselves, because I couldn't hear them out here as I went up the stairs to the second floor. The whole place had a rough look that predated our occupancy. Pipes rattled, drywall needed smoothing and patching, and there was even the occasional hole in the wall. We fit right in.

I breezed in through the door into our office suite and found Casey manning the desk, looking up as we came in. Casey, dark of hair and small of stature, had seen some shit go down in the previous iteration of our office and was thus probably pleased that it was me and not a meta villain crashing through the door.

"Morning, boss," she said, barely sparing me a look before turning back to the magazine she had splayed across the front desk. I caught a glimpse of "**18 SEX TIPS THAT WILL BLOW HIS MIND**" as I passed, and wished I hadn't. "Gang's all here."

"Good," I said, "cuz we're about to have a brainstorming session." I stepped into the bullpen and found a quiet crew waiting. Some of them were sleeping on the floor, a few on bare carpet, a few with blankets that had come from … "Hey, that pillow looks like one I have in my living room."

"It *is* from your living room," came a calm voice from the

corner, accented with Italian, sleepy, the way she sounded in the middle of the night whenever my phone went off with an emergency call.

Isabella.

"What are you doing here?" I asked, taking her in my arms as she came up to me. We kissed, just a brief peck on the lips, then broke.

"It was all hands on deck," she said. "You expect me to stay below?"

No, I did not expect that, would have been the smart thing to say. But I did expect her to stay out of danger, though I would not wish to say that aloud either. So instead I just furrowed my brow, and looked at her. "No."

Simple. Easy. Not too much of a lie.

"You are not telling me the whole truth," she said, her brown eyes narrowed at me. Uh oh. I knew that look. It was not a good one.

"I just … there's a lot of danger out there," I said softly. "Don't want you in the path of it, whenever possible."

Her beautiful eyes flashed. "And I don't want you in it, either, but off you go all the time, throwing yourself into it."

"We caught the guy," I said, anxious to change the subject, as Andy marched in robotically, under his own power.

Everyone caught it, or at least those that were awake. Those who were sleeping stirred. Olivia Brackett jerked to consciousness in a heavy chair that she'd pulled out of the conference room, and it shot out from underneath her, propelled by her powers into the wall at high speed. It buried itself into the baseboard and drywall, and she hit the ground and then flashed up into the air to nearly the ceiling. Landed on her feet, though, and fully awake by that time.

"Whoa," Augustus said. "Does that happen every morning?"

Olivia stretched, gingerly, like she was testing her balance, her blond hair a mess from sleeping and multiple slingshots around the room. "More often than not."

"I'm guessing a relationship is going to be somewhat difficult for you," Augustus said, causing Olivia to draw her light eyebrows together in a tightly knitted frown. "Man goes to give you a hug, gets jetted into the next county, boom."

She maintained the ireful look a second, then it faded. "You're not wrong."

"So good to have you back, boss," Tracy Brisco said, making his way through the cubicles and stopping just in front of me. Tracy was a good head taller than I was, but he stooped and hugged me around the ribs before awkwardly pulling back. "We tried to carry out your orders as best we could in your absence."

"Oh?" I looked around, everyone stirring to life. Some slower than others. Chase, for instance, still had the imprint of the carpet imbedded in her cheek from where she'd fallen asleep on it, no pillow or blanket. She was a tough lady, and as she rose the red faded thanks to her metahuman skin plasticity. "Where are we on … everything?"

"We've been waiting and watching," Scott Byerly said, slipping out into the gap of cubicles where I was standing. His dirty blond hair looked more brunette in the weak light making its way through the windows. Friday lurked a step behind him, only partially hulked, arms folded across his bulging chest like a bodyguard. "Nothing from the prison yet to indicate a problem," Scott said. He took in Andy Custis with a look. "Who's the prisoner? And does he need restraints?"

"Oh, no, he's being a good lad," Eilish said, patting Andy on the shoulder. "Aren't you now, Andrew?"

"I am being a good boy," Andy said mechanically.

"That's creepy, Irish," Veronika Acheron said. "Is this your sex puppet?"

"I don't have one of those," Eilish said, blushing furiously.

"Oh, you do, don't you?" Veronika asked with a laugh, doing a little stretching as she padded into our little impromptu circle, lacking shoes, socks, pants and …

"Good grief, Veronika," I said. "If we had an HR department, they'd be all over you for … lack of clothing."

She stretched, hands over her head, mismatched bra and panties suggesting to me that she was just being immodest, not purposely provocative. "It's hot in here, and I sweat in my sleep. I don't care who looks, either, so long as you don't touch.

I'm a little old to be all horrified that some of you might see me wearing roughly the same thing you'd see me in if we went to a swimming pool together." She put her hands in front of her perfect abs and raised her voice mockingly high. "Oh, no, what if they see my belly? Heavens, what will I do?"

"Hey, Reed?" came a voice from the corner. It was J.J., parked in front of his computer. "I'm getting a whisper of something across the net—"

"Whoa," Jamal said. "The whisper just became a flood." He must have picked up on it, too.

"What?" I asked. "What is it?"

"It's—"

"AHHHHHHHH!" Casey's scream was loud, echoing down the short hallway into the bullpen. Greg Vansen was closest to the exit, along with Angel, and they both turned immediately—

But not fast enough to head off the person who came running in.

She was blond, hair tangled, pale skin beaded with sweat across her face. I could smell the aroma of a long run through warm air. Her eyes were darting, dark and furtive under the shadowy lighting in the bullpen, but she found me, anchored her gaze there, and her hands fell to her side, bare, tattooed arms at odds with her …

Orange pants? And a jumpsuit that was tied, neatly, around her thin waist, a dirty and soaked tank top covering her upper body.

"Make ready, everybody," Scott said, stepping forward, distortions around his hands as he summoned water out of the air, as well as out of the cups around the office. "That's June Randall."

I knew that name. "What the hell is she doing here?" I asked, my voice dropped to low, anger bleeding in. Isabella laid a reassuring hand on my right arm. It was fine; nowadays I could blow June Randall through the roof without displacing Isabella, and she knew that. Plus, I could step between them if Randall presented any hint of trouble.

"Why don't you ask her, the person who would know, instead

of us, the people who don't," Veronika said. "She's a human. Worthy of a word."

"She's not worthy of shit," Kat Forrest said, stepping out, perfectly primped, from somewhere in the back of the bullpen. She raised her hands … and there was a gun in them, leveled at June. "Except suspicion and maybe a few bullets."

"Whoa," Friday said, turning to look at our once-placid Persephone. "Feel the rage of the dark side flowing through Kat."

"She's earned it," Kat said, not taking her eyes off June, the gun barrel wavering not a centimeter. "She shot Sienna in Florida last year. Damned near killed her."

"What the hell are you doing here?" I asked, looking her up and down. The orange jumpsuit was an interesting fashion choice. Or not, since she was supposed to be a prisoner at the Cube, and that was, presumably, their uniform.

"Yeah, it's cool, I ran like twenty miles to get to you guys, don't anybody rush to offer me a chair or a drink or anything," she said, raising her hands, signaling surrender.

"Would you like a drink?" Kat asked, pistol steady. "Because we could have Olivia get it for you—"

"Kat," I said, waving her off, imagining Olivia trying to hand June a cup of something and … propelling her into the fifth dimension in the process. "Okay. You've escaped the Cube. Run here. To my office. Why?"

"Which is not easy to find now that they've done away with phone books and public phones," June said. She was drawing slow breaths, and her hands were raised, her palms facing the ceiling. Her power to generate clouds of poisonous gas was hardly at bay just because she was pointing her emitters in a nominally safe direction. I side-eyed Kat and Scott. They both got it. "I need your help with something," she said. "And I come with information. First of all … Sienna's gone."

I blinked. That … was a surprise.

"And second …" she said, just as breathless, riding right past that first point of interest, "I need you to arrest me. Now."

7.

Sienna

I laughed.

Then I laughed harder.

Then I laughed some more.

"Lemme get this straight," I said, finishing up slapping my knees, because I'd doubled over with laughter at Vlad's *Come to my evil castle!* proposal, "you're going to tell me everything about why you've been trying to kill and destroy me for at least the last two years … but only if I come with you into your dank, musty, Bond-villain-lair castle over there." I laughed once more. "Yeah. Okay."

Vlad took my insulting laughter unflappably. He made a show of looking at the castle, then nodded. "I suppose it is a bit … Blofeld-esque, my home.

Sophie, once more, evinced a hint of irritation. She was good at giving off the hints. Or I was just so severely annoying she couldn't hide her aggravation with me any longer. "This is a serious offer. We infiltrated the Cube and broke you out, saving you from death, at worst, and a lifetime in captivity at best."

"In exchange for what?" I asked, getting down to brass tacks. "So I can become your … new minion? Like this triad?" I pointed at Sophie, Yvonne and Arche. "Because I'm gonna tell you right now—there is no way I am having my sense of

like my own personal European, slightly vampiric (he was definitely not a meta vampire, though) chauffeur.

"You're not going to learn anything standing out here," Sophie said, and she shuffled away toward the limo. Arche and Yvonne followed, each casting me a look that was mostly curiosity. And not all that serious, either. They were paid. Whatever Vlad was up to, they were mercenaries, not staunch loyalists. Which told me a little something about him.

Either he wasn't an ideologue, or he couldn't attract anyone to his ideas. Other than maybe Sophie. It eliminated a key motive from my normal line up. Yeah, I was applying my limited investigative skills here.

And if I got back on the plane, my investigation was over. Probably along with my life, because … I had nowhere else to go at this point.

"All right," I said, taking the slow walk over to where Vlad was waiting, holding the door. Credit to him—he must have either been prepared to hold it awhile, or he'd known I'd cave quickly.

"Excellent," he said as I climbed in with the ladies, and he got in after us. He moved reasonably quickly, not meta-speed, but well for a man of his age. Once in, he closed the door and knocked on the glass partition to the driver. The limo lurched into motion.

I sat there, on the back bench, the others spread out around the compartment, Vlad up by the glass divider to the driver, Sophie sitting just to his right, Arche and Yvonne on the long bench to the left—and looked at my new … warden?

Employer?

Enemy?

I didn't know yet what Vlad was, or what he was to me. But as the limo rolled along the tarmac toward the exit, the city of Bredoccia rising into the distance ahead, I had a feeling it was going to be that last one.

8.

Passerini
Washington DC

Now the Situation Room was quiet. A little background chatter came from the speakers overhead, where he was hooked in with the Pentagon, and his various analysts and commanders were doing their thing in real time over there, while he sat here, feeling about as useless as the operator of a surveillance drone watching when the shit hit the fan for men below.

"I'm not predicting a good ending for this." Like him, SecState Ngo was riveted to the screen. There were only a couple other observers now, both tucked into their own work, scrawling on paper or reading reports.

"It is looking a little dismal," Passerini said. "It looks like a dry hole to me, too. If the president won't see the light …" He shook his head. He hadn't voted for Harmon or Gondry, but he'd been stuck with them both for the better part of a decade now. "Well, we just keep on keeping on."

"So inspiring." Ngo had a half-smile. "Like you've been under this particular gun before."

Passerini smiled, too, lifting his cold coffee to his lips and taking a sip. "Not a big secret … Harmon wasn't a fan of the military, either. But he'd at least listen. Gondry …" He shook his head, looking at the two men scattered around the table that weren't partaking in their conversation. One shot him a tight smile. He had short, dark hair and was wearing an army uniform, with the bird that indicated he was a full colonel. He looked a touch young to be a full-bird colonel.

"He seems to be thoroughly trapped inside his own conclusions and priorities," Ngo said. "Like he came into the office with a fully-formed worldview, and nothing he's learned since has made a dent in it."

"You should, uh …" Passerini nodded at the other two. The colonel worked for him, probably his new adjutant, though he must have filtered in during the night. But who was the guy at the end of the table? Secretary of Transportation, wasn't it? Passerini wasn't about to trash talk his boss, even on his way out the door, in front of peers.

Ngo picked up on what he was trying to get across and picked up her sheaf of papers. "I doubt I'm long for this gig, either," she said. "Which is funny, because I've spent a lifetime in the State Department. Got the nod to move up under Harmon and … then Harmon's gone. I believed in him. He listened. Tried to take it all in, and sometimes … he'd go his own way, but mostly he listened and let us run our shop. Gondry, though?" She lowered her voice. "Good God."

Passerini chuckled. "You and I are at odds, then, up till now. I didn't like Harmon at all, but I didn't work directly for him. He was Commander-in-Chief, I was just an admiral. Getting orders you don't like is part of the service. But Gondry … I don't know who he's going to replace me with, but I doubt they'll have a worthwhile background." He shook his head. "Probably going to be a heck of a reduction in force if he carries forward even half of what he's talked about."

"You think peace is a bad idea?" Ngo's smirk suggested her tongue was fully in her cheek.

"Hey, if you want to orchestrate some peace here, I'm very open to it," he said, pointing at the satellite display of Revelen, "I'm just not sure they are."

"Trust me," she said, "I know the importance of the stick in diplomacy. I like offering the carrot, but I've been doing this a long enough time not to be naïve." She shifted her gaze to the overhead view of Bredoccia and the outlying area. "I see the value in having a big stick, as TR said."

"Yeah, no one ever complains about having it when a lion comes along," Passerini said, glancing at the screen again. Movement had caught his eye. "They only ever complain about the cost." There was a lot of movement, it being mid-morning in Bredoccia, but …

What was that?

"I think there might be more to the argument than that," Ngo said. "But I'm not unsympathetic."

Passerini reached for the nearest control and flicked the button to activate his mic. "Pentagon … zoom in on Grid H-4, please."

"What is it?" Ngo asked.

"Private plane at the airport," Passerini said, pointing at a newer model Gulfstream. What was that, a G6? He didn't know civilian planes as well as he perhaps should, but the air force had a few Gulfstreams in their inventory. The overhead satellite zoomed, the resolution increased.

"That's … interesting," Ngo said. Someone was coming off the plane. Several someones, all female as near as Passerini could tell, and being met by a male someone with a hell of a widow's peak at the summit of his dark hair. "That the main airport?"

Passerini shook his head. He'd read the briefings on the local geography before a series of planning meetings where his subordinates suggested targets for air strikes, should things come down to war. "No, Bredoccia's main airport is on the other side of the city. This is the one that services the big wigs. CIA has it under orbital surveillance 24/7 right now, in fact."

Bzzzzt.

"Priority message," Ngo said, lifting her phone to look at the screen. "CIA is taking an interest in the plane, too—and the passengers." She looked up. "Got a color display option here?"

"Hm? Yeah," Passerini said, and then flicked the mic button for the Pentagon again. "This is Hammer. Give me the photo lens option, please."

A moment later, the satellite view flipped out of the black and white it had been left on when night had ended and they'd switched out of thermal mode. Now it was full color.

"That woman's wearing an orange jumpsuit," Ngo said. "CIA flagged it. They're tracing the plane to the flight's point of origin now."

Passerini stared at the woman in orange. It looked a lot like a prison jumpsuit. And she was dark-haired … He flicked the mic again. "Pentagon, Hammer. Can you get me a closer view of the female subject in orange? I want to see what's on the back of her jumpsuit. Looks like lettering."

"Roger that, sir."

Passerini stared. He was getting the back of her head pretty clear, and could see her forearms—pale was all he could discern from that. The camera zoomed again, on the back of her jumpsuit, which said—

BUREAU OF PRISONS

Passerini almost smiled. Almost.

"Well, well, well," Ngo said, "looks like we found a little something here that might pique the president's interest."

"Indeed, we seem to have found a hobby horse he might just want to ride," Passerini said, and hit the button on the mic again. "Patch me through to President Gondry." Now, he smiled. "Tell him we've found Sienna Nealon."

9.

Sienna

"So this is Revelen," I said under my breath as we rode along. I stole glances out the window while keeping most of my attention focused on the people sharing the limo with me, because …

Well, duh. Because I couldn't trust a one of them.

"Indeed," Vlad said, smiling thinly. I wondered if he'd ever smiled sincerely and fully in his life. It would probably be a fearsome thing if he did. "From the wreckage of the Second World War to the devastation left in the wake of the Soviet Occupation, we have arisen like a phoenix—"

"Readying yourself to burn all of Europe and everyone standing close by," I said.

Sophie clicked her teeth together. Then ground them slightly. "You don't know us. Stop jumping to conclusions about our intentions."

"I'm sure you're establishing a very honest, open state here in the hinterlands of Europe," I said, nodding along. "Say … when was the last time Revelen had free elections?"

"Is that the sole measure of country's worth in your view?" Vlad asked, still with that thin smile.

"The people having some say in their governance?" I asked. "Yeah, I rate that as kinda important."

"How free and fair has your country treated you of late?"

Vlad asked, and … yeah, now he was probably smiling sincerely, and it was, as I expected, terrible. "Surely with all those elections you have gotten a … fair shake."

"Low blow, Vlad," I said, stealing a sideways glance at Yvonne. She'd been there at my trial. She was suppressing a smile at the dunk he'd scored on me.

"Ah, but the truth is a high and noble thing, is it not?" Vlad asked.

"That's a chocolate delicacy of richness, considering my current company," I said. "I don't know the real names of any of you. Lies, all, and I doubt it stops with just your name, which is the first thing you exchange when you meet with someone."

"I thought it was phone numbers these days," Vlad mused. "For hookups and whatnot?" He glanced at Sophie, who shrugged, rolling her eyes.

"I don't hook up, and I don't know," she said.

"I don't know who any of you people actually are," I said.

"I told you, I'm Yvonne," the woman formerly known as Owens said. "Real name."

"Not knowing us … a convenient theme," Vlad said. "For really, after Scotland, after Rose … what she did to you, what she took from you …" He leaned forward. "Do you even know who *you* are anymore?"

To thine own self be true. Harry's words bounced back to me again; I'd thought they were a reminder for while I was in prison, but they were starting to sound more multipurpose, and I clung to them like a life preserver, as though I were in the middle of an empty ocean all by myself. "I know who I am. Doubt many others do these days, though."

"Now we come back to reputation," Vlad said. "You refer to how you are seen by others, the world over, yes?"

"Yeah, it was an offhand reference to being thought of as a villain," I said. "Don't make too much of it, though, because I know you're the actual villain of this piece."

"How easily you judge me," he said. "But you don't know me. You have admitted as much."

"Dude, you're the man behind the legend of Dracula," I said. "Unless you were impaling people with kindness, I don't think your rep is so very far off the truth as to put you in the 'hero' category."

"But you said it yourself," Vlad said. "You are perhaps a hero in your own eyes? But a villain to the rest of the world? How do you explain that contradiction in terms?"

I looked sideways out a window. We were rolling through Bredoccia's downtown. "It's subjective, obviously. There's room for interpretation. And the people telling my story hate me, so—"

"Well, I would argue I received the same treatment," Vlad said. "I am sympathetic to your troubles on that count alone."

"Heh," I said. "Did you just say 'count'?"

It took Vlad a second. "Ah. Count Dracula. Very good. Never a title I held, 'Count.' But funny." He grew serious once more. "We have both been ill-defined by others who hate us, fear us. You are, after all, a succubus. Despised among the metahuman kind for thousands of years. You did not live through the worst of it, when your kind were hunted, run out of cities and countries. Killed, burned, stabbed, torn apart … Were all those incubi and succubi evil? Villains?"

I shrugged. "The ones I've met? Sovereign? James Fries? My aunt Charlie? Rose. Yeah, kinda. They were all villains."

"What about your mother?" Sophie asked, staring at me with a strange intensity. "Was she a villain?"

My lips tightened as I tried to keep a swarm of feelings down. Like Sophie maybe was at all times. "Well, she locked me in the house until I was almost eighteen and imprisoned me in a metal box to keep me in line, so … yeah, I think a lot of people would class her as a villain."

"Do you?" Sophie asked. She didn't look away.

But I did. "Depends on the day," I said, staring at that skyscraper that stretched up so high above us I could see it through the moonroof. It came to a sharp point, a massive antenna up top stretching like it was trying to compete with the big leaguers in New York or Tokyo.

"As you said, everything is subjective," Vlad said. "To some, I am perhaps a villain. To the press of Dracula's day, my story is a tale of villainy and woe. But that is not my story, nor my telling of it. I have been wronged many times in my life, and many times it was … extremely personal." He brushed his hand against his flawless white shirt, almost self-consciously. "But I doubt that I have ever been wronged as thoroughly as when my likeness was bent to the perversion that is Dracula."

"Plus, I haven't even seen any fellow vampires here, yet," I said. Back to snarky, because they'd gotten me way too close to uncomfortable sentiment, and I hated doing that with strangers. Especially lying strangers. Maudlin was not the feel I wanted right now. "Hell, I think I'm paler than you."

Vlad looked at his hand, which was somewhat tan. "It was not always so, but I venture out of doors a decent amount these days." He held up his hand and smiled. "Still … if I had been locked away for a time, our skin tones might be very much the same, I think." The limo pulled to a stop. "Ah. It is time."

I looked out the window as Yvonne threw the door open and got out. We'd pulled up to the curb and were parked there, limo's engine still idling. "This is where I'm doing my talkabout?" I asked, peering out. It looked like a business district, office buildings all around, a steady flow of people ebbing on the sidewalks.

"If you wish," Vlad said. "At the very least, it is a nice place to start."

"Fine," I said and stepped out. I leaned back down. "But don't think this is going to convince me you're not a villain, no matter what some man on the street says."

Vlad's eyes almost twinkled in the shade of the limo interior. "I wouldn't think that the well-trained suspicion of Sienna Nealon would be dissolved in the course of minutes. We have had years of antipathy and misunderstandings from afar. This is but a first step in what I hope will build trust. Perhaps."

"You got a lot of steps ahead of you, then, bub," I said, and he chuckled, nodding. "Don't go anywhere."

"We'll be waiting," Vlad said as I stood, losing sight of him.

I started to shut the door but someone caught it. Sophie squeezed out of the limo to stand next to me, then closed the door, carefully, herself. "I didn't ask for company," I said.

"You get it anyway," she said. So cool. So calm. Those eyes

like icebergs coming to capsize me.

"Don't cramp my style, Sigourney." I turned to walk into the crowd. "Keep your distance, because I don't need something slimy busting out of your chest and getting my prison jumpsuit all grimy."

I heard her sigh as I walked away, but I also heard her steps, following after me a few seconds later.

This was going to be fun.

10.

"Hi, what's your name?" I accosted a man in a suit not five steps away from Sophie. He looked to be middle-aged, and the suit wasn't exactly high end. Middle management, at best, I figured. Maybe lower.

He blinked at me in surprise. "Milosz. Say, aren't you—" His English was accented heavily.

"What gave it away? The prison jumpsuit?" I flaunted my outerwear. It was not a great look for a random street in Eastern Europe. Or anywhere, really. "Yeah, it's me. I have questions for you."

"I would be happy to answer any questions of the great hero Sienna Nealon," he said. There was a tone of awe in his voice.

Wait … what?

"What'd you call me?" I asked. Sophie eased up behind me, and I looked to make sure she wasn't about to bushwhack me. She was just standing there, scanning the crowd flowing around us, returning steely looks when someone would shoot ones of curiosity at me. No threat there—for now.

"You are a hero," Milosz said, and now his dark eyes were lit. "We see your exploits on the news. You get, uh … what do Americans call it? A bad rap. Like us." He nodded, smiling. "Glad to see you escape."

"Yeah, it's been a joy dodging that trouble. Listen, uhm … that *hero* thing you said—you're a … weird person here, right? Like a true contrarian? Bucking the tide?"

His smile faded to blankness. "How do you mean?"

"You're the only one who thinks I'm a hero, right?" I asked, forcing a smile of my own to put him at ease.

"Hey … this is Sienna Nealon, yes?" Another man came up to me, smiling pointing, speaking loud enough to be heard over the buzz of the crowd. A lot of heads turned. "Heyyyy!" He said, pointing at me. "Look! Look! Is Sienna Nealon!"

Sophie sighed. "Now things are about to get interesting."

"I—what?" The crowd milled around me, coalescing. They weren't flowing as a crowd normally does on a sidewalk, numerous people heading to their own destination.

They were coagulating, like white blood cells around an infection. Which was me.

"Sienna Nealon!" Someone shouted, pointing over the crowd. "Can I get autograph? Or selfie?"

More shouts for autographs and selfies came.

"Wow," I said as Sophie was bumped gently against me by motion of the crowd. "I was in another crowd not too long ago, outside a courthouse in Minneapolis. They were not nearly so complimentary as this bunch." Someone thrust a piece of paper and a pen at me, and I squiggled something approximating a signature and handed it back. Five more got pushed my way.

"Please, please, my daughter is huuuuge fan—"

"Love what you did in London that one time. I read the untold, secret story—"

"Thank you for not letting Chicago be destroyed by asteroid. Have always wanted to see Sue the dinosaur."

"That … is an interesting reason to not want Chicago destroyed," I said under my breath.

"Get off me," Sophie said behind me, pushing at someone who was all up in her business, "or you'll regret it."

"You want to wait in the car?" I asked.

"No," Sophie said, elbowing someone else—more gently—out of the way. "Because if they get too close to you—"

"Relax, I'm not draining any souls today," I said, then looked back at the limo with a little significance. She caught it. "Maybe. The day is still young."

"Your threats would be funnier if I didn't know you were so quick to commit violence," she muttered. I barely heard over the crowd and didn't have time to address it before I had to sign five more papers.

"Seriously, this is the best reception I've gotten anywhere since the Gail Roth interview bullshit," I said, handing back another piece of paper. "What's up with this?"

"The press here doesn't paint you as an enemy," Sophie said, shoving someone else back that was edging too close to either me or her. Couldn't tell which. "And the people of Revelen have tasted enough neglect and spite from western news pointed in their direction that they don't trust it anyway."

"Are you sure we're not in the American heartland?" I asked, getting a blank stare in return. "Kidding. I guess almost everyone hates the American press."

"Probably because they're self-important douchebags who spend more time whining about their status and giving each other awards to show how very, very vital they are than they do actually tracking down the truth and reporting on it."

"Plus, clickbait," I said. "Nobody likes clickbait. You just feel dirty after clicking it, you know?"

"No, I don't know," Sophie said, shoving someone else back. They didn't seem to take umbrage, hooking around her and thrusting a pen and paper in my face.

"I bet Vlad knows," I said. "He seems pretty up on the world. You know, for an old, old—several more times old—guy."

"He likes the internet," Sophie said, turning her back to wall me off from an aggressive woman and her young children. She snapped something in the native tongue, and the woman halted, keeping her distance as though Sophie had spit fire at her.

"Here," I said, and took the papers in the woman's hands. They were napkins. I signed every one of them, and made sure there were enough for each kid, plus her. I handed them out individually, tried to make eye contact. Basically bucked my nature every step of the way. "Here you go," I said gently. "Do you like it here in Revelen?" I asked her.

"Is even better now that you are here," she said, gazing starry-eyed at the napkin with my autograph. "Will you be staying long?"

"Will you stay forever?" said a little dark-haired girl with a scarf over her head, a little mop of hair sticking out the front. "Please?" That accent—so cute.

"Forever's a long time," I said, realizing I was interacting with a child, not something that was uber comfortable for me. But my exposure to Eddie Vansen had made it … easier. A little. "But we'll see."

A rough cheer rose up from the crowd.

Sophie seized my hand and started to drag me away, but not too roughly. I could have broken away if I wanted to. "That's all for today," she announced, and the crowd mellowed a little as she pulled me to the limo and threw open the door.

"Uh, thanks, guys," I said, waving at them as we came to a stop at the door. They were all holding position, either too cowed or too polite to follow us right to the edge of the car. "I haven't been welcomed like that in … a long time."

They burst into spontaneous applause, and it was kinda cool. I waved and got back in the limo, still waving as Sophie squeezed in behind me and shut the door. She wore a hell of an expression, and I couldn't tell if it was because she was pissed at having to be my bodyguard, or if she was just irritable in general.

Throwing herself back into her seat, folding her arms across her chest, she looked straight ahead at Yvonne, who mouthed, "What?" to her.

"Nothing," Sophie said, then turned to Vlad. "Can we go?"

Vlad, for his part, was just sitting there with a cell phone in his hand, browsing the 'net. He looked up at me with those glossy blue eyes. "If she says it is okay …?"

"Yeah, let's roll on," I said. My words were promptly followed by a faint rumble from my stomach. I hadn't eaten in … days? Vlad rapped the divider, and off we went. I watched the crowd as we cruised to the next corner and turned. They stood there, just watching us go, as though someone important were in my car.

Someone worthy of respect.

Someone … worthy, period.

It was a weird feeling, and though it could easily have been directed, unbeknownst to me, at Vlad …

I thought … maybe … just maybe, against all odds, in defiant opposition to how the rest of the world saw me …

… Here in tiny Revelen, thousands of miles from home …

I actually was a hero.

11.

Reed

"My sister is a damned hero," I said, stalking back and forth in front of June Randall. She was bound to a chair—at her request, cuffed tightly to it, and she'd just finished telling me a hell of a story.

Light was streaming heavily through the windows, the full light of day flooding in from a high-risen sun, and I could see motes of dust floating in the sun rays. There was a tightness in my chest that hadn't been there before I'd heard what Sienna had been through since I'd left her with cops in that quarry in Maple Grove.

I never should have done what she wanted and given her over to the police.

"Guilt is not going to do you any good right now," Isabella said, sotto voce. Everyone heard her, anyhow. We were all metas.

"It's not your fault, Reed," Scott Byerly said, easing up to me. "She chose—"

"What?" I asked, wheeling on him. Scott didn't flinch; he knew he wasn't the real target of my rage. "She chose a show trial that lasted minutes? She chose to be accused of crap she didn't actually do? She chose to start a prison riot—"

"She actually did choose to do that," June said. "That was totally her choice."

I froze mid-rant. "Okay. She didn't choose the other stuff, though."

"Reed, we're with you, okay?" Scott said. "No one is here who's not on the Sienna train."

I looked around for opposition, then frowned. "Where's Gravity?"

"She left," Friday said. "She wasn't so much on the Sienna train. Said something about not wanting to be away from her kid anymore, or her friends, or her business. I think the Scotland thing kinda did her in."

I stood still, thinking. "I guess this whole thing … it's asking a lot."

"Yeah, but those of us who are here," Scott said, "we're in. Don't even worry about it."

"So who's this doctor?" I asked, looking at Jamal. "And this prison guard, Owens? Do we have a line on either of them? Where are they taking her?"

Jamal shrugged. "I was, uh … caught up in the story."

"Hey, Reed," J.J. piped up from the corner. "I've done a little digging in the government files … personnel files for both look like fakes, inserted into the system by someone with a little skill."

Jamal lifted his phone, and his eyes flitted back and forth, like he was reading blank air. "Whoa."

"Good whoa?" Augustus asked. "Or bad, like 'woe is us'?"

"How much longer is this meeting going to last?" Chase asked. "Ballpark? Because you guys woke us up, and I haven't had a chance to pee yet."

I blinked. "Uh, just go." Thought about it a sec. "To the bathroom, in case that wasn't clear. Not … here."

She stared back at me. "I'm not Friday. The second part was just implied."

"You could be Friday, though," Friday said. "Friday is just a mask. A symbol—"

"Yes, a stupid, phallic symbol," Veronika said. "Witness the rise of Dickheadman."

"I'm going to take that as a compliment," Friday said. "Phallic symbols are strong. That's why we say, of people with courage, 'they have balls.'"

"Mmm, that's not what I think of testicles," Veronika said, almost giggling. "I think … 'those look like a weak target'—"

"Can we get back to 'whoa' or 'woe'?" I asked, focusing in on Jamal. "You have something J.J. didn't get?"

"Just recognizing the signature on this personnel file hack," Jamal said, coming out of his cybercoma and looking me in the eye. "An old friend did this—ArcheGrey1819."

"The same lady that landed you in jail in DC?" Angel asked, frowning. "Hell of a friend."

"She didn't land us in jail," Jamal said. "Just set us on the path to the clash. She actually helped us out of it." He looked at me. "And she was trying to help us get to the Custis family. Tipped us to their existence." He shot a look past me to Andy, who was just standing there by Eilish's side, utterly sedate. "Which worked. We wouldn't have the video if not for her."

"And now she's helped orchestrate my sister's escape," I said. "Why?"

"No idea," Jamal said.

"What do we know about her?" Veronika asked. "What's her deal? Where's she live? What's her real name? Cuz ArcheGrey1819 sounds like teenage boy gaming in his parents' basement."

"Finally, someone asks the brave, tough, probing questions," Friday said. "Like a penis." Veronika just rolled her eyes.

"We know she's a hacker, and Jamal has a big-ass crush on her," Augustus said.

Jamal looked like he was torn between smacking his brother and crawling under a desk. "I do not have a crush on her, okay? She's just got skills, that's all."

"I kinda have a crush on her," Abby said, from over in the corner of the room, hidden behind a few cubicles, with J.J. "Her work is A+."

"She was involved in the New York attack," Scott said, brow furrowed. "The one that brought down the US Attorney's office and FBI HQ. The one that eliminated the evidence against Nadine Griffin and let her skip out of trial."

"She freelances a lot," Jamal said, still sending his brother some side-eye. "Works out of Eastern Europe." He stared me down. "Most likely Revelen."

"There's that name again," I muttered, and Isabella squeezed my arm sympathetically. "So … is this straight out of Revelen, then? We've been getting a lot of noise, a lot of mess out of that country over the years. Is this the final play? Grab Sienna and … what?"

"Have a lovely tea party with her, surely," Augustus said. But his whole body was tense, and I could tell he was only joking to diffuse the very real worries he was feeling.

I knew those feelz.

"What do we know about Revelen?" I asked. "They've had that serum flowing out of them. They've been sending us trouble since that guy Benjamin that Augustus and I dealt with. The one that blew up the Minneapolis airport customs line."

"That was not a great time," Augustus said. "I got my back broken."

"They absorbed the nation of Canta Morgana not that long ago," J.J. said. "Just annexed a neighboring country for Baltic Sea access. They border Russia—"

"Stop reading the Wikipedia page," Abby said. "I think Reed was looking for stuff that's a little more practical. Like: a huge number of the world's mercenaries run through there. A lot of hackers, too. They've got a flourishing black market there."

"Why?" Scott asked.

"Low enforcement on cyber crimes?" Jamal asked, shrugging. "Or they've got a considerable cyber army, like China and Russia. It kinda works as an alternative funding method to taxes. Lots of identity theft for profit, that kind of thing."

"I, uh … know some stuff about Revelen," Friday said. His voice was quiet, subdued—which was the main reason I noticed it.

"The only thing you know is dick," Veronika said. "And even in that, really, you only know your own."

"Hold it," I said, looking right at Friday. He was maximally shrunk now, skin and bones, a ninety-eight-pound weakling. Friday never shrunk all the way. "What do you know about

Revelen, Friday?"

"Been there," he said, as Chase re-entered the room. She paused at the outside of the circle we'd formed in the middle of the bullpen, listening. "We both have," he said, nodding to her.

"What? Where?" Chase asked. "And please do not say 'Pound town.' Because we have never visited there together, ever. And I question whether you've visited it at all."

"Validation," Veronika breathed. "I knew it."

"Revelen," I said.

"Oh, yeah," Chase said. "We've been there. Grim-ass place. Lunchbox here didn't talk for two weeks afterward." Her eyes glimmered. "It was the best two weeks of our acquaintance."

"Oooh, can we go to Revelen?" Veronika asked. "With Friday?"

"Hold it, hold it," I said, and Isabella let loose of my biceps. "Friday—what happened in Revelen?"

"He got separated from the team and got scared," Chase said, after Friday didn't answer for a beat. "When we found him, he was catatonic, and his pants were shat."

"My pants were not shat," Friday said in low, raspy, Batman-voice. "I did not shit my pants."

"Fine, someone else must have shit his pants for him, then," Chase said, shaking her head, "because they were definitely shat."

"Dude," Augustus said, "that ain't even right."

"What did you see, Friday?" I asked, closing in on him. But not too close, now that Chase had said the thing about pants being shat.

"I didn't see anything," he said.

"Oh, he's lying," Veronika said.

"Am not!"

"Look at his eyes darting beneath the gimp mask," Veronika said. "He's like a bird trying to find a direction to fly away."

"Friday," I said, lowering my voice, "this is your niece we're talking about. She could be over there, right now—and I need to know what you know. I need to know what she's dealing with—"

"It's Vlad," Friday said, the words coming out like an abrupt squeak. "Vlad the Impaler. Vlad effing Dracula. That guy."

"That … is not what I was expecting," Augustus said. "Vlad … Dracula?"

"The guy he's based on," Friday said. "And I can tell you," and he sounded so haunted I wouldn't have been surprised to see a ghost come flying out of his ass right then, "having stood in his presence … having been threatened by him … his legend is earned." He looked me right in the eye, all the normal Friday bombast absent. "That man … is the single most dangerous and frightening human being on the planet."

12.

Sienna

"Would you like us to stop off for some cotton candy, perhaps?" Vlad asked. "A cappuccino? Cucumber sandwiches? A little spot of lunch? I could have the chefs back at the castle prepare something to your liking."

I sat in the back seat, staring at him, the window divider like a dark mirror reflecting the entire back seat's scene for me. Sophie sat to my left on the bench that stretched along that side of the limo. ArcheGrey and Yvonne/Owens were sharing the bench to my right, and I sat staring at Vlad as he made his curious offer.

"I am kinda hungry," I said, getting an idea. I looked to my left, and saw a little café coming up through the smoky, tinted glass. "How about we stop right here?" And I pointed.

Vlad evinced a little surprise, brow rising, and then knocked on the window divider and said, "Stop here." And we stopped.

I opened my own door before Sophie could manage to surge in front of me and got out before her. "Oh, sorry," I said, not sorry as she stepped out behind me. "What are you, my bodyguard?" I had a darker thought about what she was doing, but I wasn't prepared to share yet.

"Well, you do get in a fair amount of trouble," she said, clearly trying to pass off her actions as no big deal.

"Just as long as trouble doesn't get into me," I said, walking through the open door of the café. It had a little sign out front with *Café* written on it, and above that, probably the local translation. I couldn't read it. "I'm seriously germaphobic."

"Why? Your immune system makes you practically invincible to conventional illness," Sophie said, following a step behind me. "And you don't fool me, you know. Or him."

"Whatever do you mean?" Damn. She'd figured me out.

"You think this whole experience is a Potemkin village," Sophie said as we stepped inside the café. It was a nice place, a little worn, with some dirt around the edges. The booths had seen some mileage, and the chairs were kinda banged up. "That the crowd we encountered was mind-controlled or prepared for you. That's why you asked to make the sudden stop, and it's why you don't like me following you. You think I'm mind-controlling people to give you the reaction you're looking for."

"The thought did cross my mind," I said. Lie. It was top of mind. "Points for using 'Potemkin village' in everyday conversation, though." I headed for the counter.

Apparently, the lunch rush had either died down or never existed at all. There was a woman behind the counter peering at me as I walked up. She was probably late twenties/early thirties, and had the look of someone who'd seen a fair amount in her time. Jaded, I guess you could say. She was trying to decide how she knew me as I walked up to her and thumped my elbows down on the deli counter, glancing into the glass display below. "Hiya."

"Hello," she said, frowning in concentration. She was trying to place my face. I got that a lot. Maybe the jumpsuit was throwing her off, orange not really being my color.

"Nice place you got here," I said, looking over my shoulder and out the window. Past where the limo waited at the curb there was an expansive square with a few people scattered around it on benches, grass growing out of the triangles of space that were cut through by sidewalks. A few trees dotted the green sections, and a statue I couldn't quite see dominated the center of the square. "Got any specialties on the menu I should try?"

"Ahhh … the Reuben sandwich is good," she said, clearly

still trying to place me. "Westerners like it. You … Canadian?"

"What the hell?" I asked. "Do I look like a maple syrup guzzling lumberjack to you? Because that's all Canada is. Lumberjacks and maple syrup. And toothless hockey players." I fake smiled at her. "See? Still got all my teeth." Only because of my powers, though. If not for my regrowth abilities, I would have had a smile like a centenarian sugar addict with an aversion to tooth-brushing.

She laughed weakly, probably trying to decide whether I was serious or not. "Your accent … sounds Canadian."

"I'm from Minnesota," I said. "It kinda bleeds into Canada, so I guess that's an honest mistake. But I'm way less polite than a Canadian, so … anyway, I'll take that Reuben."

She nodded, then jolted upright. "You—Sienna Nealon?"

I smiled. "There are some who call me that."

She blinked. "What … do others call you?"

"Nothing I'd care to repeat in polite company," I said. "Reuben, please?"

"Yes, of course," she said and rushed to work. "I have watched you many times." She pulled loose, clear plastic gloves on and started to fuss with the sandwich bread.

"That so?" I asked. "Not from outside my bedroom window at night, I hope."

"Mm? Oh, no, no," she shook her head, smiling at my little joke. "I am, how you say—great admirer of you. You are fine exemplar of what we can accomplish. You inspire me to live at best possible level."

I tried to suss out what she was saying there, but it was lost on me. "How do I inspire you?"

"You want sandwich toasted, yes?" she asked, and I realized … she was done. She'd made that whole sandwich in the seconds I was mulling how I inspired her.

"Uh, sure—"

Taking the glove off her right hand, she lit a flame out of her palm and held it over the sandwich, flipping it with the other and then applying the heat again, slowly, evenly, until the bread was nicely crisped. That done, she slid it onto a plate, sucked some of the excess heat out of it, and nodded at a display of chips behind me. "You pick one of those—and also drink." She slapped a cup next to the plate.

"Huh," I said, "you're a Gavrikov."

"It's a very common type in those of Eastern European and Russian extraction," Sophie said quietly. "Not quite Hercules common but common enough around here."

"Natural or serum?" I asked, looking at the cashier.

She shrugged. "I ended up with powers at age twenty-seven. Two years ago."

I looked at Sophie. "Serum."

Sophie did not respond. I took that as its own answer.

"Do you know a lot of people with powers?" I asked.

The cashier nodded. "Almost everyone here has powers now. We are … very special country."

I had been just about to pick up my sandwich and froze. "… Everyone?"

"Almost," she said. "Maybe one in five not have powers of their own? Is very sad when that happens, but … it happens."

I stared at her across the counter. She stared back at me. Eventually, she pushed the plate to me. "You … want your sandwich? Is 'on the house,' I think you say?"

"Sophie, pay this lady," I said, and Sophie evinced a flash of irritation. I didn't have money, and I figured she did. She fumbled in her pocket and produced a roll of the local currency. Whatever she put on the counter, it sure made the cashier happy. That done, I started to walk away.

"You not want your sandwich?" she called after me.

I didn't look back. "Sorry. I just lost my appetite," I said. Because I had.

An entire country of people with metahuman powers?

Suddenly … I did not feel nearly so safe as I had a few minutes earlier.

13.

Vlad looked up from his phone as I got back in the limo. What was it with this guy and his electronics? Maybe he was a Thor type, though he seemed to part with it fairly easily when I sat down, and he was actually looking at a lit screen. Jamal didn't always. He also held his finger over the charging port to allow direct access to the net using the phone's antenna. Vlad held his phone like a normal person.

So probably not a Thor. Or at least not the kind that manipulated electricity at the digital level.

"I thought you were getting something to eat?" Vlad asked, those black eyebrows dragged down in the furrow of his brow line.

"Lost my appetite when I found out you've dosed your entire population with meta serum," I said. Sophie took her seat and Vlad knocked on the window, causing the limo to slide back into motion on the quiet street.

"This bothers you?" Vlad asked. He looked concerned. "The idea that so many people here are like you—this disturbs you in some way?"

"Maybe a tad," I said. It was more than a tad. It was a lot.

"Is this not the purpose of your Second Amendment?" Vlad asked. "To see that the people are suitably armed against all threats that may come their way? To give them—how do you say it? Right of revolt should your government become too overbearing? To allow them to defend their families should dangers come to their door?"

"Yes, that is the philosophical underpinning," I said, "and I suppose I shouldn't be surprised that a guy who was alive during the Revolutionary War would know that. But we don't allow rocket launchers on our streets, and a whole lot of metahuman powers are way more dangerous than your garden variety gun. Like that girl back in the café who made me a sandwich." I chucked a thumb behind me. "She had Gavrikov abilities. It was nice that she was able to toast my Reuben for me. It was cool. Looked good. Kinda wish I'd picked it up and brought it with me, because now that I'm over the initial shock of you experimenting on your entire population with metahuman drugs, I'm hungry again—"

Sophie lifted a white plastic bag in front of me that I hadn't even seen in her hand. She'd gotten my sandwich boxed by the girl in the café. One of her eyebrows was slightly above the other. She was definitely annoyed at me.

"Thanks," I said, taking it up from her and setting it on the seat next to me. "The point remains, though—that girl used her powers for good. But what if she decided not to? What if she decided to—I dunno—blow up the tallest building in Revelen?" I nodded at that under-construction skyscraper, which was now out my right window, looming in the middle distance.

"The 'Dauntless Tower'?" I must have given him a funny look, because he shrugged. "It loses something in the translation. If she did that, then she would be arrested, tried, and punished," Vlad said, very calmly. "Just as we would do to any other criminal."

"But the loss of life—" I started to say.

"Would be terrible," Sophie said calmly. "But what would you have us do? Lock them all up ahead of time? Round up anyone you deem 'too dangerous' before they even act?"

"No," I said, "I would have not given them powers to begin with. Duh. That's what I'm arguing."

"But you have powers, do you not?" Vlad said, leaning forward, eyes sparkling with amusement. So help me, he was actually enjoying explaining this to me. "They allow you to have an advantage over others? In any situation you walk into with a human, there is a power differential, yes? You could enforce your will upon them. Make them do things against their own will with greatest ease. This is … dangerous. Unfair."

"Inequitable," Sophie said.

"Consider at its base, what you fear," Vlad said. "Your fellow man. His actions. The danger he brings. And you are right to fear, for we have all, at this point, watched enough of *The Walking Dead* to realize that the true threat is not the walkers—it is the humans."

I blinked. "Did you just—?"

Vlad smiled. "You fear the brotherhood of man more than any other threat now. We all do. We prey upon one another. The strong take from the weak. Might makes right, yes? Allows those with more tanks, more planes … to simply run over those without. The rule of the sword—or the missile, now, yes? This is the principle that governs our world. Police with guns enforce the peace at the community level, and America enforces the peace as it so chooses across the world, hm? Or at least their version of it?"

"That's … a vast oversimplification," I said.

"But it works in general, yes?" Vlad was smiling, not quite smugly, but confidently. It was borderline.

"Dude," I said, feeling like a headache might be coming on, "you experimented on your people. Put serum in their water—"

"Good guess," Sophie said. "How did you know it was the water?"

"It's how your agents did it in the US every time that stuff came up," I said.

She shook her head. "That wasn't us."

I let my shoulders sag as I rolled my eyes. "Yeah, okay, liars. It all came through and from Revelen."

"We certainly have the substance in question," Vlad said, "the serum, you call it. But it was not us that have been shipping it to the United States, inserting it into your water, causing your problems."

I narrowed my eyes at him. "Remember the guy that tore up Minneapolis back in January? He killed Eric Simmons, ripped up the Chesapeake Bay Bridge after Simmons destroyed the USS *Enterprise* in its graving dock?"

"Ah … That was us," Vlad said. "The *Enterprise* thing."

"Well, the guy—I called him the Predator," I said, "he was terrified of you. Warned me about you. Said you experimented on him."

Vlad shrugged. "Not exactly, but we certainly empowered him. His name was Stepane."

"I know. Why was he so scared of you?" I asked, staring Vlad down. "Why was Friday so frightened of you? I'm sitting here and you're offering me cotton candy?" I looked at the takeout box next to me. "And thanks for the sandwich." I tore open the box and hefted half the Reuben. It was still warm, tasted great. Fresh sauerkraut.

"*I* bought that," Sophie said, sounding more irritated about the sandwich than she had at anything else so far. "That was my money."

"I will reimburse you if you like," Vlad said, smiling, clearly getting a kick out of this. "Present the receipt to the accounting department and—"

"In four to seven years I'll get my money back," Sophie said, rolling her eyes, then fixing on me. "Fine. My gift to you."

"Thanks," I mumbled, mouth full. "This is way better than that prison food. Probably better than the food before that, too, though it's hard to remember that far back …" I took another bite.

"It's been all of four days," Sophie said.

"A lot's happened since then," I said, "and I had a really trying night before the whole prison ordeal, okay?"

"Indeed," Vlad said. "I hear they are still removing bodies from that quarry in Minnesota."

"That was lit," Yvonne said.

"Yes," Vlad said, "Very … lit. Now, you asked a question, and I think it is time that you receive an answer." Then he clammed up.

I paused chewing for a second. "And the answer is …?"

"Not here," Vlad said, as the limo cruised through the streets of Bredoccia. "For this, some classic rules must be observed. I will tell you in my lair." His eyes gleamed, and he let loose with a cackle that made the tiny hairs on the back of my neck stand up. "How was that for a maniacal laugh? I have been practicing, you see, in front of the mirror sometimes. For my own amusement exclusively, I assure you."

"It was pretty good," I said, the Reuben paused in front of my lips. "Please don't do it again while I'm eating, because it's very creepy and put me off my food for a second. Oh, wait, here comes the ravening hunger again." I took another huge bite. "Seriously, though … don't do that. It's terrible. Very Dracula."

"As you wish," Vlad said. "But the explanation, it will come very soon. And I think it will answer so very many questions you have had. Perhaps …" His smile actually reached his eyes, and for the first time—and in spite of that horrifying laugh—he seemed rather paternal. "Perhaps it will even allow you to see me … differently."

We lapsed into silence, the limo quietly humming as we made our way back to his dark and spooky castle lair, and I finished my Reuben in the silence.

14.

Dave Kory
Brooklyn

"Oh, man," Dave Kory said. The clicks. His Sienna Nealon story and the listicle follow-up were churning traffic through the flashforce website at higher volume than he could ever recall seeing. The counter was spinning up by the millisecond, zooming higher and higher—

"Dude," Steve Fills said, walking past with a kombucha in hand, "you're gonna crash the site if you keep writing articles that bring the heat like that."

"That's my goal," Dave called after him. "Bring it down, baby. I mean, not really, though." The site going down meant no money for clicks. That would be bad. He had to manage the server load so as to avoid that, and it might require a little extra bandwidth on a day like today. There were probably parts of the country where flashforce was currently loading very slowly. Not optimal.

Dave dashed off an email to web services, making sure they knew to keep things rolling. He was halfway through writing another follow-up story, this one even thinner on substance, and he'd shot a couple requests for comment to contacts he had in the government: the White House Press Corps, the Justice Department—hell, even Director Chalke's office over at the FBI. That one was just a formality, though.

Bzzzt. Dave's phone buzzed, and he picked it up off the white plastic desk. It had an alert on the notifications—from what looked like a game app, Escapade. It read: IT'S TIME TO PLAY!

"Ooh," Dave said and looked around. The office was getting pretty full, so he took his phone and headed for the bathroom. The entire office was just one big open bullpen, to allow for better collaboration. There were a few conference tables around the edges of the room on two sides. A bank of windows filled the other, giving a nice view of Manhattan in the distance, past the East River. The exit covered the fourth wall, and the bathrooms were this way.

Dave popped into the "Executive Washroom," clearing the locked door with a keycard. The exec washroom was the sole privilege accorded to him and a couple other high-ups here, and it had a little secret inside, where no one could really see it . . .

A couple privacy booths that locked when you were inside. Opaque black glass, floor to ceiling, just around the corner from the entry. Not for when you wanted to take a dump, but for when you needed the privacy that open bullpen couldn't provide.

Dave entered one and shut the door, clicking the lock. Now he was in a soundproof, witness-proof space. The light above was faint; it shone down right on him, but dimly. He unlocked his phone and touched the Escapade app.

It popped onscreen, requesting a sequenced code entry. Twelve characters, including caps, lower case, numbers, and special characters. It had been annoying to memorize, but he had it down now, and it was soooo worth it.

The app flared to life once unlocked, presenting him with—in this case—a text string. A conversation with a half-dozen participants, each denoted by name.

RUSS BILSON: Hey Dave

HEATHER CHALKE: Nice work today, Dave. Don't expect a comment from my office.

Dave typed his own reply, ignoring the other salutations of greeting in favor of talking to Heather: Didn't figure I'd get one, but I have to cover the bases, you know.

HEATHER CHALKE: I know how the game is played.

RUSS BILSON: This is not exactly going how we planned. Sienna Nealon was supposed to be dead by now.

HEATHER CHALKE: Our contact, Berenger, over at the Bureau of Prisons failed. So did the warden in the Cube. The whole place is a disaster area, but it looks like Nealon got out by way of an old air duct—do not print that, Dave, or anybody else.

A few "Understoods," or their equivalent popped into the conversation string. Dave added his own, just to cover his ass. He added: "You've got to give us something. To stir the pot, you know."

RUSS BILSON: The pot is pretty damned stirred already.

JAIME CHAPMAN: I've got a little rumored something, but can't confirm. DoD has spotted Nealon from overhead satellite imagery in Revelen.

TYRUS FLANAGAN: Whoa.

RUSS BILSON: That's problematic.

HEATHER CHALKE: That's way outside our conventional reach. But can confirm. Off record. She is in Revelen.

RUSS BILSON: And you didn't lead with that when we all logged on?

HEATHER CHALKE: Would have gotten to it eventually.

Dave snorted in the soundproof booth. No she wouldn't have. Chalke was always a half-hearted participant in this information-sharing exercise. She fed them stuff when she wanted to, or when it was convenient. But Dave wasn't going to call out the FBI director, because her stories had personally driven a ton of traffic to his site. You didn't shoot the golden goose until it stopped producing eggs. Then it could be dinner. Or in this case, *she* could be the story.

DAVE KORY: No problem. Will note as anonymous source in the CIA. They'd have this, right?

HEATHER CHALKE: Yes, but be careful. Was considering bringing their director in on this. Do not want to alienate the agency.

Dave thought about it. Came up with another answer.

DAVE KORY: NCTC?

That was the National Counterterrorism Center. They were cleared pretty high up.

HEATHER CHALKE: Better still, Pentagon. And you can add this—SecDef Passerini is on his way out the door, at the pleasure of the president. Big blowup in the Situation Room, Gondry told him he was fired as soon as a replacement could be found. I wasn't there, but heard about it. Sounded amazing.

Dave chuckled. He wasn't a fan of Passerini, either. The guy was a no-brain military knuckledragger. But whatever dim opinion he had of the man, it was generic; Chalke's was colored with some kind of deep loathing that Dave didn't know the source of. He must have really peed in her cornflakes, because she hated the Secretary of Defense the way Dave hated people who mocked kombuchas and soy lattes.

DAVE KORY: Pentagon, got it. Anything else you want to add? Or anybody else want to confirm this? I could use a second source.

He waited, but no one stuck their neck out. That was fine; anonymous sourcing didn't bother him. It got him the news, allowed him to get it out before anyone else. Got clicks, got traffic. And especially on this story, being so far out in front was going to paaaaaaay.

HEATHER CHALKE: I can push someone your way that you can confirm with. That Bureau of Prisons clown Berenger owes us after the Cube screwup.

Dave blinked, then typed his reply: Was she there for it?

HEATHER CHALKE: No, but she'll confirm anyway, and then you can run it with a clear conscience.

Dave shuddered, but only for a second. Two single-sourced stories in a day. He may have protested to Mike Darnell that it didn't matter, but it did matter to him, at least a little. He wanted this one, but … he needed to be a little careful about stepping out on this limb constantly.

He'd met Chalke on a few occasions and could imagine her grinning as she typed all this. He started to reply with a question, something that might push her in the direction of getting him a legit second source, but—

Really, did he want that? This little horse-swapping thing they had going on here … it was designed to fly way below the radar. If he made her bird-dog a second source for him, a truly legit one, not this Bureau of Prisons patsy who was basically just going to confirm what she said without having seen or probably even heard it herself—it would probably blow up the story. Or at least delay it.

Chalke had seen what she was telling him about, Kory knew that. She didn't put stuff out to him without making sure it was legit, which meant if she said Nealon was in Revelen, she was in Revelen. Digging up another person in that classified loop that was in the know, just to confirm what he already knew, that Chalke was telling him the truth? It'd put someone else's ass on the line and jeopardize the good thing they had going on here.

Nealon was in Revelen. There wasn't a doubt in Dave's mind about it. Getting a second source was just covering his ass, however it was played. Talking to the Bureau of Prisons source would cover his ass just fine, because he could plausibly deny, in a court of law, in front of a jury of his peers, that he was being played. And who would know differently?

Not a damned soul, that was who.

Decision made.

DAVE KORY: Okay, I'll break it as soon as I get back to my desk and write it up. Have your contact call me.

RUSS BILSON: Awesome. Get it done. We've got a new narrative to shape. Stir the dogs up against Sienna Nealon again. I think we can all see how maybe this goes, if we do it right. And we'll all find ways to make out like bandits from this situation.

Dave just nodded, locking his phone and standing up in the darkened privacy booth. He certainly would be making out like a bandit. If the click counter had moved up like it was propelled by a rocket thus far, imagine how it'd move once he broke the exclusive story that Sienna Nealon was hiding out in a place no one had even heard of?

15.

Sienna

"Welcome to my humble abode," Vlad said once the limo had made its way up the curving switchbacks, up the mountainous hill to his castle, across a wide tarmac-like space, and pulled into his underground hangar beneath the castle. There was no other way to describe it besides that. Military equipment was pretty much everywhere, and included T-72 main battle tanks from Russia, a whole boatload of army trucks, a couple Bradley Fighting Vehicles from the US alongside a plethora of Humvees. Some of them even had turret-mounted weapons like Mk 19 grenade launchers and Ma Deuce 50-cal machine guns, which was not something you typically saw on the ones that cruised around in US cities. Though they might have been useful in LA traffic, especially the grenade launcher.

Also … the dude had cars. Cars enough to make Reed and Scott jealous. Mercedes, Ferraris, Lamborghinis, and even some classic Fords, Chevys and Dodges were represented in Vlad's car collection.

"Compensating for something, Vladimir?" I asked as I stepped out of the limo next to a 1970s-era Dodge Charger. American muscle, Transylvanian vampire. It didn't quite make sense to me, but there it was.

"Yes," Vlad said, nodding. "I am compensating for the fact that I cannot fly and sometimes wish to get places very quickly." His eyes sparkled again, and he strode past me, a slight limp slowing his movement. I hadn't noticed it before. "Come, and I will explain all."

"About overcompensating?" I asked. "You can go ahead and leave that part out."

Sophie elbowed me, lightly, in the back, and I looked back to see her staring at me with thinly pursed lips and narrowed eyes. "Enough."

"Am I finally getting to you, 'Sophie'?" I asked.

"Nothing 'final' about it—yet," she said.

Ooh, menace. I liked that. I made a kissy face at her, and she steamed, though she barely showed it.

"This way," Vlad said, leading me through the strange hangar deck of a garage. It was massive and reminded me of Greg Vansen's enormous garage/hangar that he had built into the wall of his house. Though technically it was smaller than an electrical socket, the treasures it housed were incredibly impressive.

"Your lair is beginning to look more and more like either a James Bond villain's digs or a third world king's palace," I said as he led us to an elevator in the corner of the room. I looked up. Stalactites reached down from a hundred feet above, the cavern's natural ceiling hemming us in there. "Or the Batcave, possibly. You're like an Eastern European dictator Bruce Wayne, maybe. With pointier hair."

"I like that one best," Vlad said with a smile. He pushed the elevator button himself after I got in with the rest of them. There were a few people walking around doing things in the garage, servicing vehicles and whatnot. I even caught sight of a few guards with G36s and AK-74s, doing their rounds.

"Are there any bats hanging out in the stalactites?" I asked. "Because then you'd definitely have a better claim. Unless they're vampire friends of yours, in which case …"

"I'm afraid I don't have any shifters here in my employ," Vlad said, "though I have known a few."

The elevator thrummed, moving fast. We'd entered through a massive garage door in the side of the cliff. It was big enough to pull a plane through, though there were none nearby and no runway near enough to use, though that expansive tarmac would have made a pretty nice helicopter landing zone.

The castle itself was up a cliff face a few hundred feet, meaning this whole ground level was excavated later, long after the castle was constructed. Again, I was reminded of Edinburgh Castle. Built on a huge rock, they'd tunneled into it to build basements and whatnot, though Vlad had clearly gone much farther here than the Scots ever had there.

After a few seconds the elevator whooshed to a stop. It dinged and opened on a floor that looked like it could have been torn out of any office building the world over, save for the lack of windows. "This is us," Yvonne said and moved past me. Arche followed her, shooting me a sly look as she passed. She bumped me with her right arm, and I felt the stiff, unyielding sensation of something thick and metallic wrapped around her right arm.

When last we'd met, she'd had a neato mechanical retractable arm up the sleeve of her trench coat. She controlled it directly with her electrical powers and could use it to choke a bitch, as Dave Chapelle would say. Or like a grappling hook.

Clearly she was still wearing it, and apparently she wanted me to know, because she gave me a thin smile after bumping me with it. "Nice to see you again, too, Arche," I said as she got off the elevator, leaving me alone with Sophie and Vlad as the doors closed.

"They're very good employees," Vlad said, "especially at what they do best."

"Destruction, right?" I asked, starting to get a possible picture of what he was talking to me for. "That's what they're best at."

"They get the job done," Vlad said. "Whatever the job is. Like Sigourney here."

I blinked, and Sophie's face hardened. "Did you seriously just forget her made-up name?"

"It is, as you said, made up," Vlad shrugged. "How am I to remember these things? I am … very old." He waved a hand around his head.

"You going to tell me the reason for all these lies yet?" I

asked, as the elevator hummed again. It seemed to be really moving, like a skyscraper elevator.

"In moments," Vlad said, holding up a single, thin, long finger.

"Fine, let me ask this while we wait—why have your people try and kill Friday a year ago?" I asked. "And why spare his life when he came here?"

Vlad nodded thoughtfully. "That is a longer story, and one which I am more than glad to answer, but perhaps the other truths first?" The elevator dinged again and opened onto a hallway with dim lighting, solitary bulbs strung one after another like runway lights from the ceiling. The hallway stretched for some distance, all stone and medieval construction. This was the older part of the castle, clearly one of the classics of Europe. Rooms lined either side of the hallway, and Vlad indicated I could step off the elevator first if I so chose.

I so chose, keeping an eye on both him and Sophie as I got out. I had to admit, Friday was right: the ambience in this part of the castle was creepy as hell.

"This way," Vlad said, taking the lead again. Sophie walked beside me, me eyeing her, her eyeing me, neither of us really trusting the other. I also listened very carefully for footsteps to make sure someone didn't bushwhack me from behind. Vlad might have been disarmingly nice thus far, but nothing about his tour or his answers had made me forget that he was both a legend for the worst reasons and also someone who had a strong connection to the all manner of hell that had rained down on me in the last few years.

We walked until the corridor turned abruptly left at a ninety degree angle, passing modern wooden doors that didn't quite fit the stonework and aged frames. This really was an old, castle, every bit of it—

Until we turned the corner.

Here the local carpenter had put in his best work, adding some frames and whatnot that were actually shimmed properly into position around the doors. One door, specifically. It was taller than the others, and I had a feeling it might have been a throne room or living quarters for the biggest cheese in Revelen at the time of its construction.

"I see you live in the renovated wing," I said as Vlad opened the door and held it for me. Such a gentleman. A bloodsucking gentleman.

He smiled again, and I stepped inside to find—

I let out a low whistle without intending to. This was definitely the modern wing, antiquity be damned.

A lushly appointed living room the size of a small barn awaited. The typical tiny castle windows had been ripped out here and replaced with an impressively large glass pane, which looked out over Bredoccia in all its rising glory. Despite its size, the room looked … homey, with couches and chairs that wouldn't have been out of place in a rustic lodge. There were even a few animal heads on the wall, though not too many, a couple of really big deer, one bear, both of which looked like local species rather than the North American varieties I was used to.

"Little bit of a hunter, there, Vlad?" I asked, strolling past to the window. The view of Bredoccia was amazing, and I shuffled up to the edge of the floor to ceiling window. Nothing was visible below save for the tarmac, which suggested the hangar deck was immediately below. After a several-hundred-foot section of castle wall and sheer cliff.

"Those trophies are mine," Sophie said.

I looked at her. A little query. She looked back at me, solidly indifferent. Sophie didn't seem to me the type who enjoyed hunting animals. I had her figured for the sort that preferred hunting the most dangerous game, man.

"So … you two live together?" I asked. Should have seen that.

"Not like you're thinking," Sophie said.

"I'm not thinking anything," I said, "except that you're both of that certain age where maybe looks aren't as important as finding that special someone who enjoys megalomania and murder as much as you do."

"I don't think you're losing your looks at all," Vlad said to Sophie, nodding at her in a very reassuring way. "I, on the other hand, have been on a bit of a downhill slide for … many years now, shall we say."

"It's good that you acknowledge it," I said. "Once you've confronted the problem, you're ready to take steps to fix those certain things that start to go wrong. Like, for, instance, have you considered Hair Club for Men to maybe smooth out the knife point thing you've got going on there …?"

Vlad chuckled, hardly menacing at all. "You really are quite amusing. I should perhaps look into that, but it is something of a signature at this point, is it not? Part of my … how do they say it these days? Brand awareness?"

"Dracula's got brand awareness and self-awareness," I said. "This is not what I expected. At all." Because it wasn't. A guy as old as Vlad, I would have thought he'd have missed the train on irony. But surprisingly, none of my insults or jibes was going over his head.

However old he was, he was still sharp. And sharp … was way more dangerous than dull.

"Can we get down to business?" Sophie asked, folding her arms in front of her and pacing toward the big window. She was twitchy, at least for her, but she moved to give me space. It wasn't exactly a sign of trust, since, again, I didn't know her powers. But psychologically, it was a nice gesture.

"Ah, yes," Vlad said, and he took a tentative step toward me. He was only a few feet away, just out of arm's reach, and offered me his hand, palm up, keeping the other where I could see it was empty. "Would you mind?"

I stared at his proffered hand, then up to his eyes. They glistened bright blue, brighter than the sky out that window. "You want me to … take your hand?"

"Yes," he said. "Exactly."

I looked at it, looked at him. Well, this might solve more than one problem. "Okay, bub. But if you want to hold hands, I'm just going to go ahead and warn you—this is gonna hurt you more than it hurts me."

He just smiled, and I hoped he wasn't about to reveal Gavrikov powers and burn off my hand.

I slapped my mitt right in his, and he held onto it—gently.

He gestured toward the window, and we took a couple steps toward it. Enough I could see pretty clearly out of it, not so close he could yank me around and defenestrate me without giving me enough time to react. "Nice view," I said, counting the seconds in my head. Five … six … seven …

"I chose to build here because of the commanding views," Vlad said. "I came here long ago. These lands were all controlled by local tribesman back then. The local wars were brutal, and there were no metas to speak of. Oh, some would pass through every now and again, looking to pillage and conquest, but … they were easily dealt with."

Ten … eleven … twelve … oh, shit …

I put a hand up to my face, blocking the light from my eyes as I groaned.

"You start to see now, yes?" Vlad asked. Boy, he was chipper.

"Damn," I muttered.

"What?" Vlad asked. His voice held traces of genuine wonder at my reaction.

"Another incubus wants me for his bride, yay," I said, pulling my free hand off my face. The other was still clutched—still gently—in Vlad's.

No burn.

No sting.

No powers working.

"You guys suck, and I mean that in the worst way, not the garden-variety soul-sucking kind," I said, words tumbling out in a rant. "You—none of you assholes—can even be bothered to get down on one knee. I mean, seriously, learn about what women want. I'm beginning to suspect you bastards all just want me for one thing—"

"No," Vlad said, shaking his head quite rapidly, vehemently. "No, no. I am not like Sovereign." He cringed, and his lips pursing together in utter disgust. "Not at all. This is not—*not* my reason for bringing you here, to be … that." He shook his head. "No."

I raised an eyebrow. "No?"

"No." He pointed at me, then himself. "We are family, you and I."

Eyeroll from me. "I'm sure, yeah, way back up the tree, fifteenth cousins eighteen times removed or whatever—"

"No," Vlad said, taking a step closer to me, voice a low and certain whisper. "No, Sienna … I am directly related to you. I am your great-grandfather. You wanted to know my name, my true name? It is not Vlad—"

"Bull*shit*," I whispered. My great-grandfather on the succubus side? I knew his name, and he was right … it wasn't Vlad.

It was …

"I am not an incubus at all, you see," he said. "I am … the father of all incubi and succubi … the first avatar of Death. I am—"

"Hell," I whispered.

He blinked, eyes moving as he processed what I'd said. "No." He shook his head gently. "*Hades*, not hell," he said, correcting me as though I'd merely misspoken, awareness of what I was actually trying to say sailing over his head for once. He spoke again, apparently proud of his title: "Hades.

"The God of Death."

16.

"Oh, man," I moaned, sinking a little inside. "You're supposed to be dead. Everyone told me you were dead."

"Who told you that I was dead?" Hades asked.

"Janus," I said, then I sagged. "Janus, you know. The lying-ass, two-faced god of doorways and bullshit."

"In fairness to my former son-in-law, he probably thought I was dead," Hades said. "He did, after all, come along with my brother, who certainly wanted me dead had the deed not already been done. It was not either of them that did 'the job,' however—"

"I don't remember who told me," I said, moving a step past him and staring out at Bredoccia as I brushed my hair back behind my ears, "whether it was Hera or him, but … they said Persephone did it."

"Indeed she did," Hades said, unbuttoning his shirt in the middle and pulling it open for a moment to show a chest that had a very immense scar right in the middle of it, a lumpy ridge of flesh in a circle right above the heart. "She did not miss when she aimed a root at me. She was trying to still my rage over—"

"Your granddaughter," I said, filling in the blank. "The one that had been killed by that mob in the square in some little Greek town."

"Exactly," Hades said, re-buttoning his shirt. There were other scars there, too, but I didn't inquire about them. Some kind of burn mark. He caught me looking, though. "You see this?" And he pointed to a mark, one of those burn scars. "This … is where my brother, Zeus, brought me back with his powers, some hours after my wife killed me."

I was blinking in surprise. "Uhmm …" This was all in utter contradiction to everything I'd ever learned about Hades, about Zeus, about … anyone, really. "Why?"

Hades smiled. "Because in spite of all that Zeus was—an assclown, I think you would say these days?—he was still my brother. And because my other brother convinced him to do it. In the name of mercy." He finished buttoning his shirt and walked over to the window, putting a hand against it and looking out. "And so, some hours after my wife stabbed me through the heart, putting an end to my … unquenchable rage … I awoke in a wooded grove, surrounded by my brothers and another, shall we say, interested party … and they presented me an ultimatum."

"Leave Greece and never come back," I said. "Under pain of … you."

Hades smiled, thinly, still looking out the window. "If I returned, I would experience death on a somewhat more permanent basis, yes. For keeps, this time."

Man, my head was spinning. "Okay, so, you were expelled from Greece. Fair enough. Then you came here?" He nodded. "Okay. But … why not, say, in the modern day, go … elsewhere? Rear your ugly head again? Why stay cooped up here in Transylvania?"

He shrugged. "This is my home and has been for as long as I can remember now. Why would I leave?"

"I dunno," I said, "to recapture some of that ascendant godhood you left behind in days of yore."

He smiled. "I am content in this place. From Revelen I can reach out with my influence. Try to steer the course of events in certain directions—"

I closed my eyes and bowed my head for a moment. "You sat out the Sovereign fight."

"I did not, in point of fact," he said. "I prepared Revelen as a stronghold against Sovereign and the threat he brought. We were prepared to fight, and did, killing several members of Century and eliminating many of their telepaths when they moved in Eastern Europe."

"But you didn't fight in North America," I said under my breath. I clenched my jaw. "I could have used some help back then, Great-Grandpa Death."

"I was forbidden to interfere in North America directly," Hades said quietly. "You are, I think, unaware of the forces that still slither about the world from days of old. Trust me when I tell you that more of our kind survived Sovereign's attacks than you have perhaps thought." He rubbed his chest. "Magni and Modi were very clear and unequivocal in spelling out what would happen to me if I involved myself in North America." He smiled. "They did allow the very slight accommodation of not killing me on sight, and thus in 1990 or so, I was able to visit Disney World in Orlando. Have you been?"

"I've been to the parking lot," I said, and put all thoughts of happy theme parks out of my mind. His little revelation had caused the steely chill I was feeling to be replaced by a slight boil. "So you fought in the war?"

He nodded. "I fought. *We* fought. I gathered metahumans here and we became a stronghold of Europe. Sovereign's attempts to enter our borders with his forces were all repelled. He was, of course, planning to come back at us, again, later, but … you stopped him and his army first. To which I say … Thank you. For saving the lives of my people. Many would have died doing what you did easily."

"It wasn't that easily," I whispered. "We lost people." I bowed my head. "I … lost people."

"We all lose people sooner or later," Hades said softly. "It is the human condition to always be losing. Friends. Family. Our lives as they slip away an inch at a time, day by day. I am sorry for your losses. Sorry I could not do more to help at that time, though I had very little idea that you were even in the fight."

I looked up at him. He stared back and seemed … probably sincere, though I couldn't really tell. "How could you not know?"

"Because he wasn't over there," Sophie said, her eyes fixed on me, but calmer, less angry than usual for her. "That war was a war of secrets, a war of silos—a fight going on over here, another over there—there was no central front, no communication between the players, no union between those of us against Century. It was a quiet war, up until that last bit with you and Sovereign showdowning over Minneapolis."

"It was a whispered thing before that, though," I said. "People knew. Omega knew. Governments knew—"

"If I had known you were fighting that fight and could have intervened, I would have," Hades said. "But … because I did not, because I could not … look at you now. You have ever stood on your own, have become great in your own right." He turned his eyes away. "Your strength … it is inarguable. You are feared the world over, and not because of the legacy you represent. You are feared, not because you are one of my progenitors, a succubus, the way so many of your forebears were. The awe with which the people look at you," and he stepped closer, eyes burning, "has nothing to do with your powers, with the social stigmas of your kind in the meta community, or with me—my legacy of—"

"Death," I said softly.

He nodded, but did not look pleased about the title. "You are your own person, Sienna. The most famous metahuman on the planet. And," here he smiled, a hint of pride swelling his chest—just a hint, "the most … dangerous? Most deadly, perhaps. Certainly the most feared."

"That's not who I am," I said.

"It is," Sophie said.

"I mean … that's not all of me," I said. "That's just the … brand awareness I use to scare people off when they try and do something stupid, like cross me. I'm not you. Not … Death. Why did you bring me here?" I asked. "Just to tell me this? Just to explain—what? 'Psych! We're actually family, and I mean you no harm'?"

"I do not mean you any harm," Hades said. "I have tried to help you—"

"I appreciate you getting me out of prison," I said, face

burning, but some of my emotion spent, "but … I don't know that I believe you when you say you've been 'helping' me. Helping me how?"

"I've been keeping an eye out for you for a long time," Sophie said. "Trying to keep some trouble off your back that you weren't ready for."

"At your command?" I asked, looking right at Hades.

He nodded, and I sensed there was more to it than he let on. "Yes."

"And you did this because … you serve him out of the goodness of your heart?" I turned on Sophie, and she evinced just a hint of surprise around the eyes.

"Not exactly," Sophie said, getting her reaction back under control. "We're both in this for our own reasons."

"What is your reason?" I asked. "Money? Ideology? Creed? Ego? Cuz those are the four big ones."

Sophie chuckled softly. "I'm quite wealthy. I don't care deeply about any political order or religion, nor does my ego need burnishing, thank you very much."

I felt the little grind in my heart, lowered my head, looked at the floor. "Yeah. That's what I thought."

"What did you think?" she asked, sounding a little careful about the question, as though she were afraid of the answer.

"You're a grade-A badass," I said, looking her right in the eyes. Blue as the sky, a few little flecks of green in there. Skin as pale as if she'd been raised in a cave—which I suspected she had. "You look like you could wipe out Hades with one hit."

Hades sort of shrugged. "I suspect it would take at least two."

"You're not his girlfriend," I said, and she blanched, almost imperceptibly.

She held my gaze. "What … do you think?" Waiting.

For my pronouncement.

"I think you're another person who was supposed to be dead," I said, looking *her* right in the eye. "I think 'Sigourney Weaver' was as good a name for you as 'Sophie', and that there's a damned good reason you haven't told me your real name. That you don't even go by your name anymore—"

"Most people couldn't pronounce it in the original tongue,"

she said. "Couldn't read it."

"'Lisa' was as close as you wanted to get, right?" I asked. "Because the real name—the anglicized version—some people would know it. Educated ones—"

"Education isn't what it used to be," she said.

"And neither are you, Lethe," I said. "Or did you prefer … Valkyrie?"

She froze. "Either would do. Just don't call me Lisa, I—"

"But that was your name," I said. "Wasn't it? Lisa—"

"Don't say it."

"This is getting interesting," Hades muttered under his breath.

"Shut up," she warned him. "It's not funny."

Hades held out his thumb and forefinger a few centimeters apart. "It's a little funny."

"Lisa Nealon," I said, and she sagged, shoulders falling. "That was your name. When you were my grandmother, that was your name. That was your name … before you died."

"Yes," she whispered, not daring to look me in the eye.

I stared back at her, a thousand questions bubbling to the surface of my mind, to my lips.

Only one made it out.

"… Why?"

17.

Lethe
Michigan
December
1989

"The Iron Curtain is falling," Hades said, looking around the living room, picking up a Hummel figurine of a little girl with an angelic face, staring at it for a moment, then replacing it on the shelf with the others. "This presents me an interesting opportunity, you see—"

"To die? For real, this time?" Lethe asked. She looked upon her father's face with a mixture of weariness and exasperation. She felt wrinkled even though she wasn't, at least not much. Over two thousand years she'd lived, and this—this middle-class living room in this middle-class town—this was her reward.

"I would prefer not," Hades said, looking away from the wall of figurines. "It is a nice collection, I think. Hardly the prize of your existence, though. Is this what you feel you have come to after all this time? From battles on the frontiers of the earth, from pushing the very boundaries of our existence to … collecting ceramic idols?"

"They're not *idols*," Lethe said, crossing the room to stand by him. His mere presence used to be intimidating. A lot of that luster had died when he had, so long ago. The man who had come back …

She picked a Hummel, standing next to him without fear. She'd never feared him for his powers the way others did. He could latch onto a soul at great distance; standing in the room with him while his full attention was upon you? More than a few weak people had been driven to death by the mere vibrato of his powers, even at a distance.

"I didn't mean it in the worshipful sense," Hades said, looking at the collection. There had to be a hundred of them, lining the wooden shelf. "I didn't think you were bowing to them at night, making sacrifices at an altar before them, doing missionary service in their name—"

She brought the Hummel in her hand to the shelf, a little too strongly. It shattered, sending porcelain dust all over the place. "I don't do missionary service in anyone's name anymore."

Hades cocked an eyebrow at her. "Not even James Fries, then? Because I had heard—"

"Don't be a pig," she said, giving him a deathly look all her own. "He's … a distraction. At most."

"He is some distant cousin of yours, I believe," Hades said, full of mirth. "Not that I judge. What you do in that arena is of little consequence to me save for the fruits it produces."

"I'm past my days of bearing fruit," Lethe said, glaring him down. He didn't even blink; hardly a surprise. The man standing before her had been glared down by the gods of old. Lived with them, died at the hands of one of them. "Modern science sees to that."

"I wouldn't put all my faith in medicine if I were you," he said. "Still … I suppose it has been difficult this last two thousand years." He picked up another Hummel.

She slapped it out of his hand, obliterating it. "Oh, you think it's been difficult? Being a succubus? Why yes. Yes. Yes, it has. Doomed to not touch lest I take—"

"I did not come here to argue with you."

"Maybe I'm just glad you're here so I can slap at you for a time for this curse you visited upon me." She did not remove her glare.

Hades did not meet her eyes. "Your mother and I had many

discussions in those days about what would befall our children out in the world, given how despised I was, given what you could do. I am sorry that I had no better answer than to send you, at your request—"

"With a monster as my guide," she breathed.

"I sent Wolfe with you because you needed … tempering," he said. "I did not realize that you would become more dangerous than he. That you would almost put him to shame. But … those days are gone, are they not? You hardly wreak any havoc anymore."

"It's not as easy to get away with it in the modern world. You should know this."

"I do know this," he said. "And that is why I have come to you. I know you have struggled with a path. Tried to find your place in the world … I was sorry to hear about Simon's passing—"

"No, you weren't," Lethe said. "You never liked Simon Nealon. You never thought he was good enough for me."

Hades shrugged. "A common sentiment among fathers, I think. But … I wished him no ill. In fact, I met one of his children of another liaison not so long ago. He came to my castle, in fact."

"Oh?" Lethe looked up from the dust of shattered Hummels. "Did you kill him, too?"

"No," Hades said. "I let him live, though I expect he will be quite reluctant to speak of our meeting."

"You should have killed him," Lethe said.

"That would seem more your grievance than mine," Hades said. "So I let him go, him and his … friends. You may feel the need to track him down, scourge him from the face of the earth if you would like. I would not complain; I would even lend you help if you needed it."

"I don't need your help, thanks," Lethe said. "If I want to kill the last things that remain of Simon, the things he made while he was catting around without me, I could do it myself."

"I have no doubt."

"I don't need to, though," she said. "I've long since made my peace with his … dalliances."

"The baggage behind which, I assume, brings us to young Mr. Fries?" Hades asked, one eyebrow perked up. "Is this really all you need anymore? A physical relationship with some young—"

"I just wanted to know what it would be like," Lethe said, almost hissing her answer. Her face burned. "This isn't something I want to discuss with my father, even one as distant and uninvolved as you."

"I am only distant because your mother's friends are very clear about how welcome I am here in your new homeland," Hades said, touching another figure. This one was a little bigger, two kissing little cherubic creatures. "Otherwise, I assure you, I would have visited long ago."

"You know she's alive, then?" Lethe asked.

"Of course."

"Then you know why I'm still here," Lethe said and ground another Hummel to dust out of pure spite.

"Your daughters," Hades said. "Charlie and Sierra. Quite an interesting pair, those two."

"Have you met them?" Lethe asked.

He nodded subtly. "They don't know it was me, of course."

She rolled her eyes. "Of course. But if you've met them, you know. Charlie's going to need my help to keep out of trouble—"

"I find her madness rather … endearing," Hades said. "I doubt many would see it that way, but … prerogative of my blood, I suppose. What does Persephone think?"

"That she's batshit crazy and dangerous, the worst sort of succubus. She doesn't want Charlie to cross her or anyone else she knows."

"A fair assessment. And Sierra?" Here his eyes twinkled.

Lethe barely looked at him, but knew what he was thinking nonetheless. "Leave her the hell alone, Father."

"I would hardly dream of interfering in her life," Hades said. "Not in any … large ways. She will have enough trouble come her direction, I expect, from her personality alone." His eye truly did twinkle. "She doesn't know when to quit."

"Yeah," Lethe said. "Maybe she got that from her dad."

"I doubt it," Hades said, making his way over to the couch,

which had a checkerboard pattern on it, each square only a centimeter wide. There were thousands of them. He sank down. "Ah. Modern upholstery is so much more comfortable than …"

"The cave?" Lethe asked.

"Or even the simple wooden items of my upbringing. Straw beds. Terrible." He shook his head. "I am intrigued to see what they do next with mattresses. I feel there might be great strides in them over the next decades. Comfort is a priority for this late-stage society. The comforts always become great just before a fall."

"You would know."

"From experience, yes," he said, "and this couch is … very comfortable. And the society in which I find myself ruling? Well, it is experiencing an upheaval of its own right now. Revelen will come through this crisis, though, and these Soviet pet puppet masters who I have pretended to bow to over the last few years? Well, they are being swept away even now. One curtain falls—iron, you see? Another must rise to take its place, if I wish for Revelen to continue to be my haven."

"Why should I care about any of this?"

"I know you have a comfortable life here," Hades said, adjusting himself on the couch. He wore a suit, and quite a flattering one at that. It looked like something he'd picked up on Savile Row in London. Perfectly tailored. New, too, which meant he'd dressed up for this. "Living in your widowhood. Enjoying your … creature comforts … couches and Fries and …"

Lethe turned her back on him. Stared at the Hummels.

"… figurines?"

Something about that plinked a chord in her as surely as if he'd reached in with his soul powers and plucked at her heart. He didn't—because he couldn't—but he was her father, and he knew her as well as anybody ever had, even in spite of their long estrangement—

Lethe lashed out at the shelf and shattered the Hummels one by one.

One for cheating Simon, damn him. She'd tried; truly tried, for the first time, and her best as a wife, as a lover—

It still wasn't good enough.

One for Charlie. Crazy Charlie, doing all the stupid things Lethe had done in her youth, but under the gun of modern society and all its restrictions. "You can't do this nowadays," she'd told her youngest daughter, but it fell on deaf ears and Charlie went on drinking and ripping the souls out of men at random—

Not good enough.

One for Sierra. Tightly buttoned-up Sierra, who'd looked her mother in the eye and said, "I don't need you. I don't need—"

"Not a good enough mother," Lethe said, smashing the Hummel to smithereens, and then shattering the shelf. "Not good enough at anything—not even for Wolfe anymore, too tame, too—"

"Shall I come back later?" Hades asked. She rounded on him, and he was just standing there, thumb at the door. "Would like some more time to destroy your possessions? I can come collect you in a few hours if you would prefer …"

Lethe kicked back like a mule and the whole shelf shattered down. "What makes you think I even want to come with you?"

Hades just stared at her, blue eyes glimmering in the shadows of the room's half-light. "Call it an idle suspicion, but I sense your despair. You have lived a long life, and now … you come to the point of questions, yes? 'What is the meaning?' You have lived a full life … lived more perhaps than most even your age. Killed more, for certain, than almost any your age."

She bowed her head. "Not more than you, though, have I?"

"Perhaps," he said. "Only an amateur would keep count."

She looked up. "What do you want from me?"

He smiled. "I had the same questions you now face, when I reached my … middle age, they call it now? A cute title, I think. We were gods, my daughter. Now … you are nothing, yes? You see yourself struggle with the role of … wife? Mother? Selfishly, you think, becoming perhaps a true lover for the first time? With Fries? Becoming something you couldn't even be with Simon?"

"Screw you," she said. "You made me this way."

"I did not," he said. "If it were down to my choice, I would have made you like me, not this hybrid between your mother's powers and mine, unable to touch, unable to feel, unable to live between the moments when you embrace your destiny, your power. Yours is without doubt a harder road than even mine—but that has made you strong, my daughter." He crossed to her. "You know the darkness of misery. It has tempered your soul. Gone are the days when you sought easy death, easily inflicted on lesser men. You are more now. You should be more than a housewife, a lover, a mother to ungrateful children who have not lived in the world as we have lived in it—"

"What do you want?" she asked, sagging into the couch. Annoying as it was, he was right: it was comfortable.

"I want to help you," he said, and here he offered her a hand, open, his palm waiting for her. "I have experienced what you feel now. That dooming despair that comes when you realize all you have loved is lost. All you have known, all you have wanted is now forever outside your reach." His hand wavered. "I want to show you what I discovered that saw me through those dark days. I want you to believe again. Perhaps, even … in me? Though if not, that is fine, too. It would just be nice to see my favorite daughter …" The corners of his eyes crinkled as he smiled. "… live again."

"I am living," she said, looking up at him with sharp loathing. "Or … at least I thought I was. With Simon. With Fries. With Charlie and Sierra."

"Wife? Mother? Lover?" Hades shook his head. "These were never the words that defined you. You were always so much more."

"You better not be saying the best I can be is 'daughter,'" Lethe said, glaring up at him.

"Hardly," he said. "Come with me. Find out for yourself. Let us get back to finding you a path, yes?"

She stared at his hand. It was … inviting. He'd never struck at her, never hit her … and if she touched him …

He wouldn't die. Unlike … so many others.

Minutes passed. She stared at him, he stared at her. Patient.

Finally … she took his hand.

"Now," he said, as she rose to her feet, "we just need to deal with the trivial matter of making sure that Mr. Fries and his employers think you are dead. For I want complications with Alastor like I want a kick in the groin."

"How are you going to manage that?" Lethe asked, looking around. The Hummels were shattered, the living room a mess. Good thing she'd just given up on the role of housekeeper, because cleaning this up? Would suck a lot.

"I have the body of a woman your height, your weight, in my trunk," he said.

"Were you carrying that around for fun or did you pick it up specifically for this?" Lethe asked.

Hades's eyes twinkled. "Wouldn't you like to know. I found her in a morgue across town."

"How did you know I'd say yes?" Lethe asked. There was a peculiar weight on her shoulders. "What the hell were you going to do with her if I said no?"

"Leave her in a Christmas display and let the cops chase their tails for a while, probably," he said with a shrug. "I think we leave her here … set a small fire … and … as the French say, voila! You are now dead. Lisa Nealon will die here, today. All her obligations, all her fears, all her troubling decisions. All you need to decide is what you want to bring with you."

"Not a damned thing," Lethe said and walked away, passing a picture of Sierra and Charlie, as girls, hanging on the wall. She didn't even look back. "Let it all burn."

18.

Sienna

"Is everyone I thought was dead still alive?" I asked, staring at my grandmother and great-grandfather as she finished her story about evading James Fries and Omega in Michigan back in 1989. "Seriously. Is George Washington going to come strolling out here, fresh as a daisy?"

"I think we can safely say Washington is dead," Hades said. "Though I did not witness the event myself, I am informed, reliably, he was human, and did die."

"Dead is usually dead," Lethe said, a bizarre melancholy hanging over her, making her way more sedate than even usual. "Hades and I had good reasons to fake our deaths. His brothers' threat in his case, and … Omega and Fries in mine."

"Why not just take on Omega?" I asked. "Why not whip their asses? I did."

"Is that why Janus is still rebuilding it from the ground up?" my grandmother asked with a small smile. "Cut off one head …"

"Captain America fan?" I asked. "You'd get along great with my brother."

She rolled her eyes. "I doubt it. I don't 'get along great' with much of anyone."

"Well, you haven't made me kick your ass yet," I said. "That's something."

"Oh, we've fought, granddaughter," Lethe said. "You just don't remember it."

"Why don't I remember?" I asked. "Because you're the stronger succubus?"

"No," she said, "I don't know which of us is. Rose was stronger than you, though, and she took your memory of it. Clearly. Because it was a humdinger of a brawl. Best fight I've had in a few centuries." She brushed her jaw.

Damn Rose, stealing my memory of kicking my grandmother's ass. And meeting her before, in general. "Seriously, though—who else is alive?" I asked. "Is my mom?" I knew the answer already.

"No," Lethe said. "She's quite dead. You saw the body."

"Yeah," I said. "Of course. As is Charlie." My grandmother reacted, almost imperceptibly, but I couldn't tell quite what she was thinking.

"I am … somewhat late in saying this, I think," Hades said, "but … I am sorry for the loss of your mother. She was everything I have come to be proud of in my brood … and I am sorry I never got a chance to know her better."

"You had a chance," I said under my breath. He could hear me, of course. "You chose not to."

"Not exactly," he said. "The same goes for you. The first we knew of you were rumors, really. From Omega expatriates seeking sanctuary in Revelen during the war. The rest—"

"You're telling me you didn't know about me at all?" I asked, staring him down. "About my fight?"

He shook his head. "No. Only whispers, until just before your battle with Sovereign. Imagine our surprise to find out one of ours was leading the charge."

"I tried to help," Lethe said. She was fixed on me, looking me dead in the eye. "I was on my way up to Minneapolis when you fought him, after you killed Century. I was hours away when I got the news he was dead. That you won."

"Did I make you proud?" I asked, as snarkily as I could manage.

"Yes," she said and … shit. I think she meant it.

"It was indeed a proud day," Hades said. "But also a sad one;

Sovereign, for all his faults, was one of my brood as well. A shrinking number, to be sure. I found no joy in his death, but I did find pride that you proved yourself strong enough to handle the threat he posed. Sovereign had a world-killing, world-ending organization, and you …" Hades smiled. "You countered it. Eighteen years old, and you defeated a man who had walked the world for over a thousand, defeating all comers in that time. It was an impressive accomplishment, and the first of many, if I do say so. So, yes, we are … proud of you and all you have done. I only wish we could have met sooner, but … this is the time we have."

"Why couldn't we have met sooner?" I asked. "You've been here all this time. I've been on the run from the law for two years. Hell, I was a few hundred miles away last year, up to my eyeballs in trouble with another of your 'brood' in Scotland—"

"Yes," Hades said, nodding, "it was unfortunate that your greatest battle came at the hands of another of our own. Tragic that we have seen so much internal strife when the world largely hated us all along." He shook his head. "This is why I have brought you here now, in fact."

I raised an eyebrow. "So it's not just because I'm super special and needed a way out of prison?"

He shook his head. "There are so few of us left now from the family. And so many of us have fallen in the last years. Sovereign. Charlie. Rose. Your mother."

"Your boy Raymond," I said.

Hades blinked. "Who?"

Lethe thought about it for a second. She muttered something in Greek. "He had started going by Raymond."

"Ahhhhh," Hades said. "He was still alive? How unfortunate, I did not know, but this merely illustrates my point. Our family has long been under attack, especially those of you with the power of incubi and succubi. We have long seen you hunted by a jealous and fearful world. Here, we will watch each others' backs. Put aside pointless dominance games and live in peace. Together, we will forge a new society, and a new future for our kind." A smile tugged at the corners of his mouth. "Here … we will be family again. Just as it was in the days of old. And you, Sienna … to you, I say …" He extended his arms wide. "Coming here … this was always to be your fate. Welcome home, Sienna Nealon." He smiled, and it was … less terrible. "You need never fear again."

19.

"Great-Grandpa is a little grandiose, isn't he?" I asked Lethe. We were walking down the hall of the castle a few minutes after Hades had made his pronouncement of how I was home at last, and was oh-so-welcome. We'd exchanged a few conversational pleasantries after that, nothing major (because I'd been a little stunned by everything), and he'd asked Lethe to show me to my room so I could rest after my long journey.

So now she was showing me to my room, and I was looking to get the straight dope from my grams.

Lethe just smiled at my observation. "He was the God of Death for an entire civilization. Even in exile in the caves—the underworld—yes, I suppose being who he was lent a certain grandiosity to everything he did."

"Hm," I said. "What about—"

"Here," Lethe said, and we stopped outside a wooden door. She opened it, and it gave way to a nicely appointed room. The stone walls were hung with some paintings and such to make it look less medieval, and there were blankets and pillows on the bed to give it a homey touch. All in pink. Like they'd just found out I was a girl and tried to decorate appropriately.

"Wow, I'm so excited to get my own room again." I said it deadpan, but honestly … I was kinda glad. I'd shared with June Randall for the days before this, Harry before that, and getting one without a lock on the outside? Even better.

"We can personalize it some if you'd like," Lethe said, giving it the once over with me. "Lots of tradesmen and merchants in Bredoccia have some nice touches that could spruce things up. Interior décor was never my strong suit, but … there are options available. And a nearly unlimited budget."

"Cool, I'd like a nuclear silo over in the corner, and a vault to store my Fabergé egg collection over here—"

She evinced a little surprise at the words "nuclear silo," just a flash of the eyes.

"I was totally kidding about the Fabergé eggs. Unless you're cool with me buying some."

"Well, we're not exactly an Emirate here," she said. "Our budget isn't entirely unlimited, I suppose I should have said. As to the other thing … were you kidding?"

"No, I want some nukes to wipe out all my enemies in a scourge of fire—of course I was kidding," I said. "I was listing expensive things. But you have nukes here?" I asked, and she grimaced, confirming it. "Wow. When did that happen?"

"We have an entire country of metahumans," she said, looking around the room as though there were an escape hatch available. "There are powers at our disposal that have allowed us to—"

"Go nuclear?"

"To take over Russia," she said, apparently deciding somewhere in the middle that honesty was the best policy. "Dammit. We were going to tell you all this a little later. Hades had a whole briefing planned."

"I'll try and act surprised when it comes up." I deepened my voice to imitate my great-grandfather's timber and accent, crossing it with the traditional Dracula. "'Ve have taken Moscow. Ze Russians are now our bitches.'" Back to mine. "'Yay! That's so amazing! Can I be Czaress'?"

Lethe arched an eyebrow at me. "Well, you wouldn't do any worse than Stalin."

"Let's not be so sure of that," I said. "I have a firm hand. An iron one, one might say. I bet I'd be a bloodthirsty dictator." I let my amusement dissolve. It was mostly forced. "You know invading other countries isn't cool, right?"

"We didn't invade them," she said. "We put a skinchanger in

charge. He looks like the old—"

"Douchebag."

She stared at me in question. "You mean us or—"

"The other guy," I said. "He was a douchebag. Dmitry Fedorov was a tyrant. Though, based on *your* reputations …"

She looked away. "I know." Then her gaze fell back on me, like she found her courage with a new line of attack. "One could say the same of you."

"You're kinda hurting my feelings here, Grandma," I said.

Lethe didn't quite blanch, but her eye twitched some. "It might take me some time to get used to you calling me that, at least in such a cavalier manner."

"Well, I'm always cavalier. Flippant, even."

"No doubt," she said, and walked over to a high dresser, messing with the doily atop it, cringing a little at it as she picked it up between her fingers. "There's no one innocent in this room, Sienna. The standards of the world were different in our day. It was not the civilized place it is now. It was tribal warfare; no one trusted anyone, at least not without good cause. That led to conflict. Neither I nor Hades much cared to lose."

"I, too, do not care for losing," I said, pursing my lips. "Fine, I won't judge you based on your reputation from thousands of years ago. But we're still going to have a talk about all the crap that's flown my way the last few years out of Revelen. It's a long list."

"Agreed," she said, wadding the doily up and tossing it in a nearby trash bin. "I assume you didn't want that?"

"But it was so pretty," I said. "Kidding. So … how many souls do you have under your command?"

She shrugged. "I don't know. None, really, at least none active. They've all been dissolved away given how long it's been since I've taken one in. The power …" She shook her head. "It's a burden. I'm not Charlie. I'm more like your mother. I only use it when I absolutely have to, and I haven't found cause for quite some time."

"But when you were younger …" I watched her carefully.

She nodded. "Yes. I killed … countless. Absorbed so many. Took my enjoyment wherever I could. Felt the rush … used it." She bowed her head. "Sienna ... you have to understand ... the things you can do ... with your boyfriends ... I couldn't."

I frowned. "Hey, wait. I don't need to hear—"

"There was no easy way for me to touch another human being without taking their soul," she said, looking right at me, "until the invention of—"

"I don't need to hear this."

"—latex—"

"Really, really don't need to—"

"Imagine going through your whole life not being able to—"

"I—please—stop—"

"I mean, you think *you* have it bad—"

"No. No. Noooooo."

"—the things you can do with your boyfriend now? Younger me would be jealous. And probably try to kill you, because ... that's just how I did things."

I realized one of my eyes was tightly shut. "Oookay. Are we done with this now? Confession may be good for the soul, but even the tangential details of my grandmother's tragic sex life, even with lots of blanks not filled in? Terrible for my brain."

"What's that clichéd phrase? 'Just sayin'?" Here I caught a glint of amusement in her eye, a slight twitch to the corner of her mouth. "In that one small area ... you don't have it so bad living in the modern world." She looked away, toward the small window out of the castle wall. "Actually ... there are a lot of wonderful things about the modern world."

"Indoor plumbing, right?" I asked. "Gotta be high on the list, given the state of latrine technology when you were a kid."

"We lived in a cave for most of my childhood," she said, making her way to the window. "We can get this torn out and replaced with a bigger window if you prefer. One like Hades's."

"Yeah, I'm not a vampire, so, that'd be great."

"I'm a soul vampire," she said, lifting a bare hand. "Technically, so are you."

"Well, like you said ... I don't enjoy sucking. At least not souls." I said. "Maybe a lollipop."

"I like those, too," she said. "Another boon of modernity."

She lowered her gaze to the floor. "I'm sorry that you had such a rough upbringing. And … young adulthood. And life, in general."

"Well, that's the way things roll," I said. "My childhood, all that, it wouldn't have been my choice—"

"Yes, it would," she whispered.

"Um, no," I said.

She raised an eyebrow at me. "If you say so."

I frowned. "It was what it was. What about you? What's your path these last … however many years? You're still working the family business, still dealing with … I'm having a hard time not calling him 'Vlad'—"

"He won't care if you call him that. I don't know if you noticed, but he's annoyingly self-aware and very into trends. The whole Dracula thing? It amuses him, though he's … well, he's not what you'd expect of Dracula."

"Not as bloodthirsty as I would have expected from Dracula, true," I said. "Didn't really anticipate being offered cotton candy by Vlad the Impaler."

"He's still not someone you would want to cross," she said, "but he's different now, for this different age. Bloodthirsty played well in the old world. If you were facing a legend like that? Who wants to storm that castle?"

"Elizabeth of Bathory, maybe?"

"She was an actual vampire," Lethe said, "and not a nice one. The day I helped kill her—"

"My family was involved in making history by killing people, so interesting," I muttered.

"It's a family trade," she said with dry humor. "You seem proficient in it yourself."

"I have done things I am not necessarily proud of," I said, looking around, catching a flash on the flatscreen TV mounted above the fireplace. For a second, I thought maybe it turned on and off. "But I'm a little low on regrets, to be honest. Going to Scotland without a portable howitzer might be one of a very, very few."

"I have … so many," she said, staring off into the distance.

"Oh, yeah?" I asked. "Name one."

"Not killing your bastard Uncle Friday is right up there, some days," she said, eyes flashing.

"So you did order that," I said, staring her down. "I hope you don't plan to try it again, because—"

She shook her head. "I'm over it. Mostly." She looked away. "Your grandfather, Simon … we weren't good for each other. His behavior reflected the gaping flaws in our relationship." She looked me right in the eye, and … yeah, there were hints of pain. "It wasn't like it is now. I thought we could have a solid relationship without … those certain things you probably wish I wouldn't talk about—"

"Yeah, let's steer clear of your sex life, please, thanks, bye."

"Anyway, even with that, I wasn't able to …" She shook her head, looked away. "I guess I had other problems by that point. I always thought if I could just touch I would be able to … be …"

"Normal," I whispered.

She looked up, sharply, surprised. "Yes. Normal. Have a normal relationship. After … thousands of years of … not."

Lethe shuffled to the window. The sun was starting to fade toward sunset. "But it turns out that thousands of years of pushing people away or draining their souls? It leaves a mark on your personality. I think you might know something of that."

"What? Nooooo," I said, joining her by the window. Her eyes were fixed in the distance, past the Dauntless Tower, and there was a longing there. "All my relationships have turned out wonderfully, thanks. I've definitely never driven away men by dint of my personality, which is all sweetness and light … and woe betide any son of a bitch who says differently."

Lethe cracked a smile. "You sound like …"

"You?" I asked.

"And your mother," she said, looking away again. "She and I … we butted heads. Big surprise, right?"

"She and I did the same," I said. "Constantly. She kinda tried to … break my will. It didn't take."

"I don't think she tried to break your will, Sienna," Lethe said, putting a hand on the window, palm on the glass. "I think she did what she had to in order to keep you safe. No more, no less."

"She might have done a little more than was strictly necessary," I said. "But … it's hard to quibble with the 'keep me safe' part, given what I've gone through since I got out."

Lethe nodded. "You miss her."

"It was the question, wasn't it?" I asked. "About whether she or not she was dead? That was the giveaway? Because most people assume I hate her."

She didn't answer, just waited.

"Yeah, I miss her." I nodded. "Weird, isn't it? She imprisoned me for a decade. Hammered me. Locked me in a metal coffin when I pissed her off—"

"When you pushed at the boundaries she'd set for your safety," Lethe said.

"Way to justify child imprisonment, Grandma," I said. "Lemme guess, in your day, they boxed you up every hour on the hour, whether you needed it or not?"

A faint smile appeared on her lips. "I was raised in a cave, guarded by Wolfe and his brothers, so … my upbringing is not one you want to look to for a favorable comparison. I didn't see the light of day until I was a woman grown."

"You and Bane both," I said. "Bet you have dynamite night vision, though."

She rolled her eyes. "We all do. But the point stands. We were both prisoners growing up—you because of Omega and the others who would have wanted you. Me because of my father's enemies, who were legion. An entire pantheon, actually."

"That does suck," I said. "I can sympathize with the 'no light' thing. I mean, I had electricity, and Mom let me get away with looking out the back windows, but other than that …" I shook my head. "I didn't see the sun, really, until … the day I was standing on the roof of the IDS tower having just drained Aleksandr Gavrikov."

She nodded. "I know these feels, as you kids say."

"It kinda creeps me out that you and Vlad use these extremely modern terms," I said. "I'm all set to take you seriously as these epic, legendary murderous badasses, and then you bust out the tweener-speak. I figure you're about two sentences away from saying, 'We're literally gods over here, you guys.'"

"We try to keep up," she said, smiling. "With the changing times. It's easier now, with the internet."

"Well, congrats on being the 'cool' grandparent," I said. "And also the only living one."

"Lucky me," she said softly, "I've got you all to myself—for now." That could have sounded really threatening in someone else's words, especially given Lethe's track record of murder and mayhem, but it was so laced with regret that it sounded almost … sweet.

Like she was actually grateful to be standing here with me.

My throat got a little thick just then, and I coughed a few times. Not out of emotion, you know, just … "The air's dry here," I said.

"Sure." She coughed, too. "If you want, I can leave you be for a little while. Let you get some rest."

"I probably should," I said. "It's … been a day, y'know. Lots of revelations. And I just got out of prison like twelve hours ago or something. Maybe more like twenty now. I dunno."

She started a slow retreat toward the door. "If you need anything, just …" She pointed at the phone on the desk. "There are servants. Chefs on duty. Just dial zero."

"Nicest hotel I've ever stayed in," I said, looking at the bed. "No mint on the pillow, but still … very nice."

"I can get turndown service for you, if you'd like," she said. "Pretty sure there's chocolate in the castle somewhere. Your great-grandfather has a sweet tooth—"

"I'm good for now," I said, waving her off. "Like you said … I probably just need some chill time. I'll probably collapse the moment you're out the door."

She walked over to the phone. "Come here a second."

I did.

There was a nice laminated series of numbers there, and she pointed at one. "This is the castle phone number. It's been the same since the 1950s, when it was first installed." She looked me right in the eye, with strange intensity. "Memorize it, will you? You might need it."

"Uhm, okay—"

"If you ever need me—ever, at any time—you can call this number," she said, staring me down. "Any time. Even overseas."

"Am … am I going overseas?" I asked.

"Any time," she said with strange emphasis. "Memorize it now. Country code, too."

I looked down at it, and stared. It was a three-digit country code, and then 0000 0000. "Uh. Well. Got it, I think. Simple enough. I guess we know who the earliest adopter was in this country."

She nodded. "Call any time. Just ask for me at the switchboard."

"Do you really think I'll be needing it soon, then?" I asked. "Aren't I staying a while?"

She smiled tightly. "I doubt you'll need it immediately, but … it's important to me that you know …" She put her hands on my shoulders, and looked me right in the eye. "You are family to me. And whatever you might think of me … of the things I've done …" There was a glint in her eye. "I am and always was a tigress when it came to my kids and grandkids. You can call me anytime. *Any*time." She repeated. "And I will help you. Okay?"

"Anytime I need help, I call you," I said. "Overseas. On the moon, maybe, even? And you'll come running."

She nodded, making her way to the door, which was right next to the desk. "Exactly. Any time."

"Understood. I think."

Lethe opened the door. "If you need anything …" and she pointed at the phone. "My extension and Hades's are both over there. If you can't sleep, feel free to call. If you need someone to talk to. We keep odd hours here."

"Sure, because of the vampirism." She smirked, and I felt the need to respond more seriously. "Yeah, no, I'll definitely …" I caught movement out of the corner of my eye the moment she was through the door, but I didn't turn to face it because it was on the TV.

Simple text. Green on the black background.

"See you tomorrow," Lethe said, and she shut the door, oblivious to what I'd just seen.

"Yeah," I said, reading while I formulated an answer. "See you tomorrow …" The door clicked closed softly.

HEY SIENNA, the text on screen read. **GLAD YOU MADE IT.**

"Oh, shit," I muttered to myself. "No, not …"

THAT'S RIGHT.

"Dammit."

IT'S CASSIDY.

"Like I didn't know that."

And then another line … one that caused me to sag.

ARE YOU READY TO BEGIN?

20.

Passerini
The White House

"You'd better not be wasting my time with this, Passerini," President Gondry said as he walked into the Situation Room. His lips were tight, hemmed in by his grey goatee, eyes dark in the dim lighting.

Passerini was waiting by the biggest screen in the room, the satellite image already zoomed in. *Or what?* he thought. *You'll fire me?*

But Bruno Passerini was way too buttoned down to ever say anything like that to his Commander-In-Chief, even a REMF like Gondry. Instead: "Sir, we've located Sienna Nealon. She's in Bredoccia." And he pointed at the image on screen.

Gondry paused just inside the door. Someone had definitely given him the bullet point, but as his eyes, hidden behind the reflected glare on his glasses, took in the sight of a somewhat blurry, dark-haired girl in an orange jumpsuit on the screen, he brought a hand up to his chin, fingers stroking the goatee. The president made his way to his seat, albeit slowly, never once turning his head from the screen. "Well, you've certainly piqued my interest. What else have you got?"

"Sir," FBI Director Chalke said, drawing his head to turn in her direction, "we can confirm that the jet in the satellite imagery originated at Eden Prairie airport. We traced the flight path, and our agents on the ground in Minneapolis have visited the airport and picked up the flight logs. It all checks out."

"Good work, Chalke." Gondry nodded. "You are on top of this situation." He leaned on his elbows. "Her escape is the blackest of black eyes for this administration. And just days after we announced we'd captured her. The public could finally sleep safe in their beds, sound in the knowledge that this menace was off the streets …"

Passerini stayed silent, but felt his eyebrow quirk up almost inadvertently. He had strong doubts that many people were losing sleep over Sienna Nealon, at least outside of whoever in the DoJ was tasked with catching her. Passerini tended not to pay as much attention to domestic issues, but had Sienna Nealon ever actually killed anyone who didn't have it coming—at least a little? He couldn't recall seeing anything on the subject, but it wasn't really his bailiwick.

"This is priority one, people," Gondry said, and again his eyes settled on the screen—or so Passerini thought until the president spoke to him. "What are our options?"

Once he'd realized that Gondry was talking to him, specifically, Passerini lurched into action. "Well, sir, they're unfortunately few, unless we want to potentially provoke a war."

"Nonsense," Gondry waved him off. "We sent a SEAL Team into Scotland for her. Last I checked, we're not at war with the United Kingdom." He chuckled.

Passerini's blood ran cold. That had been done over his objections. "We were lucky on that one, sir. I don't know the full story, but I think Scotland might have been under some different governing circumstances back then. CIA could tell you more than I could." It wasn't a huge secret that the UK had gone through some bizarre period of governmental estrangement in Scotland last year. No one seemed to have a good pulse on what was going on, but it was apparently in hand now.

"I'll make this simple: how do we get Sienna Nealon out of that flyspeck country and back into our prison?" Gondry asked. "Or dead. I'm not particular. Making a move like that, bombing some failed second world state might net us a foreign policy win with the American people. With little reprisal."

"Ah, that might have been true six weeks ago, sir." Passerini gestured at the screen. It zoomed out, and he looked down the table. That young colonel in the army uniform, his new adjutant, nodded at him, hands poised over a computer. "It's not true now." He pointed at the overhead map on the screen. "Revelen has become a nuclear power. In addition to the silo emplacements for the defensive system, they now have their own nukes. Here, here, here—"

"That's ridiculous," Gondry said. "How did they manage that without us noticing?"

Passerini blinked. "Well, sir, we did notice. That was the content of our briefing just yesterday."

Gondry sat back in his chair. "Countries do not become nuclear powers overnight, Mr. Secretary."

"That may have been the case in the old world, sir," Passerini said, "but it appears things have changed. Much like with their new anti-ballistic missile system, they excavated silos and built them from the ground up in less than forty-eight hours." A different picture appeared on the screen, a close-up time-lapse of a silo being constructed. Passerini blinked; he hadn't even known they had this. Whoever that young army man was, he was making Passerini look good. "One metahuman came along and dug the silo in minutes. Another ..." The scenery changed, enormous pieces of metal floating through the air in a real-time video from yesterday, "... built the silo itself with some sort of metal-control power, then emplaced the SS-19 Stiletto ICBMs that came in via the port of Canta Morgana." The last shot showed the rockets hovering in mid-air as they were divvied between silos.

"Like Magneto," the Secretary of the Treasury said.

"I don't know who that is," Gondry said.

"It's from the *X-Men* comic books and movies," Passerini said. He hadn't heard of Magneto until a briefing paper he'd read yesterday. "Master of magnetism, can move metal with his mind. Stop bullets, build a silo from scratch in hours, move missiles ... that sort of thing. Choke you to death with your own necklace. Crush your skull with your glasses."

Gondry scrambled to pull off his glasses and tossed them away onto the table with a clatter. "You people could have warned me about that!"

"There's traditionally a range limit on metahuman powers, sir," Chalke said, leaning in. She'd taken the seat right next to the president, even though there was assigned seating and that wasn't hers. "You're just fine here. Out of reach." She slid the glasses back toward him.

He picked them up without a word, slipping them back on. "Just as well, I can't see a damned thing without them. All I'm hearing here are problems. I want solutions, Mr. Secretary. How do we get Sienna Nealon? SEAL Team? An attack helicopter? Tank regiment?"

"Sir," Passerini said, "if you want her extracted by force, I don't have a plan I can recommend. We have to assume if they've received Russia's ABM system, they have also received traditional surface-to-air missile emplacements, or they're coming soon. Any attempts to fly in are going to be … dicey."

"These are soldiers, Mr. Secretary," Gondry said. "This is their reason for existing. I don't care what it takes, as long as it stays within the realm of reasonable casualties. I can explain some soldiers dying to the American people, provided we get Ms. Nealon."

"Sir, the Secretary of Defense is trying to let you know," SecState Ngo chimed in, "if we attack Revelen by sending in a team, there will be reprisals. Possibly nuclear now." She leaned onto the table, looking at the president. "Do you think it's worth risking a nuclear war over this one woman?"

Gondry had to think about that. "No," he finally decided. "That would be ridiculous, I suppose. But … surely there are other options available to us." He looked around, and his attention settled on the CIA Director. "What about an assassin?"

The CIA Director looked gobsmacked. "You … want us to assassinate an American citizen … on foreign soil?"

"Don't look so shocked, Crawford," Gondry said. "This is hardly the first time such a thing has been done. This woman is a clear and present danger to national security and to the very people of the United States."

"That's not a normal request, sir," Director Crawford said. "And we have no assets in place in Revelen. None."

"Hire someone, then," Gondry said.

Passerini felt like he was in a roller coaster that had jumped the track. "Sir, we don't typically outsource assassinations ... or order them at all, really."

"That's a lie," Gondry said. "I was a history professor, you know. I'm fully aware of where all the skeletons are in our closet. We absolutely have a history of assassination, Mr. Secretary. This is very much an area of expertise for someone at the CIA. Perhaps even someone in your department. You're certainly killers."

Passerini's face tightened at the slap. "Sir, we fight wars."

"Well, I'm declaring one on Sienna Nealon." Gondry slapped the table. "So do your job and make her dead, Mr. Secretary." And he stood. "When next we speak, I want options. Military options for invasion. Clandestine options for erasing her from existence or bagging and dragging her back here to face justice. Diplomatic options to pressure them into giving her up. Everything you have, I want to hear. I'll listen, and from these options, I'll choose the best alternative for achieving our aims. And when this is all over, and the dust settles ... those who help me will be rewarded by securing your place in history.

Good God, how blinkered is this man ...? Passerini wondered as the president moved to leave. Everyone stood, and Passerini snapped to attention by force of long habit. He walked out without acknowledging Passerini, which was pretty typical for Gondry.

"You heard him, people," FBI Director Chalke said with a smile. "Let's get to work." She looked to Passerini. "Sounds like you have a lot of planning to do, SecDef. Might want to head to the Pentagon for that." Then she left as well.

Passerini burned. The president was looking for military options, and Chalke was right—he'd need to get his ass to the Pentagon and do some high-level consulting to come up with some. They were already well into war planning for the Revelen situation even before this most recent nuclear revelation, but this … this directive …

This was going to change things quite a bit.

But orders were orders, and so Bruno Passerini gathered his things, and headed for the door himself, the young army colonel trailing him, to go and try to put together an operational concept that—just maybe—he could please the president with.

21.

Sienna

"Dammit, Cassidy," I muttered under my breath as green electronic words scrawled their way across the TV screen. In all the hubbub of escaping prison and being brought to Revelen, I'd forgotten that she and I had a date with destiny here. "Your timing sucks."

CAN'T HEAR YOU, her words appeared. **NO CAMERAS OR MICROPHONES IN YOUR CELL.**

"It's not a cell," I said. "It's a …" I looked around at the fairly lushly appointed room. "It's … a kinda nice room in my great-grandpa Dracula's castle."

BUT I'M SURE YOU'LL FIND A WAY OUT SOON, she went on.

"I don't need to find a way out, genius," I said and stalked over to the door, opening it. "I'm free to leave at any time." I stuck a hand out the door and waved.

I SEE YOU. LET'S GET THIS SHOW ON THE ROAD.

"For crying out loud," I said, and stuck my head out, shaking it. "No, no, no."

BIDING YOUR TIME? FAIR ENOUGH. I CAN WAIT. GETTING DIRECT ACCESS TO THEIR TELECOM WILL ONLY ENHANCE MY ABILITY TO RUN AN ELECTRONIC INSURGENCY

AGAINST THEM.

I shook my head again. "No, no, bad idea, Cassidy."

WE HAD A DEAL.

"Miss?" A small voice reached me from outside, and I looked out to see a man in a military uniform that looked very foreign. Presumably Revelen military, unless he'd gotten very lost. "Can I help you with anything?" His accent was definitely from somewhere local-ish. Eastern Europe at minimum. Probably from here.

"I'm talking to the security camera," I said, and he blinked at me. "Gimme a sec." I shook my head at the camera. "No. No."

"This is very strange," the military man said. "I feel like I should be reporting this to someone."

"Have at it, then," I said, looking at my TV screen.

WHAT ARE YOU DOING?

"Trying to tell you not to do something stupid," I said.

"Me?" the man asked.

"Not you," I said. "Why, are you contemplating doing something stupid? Because you shouldn't."

"Ahhh … well, I was going to call the boss and let her know you're talking to a security camera … but … I'm not sure she's going to believe me," the man said.

"What's your name?" I asked.

"Aleksy."

"Do what you gotta do, Aleksy," I said, and looked right at the camera. "Hold tight. Don't do anything dumb."

"Why did I have to get assigned this patrol?" Aleksy asked. "I bet these things don't happen on the day shift."

"Dude, you're working in Dracula's castle at sunset," I said. "How could you not expect weird shit to happen? And, as an aside, a woman talking to a security camera? As things go, not that weird."

"What do you mean, 'Dracula's castle'?" Aleksy asked.

"If you don't know, I'm not telling you." I shook my head furiously at the camera.

FINE. WE'LL PLAY IT YOUR WAY. FOR NOW, the message came back on the TV screen. **BUT YOU BETTER HAVE A KILLER PLAN.**

"All my plans are killer," I said, "because I am, by definition, a killer."

"That's … not something I really want to think about," Aleksy said. "It sounds threatening."

"Well, maybe you should grow a pair and do something about it, Aleksy," I said, kind of annoyed that he was just standing there. "I mean, what army are you part of, the Salvation kind?"

"See, we were given very specific orders regarding your latitude," Aleksy said.

"My 'latitude'?" I asked, turning on him. "What the hell does that mean?"

"You're to be given the run of the castle," he said, taking a step back like I'd threatened him. "And free reign of the country, if you so desire. There's a car and a plane on standby for you. Boats, too."

"What about a tank?" I asked. "Kidding. I think. Gimme a second, will you?"

I made the okay sign with my hand at the camera and waited for the response.

STANDING BY. DON'T KEEP ME WAITING TOO LONG.

"Oh, goodie," I said under my breath and closed the door as the TV powered off. "This can't possibly go horribly wrong."

"I'm still unclear if you're talking to me or—" Aleksy said.

"Not you, dude," I said.

"I'm the only one here, though."

"Hardly," came a voice from around the corner, and ArcheGrey came strolling around a moment later, her overcoat baggy at her arms. Her stormy eyes fell on me. "Was that you?"

"Because I have heretofore undisclosed talents for hacking security systems and televisions?" I said, and she scaled back the hate glare a degree or two. "No, it wasn't me. But it was aimed at me."

"It wasn't Jamal's signature," Arche seemed to decide right there, lowering her head to bathe in thought. "And he couldn't find us in any case …" Her head snapped up. "Cassidy Ellis?"

"Nailed it," I said. "She's still a little peeved about that

Chesapeake Bay Bridge thing where you guys loosed the nutbag that killed her boyfriend."

"We didn't loose a 'nutbag,'" she said, shaking her head. "Stepane loosed himself."

"The point remains," I said with a shrug, "he killed her boyfriend, and she's not the forgiving type, so …" I shrugged again. "Might want to batten down the e-hatches, Arche. I having a feeling there's a storm brewing."

"I am so lost right now," Aleksy said. "I should have gone left at the last turn on my patrol. It was up to my discretion. Why did I go this way?"

"Because it's fate, Aleksy," I said, turning on him. "You know that latitude you mentioned?" He nodded. "Howzabout using it to tour me around the castle?"

"I need to report this intrusion to Hades," Arche said, fiddling with a tablet she pulled out of her coat. "Do you have anything else you'd like to tell us?"

"Yeah," I said, "you look like a flasher in that outfit." I gave Arche a thumbs up, and she blinked at me, looking away from her tablet for a second. "I'm going for a look around. Come on, Aleksy. Show me the sights." I snapped my fingers.

"Now I'm a tour guide." Aleksy shook his head. "This … this is not what I signed up for."

"You jonesing to be part of a battle?" I asked, as Aleksy hurried to catch up with me. I stalked past him, leaving Arche back at the intersection, glaring at me as she held her finger to the tablet's socket. Communing with the e-world, even as she glared, no doubt. "Stick with me, bud. Because trouble always seems to be coming my way." I narrowed my eyes as I walked down the corridor. "Whether I like it or not."

22.

"… And these are the dungeons," Aleksy said, waving his hands expressively. What was he expressing? A clear desire to be anywhere else so long as it involved not being near me, or in charge of me, or in my presence, at all. We stood in a hallway under the castle's rock, five levels down from where we'd started, the only light coming from the dim overhead bulbs.

He was officially the worst tour guide ever.

"No shit, Sherlock," I said, looking around at the dull stone walls with a sigh. He'd taken me past the kitchens, given me a very perfunctory tour of the guard barracks, which was inhabited by a lot of guys who looked kinda like Aleksy himself, down to the long-tailed-cat-in-a-room-full-of-rocking-chairs look on their faces. The armory was locked, of course, the gym was filled to the brimming with army guys using metahuman weights, the kitchens were surprisingly quiet (probably because of the hour), and now …

Now we were in Dracula's dungeons. Where there was no screaming, no wailing.

"Do you guys have any prisoners down here?" I asked. I doubted he'd tell me the truth.

"No!" Aleksy said, looking all offended I'd asked. "This is vestigial, from the days when this was the governmental center. The justice bureau handles prisoners, and they are down in Bredoccia. This is … uhm … how you say it? Historical site, now. Nothing down here except empty cells."

"Oh?" I brushed past him and threw one open. Sure enough, it was empty, didn't look like anyone had been down here in a while. There was no bedding, no toilet facilities, just some boxes piled in the corner. "Huh. Guess it's a storage room now." I walked over to one of the crates and popped it open. There was a stack of plastic cafeteria chairs inside, never unboxed, the kind you might find in a corporate lunchroom. "Well, that's … kinda dull."

"It takes a lot of logistics to run a castle, you know," Aleksy said. "It's not all dungeons and torture chambers. There's probably a storage room around here just for stewed beets." He rubbed his stomach. "Best meal the cafeteria makes."

"That makes me so sad for you." I rolled my eyes and opened another crate. Styrofoam cups waited within. "Yeah, these dungeons have seen better days."

"If you'll excuse me, miss," Aleksy said, "you seem almost disappointed that are no prisoners."

I *was* almost disappointed. Because I'd come to Revelen expecting a fight, and great evil—the country was run by *Dracula*, for crying out loud.

Instead I'd found my long-lost grandmother and great-grandfather. Talk about defying expectations. I tapped my fingers on the wooden crate. "Well, balls."

"Miss?"

"Nothing," I said. "I'm totally not disappointed."

Aleksy made a face. "You know we have sarcasm in this country, yes?"

"Don't be a pain in my ass, Aleksy."

"Yes, ma'am."

I slapped the box tops back on the crates and walked out of the storage room, leaving the door open. Looking down the hall to my left, I saw more of the same, as the corridor wended out of sight. "Let's go this way."

"Oh—okay," he said, hurrying to catch up with me. "I … I am so going to get busted down to private for this."

"Like that's a big deal," I said, walking down the corridor, my crisp steps echoing against the stone.

"It's a big deal to me!" he said. "I've worked my whole life to become an officer, a lieutenant." His face was red, worry lines creasing around his eyes.

"Look, Aleksy, I'm tightly related to the big boss here. Don't sweat it, man. I'll make sure you're not busted down to butt sergeant or whatever."

"What is a butt sergeant?" Aleksy asked.

"Hell if I know, I just made it up," I said. "Come on, this way."

I led him, still fretting, around the curve of the corridor and stopped as the end came into view.

"Oh, no," he said under his breath.

Oh no, indeed. Ahead was a giant double door, taking up the whole wall of a chamber. "Well, what do we have here?" I asked, stifling a grin.

"I don't know, but I have a feeling it's not good," Aleksy said. "I mean, it looks like it dropped out of one of your American horror movies."

"You're not wrong, Aleksy," I said and walked across the chamber. It was about thirty feet or so in length and width, and the ceiling lifted about the same, a cube of stone with gothic arches lining the sides. This door was almost twice the height of any of the others along the corridor, and also doubly wide, since it was two doors. The grandiosity of the architecture compared to the blandness of the rest of the dungeon could not be overstated. It was way, way out of place.

"This is not on my patrol route," Aleksy said. "I am very out of area, and very uncomfortable."

"That makes two of us," I said, "but I have a feeling I'm about to get to the heart of my troubles here." Because I had some serious troubles in mind. There was just too much going on here that I hadn't expected, and this—this foreboding door—this felt like the key to getting back on smashy, face-punching track. I reached out for the handle, sure that I was just seconds away from discovering Vlad's darkest secret, the one he totally was going to tell me about anyway, for sure, for sure, except not really.

I grasped onto the door handle, felt my thumb slip onto the push tab, smiled as I realized—yes, this had to be it. Whatever he was hiding, it was in here. With slow pressure, I pushed to open it—

And it clicked. Didn't move.

Locked.

"Well, damn," I said.

23.

Reed

"Revelen," I muttered under my breath. We'd gone through the full boat of info, the profile of the country, a brief recap of all the hell that had flowed out of there toward us in the last year—I'd forgotten about the guy Sienna had called the Predator, who had wrecked every one of our asses in Minneapolis only earlier this year—and now there was silence in the bullpen.

"You want to go," Isabella whispered, still by side. She hadn't left during the whole group chat session. "To charge into danger, all … how do we say it? Willy nilly?"

"Nobody says that," I said.

"I always do my danger charging willy nilly," Friday said. "With my willy, especially."

"Okay, because he says it, no one else should," I said. "And I don't want to charge into certain danger without knowing for sure that Sienna is there. Let's face it—we'd be flying over most of Europe to get there, and they've got that whole meta ban thing that, uh … someone caused."

"Yeah, that was you," Augustus said. "Way to go. If not for that, we could slip into Germany and hang out drinking the best beers of Oktoberfest while we wait for confirmation Sienna's actually there, then saddle up and roll in."

"It's June, not October," Friday said.

"What? It wasn't me," June Randall said, looking like she just snapped out of sleep.

"It wasn't *only* me that caused that," I said. "And that's not something we should be focused on right now." I looked around for J.J. or Jamal or Abby, and found J.J. first. "Okay, we're up to date with the threads that tie Sienna—and us—to Revelen. What's the current status there? Diplomatically, militarily … Can we waltz right into the country if we decided we wanted to take a flight?"

"I think commercial flights are still going there, no problem," J.J. said. Abby tapped him on the shoulder and tossed something over to his monitor like she was flicking it. That was a neat trick, not something I could do with my PC. "Oh. Oh, wait. No. Okay, this is weird. It looks the State Department is preparing to issue an advisory on Revelen, but the text is not up yet."

"Which is especially strange since there's literally no news out of the country," Abby said. "Not a peep."

"Well, I doubt there's a lot of embedded reporters from western agencies in Eastern Europe right now," Chase said, stepping over to look at their screens. "It's not a high priority area for them, what with the Middle East in perpetual chaos. If they want to capture American viewers' attention with war photos, there's that whole Saudi/Yemen conflict going on that's probably much sexier. And which they're mostly ignoring anyway."

"I bet if word got out Sienna could be in Revelen, you'd see some reporters hopping a flight pretty quick," Scott said.

"I think we're about to find out," Abby said, and suddenly the TV switched on in the corner, and the inputs were adjusted. "Check this out. Boom."

A webpage loaded on the flatscreen, huge, with a glaring headline:

SIENNA NEALON ESCAPES TO REVELEN

"Whoa," Scott said. "When did that go up?"

"Twenty minutes ago," Abby said. "On flashforce.net. It's already going viral."

"What the hell is flashforce.net?" Olivia asked.

"Sounds like one of those dance mob sites," Friday said. "Dangerous."

"Flash mobs are dangerous?" Jamal asked.

"You never know when they're going to appear, and you just get sucked up in the dancing and completely forget yourself," Friday said. "Flash mobs are the single greatest threat to humanity. Other than Vlad."

"It's not about dancing," Veronika said. "Other than maybe dancing on graves. It's a news site, putatively. And not to go all old on you, but in my day, this crap was tabloids. Flashforce makes the *Weekly World News* look credible. The sheer volume of their retractions makes me a little ill to my stomach."

"Were you a journalist at some point?" Scott asked.

Veronika rolled her eyes. "Yeah, briefly. Back when standards were a thing, and the different outlets weren't in such a knife fight for clicks and eyeballs and ad revenue rather than, y'know, correctly sourcing a story and getting the details right rather than rushing to publish now and having to stealth edit it later to hide your embarrassing screw-ups."

"Someone feels strongly about this," Scott said.

"Shh," I said as I read the text of the article. Abby slowly scrolled it down the TV screen, but it was extremely light on confirmed facts. "'Anonymous Gondry administration sources say' …" I sighed. "Doesn't anybody go on the record anymore?"

"Probably not when you're leaking classified information," Augustus said. "Tends to be a little detrimental to one's career advancement, unless it's okayed by higher ups. Which I doubt this is."

"Still, if this can be believed—" Jamal said.

"Questionable," Veronika said.

"—then the government has confirmed that Sienna's in Revelen," Jamal said. "Which they should have been able to do, really."

"Okay," Scott said, folding his arms over his chest. He'd shed the suit jacket at some point in the last few hours, and his sleeves were rolled up to show his arms. "Let's say that's all true, that Sienna is in Revelen. Under the control of Vlad the

Terrifying—"

"I hope she brought a change of pants," Friday muttered under his breath.

"—then … where does that put us?" Scott asked.

"Not flying commercial," I said, and looked to Isabella. "You're right. I do want to charge in, all willy nilly."

"Your willy is totally nilly compared to mine," Friday said. "Everyone's is, actually."

"Uh, no," Augustus said, "and on the matter of us invading Revelen … hell, yeah. This war is going to be lit AF."

"War?" Greg Vansen asked, kind of out of nowhere. I wondered if he'd shrunk down for a nap.

"I think we have to go," I said, nodding at the circle formed around me. "We can jet over there, and if for some reason she's not there … we can always come back. At supersonic speed."

"Yeah, let's get within striking distance," Scott said. "It doesn't make sense to just sit around here, waiting."

"You guys, we're chasing an unconfirmed, anonymously sourced news story that comes from an internet outlet best known for listicles like 'The Ten Best Wombat Videos on the Internet Right Now' and 'Sienna Nealon Has Just Nuked a Mexican Restaurant in LA, and Six Nutbags on Twitter Think It Confirms She's Inherently Racist,'" Veronika said. "You want to take us halfway across the world for that?"

"If I get a vote," Eilish spoke up, sitting between Andy Custis and June, who was still bound to her chair, "I think we need to address our rapidly increasing number of prisoners, because I'm not sure we want to ride into … whatever … with two unreliable people here."

"I can handle your prisoners," Greg said, walking over to Andy and taking him by the hand. He pulled something out of his pocket and Andy suddenly disappeared, down to the size of a pencil eraser. I watched him squirm, miniaturized, as Greg put him in a little opaque thing the size of a test tube and corked it.

June watched him disappear and her eyes widened. "Uhm … can I just go back to prison now? Because that was my intention all along. I'm just a messenger telling you what's up, that's all. I really don't need time added onto my sentence for this, and I definitely don't want to get shrunk."

"Abby …" I said.

"The Cube is still in lockdown," she said. "Definitely not pacified. It's questionable whether they're even going to attempt to go in anytime soon. I can't see deep into their systems, but—"

"I can," Jamal said, closing his eyes. "It's still chaos in there."

I smiled sympathetically at June. "Looks like you're coming with us—for now."

"Please don't shrink me like that," she said, as Greg took a step toward her. "Please. I don't want to be miniature—"

I waved him off. "She's on her honor. Unchain her." I nodded at Eilish, who shrugged and fumbled for keys. "As for the rest of us …"

Isabella touched my arm. "Are you sure?"

I nodded, and knew that everyone was hearing me. "Saddle up, people. We're heading for Revelen."

24.

Sienna

I checked the door again; it didn't budge. Big and bold and just standing there as tall as the extra-high ceiling, it was solid as if it were built into the wall. The handle was cold to the touch, and I let a finger slide across it, a sniff of oil or something mechanically greasy exuding from beneath it, or from the seemingly impermeable crack down the middle.

"What is going on here?" came a voice from behind me. Sharp, female, no-bullshit, it made me turn my head immediately, my internal threat radar pinging all to hell.

"I'm trying to open a door," I said, rounding on a small-ish European woman. She had the local accent, was shorter than me(!), and wore a uniform like Aleksy, but with a lot more ribbons and decorations... what do the military guys I know call it? Fruit salad? She'd been doing this job a lot longer than Aleksy. "Didn't happen to bring a key, did you?"

Her hair was a short, blond bob that tapered off just above her neck, and her face looked like it had been permanently frozen in purest bitchiness, like someone had lit the fuse on her tampon and snapped a picture at the moment when the bomb went off. Now, I assume, her face had frozen like this forever, as a warning to children everywhere that their moms were, indeed, right about that face freezing like that thing. "Step away from the door," she said. Some people, you hear their voice and you think, *Man, that does not match their look.* Huge guy, high, squeaky voice? What a mismatch.

This lady, though, with the Frozen Bitch Face … her voice was like the cracking of a whip across the back of your neck. The hairs raised on mine, which annoyed me to no end. Perfect voice/face match. A cop I'd worked with one time called it, "First Ex-Wife Voice."

"General Krall!" Aleksy said, snapping to attention just a second late. His features were wide with horror. I rolled my eyes; it wasn't like he'd gotten caught sleeping with me on the job or anything.

"Explain yourself, soldier," she said, marching up the hall toward us with measured steps.

"I was escorting her around," he said, looking like a train was barreling at him and he was riveted to the tracks by both feet. "She … she demanded it."

"I don't see a uniform on her," General Krall said. She didn't look a day over thirty-five, which told me something else about her, given that in the US military, it was rare to find a general younger than their late fifties. Sure, maybe she was a prodigy, but more likely, in this land of nearly-entirely metahumans, she was one as well. "Why would you take orders from this piece of blown-in trash?"

"Ooh, she fires the first shot in the war of words," I said. "Welp, that's it—now I'm free to fire off all the unkind observations I have about you, which is going to be such a relief, because I'm telling you—boy, have I got them for you. And that's number one, by the way—it's the hair, General Krall. Seriously. Which boy band are you part of?"

She was still marching in her steady cadence, and she'd made it almost across the big room. She wasn't moving meta speed, she was taking her time getting to me. Still, her eyes were on mine, and a smile that I could only describe as savage broke out slowly across her face. "Lieutenant?" she asked, not sparing a glance for Aleksy.

"Yes, ma'am?" His reply was immediate, meta-speed, and his boot heels snapped together.

"I am going to teach this interloper a lesson about manners,"

General Krall said, stopping in the middle of the high-ceilinged room as though it were the center of an arena. "It is long-needed, I think … and you will stand aside." She unbuttoned her jacket front swiftly, slipping it off to reveal very petite shoulders underneath, bared by a tank top that was a deep grey covering a chest that was so sunken a pirate would jump for joy at seeing it.

I shared those thoughts with General Krall, whose expression became slightly more crazed, her smile twisting wider as I stepped opposite her. "Also," I added for good measure, "your singing voice sucks, so whichever band you were part of, guy, I feel certain this is why they dropped you like a vat of bad sauerkraut. Which you smell like, by the way." That last part wasn't true. She did smell a little spicy, but it was like a potato dish of some stripe. Couldn't place it.

She dropped one shoulder low, in line with me, setting her posture for an attack. "It is going to be a pleasure to drag the screams from your lips."

"Bigger people than you have tried, short round," I said, doing a little stance correction of my own. "Want to know how it ended for them?"

Her smile got wider, exposing some serious deficiencies in her dental work that seemed to predate her meta powers. "The same way it will end for you—in tears." She looked sideways at Aleksy. "Salute me." He snapped to attention. "Remain that way through the battle. If you drop your hand or fail in your posture, you will be removed from the service."

Aleksy's eyes got wide, but he stayed in position. "Yes, ma'am."

"That seems unfair, especially if he accidentally gets hit by your flying teeth as they leave your mouth," I said.

"I deem that unlikely to happen." She just kept grinning. I imagined her without the teeth. It was going to be an improvement.

"Yeah, well, I deem you a waist-high pile of shit unworthy of my attention, but you don't seem to be going away, so that's what 'deeming' gets you—"

She came in low at me, a kind of squat crab-walk at meta

speed her vector of attack. It was a little alarming, not gonna lie, seeing this crazy little lady with a hideous smile coming at me like a spider monkey. She even hissed.

I kicked at her, losing my cool just a little. I was used to fighting guys that felt like they were twice my size. Hell, sometimes Friday was twice my size.

Krall was probably a few inches shorter than me, maybe five foot at most, but stooped over in a gorilla stance, she seemed even shorter, and her shoulders from side to side were about as wide as a sedan's hubcap. Added to that, she moved alarmingly fast in that crab-walk, sweeping in at me as I kicked to fend her off.

She caught my leg.

Nothing good happened after that.

Between the wrenching of tendons and being yanked off my feet, I did, unfortunately, scream. There was nothing for it, because I had my balance aggressively ripped away from me by a crab-walking spider-monkey. She dragged me toward her with alarming force, slamming an elbow into my ribs and bending me almost in half. I tried to get her with an elbow as I folded, but it was a glancing blow at best, and she snapped me forward as she took my legs from beneath me.

I vaguely recognized her style as something in the vein of jiu jitsu, but by then I was hitting the ground, thrown at meta-force, back first. I slammed into the stone, all the air left my lungs, and a dancing, flashing series of lights exploded in front of me. Mom had never taught me jiu jitsu; it was something she didn't know, so it was beyond her ability to teach. She'd focused on a lot more of the kicking arts, probably figuring my meta speed would give me an advantage against most comers.

But once your kick got caught, and your legs got ripped from beneath you? Well, that brought you down to the mat. Against most metas, who didn't know shit about fighting technique? There were a few things I could do.

Against a crab-walking, boy-band-playing spider-monkey with jiu jitsu training?

Like I said … nothing good happened.

She broke my right arm at the elbow before I even realized

she'd done it. She executed some sort of arm bar submission swiftly, but instead of giving me a chance to submit she snapped my elbow so it was bending the wrong way. Not stopping to celebrate her victory, she then proceeded immediately to skittering around my back while I was busy realizing that something was very, very wrong with my elbow joint and being hit by a ton of pain.

By the time I really felt it all, she was already behind me and had a rear naked choke locked in. But she didn't throttle my esophagus and windpipe, oh no. That was amateur shit. This lady was a pro. She went for the jugular vein and carotid artery.

Her legs locked around my waist like steel cables, trapping me on my side. She had her wrists perfectly positioned, bare arms against my shirt, creating an artificial collar and keeping me from touching her. I reached up, panicking, to grab her, to employ my powers against the bars of iron she seemed to have placed against the sides of my neck.

But it was way too late for that. I didn't have my head about me, and my vision was already blurring because she'd cut off the blood flow to and from my brain.

Lack of oxygen makes things hazy, fast. All I could muster in terms of resistance was a light slapping on her arm.

"As pathetic as I expected," General Krall whispered in my ear. "You are not what they say you are. You are not …" Her breath brushed away my hair from my ear, "… worthy of the mantle."

If I could have seen straight or formed a thought, maybe I'd have argued. As it was, blackness was pushing in at the edges of my vision, and I choked off a reply because I couldn't think of one.

Then I passed out into darkness.

25.

I woke with a gasping breath, surging upright in a soft bed, darkness all around me, the only light a dim glow of blue across the room.

There was a scent of fresh laundry soap near me, and something else. A click sounded like a gun's hammer pushing back, and light flooded the room like a shot going off in the darkness—

It was just a lamp coming on, washing my castle room in a dim glow. Vlad was sitting in a chair by my bedside, hand still under the lamp shade, a warm note of relief on his gaunt, pale face. "Ah. You are all right, then?"

"Your spider-monkey general choked me out," I said, bringing a hand to my neck. "So no, not really."

"General Krall is a thoroughly humorless woman," came a voice from across the room. Lethe, of course, looming—as much as a woman around my height can loom—next to the window, looking at me out of the corner of her eye. "Still, you didn't suffer any permanent damage, so it seems she doesn't entirely detest you."

"Oh, is that a boon she grants to those she doesn't 'entirely detest'?" I asked. "Lucky me." My neck still hurt where she'd applied the choke to either side. Her precision was on point, though; I didn't feel anything on my windpipe.

"We were worried about you," Hades said.

"Maybe control your attack dog a little better and you

wouldn't have to worry," I said, stinging from my defeat. In all ways, because my pride? Not in a happy place after losing a fight, especially that badly. Man, Aleksy must have had a hell of a show … for the five seconds it took for Spider Monkey the Boy Bander to whip my ass.

"May I suggest, alternatively, you listen to General Krall's orders in the future?" Hades asked, a hint of amusement lifting his brow and the corner of his mouth.

"Hey, man, you gave me the run of the castle," I said.

"I did not, in point of fact," Hades said.

"Well, you didn't tell me not to, and you've got to know by now that I'm a free-thinking, not-bound-by-barriers kind of person, so … I'm going to put this one on you for not offering the direction to stay in my room," I said, sliding sideways out of bed. I was still wearing my prison jumpsuit, and the pants portion was smeared with dust from my dungeon brawl. It was the sort of thing Reed would have found especially amusing, like something out of one of his old games. *You have encountered a miniature dungeon goblin. It grips you around the neck and chokes all of your hit points away!*

Hades and Lethe traded a glance. "Fair enough," Hades said. "You may roam the castle as you will, but perhaps stay away from that room … and a few others … just for now."

I was surprised he buckled that easily. He must have really been trying to make a good impression on me. "Is there a reason why?" I asked, deciding not to push it for once in my life. Maybe the choke-out defeat had humbled me.

"Everything will be explained to you in its own time," Hades said. "Everything. There will be total truth between us, at least from our side. However, there are things in motion that require my attention, and certain questions have deeper answers than I can easily give at the moment. Suffice it to say, if you can be a little patient … you will know all."

"Know all, huh?" I drew my hand from my neck. "That sounds promising, especially if there's a weight loss formula in there somewhere that involves eating all the cheesecake ever and still maintaining your figure. I might be motivated to have patience for that."

"Okay, well, we're not quite at that level of advancement yet," Hades said. "I'll put some of my scientists on it, though. It seems a worthy endeavor."

I blinked. He seemed serious about that scientists thing, I thought. And I'd seldom worked for people who could actually put scientists on such a crucial project as weight loss with infinite cheesecake. It would change the very nature of humanity, and for the better, I'd argue, mostly because I'd had to work my ass off to not eat all the cheesecake in the world. "Uh. Good, then."

Lethe just rolled her eyes. "This is the dumbest exchange in the history of dumb exchanges. And I'm including Manhattan for beads."

"All I ask is patience," Hades said, looking me in the eyes. "We are working toward a purpose here. To make this country strong. To allow it to stand on its own on the world stage. We are … so very close," he said, holding up his thumb and forefinger an inch apart. "This can be a homeland for metahumans, the next phase of development. Bring peace and prosperity to our people in a way that they have not experienced in quite some time—"

"The hell?" I asked. "Our people have generally been some of the wealthiest and most powerful people on the planet. With power comes the ability to insinuate yourself into government, and other power structures. Hell, the president of Russia is a meta now, thanks to you guys."

He traded a look with Lethe, and she shrugged. "She asked, I told her," Lethe said.

"What you say is true, to a point," Hades said.

"We were gods," I said. "You … were a god. Both of you—"

"I was never classed as a god," Lethe said, a little darkly.

"If you say so, Valkyrie," I snarked. She rolled her eyes and looked back out the window. "Point is, you guys have had wealth and power throughout human history. Metahumans have always been able to climb the heap a little better than the average Joe, okay? I realize we got knocked down a little bit these last few years, what with Sovereign killing, uh … most of us, but … come on. We're doing all right. Except for all these new Johnny-come-latelys you've been creating out of the human population. A lot of them are ending up in jail or dead. But those of us old-schoolers that have survived? We're doing fine."

"We have lost the seats of power we once held," Hades said. "And our strength is not what it once was. After the Great War—"

"I can always tell how old a meta is by whether they refer to it as World War I or 'The Great War,'" I muttered.

"We're your elders," Lethe said. "I don't expect you to respect us any more than you respect anyone, but if you listen you might learn something."

"We are not what we once were," Hades said after I clammed up. "Yes, some of our people have done well individually, but there are so few of us left. That war wiped out so many of our number. We were cannon fodder in our own armies, the ones who led the field. We lost entire generations of our kin in that war." He stared into the distance. "Here in Revelen we were fortunate to stay out of that conflict—there were few enough of us in any case, your grandmother having been … ahem …"

Lethe rolled her eyes. "I see what you're getting at." She refocused one me. "He means that we were the only two metas here back then, and that I was abstinent by necessity and choice, and he's old and used up, so …" She faced back toward the window.

"That was … deeply uncomfortable to hear," Hades said, "and also unfortunately true, for the most part."

"I don't know want to know which part wasn't true unless it involves abstinence by you, too," I said, about a half-step from putting my fingers in my ears and humming really loud until this whole expository speech was over.

"As uncomfortable as it is," Hades said, not meeting my eyes, "this is the truth—family was vitally important to me for reasons that you might not understand at your age." Here, his striking blue eyes looked into mine. "You … you and so very few others remain to carry on my legacy. I am, as she said … old. Used up as well, perhaps. I do not deny it." He smiled faintly. "To look in the mirror every morning is to realize I have more days behind me than ahead. Perhaps many more behind me than ahead. I did so much to try and leave a legacy in this world. I had many children with your great-grandmother, and yet almost all of them are dead." He looked away. "Almost all of your kind … have passed on."

I took that all in. "'kay …" I was waiting for the other shoe to drop.

"Your grandmother and yourself are the last two succubi that I know of," Hades said. "And I know of no incubi remaining. That makes you …" His smiled faded. "My heirs."

I blinked. "Uh … so … are we just going to disregard all those Persephones out there as not your kin …?"

He shook his head. "Very few are related to me in any way … if at all."

"Nearly all of the children of Persephone and Hades were either incubi, succubi, or Hades types," Lethe said. "The Persephone genetic code is apparently not dominant. Which is why most of their offspring ended up being an amalgamation of the death and life that comprise our power. Death bound to the skin instead of life bound to the skin." She turned back toward the starry night shining in through the window. "There was only one Persephone born to Hades and my mother, and I think … it is questionable whether that child was even his." She didn't look at Hades.

"Ouch," I said. Hades was looking right at me, unembarrassed.

What the hell did you say to that? "Sorry you got … cuckolded," was what I came up with.

That … probably wasn't the thing to say. Lethe shot me a dark look from the window.

Hades quirked an eyebrow in amusement after a moment. "Well … it was hardly the worst thing she did to me." And his hand fell to his chest, where that scar lay under his shirt. "And it was a very long time ago."

"So … basically you're saying that, uh … with Rose dead," and I saw him blanch only a little, "Grandmother and I are your only living descendants."

He nodded. "Indeed." He smiled again, though it was sad.

"You are the only evidence I leave behind that I ever existed, which … considering how long I lived is perhaps not how I would have preferred it, but here we are. I will, as they say … play the ball where it lies."

"Big golfer, huh?" I asked.

"I have always wanted to learn," Hades said, "but no. You and your grandmother are all that remain of my legacy, other than whispered legends and myths. My days grow toward an end, and with that end …" He looked up at me again. "I want to make sure that the few things I leave behind are well protected. That my legacy is secure."

"This better not involve a box of any sort," I said.

"No box," Hades said with a feathery laugh. "But … a country, yes. Here, I am a king. And someday very soon … your grandmother will be—"

"Queen," I whispered, getting it. Finally.

"Yes," Hades said. "And she has many years left before her—"

"If I can avoid getting into a fight with General Krall," Lethe said, not turning from the window.

"She really is a hardcore bitch," I said. "Do you just look at her and want to punch her in that saucy beast-face, too …?" Lethe nodded, almost imperceptibly. "Thank God, I thought maybe it was just me being ornery," I said.

"—but regardless of how many years your grandmother has," Hades went on, apparently well used to talking over us by now, "someone has to take up the role of—"

"Apprentice?" I asked. "Because there's always two Sith, right?" Reed would have been so proud of me.

Hades chuckled under his breath. "Movie metaphor aside … there needs to be an heir waiting in the wings. This country may be small, but it will not remain so. We are growing even now—"

"That's what happens when you annex Russia, yeah," I said. "You get bigger."

"—and require a continuity of leadership behind the scenes," Hades said. "Someone to be the face to the public in times of crisis. The one they look to, the one they respect—"

"Oh, shit," I said, "that's why everyone sees me as a hero. You've been feeding them propaganda as to how awesome I am, in preparation for my arrival."

"However you want to look at it," Hades said, "here, yes, you are a hero to the people. They see you as we have seen you. A bit more idealized, I suppose. Perhaps a few of your more jagged edges filed off. But they know the good you have done, and don't automatically assume the bad the way your own press has. They have given you the benefit of the doubt, and thus …"

"I'm a hero here," I said. "And now you want to make me …" I knew the word. I was just having trouble saying it out loud.

"The crown princess," Lethe said, turning to face me. "That's what you'd be. Second in line for the throne."

"Princess Sienna Nealon," Hades said, with the trace of a smile. "It has a nice ring to it, wouldn't you say?"

26.

Dave Kory
Brooklyn

… the Eden Prairie incident, in which Sienna Nealon attacked a crowd of innocent, unarmed protestors and reporters, murdering over—

Dave stopped typing and flipped over to the click counter. His latest article was blowing up the internet, driving traffic so heavy that they'd probably have to start bringing some more temporary servers on to handle all the clicks. "Booyah," he whispered to himself.

It was his single biggest article yet.

"Hey, congrats on the big hit, Dave," Mike Darnell said, passing his cube, popping a hand on the wall as he moved by. "You're really showing us the way on this one."

"Thanks, man," Dave said. "Coming from you that really means something."

Mike stopped. "Oh?"

"Well, yeah, I mean your pedigree? Top notch," Dave said, tearing his eyes away from the click counter for a moment to look at the former *Times* reporter. "Come on. Most of the people who work here are fresh out of college or come from the blogosphere. Nobody comes from the big leagues to flashforce. Until you. I mean, I predict more of it will happen as time goes by, but, uh … yeah."

"Well, I'm a little counterintuitive," Mike said, brushing a few strands of greying hair at his temples, "and I can see which way the wind is blowing."

"Yeah, the meteor is definitely streaking toward the dinosaurs," Dave said, "so you picked the right time to find shelter in the new paradigm." Had his clicks really jumped that much in the time they'd been talking? He could barely even remember any more. The counter was just flying up.

Word was getting out. Flashforce.net was the place to go for all things Sienna Nealon.

"Can I ask about your big scoop?" Mike asked, leaning on the cube wall.

"Sure." Dave didn't want to look away from the click counter. It was entrancing, it was climbing so fast. He would have seen dollar signs, if he'd cared about those at all. He did, to a point, but it wasn't the big driver for him.

Instead … he saw prestige. This was the stuff they were making their name on. It was a warm little feeling inside, and it validated all the trust Russ Bilson had placed in him when he'd invited Dave into the Network, given him the app that was like the keys to the kingdom. Hell, yes, he was doing good work. That cross-pollination project? Was paying the right kind of dividends for his business. He hoped that Director Chalke was pleased as well. She'd certainly seemed eager to get this out. But the other connections he'd made through it … they were worth their weight in gold, in the form of clicks.

And of course, there was the feeling he got, of being connected to these important people, of rubbing elbows with the big names moving the world forward. Titans of society.

"Seems like you've got a couple highly-placed sources in the Gondry administration," Mike said. "You couldn't get either to go on the record?"

"Well, you know how it is," Dave said. The counter was moving up even faster. "They don't want to get fired for telling tales out of school."

"Hm," Mike said. "I'm surprised that the PressSec didn't confirm any of it."

"I sent him an email," Dave said. "Didn't get word back before I published."

"How long before you published did you send the email?"

Dave spun around in his chair, grinning faux-guiltily. "I dunno. A minute?"

Mike just blinked. "What the hell, man? You didn't even give them a chance to respond?"

"Why would I?" Dave asked. "I wanted to break the story. They'd just deny it anyway, so …" He shrugged, and tore himself away from the sky-rushing page load counter and flipped to his email. "Oh, look, they responded."

Mike stepped into the cubicle behind him. "An hour ago. They replied to you an hour ago, and you haven't even checked it yet …?"

"Look," Dave said, keeping his eyeroll under control, "the only way their reply is interesting is if it allows for a new story. And anything that includes, 'We have no comment at this time' is only worthy of an update. Which does not drive much traffic."

Mike's face reddened. "But … if they do have something to add, it could change your story."

"I'm not changing my story." Dave shook his head. "Look at the traction it's getting." He flipped back to the link counter. "We've hit a stage of viral here that most editors only have wet dreams about."

"But what if it's not true?" Mike asked.

"You don't think Sienna Nealon is in Revelen?"

"I don't know if she's in Revelen," Mike said. "She could well be. But you're the reporter, who's supposed to take the information he gets from sources, present it, preferably with a name attached so I, as your reader, can decide whether the info is solid or not."

"Pfffft," Dave said, waving him off. "That's not what people are looking for."

Mike's eyebrows crept up his face. "You don't think people are looking for the truth?"

"Psychology tells us people are not looking for the truth," Dave said. "Consumer behavior tells us people are not looking for the truth. This click counter tells us people are not looking for the truth—whatever you think the truth is." He leaned closer to Mike, lowered his voice. "Look … I *think* I've printed the truth here. But I don't care if I didn't, because I printed it as best I knew—"

"While ignoring any possible rebuttal from people who would tell you their name and allow you to print it, who might be saying, 'You're wrong.'"

"It's the White House press secretary," Dave said. "Come on. It's their job to spin, and let's face it—Sienna Nealon escaping their custody is a prime thing to spin. Nobody wants to tell that like it is—'We had her, we totally screwed up, and now she's in a foreign country where we can't get to her.'" He grinned at Mike. "Seriously. They're not going to say that. They're going to say …" And he clicked on the email from the press secretary.

"'The White House has no comment at this time,'" Mike read. "Look, Dave … you are obviously the genius in this nouveau world. And I'm here to learn from you—"

"Thank you, thank you," Dave said, "now hit me with the 'but' …"

"But," Mike said, "what if … and I know it's a small chance … what if the press secretary had said, 'Yeah, you're right, but here's how it actually went down, here's an amendment that changes the story.'"

Dave shrugged. "They wouldn't do that."

"You don't know that."

"Dude, I called it before we even opened the email."

"This time," Mike said. "Look, you could have this story a hundred percent right. But we used to do things differently …"

Dave could not contain the eyeroll this time. He mimed a yawn, too. "Yeah. The good old days, I'm sure."

Mike closed his eyes for a second. "Look … I'm telling you this because … doing things this way, it's … how many of these big stories do you think you can get wrong, like big-time wrong, before you blow your credibility?"

Dave just snorted. "Credibility? Dude. Look at the clicks. Credibility is for suckers. Credibility is for the *Toledo Examiner*, more worried about triple checking to be sure they never put a wrong foot forward on a story—"

"Hey, we make plenty of errors even doing things the right way," Mike said. "But when we put a story out there, it's easier to stand behind it when you can identify your sources, when you can give your readers a little more information to make their decisions—"

"That's not what our readers are looking for, Mike," Dave said, spinning around to face him, leaving the click counter behind for a moment. "Get this through your head, because—I'm thinking, man, this is the thing you need to adapt to in this 'new world.' It moves at the speed of thought. People aren't looking for some disinterested source to calmly present them the facts. They want the hottest info, the hottest takes, and they want it yesterday." He reached back and tapped on the click counter. "That's what brings them running. That's what drives up the ad revenue. Hotness. Not slow and steady, not calm and calculated. Nobody comes running for a thoughtful article about how Sienna Nealon is really not that bad, okay? They're looking for something to fire the emotions." He clicked back to his article in progress. "See? She's attacking unarmed protestors and reporters. That gets people fired up. They can imagine themselves in that situation. They can share the fear of her—which is a reasonable fear of a crazy person with superpowers, right? Who's now on the loose." Dave nodded. "See where we're going here?"

Mike just stared at him for a minute, then folded his arms over his chest. "Yeah. I think I get it. You want to move people. Generate an emotional reaction."

"Yes." Dave pointed at him, smiling. "Light 'em on fire, and they'll keep coming back for more."

"Whether it's true or not," Mike said.

Dave shrugged again. "If it's true, it'll come out in the wash. If it's not, it'll fade into the background. People have thirty-second memories these days. They'll get out of our articles what they want to get out of them. But they'll get them from us and not somebody else, and that's what's important." He pulled up a subsidiary counter to his main story one. "This is how many clicks we're getting from my latest article to other stuff on the site." He puffed up a little with pride. "That's a lot of ad revenue, my friend. A lot of people coming to flashforce.net. Way more clicks than the *Times* is going to get today, I can tell you that."

Mike nodded slowly. "You're right about that," he said, but he did not sound fully convinced. He walked away, though, back toward his cube.

He'd get it. Dave could sense his hesitation; it was the tough part of working with these dinosaurs who'd learned under the old J-school model. They didn't "get" the new world. Mike was kinda smart. And he definitely brought prestige.

Sooner or later, he'd figure it out … or he'd get gone. Dave didn't care which just now. He had an article to finish. Where had he left off? Oh, right, Eden Prairie … he searched for another word, a proper adjective to describe Sienna Nealon's attack … he settled on 'bloodthirsty,' and he was off and writing again, hurrying to finish his next scoop to keep those clicks coming.

27.

Sienna

"Lemme get this straight," I said, looking at Hades, who sat by my bed, earnest, pale and commanding, and Lethe, who stood by the window, almost as pale, almost as commanding, and reminding me—just a little—of Mom, "you want me to be … your …?"

"Princess," Hades said, nodding. "Crown princess."

"Sorry, I had to hear it repeated because I've never been anyone's princess before," I said. This was really having trouble getting through the bullshit filter.

"Well, it is a unique circumstance," Hades said.

"Unique." I blinked at him, trying to get my head around his … offer? Request?

I'd been certain I was coming to Revelen to kill Vlad the Impaler, whoever he was. I predicted battle, carnage, a tough fight against a metahuman older than much of the earth's dirt and so mean that he'd developed enough of a reputation for bloodthirst that legend said he literally drank it.

Instead, I was here with my great-grandfather, who was presently trying to dub me the crown princess of his country.

"This is so damned trippy," I said under my breath.

"We can hear you, you know," Lethe said, turning slightly to look at me. She still wasn't smiling.

"Well, this isn't exactly how I planned my trip to Revelen

going," I said.

"Oh?" Hades asked. "How did you see it going?"

"To be brutally, viciously, Sienna-y honest, I figured I'd be knee-deep in kicking your asses by now," I said, sliding off the edge of the bed. Hades moved to help me, and caught my elbow, which he held—gently—until I took up my own weight. It was a very grandfatherly thing to do, I thought, based on my limited experience of never having a grandfather. "Instead I'm being asked to be your princess."

"Crown princess. The crown is important," Hades said. "And literal. It has many diamonds."

"I get to wear an actual crown? That's badass," I said, touching my head, which ached just a little. "But … I just told you I came here to kick your ass."

He shrugged. "My wife killed me. My brothers wanted me dead. This is hardly a new experience for me."

"Gah, we really play *Family Feud* a different way, don't we?" I asked, looking up to see Lethe almost—almost—smiling. "I've fought my mother, fought you, apparently," I nodded at Lethe. "Like for real, fists a flying, fights. Knocking out teeth and making each other bleed."

"It has always been rougher among metahumans," Hades said, almost reassuringly, "because we are more sturdy than humans. This is how we settle our disputes. Low-intensity punching. And maybe sometimes high intensity."

"You guys … you really have sent trouble my way that you haven't explained yet," I said, eyeing Hades. "I know you say you didn't, but … I'm sorry, but it's just not true."

Hades shrugged. "Ask about your troubles. We will explain as best we can."

"Fine, starting at the beginning," I said, "ArcheGrey and the Glass Blower—Yvonne, I guess—mounted an attack on New York, destroying evidence for—"

"Contract work," Hades said. "A job for Nadine Griffin. We did not set them to the task. Indeed, they were not even in our employ yet, though once we realized what we had with their skill sets, we hired them immediately. You don't let talent like that go to work for the enemy."

"Benjamin … uh … I don't remember his last name," I said. "Normal American when he left Minnesota. Comes back home, has an emotional meltdown, and goes full Gavrikov on the customs line at MSP airport. Kaboom, I mean—"

"I understood that reference," Hades said with a slightly smile. "All the references, usually."

"—he was a wild card who killed a lot of people and caused a lot of damage to my state," I said. "Why would you give him powers?"

"We didn't do it intentionally," Lethe said. "He must have been visiting during the time when we first opened up the serum into the water supply to empower the people. Maybe he drank the local water. Everything that followed … I'm sorry for the death of anyone that he killed, but we're no more responsible for what he did with his powers than we are for you killing someone with yours."

"An argument could be made you're very responsible for me," I said, "being directly up the family line, but fine … I'll let that go. For now. Benjamin, though … if you gave him a nuclear weapon and he accidentally set it off … pretty sure you'd still be held responsible. Legally and morally."

"I'll make sure to lock up my nuclear weapons then," Hades said with a glint in his eye. "You know, now that I have them."

"That was a little disquieting," I said.

"What?" He shrugged, still amused. "We are nuclear now. Is it wrong to take some pride in this achievement?"

"I'll leave that one aside until later," I said. "The entire serum development thing."

Hades raised an eyebrow at me. "Yes? What of it?"

"Why?" I asked.

"You are not amazed by the pace of scientific progress?" he asked, and pushed to his feet. "This is a thing where we partnered with others. Your President Harmon, for instance."

"Way to go on that, by the way. He almost enslaved the world with serums derived from what you gave him."

"Hardly," Hades said. "I was in Washington, DC, when you stopped him." He pulled out a phone and flipped through pictures, coming to a selfie of him standing in front of the

White House. There were a whole lot of ambulances and police and such in the background behind him. "If he had tried to move to the next phase of his attempt … I was prepared to deal with him." He held out a hand, made a slurping noise. "I suppose I should thank you for that, because I didn't really want Harmon in my head."

"How close would you have had to be to vacuum him out?" I asked.

"Ah, now you get to the heart of the issue," Hades said, nodding, a little of his enthusiasm gone. "You ask why we develop these serums? Why we partnered with people such as Edward Cavanagh and President Harmon to produce them?" He leaned in closer to me. "We have had the base power serum for a long time. It is an ancient formulation, in fact, one that might have been used to unlock the original metahuman powers. The other serums we produced in concert with our partners, using their expertise to bridge knowledge gaps that we could not. The Skill Tree Unlocker and Power Booster, as I think your friends have taken to calling them … catchy names, to be sure, better than the dull scientific ones we had assigned … these were the fruits of our efforts, bent toward doing one thing. And one thing only."

"Which was …?" I asked.

Hades sat down, looking up at me. He took a long breath, then held it in, before answering, and I could see his reluctance in the tension of his shoulders, of his whole body. "Restoring my powers."

28.

"You have died before, yes?" Hades asked, as the thing he'd said about not having powers kind of sunk in. "In Los Angeles, in the subway tunnels, correct?"

"Yeah," I said, looking him right in the ice-blue eyes. "I got zapped to death by the LA subway. Heart stopped for … I dunno, a minute or two."

"A minute or two." Hades nodded. "A minute or two is nothing, as these things go." He turned away from me. "When Persephone killed me, I was dead for quite a while. My body had time to …" He touched his chest, where that massive scar had been, "… decay. By the time Zeus started my heart again …" He looked up. "Not all of the damage could be repaired when my natural healing abilities returned. Cell death had set in, and my powers, once able to rip life from a body miles away, were now very finite, compared to what they'd been before."

"Death, hobbled by death," I said, and he shot me just the trace of a smile. "There's some irony there."

"It was not lost on me," Hades said, still smiling faintly. "I have never returned to my original strength. My powers are but a shadow of what they once were. Like you, I could once use the souls of metahumans I took to harness their abilities in my own service. This terrified my brothers, as it should have."

"But you can't anymore?" I asked, and one of his hands twitched.

"No," he said, shaking his head. "I can feel a soul as it passes through me. There is a sensation, a bare fractional amount of what it felt like to drain souls in the days of old. But they don't stay as they used to. It is as though my brain's capacity to hold them was ruined when I died." He touched the side of his head. "Brain death, you see. Cellular shutdown, we know now. Modern medicine has given me answers for questions that have eluded me for over a thousand years."

"His brain is more than half dead," Lethe said, apparently deciding to take up the role of Dr. Helen Slaughter in order to drop some medical exposition on me. "The core functions work, probably because his brain compensated when it was brought back to life, but it was deprived of oxygen for so long that he's permanently impaired in many ways, the damage done by his death unable to be healed."

"So … you're not exactly powerless, but …" I said.

"I am much reduced," he said. "I could—barely—have dragged Harmon's soul out of his body across the White House lawn if he'd been there when I arrived, but I would not have been able to do anything else for several days. And his soul would not have stuck with me as it did with you. He would have passed through my mind with but a scream, his intelligence attempting to nest somewhere in the dead sectors of my mind, never to be heard from again." Hades touched his head, and I realized for the first time that his hair really did not look right. It looked a little dry, like a wig, even though it seemed to be bound into his skull, and I wondered if that was because the hair had died once or if he was just wearing a really good rug.

I hoped I wouldn't find out. There are some things about your great-grandfather you just don't want to know.

"All the serums … were to try and re-unlock your powers?" I asked.

Hades nodded. "The Skill Tree Unlocker … the one that releases tangential powers related to your own? I was hoping to turn loose additional abilities." He shook his head. "It did not work. Nor did the Power Booster. My range and strength remain unchanged, permanently reduced by the death of so many of my cells."

"His MRI is … impossible," Lethe said. "The fact that he's survived over a thousand years since it happened …"

"And only thanks to you," Hades said, with a small smile.

I looked at Lethe. She had her arms folded in front of her, but caught my question. "I was in Norway when things in Greece went … bad."

"She refers to my granddaughter—Janus's child—being killed in the market," Hades said. "You have heard of this, I think?"

"Yeah, I've heard of it," I said.

"I was … enraged," Hades said. "I struck back at those responsible. And then I struck back at those beyond. Confined as we were in the caves for so long …." He looked at his shoes and let a little laugh, a pretty dour one. "I think I went a bit mad."

"By the time I made it back to Greece," Lethe said, "it was done. Mother had killed him to stop the madness. To stop him from draining the world. Or at least the nearest part of it."

"She was right to do so," Hades said, still staring at his shoes, like a scolded child. "I had taken leave of all my senses."

"When I got back," Lethe said, "Janus was blocking passage to the cave." Her eyes flashed. "I didn't know him, my brother-in-law. Didn't trust him. He was there on behalf of Zeus. Keeping the family prisoner, captive, until they could decide what to do with our kind."

"I'm guessing they didn't do anything good with us," I said.

"Made us pariahs over time," Lethe said with a sneer. "Caused us to be in danger of being killed anywhere we went in the meta world, eventually."

"That was the end of our world," Hades said. "Or the beginning of the end." I saw in his eye the first glint of something dangerous, something I hadn't yet seen from him. "If I had known what was coming, I would have fought them then, regardless of consequence." He clenched a gnarled fist, the age spots showing on the back of his hand. "It was funny, because before … I had the power and lacked the will to go against my own brothers. After my own brush with death …" he smiled bitterly, "… then I lacked the power. Our family was torn asunder, forever after I died. Your grandmother dragged me off, following their wishes. Took me north, out of Greece and eventually to here. Where we have been ever since. Watching the world and watching our family … diminish." He looked up, and the glint in his eye changed. "Until you."

"Oh, geez," I said.

"What does it mean to you … to be Death?" Hades asked.

"To me?" I asked, trying to shrug casually out of it, like I hadn't been touting the fact that I AM DEATH to people I wanted to fear me for a few years now. "Nothing good, at least not for the people standing across the battlefield from me." I cleared my throat. "It's an intimidation thing I say."

"Death is frightening, no doubt, but … it shouldn't always be," Hades said. "We all come to death in our own time. It is the inevitable end to all our journeys. The uniting thread that binds us all together as humans. We are born, and someday, we die. This, above all else, should be the thing that unites us. For in knowing that death is all our ends … we should see that despite all our differences we are more the same than we usually give credit for."

"'So what you're saying is … we're all equal in the face of Sienna and her fam killing us,'" I said.

"I like how you put yourself first in that," Lethe said, "as though you're the most dangerous person in the room."

"Hey, I know I'm an amateur compared to you old pros," I said, "but I'm definitely the one doing the heavy lifting in the name of Death these last few years, okay?"

"Without doubt," Hades chuckled. "When I sat on the throne of Death, I was perhaps … too aggressive in the fearful elements of my job. Now I look back on my foolhardy youth—I was so obsessed with power, with using fear to cultivate that power, that strength—I see only the mistakes I made. Ones that led directly to my downfall. Death is, indeed, a gift we possess to be dealt out. But it is not to be used indiscriminately. And if we avoided cavalier use for intimidation and power, it would be so much stronger."

"Oh?" I asked, feeling a little like I was about to walk into a supervillain explanatory speech.

"Imagine if the suffering of the world could be diminished by our powers. Used responsibly, my gift now gives death near instantaneously." He snapped his fingers. "The soul is no longer trapped in my mind, in my body. It moves on to … wherever. If Death is my gift, imagine what good I could do for the terminally ill. No slow-acting drugs, my power works in seconds. The pain is minimal, especially if they are sleeping. One strong pull and … they are free of this life." He raised his hand. "Gone, with dignity. Freed from their chains."

"You're the breaker of chains, then?" I asked.

He smiled. "I am no Daenerys Stormborn, but in this small way, I see how I could help. I fulfill the function here in Revelen, circling to the hospitals when asked, bringing relief to those who will never recover from their ailments. There are many fewer of them now that the serum has circulated, but some remain. I remove their pain, once and for all. I get nothing out of it but the satisfaction of giving them peace." He flicked his gaze away. "And someday, perhaps … I will find that peace for myself. I suspect it is not as far off as I might wish."

"It's nice that you've turned your talents toward assisted suicide," I said. "But, uh … I can't help but feel that maybe you've only gone this way because your power got hacked off at the stem. That if you still had full Hades abilities, you might not be so much about the warm and fuzzies."

"And if you hadn't gotten your brain ripped apart by Rose, you might not be as humble and sweet as you are today," Lethe said. "You might have nuked us from orbit with Gavrikov powers. Just to be sure."

"Did you Sigourney quote on purpose?" I asked. Lethe was, as usual, inscrutable.

"'Nuke it from orbit,'" Hades chortled. "A classic. But the point remains, we are all changed by the trials we undergo, are we not? Me by Persephone and my brothers, you by Rose, a distant cousin, surely—"

"The message I'm starting to get is, 'Don't trust family,'" I said. "Not sure that was your intention, but …"

"We change, princess," he said, and it took me a second to

realize that there was nothing sarcastic in his use of "princess."

"I hope I have learned from my adversities. Being humbled is a gift of its own sort," he said, nodding. "You are correct. I would not be the man you see before you, working toward a better end, a better use of powers had I not been humbled. Just as you would not be here now, standing where you are if you had not been brought low in Scotland."

"Thanks to you," I said, and he looked away. "Rose had the serum. Tons of it. She was giving it to people, harvesting their powers, making herself an unstoppable goddess. I got stuck under her wheels, true, and eventually stopped her, but … you had a plan to deal with megalomaniac Harmon." I looked at Lethe, who was back by the window. "What was your plan to deal with crazy cousin Rose?"

"The same as yours," Lethe said, not looking away from the window. "You just did it first."

"Get in her head?" I asked. "Let her beat you within an inch of your life? Have a group of friends ride into the rescue at the last second and blow her brains out with an expanding micro-bullet?"

Lethe shook hers. "No."

"You must keep in mind," Hades said, "the power boost serum." He looked at Lethe. "We were prepared to give it to your grandmother … so that she could—"

"Drain Rose like a canteen on a hot day," I said, giving them both a sour look. "Boy, that would have come in handy about a year ago if I'd had a shot of that."

"You were not ready," Hades said quietly.

"And who gets to decide that?" I asked, heating up.

"You did," Lethe said. "When I tried to reason with you a few years ago and you nearly beat my skull in without provocation." She turned. "Do you know who you were after you beat Sovereign? You were angry. You've always been angry, don't get me wrong, but the fury, it just *boiled* off of you back then. Running your agency into the ground. Driving away your friends, one by one. Putting a wedge between yourself and your brother. You were testing the limits of your power."

"This is normal," Hades said. "You see it all the time in the metas you go after. But instead of becoming lawless in service of your own greed, you broke the law while following your own moral compass."

"Bullshit," I said.

"Nadine Griffin," Lethe said.

"Eric Simmons," Hades said. "You recall the video of you slapping him around for making a sexually charged remark to a waitress?"

"You kidnapped Simmons," I said. "Turned him loose against the USS *Enterprise*. Got him killed—"

"Yes," Hades said. "But don't distract from your own accounting with whataboutism. I will answer your charges … but not just yet." He pointed a finger at me. "Yours is a history beset by overreaction. You have tested the line between wrong and right, trying to find your footing. You stole hundreds of millions of dollars—"

"From Omega," I said.

"—and have killed in what you think is the name of justice," Lethe took up for him. "All of those acts could be righteous, or some of them could be. Or perhaps none of them. Perhaps there was a different way—"

"I didn't start those fights," I said.

"You left two hundred mercenaries dead or wounded in that quarry in Minnesota not a week ago," Hades said.

"They had it coming," I said.

"Perhaps," Lethe said, and she came over to stand by her father's side. "This is the point, though. You have exercised your power over life and death, substituted your judgment for the natural order—"

"The law of the jungle is the natural order, in case you missed it," I said hotly. "I do my best to put human order back in place. The law of man. You want to talk about justice? It's a human concept, and it's based on reciprocity, not some magical fairness. Someone strikes at you, either you strike back or the law does. That's human justice—"

"That's a dim view of humanity," Hades said.

"It's a little Hobbesian, I'll grant you," I said. "But what's the alternative? Let bad guys skate around, doing all the evil they want, unchecked? Because that's a recipe for more bad, lemme tell you—"

"You don't have to tell us," Lethe said.

"We have lived long," Hades said.

"We know this is true," Lethe said.

"It's creepy that you're doing this dual-monologue thing, finishing each others' sentences," I said. "Also, it feels like a tag team."

"Fine, I'll tag out," Lethe said and wandered back to the window to stare out.

"We are not trying to 'beat up on you,'" Hades said. "We are not angry with you. We do not condemn your choices. We know that you made the best ones you could in the moments you were in and were always striving to do the 'right thing,' at least as you saw it from where you stood. But time, and Scotland, and doubt … these have given you a gift of perspective you lacked in the days after Sovereign. You have tasted defeat. Clawed through adversity. Leashed your powers … limited your responses. Think of how you have been pursued by law enforcement these last years. Did you ever take a shot at them?"

"No," I said.

"Your life was always on the line," Hades said. "Yet you turned the other cheek in those moments. Admirable. You fought, at times killed those who took up arms and fought you, but only when you had to. Again, we don't fault your judgment. I did much worse in my day, at your age. You operate from a moral principle. In those times, I operated from power."

"But you are different now than you were a year ago," Lethe said quietly.

"Now … you are ready," Hades said.

"Ready for what?" I asked, feeling a cold trickle of doubt roll down my spine as I stood before my great-grandfather.

A knock at the door stopped him answering. "Come," he said.

It opened, and Aleksy was standing there, looking like he was about to stick his head in a lion's den. "I am sorry to disturb you, my—"

"It is fine, Aleksy," Hades said, shaking his head. "I hope you are well?"

"I … yes, of course, my king," Aleksy said. He looked a little starstruck and snapped to attention. "I bring word from General Krall regarding …" And he looked at me.

Hades traced his eyes to me, and smiled with deep amusement. "This is now the crown princess of Revelen, Aleksy. You need not hide news from her, good or bad."

I raised an eyebrow at that. Yesterday I'd been a prisoner. Today I was a step below queen. Man, the wheel spun fast in my life. What the hell was I going to be tomorrow?

Dead, probably, because this was batshit levels of crazy.

"The arsenal is in place, and the defensive missile system is ready for testing," Aleksy said.

Hades smiled thinly. "Tell General Krall that she may proceed when ready." Aleksy snapped a salute and started to leave. "And Aleksy?" The soldier turned, looking like he might trip over himself to show respect to Hades. "Give it your absolute best, yes?"

Aleksy snapped to attention again. Lethe nodded at him as well, and Aleksy swelled with pride, saluting her, then me, in turn. I just waved back; Lethe returned his salute crisply. Doctor, army lady … my grandmother was a real renaissance chick.

"He is a good lad," Hades said after Aleksy closed the door. I had a feeling the "good lad" could still hear him, and that he was intended to.

"Seems like a nice enough guy," I said, more to be agreeable (why, Sienna? Why?!) than anything. "Can I ask you something about this missile system?"

Hades studied me, then nodded. "Of course. It is your right as crown princess to be as involved as you choose in all the decisions of our government." He chuckled. "After all, someday this will all be yours."

I looked out the window past Lethe at the lone skyscraper of Bredoccia, hanging in the background. "Uh. Okay. So … about this missile system … and the nukes …?" He nodded, and I found my words. Or word. "… Why?"

Hades traded a look with Lethe, a complicated one, filled with significance. She nodded, just once, and Hades sat down, in the chair by my bed, a little heavily, before he looked back up at me with those crisp, blue eyes. "Of course you ask, Sienna … so bright. The question is good. Very good indeed. Why would our tiny country, so long out of the world's sight, seek power enough to place ourselves in everyone's view?"

"Yeah," I said. "I was thinking of it a little more gut level, a little more … 'Hey, Vlad the Impaler now has nukes. This sounds bad,' but … yeah. That geopolitical stuff … that's a good point. Now they're looking at us. Because of nukes. And taking over Russia, probably."

"It is a good question," Hades said, letting his long fingers stretch out over the wooden armrests of the chair, playing along their lengths. "You are the answer, Sienna." He looked back up at me. "You are the reason we sought this power. Sought to take over Russia."

"I … what?" I asked.

"You ask why we could not have brought you here sooner?" Hades asked. "There were several reasons. Humility was but one. The other … the bigger, especially now that you have made such a stir …" His gaze hardened, and I could tell as he looked at me that this was something he was serious about. "You are hated by the US government. Hunted by them. Hiding in England? They wouldn't have dared start a war with their oldest ally just for you. But us?" He put his hands out, palms up. "We are nothing to them. Almost no diplomatic ties to speak of. No treaties. Little trade. No leverage." His eyes flashed.

"The reason we sought alliance … sought nuclear weapons, sought missile defenses … is you," Hades said, and here he pushed to his feet. He moved slowly, and I did not stop him when he put his hands on my shoulders. He loomed over me, but there was not an ounce of threat in the way he stood there, casting a protective shadow over me. "You see, they are going to come for you. As they did in Scotland. But instead of finding a toothless country with nothing to bargain with, nothing to trade … nothing to fight with …" He smiled. "They now find us with power. With strength. With the ability to fight back to protect …" He held onto my shoulder with just the slightest pressure. It was …

Reassuring.

"And protect you, I shall," Hades said, "as though you were the last of my line." A flicker of sadness glowed like a dying ember in his eyes. "Because you are, Sienna Nealon. The last of our kind. And if they come for you …" His gaze hardened, and he turned it toward the window, where Lethe waited, and once he looked her, she nodded. "… We will fight them with everything we have."

29.

Passerini
Washington DC

Passerini rode in the back of the SUV as it thumped along the DC roads toward the Pentagon. It wasn't a long drive, but long enough that he could get his thoughts in a disciplined order before arrival, which given the circumstances, was something he sorely needed.

"Sir?" the young colonel across from him in the SUV spoke, pulling Passerini out of the darkening cloud that was forming in his mind. It sure seemed like they were heading toward a showdown with Revelen, possibly a war …

"Yes, son?" Passerini asked. He still didn't even know the younger man's name. "Sorry, colonel …" He looked at the nameplate. "Huh."

"Yeah, not a great name for an army guy, is it?" the colonel asked with a grin.

"No, it is not," Passerini said with a dark chuckle, tearing his eyes away from the Colonel's name plate. "What's on your mind?"

"Well, I was in the Situation Room with you, sir—"

"I noticed. Your efforts to make me look good were wasted, unfortunately, but I appreciate the effort nonetheless."

"Thank you, sir. I was wondering …" The young colonel seemed to lose his train of thought for a second, looking up as though thinking about something, "uhm … sorry … I was wondering if the president is always so … ah … looking for the right word here so as not to give offense …"

"He's the Commander-in-Chief, son," Passerini said, suddenly very serious. No pejorative term the colonel could have come up with would have sat well with Passerini. "But … I take your meaning. Let's keep these ideas out of our discussion, though, all right?"

"Sir, he fired you," the colonel said.

Passerini let a swift nod be his answer. "And he is well within his rights to do so. I serve at the pleasure of the president. If he wants my resignation at the conclusion of this crisis, I will write it out in my own blood, if asked."

"That is commitment," the colonel said. "Loyalty."

"That's the job, son," Passerini said. The Pentagon was in sight ahead of them. "We're the sword and the shield. We follow the civilian leadership."

"Even if they're leading us into a war?" the Colonel asked. "An unprovoked war?"

Passerini hesitated. "Look …"

"We're not the FBI, sir," the colonel said, leaning forward. His hair looked freshly cut. "The president seems to be trying to get you to fulfill their function, though, doesn't he? I understand loyalty—more than you know—but this … tracking down an accused person in another country … it seems over the line."

"I don't disagree," Passerini said. "But he's the Commander in Chief, and we're the grunts. I will follow his orders up to the edge of the law. Thus far, all we've been asked to do is plan, nothing more."

"But he's ordered other stuff before," the colonel said. "That attempted grab in Scotland … Harmon completely weaponized the military for use against Sienna Nealon—on American soil, no less—"

"We're not doing any of that," Passerini said, holding up a hand to stay his complaint. "We'll take it as it comes, but that … other stuff happened on someone else's watch. I'm not attacking US soil on mine. As to this other thing …" Passerini shook his head. "We'll present options, but my concern is not Sienna Nealon, wherever she is. We're not a law enforcement agency, whatever the president thinks. My concern is the Revelen situation, and specifically, how it pertains to their new-old friends, the Russians … and the nukes."

"Heh," the colonel said. "That's a little more nuanced thinking than your callsign would suggest."

Passerini smiled. "'Hammer,' you mean? They called me that because when I'd come in hot, I'd drop the hammer on the enemy. Air support for the ground pounders." He nodded at the colonel. "I'm guessing you know what I'm talking about."

"Air support is a beautiful thing," the colonel said.

"What's your first name, son?" Passerini asked, sticking out his hand. This colonel … he was no dummy, for a ground pounder. The SUV was pulling into the Pentagon, squeaking to a stop.

"Harrison," the colonel said, smiling back. He took Passerini's hand, and his grip was firm. "But you can call me Harry if you want … sir."

"We should probably stick to rank," Passerini said with a smile of his own. Formality. Discipline. These were crucial elements in the running of Passerini's world. Rules. Bylaws.

Duty.

These were important things in the military world. Still …

"Welcome to my staff, Colonel Graves," Passerini said, flicking another look at the colonel's name bar. "It's a pleasure to be working with you … Harry."

30.

Sienna

As you can probably imagine, sleep didn't come super easy after Hades's little revelation about the US coming for me. There was some tossing and turning after he and Lethe left my room, wanting to, "Let me rest," as he put it.

Rest.

Hah. Yeah, that didn't seem likely.

A knock sounded at the door and I sat up in the dark. "Who is it?" I asked, looking around for a weapon in easy reach. Old habits and all that.

"It's me," Lethe's voice came through the door. "Mind if I come in?"

"It's a free country … maybe?" I asked, because hell if I knew what sort of government Revelen actually had other than Hades as king and Lethe as princess and me as crown princess.

Lethe opened the door and stepped inside. Still dressed in her jeans and sweater, she didn't look like she'd even tried to sleep, though she'd shed the jacket that she'd been wearing earlier. She kept her arms folded in front of her. It was such a *mom* thing to do, which made me realize …

Mom had probably gotten it from her.

"I couldn't sleep, either," Lethe said, standing in the middle of the room like an awkward statue. In the faint light from the window she really did look like Mom, all shadow save for the outline of the bone structure. The voice was different, the hair was different, but … the height, the shape …

Shit.

She was just like Mom.

"Do I even want to know what's on the future queen's mind?" I asked. "Because your worries have gotta be heavier than the crown princess's."

She snorted in the darkness. "Maybe. Everyone's worries carry weight for them. They might not look heavy to someone else, but that doesn't make them any lighter for the carrier." Her tone softened. "What's on your mind?"

"How'd you know I wasn't sleeping?" I asked.

She shuffled over to the bed in the darkness and sat down on the edge, unfolding her arms. "Call it a hunch."

"Good hunch," I said, putting my legs over the side next to her. "Why do you think I can't sleep?"

She blew out air between her lips. "Why are you asking me questions like a shrink instead of just answering?"

"It's a well-honed defense mechanism," I said. "Once you let someone inside, it's really tough to go back to wanting to kick their ass, see, but if you keep them at a distance and don't bond …"

"Oh. Right." She put her hands on the bed and leaned back. "Should have known that. Fine. What's on my mind? Geopolitics."

"Sounds … weighty," I said.

She made another noise of amusement, this one deep in her throat. "It's not what I would have considered serious or worrisome if you'd told me about it when I was fighting armies of Norseman for my very life, but … it is no less perilous should things go awry."

"Yeah, I'm not sure bringing in the nukes was a great move for defusing the tension in the region," I said. "Same goes with taking over Russia. Or whatever you did there."

"We took a situation in turmoil, put a semi-popular former ruler back into the wings, then pushed him out on stage once we had some things in place to cushion his return. Once he was in place, it was easy from there because Russia is well set up for the exercise of nearly unchecked power."

"That … sounds kinda gross," I said.

She shook her head. "It is 'kinda gross,'" she said. "Realpolitik disgusts me. And yet …"

I waited for the explanation. It did not disappoint.

"I long for the days when I could just take someone I disagreed with and hack them to pieces on a battlefield or in a duel or pound the stuffing out of them in a fight," she said, getting back to her feet and pacing. "It was so much simpler back then. Might made right. There was no moral ambiguity. There was a clarity that came with strength. If you could, you did." She let out a sharp breath. "I'm not longing for those days again, exactly, because the food was terrible, the people were savage, and I've grown rather fond of civilizational progress and cell phones and whatnot, but …" She shook her head. "I do miss the simplicity. Fight, win, done."

"Yeah," I said, "we've come a long way, baby."

She looked right at me, and I could feel the irony oozing off her. "Have we?"

"Yeah, I mean, look at me," I said. "I had the might, but it didn't make me right. The US government decided I was in the wrong, boom, they come after me. Across the damned world, in fact."

"They're mightier than you now," she said. "And you didn't even really fight them."

I sighed. "I never wanted to fight them. On the whole, I do believe in that civilizational system you talked about. I believe in outsourcing our might to just causes. That instead of just me bowling whoever pisses me off or gets in my way, that there's a system, flawed as it may be, to redress wrongs. And me? Well, they decided I did wrong. Which … I *have* done wrong." A little hint of a smile pulled at the corner of my lips. "Just not the wrong they accused me of."

"Might still makes them right, if they hammer you down."

"Well," I said, "it's a collective action, at least. Not a single king doing what he wants."

"Is it?" She was smirking.

"In theory," I sighed. "There are established principles. Laws to guide us. Or there were supposed to be." I shifted uncomfortably on my bed. Obviously the law hadn't done much to guide the people who'd tried me and thrown me into prison, but …

Well, it was a nice theory, I'd thought. Until it smashed me in the face.

"How do you feel?" she asked. It came out of the blue, a radical departure from what we'd been talking about a moment before, with might and fights and whatnot.

"I don't know," I said. "Confused, mostly, I think. Like I said before, this isn't going how I thought it was going to."

"You expected a fight," she said. "You weren't expecting a home."

Boy, that word hit hard, right in the gut. I let out a long, slow breath. "You're right," I said, after most of the emotional impact had passed. "It's just been a long time since I've really had a … home."

I'd been in Minneapolis only days before, crawling through backyards and hiding from the cops. Fighting it out in a quarry, visiting old friends …

But I'd been on the run pretty much the entire time, and never once, even when I was chillin' in my old backyard …

It had never felt like I'd come home, not really. Ditto for when I'd been back in January to fight the Predator when he'd gone nuts in the city.

Was that just because I'd been running for so long, because I'd been feeling hounded? Disconnected from everything that had made Minneapolis my home? I mean, I'd been raised there, but pretty much entirely in my own house. My world growing up, from as long as I could remember, was the inside of that house and the small section of backyard I could see whenever I dared to move some furniture so I could look out the back window.

"You could have it here," she said. "With us."

There was a funny feeling that came along with that. I pushed it away, focusing instead on the question throbbing away in my brain. "What are you not telling me?"

"Quite a bit," she said, folding her arms in front of her again. "I mean … Hades and I have both lived a very long time, so the sheer volume of what we know could fill an awful lot of books individually. Combined, it's even more—"

"You know what I mean, and it ain't that."

"I know what you mean," Lethe said, stopping short of the window. "Of course there are things we aren't telling you. There's so much more going on here than anyone could know looking from the outside. But we will tell you everything. It's just a matter of time."

"Why?" I asked. "If what you're doing here is decent and aboveboard and in the name of protecting me—"

"And our people," Lethe said.

"—then why not get it all out at once?" I asked. "'Hey, this is the savage-ass shit we're into. Here are the terrible things we've done, loading our rapists and murderers into a catapult and launching them into the sea.' Actually, I might be on board with that one, depending on—"

"You joke, but …" she shifted uncomfortably, "… might makes right, and the might given to you by the modern nation-state is powerful. More powerful than the armies of my day by orders of magnitude. When I massacred Viking invaders—"

"You must be a Packers fan."

"—I had to do it by hand, with my chosen," she said. "We looked our enemies in the eye, felt the battle fury, and claimed their lives. These days, a modern police force in Anytown, USA, could wipe my old army off the map with their superior weapons. I learned this lesson—our whole species learned this lesson—in the Great War. It changed the landscape. You want to talk about people and systems and justice and rule by the masses? Well, the masses, the agglomerated power in modern nation … it beats the living hell out of the destructive power we wielded back then. No one, save for perhaps Genghis Khan, ever had that level of annihilative power at their disposal. And it's only getting heavier."

"That's dark," I said, "but it doesn't exactly clear up the secrets you're keeping from me."

"My point is," she said, "whatever reputation you think Hades built as Vlad, the things he could do back then—and they were dark, to be sure, and he has rejected them now, also to be sure—they pale compared to what your country can do almost accidentally in a war. Collateral damage, they call it. Well, any modern army, air force, navy—even a modern police force … they can create similar amounts of havoc. The examples are all around you of what an unchecked government can do to its own people. Turkey, Iran—"

"You drawing a parallel here to what happened to me?" I asked, not quite getting it.

"I'm drawing a parallel here to show you something," Lethe said. "The sheer power of a government in the modern age is something the Roman Empire would have shuddered at. It has never been easier to control people, to indulge the darker sides of our natures. However totalitarian, however barbaric we were in the past, the power at our fingertips here in Revelen now makes every empire that stood before look pathetic by comparison.

"We have done bad things, both in antiquity and modernity," she said flatly. "We will tell you all about them. Some as cautionary tales. Some from which I'm sure you'll draw your own conclusions, and they'll become the cautionary tales that guide you as you move into a future without us, eventually, your hand on Revelen's tiller. There is nothing we are not prepared to discuss with you, good or ill, given enough time to cover the subject. It's just …"

And here she hung her head. "We barely know you yet, Sienna. Forgive us for holding back on telling you all our sins, all our mistakes, right out of the gate. Because … Hades and I … for all our faults, and they are innumerable, we …" She looked up at me. "We want you to *like* us. Because really … you are just about the only family we have left."

"Huh," I said, a little … taken aback. "That's—"

The phone chirped across the room, and Hades's voice boomed through. "Sienna? Is Lethe there with you?"

"I'm here," Lethe said, swooping over and hitting the speakerphone button. She'd made it across the room in less than a second.

Damn. Grandma still had speed.

"I need you to come to the Situation Room," Hades said. His

voice lacked its usual amusement and rang with tightness. "And bring Sienna with you. We have … well, this is ironic …" The amusement returned, but it faded quickly when he spoke again, "We have a situation."

31.

Passerini
The Pentagon

"What have we got?" Passerini could read the temperature of a room as soon as he walked in, and this room was no exception. It was the Pentagon ops center, filled to brimming with bustling generals and lower ranks, all doing their assigned jobs at the edges, monitoring a variety of global situations on screens that circled the room.

In the center stood the upper echelon of each branch of the military, gathered around a planning table replete with an electronic map. The mood was tense, that much was obvious from a cursory glance.

General Floyd Marks, Chairman of the Joint Chiefs, was the one Passerini picked out immediately. "Floyd," Passerini said, "you guys all look like someone humped the bunk."

That broke the tension. "Well, we have what looks to be a problem, sir," Marks said. He wasn't quite ramrod straight, but close. He had lines on his face from his time as a grunt, sunburned all to hell. Infantrymen and SpecOps guys tended to accumulate that "hard use" look from about forty on. Marks wore it about as well as could be expected. "Lieutenant." He looked to a fresh-faced lady at a console just behind him.

Passerini moved up to the planning table, and the view on it changed as the lieutenant messed with the electronic map to bring up an overhead satellite view. It was Revelen—Bredoccia, actually, Passerini could tell from having stared at the damned place on views just like this for the last six days. The picture zoomed in tightly on something sweeping across the landscape.

"What the hell?" Passerini muttered. Colonel Graves squeezed in next to him, and the men made room. "A Black Hawk?"

"We've been tracking it for about an hour," Marks said. "It's almost to Bredoccia."

"Revelen doesn't use our helicopters, do they?" Passerini asked.

Marks shook his head. "Their military is a patchwork quilt of NATO and Russian gear, but near as we can tell, they use Russian birds. And this one …" Marks's forehead crease grew deep. "It came out of Ramstein Air Base."

Passerini swore under his breath. "It's one of ours? Who authorized that?" He looked up at the commanding general of the US Air Force, an incredibly serious former B-52 pilot named Donovan. His callsign had been "Thunder."

"Not me," Donovan said. "We didn't even get a whisper of it. I let fly some wrath on down the chain, but whoever authorized it … it didn't come through the usual channels."

Passerini thumped a clenched fist against the table's edge, and the built-in screen flickered. He didn't like showing even that much emotion in front of his men, but this crap—

He took a deep breath, closed his eyes, then opened them. Just like that, the urge to 'drop the Hammer,' as some of his former subordinates had jokingly called it, passed. For now. "Chalke," he whispered, figuring he had his answer.

"Yeah," Colonel Graves said, and Passerini looked up in time to see him nod. "It's not one of our Black Hawks. It's a civilian model. The FBI has more than a few." Graves nodded again, looking at the helicopter cutting its way slowly across the landscape of Revelen. "Dollars to donuts that's the FBI's new Metahuman Task Force."

"They'd certainly have the pull to use our bases without letting us know about it," Passerini conceded, straightening up.

His back cracked as he did so; the rigors of age. The approval could have come straight from Gondry, but dammit, he might have at least mentioned it in passing to the Joint Chiefs or the Secretary of Defense … He let out a long breath. "Double check with the tower at Ramstein. Make sure this is on the level. Confirm that everything was done aboveboard. And find out who authorized it. If it was the president …" He shrugged. "Then there's nothing we can do. I want to know if it wasn't, though. If this was Chalke running rogue again with our resources …"

Passerini felt a little flash of anger thinking of the last time Chalke had stomped all over the military. She'd appropriated one of their key assets, a meta and former Marine named Warren Quincy she'd turned loose in the US homeland to track down and capture Sienna Nealon. That had irked Passerini something fierce, and not just because he felt strongly about Posse Comitatus.

"What do we do now, sir?" Colonel Graves asked, a little stiffly. Formally, too. Good, he knew the difference between a conversation in private and the tone he needed to set in public. He really was a smart kid—though he was hardly a kid as a full bird Colonel. Must have looked younger than he was. "Anyone else you want us to … check with?"

Good guess, Graves, Passerini thought, because hell if the colonel hadn't prompted a thought with his question. "Yeah," he said, "get me SecState Ngo on the phone, Colonel." Passerini straightened his back. This was going to be a fun conversation. "We should probably let her know that the US government just invaded Revelen."

32.

Sienna

The Situation Room was fascinating, almost like something out of the movies. Video screens were everywhere, playing news both local and foreign, with paper maps pinned on bulletin boards and on tables, with push pins and tanks and soldier figurines everywhere, reminding me of a time when I'd walked in on Reed and J.J. playing some sort of tabletop war game.

Oh, the delicious embarrassment my brother's flaming cheeks had proclaimed. He always did like to maintain his image, but I knew in his heart Reed was the geekiest of geeks. For my part, I said nothing. Because it was even better to pretend I hadn't seen.

This would have put his geekery to shame, though, being as these tables were wargames for real, the center of the room taken up by a giant table representing all of western Europe and stretching most of the way through Germany on one side and all the way through Russia on the other. Lots of little figurines stood on it, too, representing the disposition of forces in the area. There was a heavy concentration of tanks and soldiers just over the border in Russia, and I could see a pretty big clump of US forces represented in Germany as well. I took it all in with a quick glance, trying to figure out the distance between them and Revelen based on the scale. I couldn't do it in my head, though, and it was a few countries away, so I gave up and followed Lethe over to where Hades was staring at a monitor over some soldier's shoulder.

"The US government has sent a chopper," Hades said, pointing at the radar screen on the monitor in front of him.

"How do you know that?" I asked. Everyone turned to look at me. Well, everyone at this monitor—Lethe, Hades, the fresh-faced unknown soldier.

"One of our empaths guarding the border called it in," Hades said with a faint smile. "They picked up a heavy helping of menace emanating from this helicopter, localized it, and informed of us of their coming."

One of the implications of having an entire population of metas had just smacked me in the face. "You have empaths guarding the borders?"

"Indeed," Hades said. "And we have boosted their powers so that they can determine ill intent when it comes our way."

"How very *Minority Report* of you," I said.

"Criticize our defensive strategies later," Lethe said, staring at the green dot on the radar. "What are we dealing with?"

"We won't know until a telepath can confirm," Hades said, "but our intelligence suggests it may in fact be the FBI's elite metahuman task force." He looked at me. "They have only one target, of course."

"Of course," I said, just dripping sarcasm. Yay. The FBI was sending their superpowered SWAT team after me. "What are you going to do about it?"

Hades took a slow breath, like he was thinking it over. "We have a few options. The simple push of a button and our new Russian-made SAM defenses could bring them down in a ball of flame—"

"Yeah, that's aggressive," I said. "Let's not do that." A vision of escalation to nuclear war popped to mind, which was the sort of thing you risked when you shot down an enemy chopper with weapons of war, even when they were invading your airspace.

"Starting to realize the implications of being responsible for an entire country?" Lethe asked, the ghost of a smile on her face as she looked at me.

"I agree with Sienna," Hades said. "The US has provoked us, but we need not respond with overwhelming force. We cannot, however, allow them to land and proceed unchecked. They may have committed an act of war, but we need not respond in kind." He smiled, too. "I think a gentler approach is called for."

Holy shit, look at Death being all merciful. "That's … good," I said, because I couldn't think of anything else to say.

"We should meet them with some force, though," Lethe said. "Soldiers. Guns …" She glanced at me. "Unless you have an objection to a measured response, one that offers them the chance to surrender peacefully?"

"I don't think they'll go for it, but yeah, we should offer them the chance, at least," I said, my conscience rattling. Things had taken an interesting turn here, what with US law enforcement invading a sovereign country to come get my fugitive self. My knees quivered a little at the thought of turning loose violence on what were basically cops doing my old job. "I'd really like to see us back them into a corner and make them surrender, though."

"I agree," Lethe said. "For both humanitarian and political reasons." I only frowned at her a little before she clarified: "It won't hurt our case to be able to parade FBI agents who invaded our country around to the world. Might sway a little public opinion our way."

"Yes, I'm sure it will counteract the bad rap we're currently getting for harboring a known fugitive," Hades said, so dripping with irony that it took me a second to realize he was being thoroughly unserious. "Still, mercy seems the best course, so … let us set an ambush, shall we?" He looked down at the kid driving the console. "Inform General Krall that we require a careful ambush." He straightened up, his eyes glittering. "And, I think, perhaps, the three of us should also participate? Just to make sure things are done to our satisfaction?"

"Oh, you want me to—" I blinked. "Wait, you want to do this yourself?"

He extended a hand to me. "I have never been much for

waiting behind the scenes when things are happening. In this, you, I think, are the same?" He glanced at Lethe, who shrugged. "I know she is. So, yes … I think we should all go together. We should look this threat in the face and defend our country, yes?"

Defend *our* country. That phrase hit me right in the belly. Again.

It hadn't been that terribly long ago—hours, maybe—when I would have considered riding in with this task force to apprehend a dangerous fugitive to be defending my country.

How swiftly the times did change.

I looked at Hades's hand. Lethe was just waiting, watching, arms folded again. It was her default posture. "We're not going to hurt them if we can avoid it," she said. "And if *we're* there, we can help to control the situation. We can leave it to General Krall, if you prefer, but …"

"She'll kill them all and let the morticians sort it out," I said, "No. Let's do this." And I took Hades's hand. He gave mine a squeeze, nodding, and off we went for the door to set up an ambush for my former countrymen.

33.

"There's only one easy way in and one easy way out of the castle," General Krall said, as we stood in the hangar bay where I'd entered earlier that ... day? "At least, if they intend to board a helicopter again to leave."

Had it really only been a day already?

The hangar was sprawling, but I noted that there were no guards save for a couple patrols lingering near the mouth of the bay. They weren't even looking in the direction of the open hangar door, and seemed to be on a slow path away from it.

The air had an oily, mechanical smell to it, which I suspected had something to do with Hades's car collection, and probably also the tanks. They were all parked in neat rows, and no one had made so much as a move to fire one up, which suggested to me that this fight was going to be somewhat more limited than General Krall might have made it if given an utterly free hand.

"You have sealed all the other entrances?" Hades asked. We were lurking behind a makeshift position secured with sandbags. A metahuman soldier with powers like Augustus's had filled them as we stood there, creating a good dozen bulwarks for our soldiers to hide behind. Cover against the coming attack.

"Sealed them and kept them under the normal heavy guard," Krall said, smiling with sharp, flashing teeth. "This hangar will look undefended by comparison. Anyone looking from overhead will have determined it is the best and most feasible entry point."

That was interesting. Krall had created a supply and guard pattern to lull anyone watching from overhead—which would include only the countries with enough wealth to have satellites and stealth drones—into believing that this was the castle's weak point. She sure seemed proud of herself, and I couldn't blame her. Keeping in mind your opponent had technological advantages and using them against them seemed very jiu jitsu of her. Surprise.

"We are not quite sure of the composition of this task force," Hades said, and he was standing with a rather soldierly bearing, hands clapped behind his back, "but you will take utmost care not to kill, general."

If Krall was disappointed in his command, she was controlled enough not to let it show. "As you wish, your majesty. We will do our very best to contain rather than destroy."

"Excellent," Hades said and carefully took a knee behind the sandbag wall. Lethe lingered just behind his shoulder. "Where is Aleksy?"

"Out front," Krall said with a stiff nod, "but not too far."

Lethe and Hades both nodded at that, which I thought was a little funny. Aleksy seemed like a nice guy and all, but …

He must have had a hell of a power if they were putting him out front. I made a mental note to watch for that, because just looking at the guy? I hadn't gotten any kind of intimidating vibe off of him. In fact, I'd thought he was kind of a goofball.

I stiffened; the whip of rotor blades in the distance prompted General Krall to shout something in whatever language they spoke here. The lights overhead went out, leaving me with a slightly dim view of the hangar. Moonlight slid in from beyond the doors, and that told me something about how desperate the FBI was to get me back. SpecOps didn't like to attack when the moon was out. It tended to expose their helos to view from the ground.

They wanted me back in the worst way, and I still didn't know quite how to feel about that.

The silence in the hangar was desperately creepy. This was what it was like being in the presence of so many metas, whose senses were turned up to hyperawareness. It felt like no one was even daring to breathe, it was so quiet, everyone so still that the chop of the Black Hawk's rotor blades just outside was the most prominent sound, even in here.

General Krall mouthed something, and I caught a hiss of radio static. She'd sent it to her whole team, who were probably wearing combat radios of some kind. I would have liked to have been listening in, but she sounded like she was speaking local, so it wouldn't have done me much good.

"Are you ready?" Hades asked, touching my forearm with his bare hand. It was a funny feeling, his rough, calloused palm brushing my smooth arm.

It was not a feeling I was used to, being touched. His hand was strong, but not aggressive, exactly.

Reassuring, again.

"Ready as I'm ever going to be," I whispered, meta-low, as the sound of the rotors reduced. The helo was parked, and we huddled beneath the sandbag wall, listening.

"Kill the chopper," Hades said, and Krall whispered something into her mic that sounded like it started with, "Aleksy," and then proceeded deeper into the depths of the local tongue.

Something groaned outside, metal straining, and the sound of the rotor blades died, the chop winding down.

"Oh, shit, mechanical failure on the chopper," a male voice called from ahead, just inside the doors. "Repeat, chopper is down."

"What the hell?" another voice came. English, of course. Rough.

"Aleksy," Krall whispered, and a torrent of swearing broke loose from the US forces as the lights snapped on.

I came to my feet a second behind the rest of them, Hades, Lethe and Krall leading the way. When I got up, I was met with a hell of a sight.

The FBI metahuman team were all staring down the barrels of their own weapons, which were hanging in the air in front of them, ripped from their very hands. Pistols, submachine guns, and grenades hovered before them, just out of reach, aimed right at their own faces.

"Surrender your weapons," Hades called over the sandbags between us. There were ten of them by my count, ten guys in military garb, their guns pointed at their own heads.

"I think they've been taken already, Grandpa," I said.

I flicked my gaze to where Aleksy had been before; he was standing there, hands extended, looking like he was barely straining.

Suspicion confirmed—Aleksy had magnetic powers.

"This doesn't need to end in death," Hades said. "Surrender, and you will be repatriated to the United States."

"We're not leaving without her," the lead guy said, nodding at me. He was … not what I would have expected from a SWAT Team lead. Most of those guys—and I'd worked with quite a few—were bulky dudes. Serious athletes who could bench press a mountain. This guy was maybe a few inches taller than me, wire-thin, his wrists about the width of a dog's leg.

"You are staring down the barrel of your own guns," Hades said, his tone indicating that he wasn't going to take any shit. "If you resist, you will not make it out of here alive, let alone with her." He spared me a sidelong look, filled with reassurance again.

Reassuring glances from Vlad the Impaler, from Hades, the God of Death and the Underworld. I was definitely living in the weirdest timeline.

"Garett," the team lead said, not looking back into his team, which was a mix of women and men, kinda unusual for SWAT or SpecOps, at least in the US. It dawned on me that it wasn't that unusual here in Revelen, though, looking around at their soldiers, who seemed to be both male and female—

"Aw, shit," I said, but I'd gotten to it too late—

The population of Revelen was all metas. Everyone had super strength, everyone had powers.

Just like this team in front of us.

"Aleksy—" Hades started to say.

But Garrett, whoever he was, because I didn't get a good look before things went down, glowed brightest white, the-sun-going-nova bright as he activated his meta power, blinding me and everyone else in the hangar as chaos broke loose.

34.

Dave Kory
Brooklyn

"I want everything geared toward Sienna Nealon coverage today," Dave Kory said, talking to the whole staff. The sun had set, and outside the windows, the island of Manhattan twinkled in the distance. Hell of a view, really, and Dave still took the time to notice it as he harangued the staff. "Anything time-sensitive or exclusive, run it now, now, now. Anything that takes a more leisurely approach, or any listicles unrelated to her, set them for publication tomorrow morning to hit the AM audience, okay?"

He looked around. Flashforce.net had a pretty good crew. He'd have the night shift cover any breaking news, or do it himself if he got a little insider buzz from the Network. Was that likely to happen? Maybe. It depended on how the situation in Revelen broke. Wheels turned slowly internationally, as far as Dave knew, and he hadn't heard anything from the Network to suggest there was anything he needed to know about—yet. At least since the big break earlier.

"How about a listicle for all of Sienna Nealon's allies?" Alyssa Brewer asked. She'd dyed her hair the color of Mountain Dew and had glasses that were so thick-rimmed they practically took up her entire face. "Names, pictures—really get it out there, these are the people she was friends with. You know, before."

"I like that," Dave said, wheels turning. He pointed at Alyssa. "But don't go with 'allies'—call them 'accomplices' or something like that."

"Won't legal frown on that?" Barb asked.

Dave shook his head. "I mean, check with them and stay on just this side of the line, but I think we can get away with 'accomplices.'" He laughed. "Screw legal. Go with accomplices. Let them try and prove they haven't had any contact with her since she broke bad."

The scattered crowd of writers got a good chuckle out of that. All except one humorless spot in the middle, named Mike Darnell. That guy, man.

"Speaking of legal," Mhairi Monroe said. Man, she was a shorty. Petite frame, too; Dave bet she would have blown away in a good gale. "I want to write a hot take piece—'Is Sienna Nealon the Worst Criminal of all time'?"

Dave tapped his chin. "I like it. But you need some work on that lede. Put some confidence into it. How about, 'Here's Why Sienna Nealon is the Most Dangerous Criminal of All Time'?"

"Oooh," Alyssa said. "That cranked up the jam a bit."

"Damned right it did," Dave said. "Make it a listicle, too, of her 'greatest hits.' I probably don't need to say it, but the LA thing needs to be near the top." Everybody knew what the top item was. It didn't even need to be said, because Eden Prairie was personal; each of them knew at least one reporter who'd been involved.

"She did some shady shit in my homeland of Scotland, too," Mhairi said, looking over at Alyssa. "Not many people noticed that at the time. You might take a look at the local reports. Fill out your list a bit more."

"Yes," Dave said, pointing at Mhairi. "More pages in the listicle, more clicks, more advertiser dollars. I like this. I mean, don't go too long, but—make sure you build to that number one atrocity, okay? I want the audience thinking she is literally Hitler by the time they click that last page."

"Want me to Photoshop her in with the little mustache?" Alyssa asked, and everybody laughed again. This was a good group. Everyone was on the same page—

Except for Mike. Again. Who raised his hand.

Dave's smirk faded, but he held in the sigh. "What's up, Mike?"

"I was thinking of writing an op-ed piece," Mike said, flipping open a little pad on his palm, going through page by page. "I don't want to soft-focus cover Sienna Nealon's life or anything, but … she has done a little good here and there. Might not be a bad idea to go over it in a piece." He looked up. "Kind of a … counterpoint."

Dave laughed, and so did the rest of the crew, but it wasn't from actual humor. "I don't think that's going to fit with our coverage." He looked around. "All right, team … let's make this happen. Come to me if you've got other ideas, and let's get things queued up for tomorrow. Shake your sources, see if anything new is developing. Scour the net, find some hot takes you can write counter pieces to, aggregate whatever's good to steal traffic for us." He smiled. "Let's be the news source and keep the traffic coming." He clapped his hands once and they broke.

Except Mike. Of course. He waited until the crowd had dispersed a little then wandered up slowly to Dave.

"Listen, Mike," Dave said, figuring he'd pre-empt what he knew was coming, "I know you're new here, so let me tell you why that piece you pitched was a really bad idea."

Mike just nodded. Hey, maybe the old dog was ready to learn a new trick.

"I'm sure you noticed the theme—the general tenor of our coverage," Dave said.

"Sure," Mike said, "it'd be hard not to. 'Sienna Nealon is the Worst Human Ever, Actually.'"

Dave paused. "Shit, that's a great lede. You want to write that story? Because I want it on the home page within an hour." He snapped his fingers and called out across the cubes. "Hey, Alyssa? 'Sienna Nealon is the Worst Human Ever, Actually.'"

"Nice lede," Alyssa called.

"Run with it for your listicle," Dave said, then turned back to Mike. "Sorry. I'm guessing you didn't want to write that one."

Mike shrugged. "I'd rather not. Mainly because it's not true.

Empirically, there have been a lot more garbage humans than her."

"Sure, sure," Dave said. "I mean, if you really want to break down into body counts, I guess. But nobody wants to do that, Mike. Nobody's looking for that level of nuance, especially surrounding a superpowered mass murderer who's on the loose. Dave talked with his hands, and they moved in front of him now in a choreographed dance that matched with his words. "The theme of our coverage colors our entire home page, right? It's a chorus, and we're all singing the same song. Different pieces layer in the harmony. That … is our narrative. 'Sienna Nealon is the worst, most dangerous threat we face today.'"

"But it's not true," Mike said. "You have better odds of dying in car accident than Sienna Nealon swooping out of the sky and murdering you."

Dave did sigh, now. "Of course it's not true. Almost all the things people worry about any given day aren't true. Why are people worried about shark attacks, which kill ten people a year, when bees kill sixty and heart disease kills six hundred thousand? They worry about them because there's *emotion* there. In these stories, they emotionally connect with us. This is what we do, okay? We sate an emotional need. People read our stories, watch our videos, they feel something, right?"

"Seems like our videos and stories tend to push them all in one direction," Mike said, index finger rubbing the page of his notepad. "Anger, stress—"

"Well, that's what people want to feel when they come to us, whether they want to admit it or not," Dave said. He could feel the exasperation just bubbling. "They want us to help them make sense of a chaotic world."

"And you're showing them only the worst of it," Mike said. "Like this Sienna Nealon business—"

"It's called a 'narrative,' Mike," Dave said. "Like I said, we're a chorus here. We're singing the same song. They come here for one Sienna article, but it doesn't totally scratch the itch. It arouses anxiety, so they click the next, hoping to douse that feeling. Except they don't really want to—they want to feel it more. It's an itch they can't finish scratching. They love it. And we get clicks and revenue. It's win-win."

"They end up stressed out and presented with only one side of the story," Mike said. "How in the hell is that win-win?"

"Look, Mike," Dave said, trying to break through this naiveté that the former *Times* reporter wore like an old coat, "it's a win because we're giving them what they want, whether they realize it or not. If they didn't want it, they wouldn't click."

"That sounds a lot like the logic Big Tobacco execs used to use to sell their product," Mike said.

"Come the eff on," Dave said, just rolling his eyes. "We're not killing anyone here, okay? That's just a ridiculous comparison."

"Like … comparing Sienna Nealon to a dictator who murdered millions?" Mike asked. The old guy had a trace of a smile.

Dave's calm evaporated in an instant. "Stick to the narrative, Mike. We're trying to do something here. It's a team effort. Don't go stepping on your team's part of the piece, okay?"

"You didn't hire me to be a chorus girl," Mike said.

Dave turned around, heading for his desk. "Damned right I didn't. You don't have the legs for it, anyway." He shot a smirk at Mike as he walked away. Stupid fossil.

When he sat down at his desk, it took Dave a minute or so to get back to Zen. That old bastard had really come at him, hadn't he?

Did he really not get it?

How could he be so damned obtuse?

There was a narrative for a reason. It gave people the continuity of coverage that they wanted. Nothing more, nothing less. And he wanted to come along and muddy the waters with a hot take about how Sienna Nealon was really not that bad? "Why doesn't he just write a hagiography of John Wayne Gacy?" Dave muttered under his breath.

A buzz on the desk snapped him back to attention and Dave swiped for the phone, then unlocked it.

TIME TO PLAY

He looked around. There was conversation in the next

cubicle, but no one was sticking their head up like a groundhog anywhere in sight. He could probably just …

Dave unlocked the phone, looking around to be sure someone wasn't sneaking up on him. He spun his chair as he logged in, ready to hit the power button if someone came walking up. They all had their marching orders, they'd be fine for a little bit. At least long enough for him to see if this was a big meeting or a little one. If it was a little one, maybe he could just sit here and pretend to be texting …

CHALKE: The FBI has inserted the Metahuman Task Force into Revelen to retrieve Sienna Nealon. Forces about to enter stronghold where we believe she is being kept.

"'Kept'?" Dave muttered, then typed it in with the question mark.

The response only took a second.

CHALKE: Early days of investigation suggest she is linked to a radical anti-Western government, has ties to terrorists who set the riot/escape in the Cube in motion. They are providing her safe harbor in Revelen.

Whoa. That was definitely a scoop, and she wouldn't have said that if she hadn't wanted it percolating out there. Now the question was what angle did he want to take to break this one …?

CHALKE: Task Force about to engage. Stand by for updates.

Dave sat forward in his chair. This was going to be interesting.

BILSON: Waiting on the edge of my seat.

So Bilson felt it, too. Hmmm.

Dave spun around and started to type out a header.

FBI CONDUCTS REVELEN RAID TO CAPTURE ESCAPED FUGITIVE SIENNA NEALON

He paused. Frowned. Edited.

FBI CONDUCTS DARING REVELEN RAID TO CAPTURE DANGEROUS CRIMINAL SIENNA NEALON

There. That was a little more properly weighted. It gave the FBI credit for being bold, thus painting them as the heroes, and it took Sienna Nealon down from 'escaped fugitive'—which sounded bad, no doubt—to 'dangerous criminal,' which sounded much worse.

Still …

BREAKING NEWS: FBI CONDUCTS DARING SORTIE INTO REVELEN TO CAPTURE ESCAPED MASS MURDERER SIENNA NEALON—LIVE UPDATES

There. It added urgency with the "Breaking," put in a cliffhanger element, a suggestion that merely by reading you could be part of something important happening RIGHT NOW. It eliminated the consonance of "Revelen Raid," which bothered Dave the second time he read it, and it escalated Sienna Nealon from criminal—which had a bad connotation, but could just indicate she hadn't paid traffic tickets or something—and put her right in the category where she belonged.

Escaped Mass Murderer. Boom.

It was all about the verbiage, whether you were in advertising or news.

Dave chuckled. Ledes were advertising. That was something else that Mike just didn't get. The whole business was advertising. *Look here! Click here! Read this!* Maybe it had always held a little grain of it, but this was one of the big changes that Dave had seen. Ledes that drew you in, pulled you across an entire webpage when you saw them, made you want to click. Only dickheads called it clickbait and wrote it off as something bad. Losers, all of them.

Winners did the things that it took to get the traffic to their site. And this little headline, Dave knew as he started typing out the basics of the story, adding a big **STORY IN PROGRESS. STAY TUNED FOR LIVE UPDATES** at the bottom of the page …

This little headline was going to win big.

35.

Sienna

The flash of that metahuman was like the worst camera bulb in the world lighting off directly in front of my eyeballs.

Times a hundred.

It was so strong, I could swear I smelled burning flesh and eye fluid as it lit off like lightning in front of my face. Blinking didn't help at all, and neither would anything else, I would have sworn, forevermore. I felt like I was permanently blind, as though somehow that meta had blasted my eyes right out of my head.

Based on the screams around me … I was not alone in feeling this.

A long scream coincided with the light abruptly going out, and I wondered if someone had snuffed the damnable bastard who'd just blinded us all. If so, I was totally going to use my crown princess powers to send them a fruit basket.

I pitched back, thumping against the concrete, and it took me a moment to realize the dark shadows I saw above me were just the ceiling and stalactites. Shouts echoed in the converted cavern, and I saw someone else writhing not too far away from me, like they were having an epileptic seizure. Couldn't tell who they were; the world's resolution had been turned down to "extremely blurry," like maybe 20 dpi or something.

"Gyahhhh," I mumbled, putting my hands up to my eyes and

finding my cheeks streaked with tears. So I did still have eyes, I confirmed by touch, and by seeing my hands move across my face.

"That was an Apollo, named for the sun god," Hades said, looming over me. "Close your eyes for a moment. Let your rods and cones reset."

"I might need to regrow retinas," I said, sitting up. Others were writhing around me. Everything was still incredibly blurry, but it was obvious that our side had taken a pretty hard hit with that surprise attack.

Hades was smiling. "You are fine, see? Which is good, because I think we will be fighting for your life very shortly."

"'We,' huh?" I asked as he offered a hand and I took it. He pulled me to my feet and up we came, back to standing. I mopped at the wetness at my cheeks and looked over the sandbag wall separating us from the FBI Task Force.

Their weapons had fallen when Aleksy had apparently gone blind, and they were trying to retrieve them.

"'Gulp,' I believe is the word for this situation," Hades said, and with a ululating battle cry, he leapt the sandbags and scrambled for the nearest gun.

"Nailed it," I said, and was after him, head feeling wobbly and my cheeks still wet.

Two of the FBI task force members were about ten feet from us, scrambling for their guns. When Aleksy had stripped their weapons, he hadn't left them at point blank range, he'd put some distance between them. That was the only thing saving us from being riddled with bullets right now, because the FBI Task force was racing just as hard as we were for their guns.

I noted nine of them still standing as I scrambled for their weapons, Hades leading me by a foot or two. Apparently he wasn't the sort to just sit back and let shit go down, which was good. Because we were desperately outnumbered, thanks to that unforced error of getting our asses blinded by the enemy.

I picked my opponent, a super-pale white lady with dark dreadlocks, like the hippie, granola-eating version of me. Her hair was hanging around her shoulders and chest, looking like it hadn't been properly washed in a decade. It lacked any shine at all, and I started to call this fact out when her hair snaked out to intercept me en route to her gun.

"Shit, Medusa!" I shouted, baseball-sliding in under the attack of the queen of split ends.

"I knew Medusa," Hades said, not slowing his roll and reaching out a hand. "She was much prettier than this one."

The Medusa froze, her hair retracting instantly as Hades took hold of her very soul in the manner that had once scared Friday into being mute for two weeks. She froze mid-step as though she were being choked, and it gave me just enough clearance to get in under her defenses—

I snatched up her gun as I slid on my back. I gave her a kick as I came in under her abdomen, and she went flying across the room a good thirty feet.

And I had a pistol. A Sig Sauer P226 government issue model. Yay for old familiar friends.

I wasted a round shooting into the ceiling, and shouted, "Nobody move!"

Yeah, that didn't work.

"I would suggest not wasting your ammunition on any more warning shots," Hades said, moving on past a perfectly good M4 carbine, apparently not down with the gun thing. "You should use that thing for real." He waved vaguely at the weapon in my hand, then brought his hand up against the next FBI meta.

"Kid gloves, Grandpa," I reminded him.

"Great-grandfather." He made an annoyed sort of grunting noise and slipped in on the next FBI agent as they went for their own gun, blindsiding them as he stooped. He struck with a knee raise so vicious that it sent the agent tumbling across the room. I cringed, because I heard ribs break from ten feet away on that one, and when he landed, I knew he was going to be down for a while.

"Get Nealon!" someone shouted from behind me with a serious Latin accent, and I spun. There was a super-serious dude standing there, fumbling for his weapon as he yanked up on the shoulder strap, which was the only part of it he had a grip on. His weapon spun as he tried to pull it off the ground and up to him.

"Don't get Nealon," I said, raising my Sig at him. "It would be a bad idea. Hazardous to the health."

Someone slammed into me with no more warning than a brief flash of motion out of the corner of my eye, and I felt the impact run along my side as I hit the ground, a thin, wiry body riding atop me like I was a magic carpet. We hit hard, their legs locked around my waist so as not to let me go. I took the impact along my flank and my ass. All on the meat, which hurt, bruised.

She took it on the kneecap, which broke. And I knew it was a she by the scream that followed.

I drove the butt of the Sig into her nose and flipped her off me, a wash of her blood running down onto my hand from the nose I'd just broken. Another pistol whip and she was unconscious, face gone slack. "See?" I asked her insensate form, not expecting an answer, "Bad idea."

I turned to face my original threat, Mr. Latin Meta. He had almost gotten a full grip on his M4 now, and was raising it up to align with me—

Damn.

This was an FBI agent, not some criminal about to dust me. I could snapshot faster than he could, and I knew I'd drill him right between the eyes with a 9mm round before he could he even line up the sights.

But I wasn't a murderer.

Just a killer. When threatened by those I deemed evil, I could respond with overwhelming force.

When under the gun of an FBI agent come to apprehend me for my evil misdeeds …

I lowered my pistol and let him draw a bead.

Somewhere in my heart of hearts, maybe I felt like … I really did deserve this for all the shady stuff I'd done.

I had no illusions about what was coming. It was going to be a bullet, and it was going to be right to the heart or damned near enough to it so as to end my flight.

Still didn't raise my gun.

He didn't smile, didn't laugh, didn't quip. Didn't do anything but raise his weapon, get it on target. It took less than a second, all things considered, and he was aiming—

The shot came, but went wide, because someone had slammed into him from the side—

Lethe had had hit him like a charging train, barreling into him with enough strength that she lifted him off the ground, sending his shot ricocheting off the pavement and far off to my right. She had him up in the air like a pro wrestler, carrying him off in her charge. Then she stopped abruptly, her face charged with intense concentration, and she whipped him down with all her strength—

He smashed into the ground and his neck snapped back on the impact. His head collided with the concrete and it was like a cantaloupe landing after a ten-story fall. Gore exploded out the top of his melon, splattering in a ten-foot burst pattern out of the top of his skull. His limp body rolled once, and stopped.

I stared at my grandmother, open-mouthed.

"What?" she asked. "You think you're fighting some noble FBI team? These are hardened criminals, given experimental serum treatments and pushed into government service. Act accordingly." And she was off after the next of them.

I didn't know if I quite believed that glib explanation, but they certainly weren't acting like typical agents trying to make an arrest. I noticed, for the first time, that they seemed to be wearing collars. Collars that didn't look unlike the sort of ankle bracelet one might wear on house arrest.

"Huh," I muttered. Had the FBI really put together their metahuman task force by experimenting on criminals and giving them powers? Because, if so … wow, that was playing with fire. My mind raced, thinking that if that were true, you'd need some sort of control mechanism like said collar, which you would fill with … what?

I snapped my attention to another task force member, who was stooping to pick up a gun. He was bloody across the top of his head, and I figured he'd gotten into a scrape with someone—probably Krall, since I could see her battling with two of the other FBI bastards not far from where this guy was recovering his gun. He was bent over, picking up a pistol, and

I drew a bead on that collar on the side of his neck. My aim was perfect, and I slowly squeezed—

BOOM! The collar exploded, taking the meta's head with it and confirming in my mind that what Lethe had said was true.

I picked myself up from the ground, the explosion having knocked me flat on my ass. "Well, that changes things," I said, and promptly shot the three nearest task force members in the head. They did not survive the hollow-points.

"So glad to see you have decided to fight for your own life," General Krall said, wrestling with her last opponent, who I couldn't shoot because she was tangled up with him, a wrist around his neck, choking the life out of him.

"So glad to see you know what 'kid gloves' means," I said.

"I have no gloves for children," she said, smiling over the shoulder of the man whose windpipe she'd just crushed. He was still alive, fighting with the oxygen left in his lungs and bloodstream, flopping wildly in her grasp like a fish that had been ripped out of the water. "For I am an adult, you see." He looked comically pathetic next to the five-foot Krall, his overlong frame bucking impossibly against hers, legs dragging against the much shorter woman.

"Well, you're not built like one, shorty," I said, turning from her to find the next threat. "Maybe someday you'll get that last growth spurt that'll put you up to five-one. Maybe give you some boobs, too, if you're lucky."

I heard the crack of the man's spine, and knew that Krall had either grown impatient with him flopping around, or decided to execute him to prove a point. I turned enough to watch her warily as she circled away from me, keeping at least one eye on me as well. "Once again, you show that you have no fight," she said.

"But I've got plenty of 'kill,'" I said, brandishing the Sig. "So don't push me, Justin Timberlake."

There wasn't much to wrap up. Lethe was crushing one guy, and Hades had another in his grip. Well, about five feet away, actually, but he held his hand out like he was force choking him, going full Vader and the guy was straining against invisible bonds.

"And so your invasion ends," Hades said. Lethe had finished her fight, tossing the limp body away with no more care than if she were chucking a chewing gum wrapper into the trash. Hades, though, seemed determined to send a message to his own foe. I wondered what the hell he was doing, and then I realized—

All these guys had body cameras. And he was speaking English for a reason.

"You have picked the wrong fight," Hades said, holding his hand out as the man clawed at his own throat, trying to free himself from the grip of death. "You send your criminals into my home, trying to take from me my own blood." He was totally posing for the camera. "You do not know me … so let me introduce myself.

His voice got dark, and heavy, and deep, and I had to force myself not to take a step back.

"I am Hades, God of Death. I have at my disposal some twelve intercontinental ballistic missiles topped with multiple independent reentry vehicle warheads." That sent a chill through me, through the room. "I have the entire army of Russia behind me." It got chillier. "I do not care for your wounded egos," he said, glaring into the body camera. "Do not care for your international politics. I am … *Death.* And if you come for Sienna Nealon again …" His eyes just burned.

The man in his thrall screamed, and fell to his knees, toppling over. Hades stooped, flipping him so as to look in the camera. "Come after her again," he said, putting every ounce of the King of the Underworld into his performance, "And Death … will come for you."

36.

My eyes were still burning, maybe for more than one reason, when we made it back to my quarters. I was surprised we didn't head for the Situation Room, but Hades and Lethe had argued that General Krall had it under control and would call if they needed anything, so off we went, Lethe at my side the whole way. Which was fortunate, because without her lead I was going to walk into something by accident.

"I made it through the fight," I said, detecting a blur in my right eye. "I don't understand why just now I'm starting to get double vision or whatever."

"Your retina took damage," Lethe said. "From the sustained assault by the Apollo. Close your eyes more quickly next time."

"Is that what you did?" I asked. I could see her face, but it was blurry, because my eyes were leaking again, tear ducts pumping out warm salty liquid that ran down my cheeks. It wasn't from emotion, I can promise you that, because the moment I'd realized that the FBI had recruited criminals that they'd had to strap with explosives, I'd known for a fact that the people they sent after us were hardcore trouble. No remorse from me for defending my life against the Inglourious Basterds.

"Yes," Hades said. "I was looking at you, and the moment I caught the flash—well. I spent enough time in the company of Apollo to know to look away when you see a blinding light. That was his favorite trick. Then he would run around while we were blinded and steal our purses and slap us on the ass. Or worse."

"Sounds like a real party guy," I said, and Lethe steered me away from a wall that I was about to bump into. She had me by the sleeve, helping me through the door into my room, which Hades held open for us.

"Indeed," Hades said. "It was an uproarious and often horrific experience, partying with my brother Zeus."

Part of me wanted to ask about the horror. Part of me didn't.

"Don't," Lethe whispered. "You really don't want to know."

I accepted her grandmotherly wisdom and moved right along. "If the FBI sent a bunch of wired-up rogue metas after us," I asked, trying to get back to focusing on the crucial things, "what's their next move, d'ya think?"

"I expect they will not let it rest," Hades said. "The president, Gondry, he prides himself on being a level-headed man. An academician."

"I think that's the Russian way of saying it," I said, still blinking away tears. Hades looked blurry, but I could see his smile. "He was a college professor. Smooth talker. Not unlike Harmon in that regard."

"But unlike Harmon, his aspirations of brilliance are, tragically, inaccurate," Hades said. "Our spy agency has thoroughly analyzed Gondry. The cool, measured approach he takes to everything is mere show. He is easily rattled by displays of violence because he has exercised no command for it in his life. Like most wilting pacifists, which he professed to be for most of his career, he thinks fighting unwise and yet has employed force consistently since becoming president. He can be backed into a corner almost immediately." Hades's smile disappeared. "And in this case, I think pride has already led him there."

"Sounds like you're calling him a wuss," I said. Lethe dabbed at my eyes with her sleeve. "But you also think he's going to keep fighting?"

"You must consider the position he finds himself in," Hades said. "For the last two years, nearly, the public has been stirred into believing you are the greatest evil that walks this planet.

Greater, indeed, than any that has existed since the days of … I don't know … Hitler, perhaps?"

"Yeah, let's just ignore Stalin and Pol Pot." I blinked the tears away, hoping they'd stop soon. Lucky my eyes hadn't started really leaking until after the fight.

"Hitler is an easier focus," Hades said, "and if you'll forgive me for saying so, your country is desperately illiterate, historically speaking. Whatever the case, for two years, concerns within your nation have built you into the greatest boogeyman, or boogeywoman, I suppose—"

"Which is funny cuz I seldom boogie."

Hades smiled, I saw it again through the tears. "They have made you into a monster. Like me. Perhaps the greatest monster of your time. Now that they have done that, created in you the most urgent and terrible threat, how could Gondry, considering himself a being of conscience and morality, simply let you walk away?"

"Uh," I said. "Wait. You think he's going to press this? After your nuclear threat? After we wiped out their criminal task force?"

"I am certain of it," Hades said, turning away, his back a dark, blurry shadow to me. "The level of cognitive dissonance required for Gondry to let you go would require he reconcile and justify to himself that he is a coward, something he does not consider part of his personality. He sees himself as brave." Hades turned. "All men do, until they are proven otherwise. And some of them, even then, must find the ways to justify to themselves how they are, truly, brave, though the facts would suggest otherwise."

"Starting a nuclear war with you over me doesn't seem particularly brave," I said. "More … stupid."

"It won't start nuclear," Lethe said. "Your great-grandfather just made sure of that."

I tipped my head back, and watery tears ran down the sides of my face. "That's why you told him how many nukes you had, and what they were on. ICBMs, MIRVs …"

"Deterrence, yes," Hades said. "If he did not believe I would use them, he would begin in a position of asymmetrical power, as your troops call it. With that threat upon the table, however, he will be forced to use craftier means. Then, potentially, escalate, as his pride calls for satisfaction."

"So you've been planning for this for a while?" I asked. My eyes were finally starting to dry, but I couldn't see him very well. His back was to me again, and he'd taken up Lethe's old place by the window while she was by my side.

"Yes," Hades said. "Without nuclear means at our disposal, there would be no way to protect you against the US response."

I blinked at that. More wetness slid down my cheeks. "You … empowered the people for Revelen for that reason, too? Used the press to move them to my side—"

"That was a good reason, but not the only one," Lethe said. "In a world of people with powers … doesn't everyone deserve a chance to defend themselves?"

"But not everyone gets powers," I said. "Sometimes the serum doesn't work. What happens to those people?"

"They are protected by the force of law and civilization," Hades said. "That is our job, you see."

I closed my eyes. It seemed to help against the burning still tearing up my vision. "Okay. So … my head hurts, and I'm not sure if that's because of the eye injury—"

"It is," Lethe said.

"—Or because I don't know what the hell is coming next," I said. "The fact that you're laying out a reasonable scenario that leads to nuclear war with the US is … uhm …"

"Terrifying?" Hades asked.

"Yeah," I said, opening my eyes. He had turned to face me, but I couldn't see his expression. He sounded somber. "'Terrifying' about covers it. The US could bomb this country into a parking lot. Fifty times over."

"This is true, but I do not believe they will," Hades said. "It was never my intention to let your president turn this into a nuclear war. I merely wished to remove that option from the table, for fear that he would … shall we say … escalate things in a certain direction."

"Have you ever heard anyone call a metahuman a 'weapon of mass destruction'?" Lethe asked. Her hand was firm on my arm.

"Oh, shit," I mumbled.

Of course I'd heard someone call a metahuman that.

They'd called *me* that. In Eden Prairie. In LA.

"You get it, don't you?" Hades asked, and I sensed him pacing away from the window. "The natural progression? If a metahuman is a weapon of mass destruction … well, the United States has only one scripted reaction to that …"

He was right. Chemical weapons counted as a WMD. So did biowarfare agents like Anthrax. The US didn't keep either of those as active options, though.

They kept nuclear weapons, only, as a response to the deployment of a weapon of mass destruction.

"Here we are, with you, we weapons of mass destruction," Hades said. "Without any nuclear weapons at our own disposal … we are powerless to truly fight back."

"That's not necessarily true," I said. "You have metas that actually could do some mass destruction-y things. One Gavrikov in the middle of New York City, for instance, and you'd be looking at some pretty hefty casualties. Hell, put Yvonne the Glass Blower next to the Empire State building and it all falls down."

"We don't use people like that," Lethe said. "Though they probably believe we would."

"Can't imagine why, after the US Attorney's office," I said.

"It will be all right," Hades said. "This method of redress is cut off to them now. If we did not have nuclear weapons, Gondry could easily use his friends in the press to spread the idea that we were weapons of mass destruction, thus justifying his use of cowardly weapons against our entire populace. We have blocked that with our preparation."

"You armed up in order to provide equivalent force against his biggest gun," I said, lowering my head. "Genius. Dangerous, but … genius. But you're assuming he would have leapt to that—"

"I do assume that, yes," Hades said.

"The argument of metas as WMDs has been floating out there for a while," Lethe said. "It's in the zeitgeist, partially constructed. All it would take is Gondry to speak the words, and most people, knowing the threat you've presented as sold by the press over the last few years … they wouldn't push back. Especially not for the population of some little country in Eastern Europe that no one's ever heard of."

I groaned. "I find this all the more disturbing because of how probable it is."

"Alarming, is it not?" Hades asked. "That one man could have such power at his fingertips? This is why I acted to offset that power. Now Gondry will be forced to come at us in more conventional ways to assuage his wounded pride."

"This is not just pride," I said.

"No," Lethe said. "It is more complex than that. But pride is the root emotion. It goes to the heart of Gondry's identity, you see? You are evil to him. If he considers himself a righteous man, how can he possibly let you escape when you're right there, within his reach? It was easy, when he didn't know where you were. He could whip the hounds against you, content in the knowledge he was doing everything he could to bring you to justice. But *now*, now that he knows where you are … now that there's an obstacle in his way, but he sees the path forward …"

"He will stop at nothing to set things right," Hades said. My vision was clearing, and I don't know if I'd ever seen him looking more serious. "Which is why … it is now time to discuss our response."

"Uh … 'gulp,' I think is the word here," I said.

He smiled at hearing his own stolen phrase parroted back to him. "'Gulp,' indeed." He reached into his suit jacket and when he brought his hand back out, two vials were clutched in his weathered fingers.

It didn't take a genius to figure out what I was looking at. He opened them to reveal two serums—green and blue.

"The power booster," I said, licking my lips, which were salty from my tears. "And the Skill-Tree Unlocker."

"It is time for you to take up your birthright," Hades said, taking a step forward and offering me the serums. "To become what you should be. Not the diluted version, the genetic material of Persephone watering down your power, locking it up within your skin … no. It is time for you to ascend to the greatness that has always lain within you. To become more than you were. To fulfill the promise that you have known … that you have whispered to yourself …" His eyes gleamed. "It is time for you to become—"

I knew the word. I'd said it often enough the last few years and heard it spoken, right into my soul by the oldest voice in my head other than my own. It came to my lips now, in time with Hades's voice, and I spoke it into being.

My legacy.

My reason for being.

My … future.

"Death."

37.

Passerini
The Pentagon

"What does this mean?" Passerini asked, looking at the monitors. They'd just gotten the feed from the FBI, the live view from inside the hangar of what had happened when the task force had taken on Sienna Nealon and her defenders, and …

Well, Bruno Passerini was left with questions.

"How can you not know what this means?" President Gondry's voice crackled on the other end of the line. Audio only, fortunately. "It means the damned enemy wiped out our task force. It means we're facing something stronger than we anticipated."

Well, yeah, that much was obvious even to egghead Gondry. Passerini shared a look with Colonel Graves, who was shaking his head, eyes rolled. He stopped when he saw Passerini watching him; insubordination wasn't a good look, and Graves, who must have been in uniform a long time, should have known better. He smiled tightly back at Passerini, who maintained his frown.

"Sir, I meant the business about him being 'Hades,'" Passerini said. "We're talking … old school Hades, right? Greek God of Death?"

"Do you know any other Hades?" Gondry snapped back at him over the open line.

Passerini kept his reaction in check for his men. This was how Gondry was when the cameras were off. The man was incredibly dignified when in the presence of any media, but the moment he wasn't …

"I guess I'm just struggling with the idea that we're facing the Greek God of Death some several thousand years after we stopped believing in him as anything other than a fairy tale and in a country some several thousand miles from his own," Passerini said.

"Fairy tales have their roots in true stories, SecDef," FBI Director Chalke's voice, dripping with smugness, entered the conversation. "We learned that when it came out metahumans were a real thing. That means yes, the gods of old had their basis in actual people. Including Hades, who is apparently still alive."

"And related to our fugitive," Gondry's tone was clipped, fury seeping out. "Great-grandfather? How did this escape our notice?"

"We knew about it," Chalke said, so smooth that Passerini only caught a hint of defensiveness beneath the surface. "We just thought he was dead. We certainly didn't know he was hiding out in Eastern Europe, running a country and taking it nuclear."

"Once again the intelligence community fails to show any," Gondry said, crackling on. He never displayed quite this much raw emotion on television, unless he was trying to make some sort of empathetic connection to a crowd. Passerini had read a bio of LBJ a year or so ago, and he, too, had been a son of a bitch when he wasn't on the record. Unlike Gondry, though, LBJ had some serious clout behind the scenes. And some brains. "President Harmon confided in me his surprise at being blindsided by this metahuman business when it all came out—"

Passerini raised an eyebrow at this. Graves snorted loudly, and Passerini frowned at him. The colonel needed to learn to control himself.

"—and it's all the fault of you idiots at the CIA, in the military, who didn't know this was going on—"

Passerini would have sooner eaten his dress uniform hat,

without so much as a condiment to cover the cloth flavor, than assume Harmon or the intelligence agencies that reported to him didn't know every damned thing there was to know about metas. Sitting here, talking to Gondry, listening to him spit out this ignorance, he was suddenly reminded of the Eisenhower quote regarding Nixon's contributions as his VP—"If you give me a week, I might think of one."

"—and now here we are, staring down the God of Death and his nuclear arsenal," Gondry said, thumping sounds accompanying his voice as if he were hitting a table for emphasis. "It's like none of you have bothered to read a book in your lives, let alone the briefing documents you've been preparing all these years."

Passerini wasn't going to stick his head into this particular fire. Better to wait and see where the president wanted to take this.

"Well, I've read your reports," Gondry said. "All of them. Here's what I want from you, SecDef. I want you to take the entire department to DEFCON 2 and dust off your war plans for an invasion of Revelen and Russia through the Fulda Gap."

A cold chill ran up Passerini's scalp, and the silence over the phone line and in the Situation Room was palpable. Those were severely outdated plans; the Fulda Gap was entirely in Germany, and was unnecessary now if they wanted to invade Russia. Had Gondry just read a book on the Cold War and gotten 'Fulda Gap' stuck in his head? Better to not point that one out. "Sir … you're talking about invading a sovereign country—"

"That's right," Gondry said. "Sienna Nealon and her family have presented themselves as the greatest threat in our modern age. Why, we don't even know what they're doing in that country. Knowing what we know about her and realizing we have no intelligence apparatus on the ground, we have to assume they're running that place with the fervor of the maddest of mad dictators. There's a reason we don't have any intelligence assets on the ground, and I think this is it. They've got that place locked up like Nazi Germany, and I think we just caught our first glimpse of their Hitler."

"Wow," Colonel Graves muttered under his breath, "we're not even on the internet, and there went Godwin's law."

"That is awfully assumptive, sir," Passerini said. "We have satellite intelligence, and there is no hint of … camps or … uh … anything of the sort." That cold feeling on his skin was persisting, and he felt an urgent need to throw some cold water on the president's plan before it got any more insane. "Could we perhaps, instead, assume that maybe—just maybe—that this threat they're presenting is more of a garden variety type, sir?"

"They've gone nuclear, Mr. Secretary." Gondry's voice was cold, chillingly so. "What motive do you think they have for that, exactly, other than to defy us while they execute their own plans? You said it yourself—they've essentially taken over Russia, and I think we can assume it was done by metahuman means, and that means they've turned our foremost adversary's entire war apparatus against us—"

"Oh, God," Passerini whispered to himself. This was what Gondry had gotten out of his briefing? All those times he'd tried to wake the man to the threat at hand, and now he'd suddenly reversed course and taken it all on board then gone twenty miles past reason? Now that Sienna Nealon was suddenly involved? "Sir, I would caution you not to read too much into this. There is most definitely a threat, but so far, it's very much in line with what we've seen from Russia in the past. We've had nukes pointed at each other for sixty years, and they haven't escalated the behavior. They've just installed some of their ICBMs from other locations into Revelen, which is a tiny country. This changes the strategic picture very minimally in terms of threat profile, sir, and—"

"This is ridiculous," Gondry said, and the hum of anger swelled to make his voice even louder. "For a week you've been hammering at me to do something about this Revelen situation. Well, I've taken your advisement, and now I'm ready to act, and here you are, sitting on the sidelines, Mr. Secretary." There was a cool moment of silence before Gondry broke it viciously. "If I'd known my Secretary of Defense was a coward, I'd have fired you sooner."

Passerini wasn't the type to go into a killing rage, but the college professor who'd never served a day in his life, the man who'd demonstrated against every war the country had ever had … calling him a chicken? Well, that was a bit much.

Colonel Graves was looking at him, slightly taken aback. "Wow," he mouthed.

Something about Graves's response cooled him right off. Passerini had been in war, had seen missiles intended for his plane streak by thanks to good fortune and countermeasures, and he would never forget what it was like to see that sort of shit go down—something Gondry would probably never feel. As a result, once the initial heat of the president's volley burned past him, Passerini's head cooled off quickly, just like it had in every fight he'd ever been in. People were going to shoot at you in war, and, apparently, in government. His job was to keep cool and prevail, not go hot and launch a flight of Slammers into the fray. Not now, anyway.

"Mr. President," Passerini said, choosing his words carefully. "I am already executing your orders to bring out war plans designed to end this conflict quickly." They'd been revising them constantly for the last week, in fact, since this situation had started. There were definitely options on the table by now, in spite of Gondry's stubborn refusal to mobilize anything until now, when his dander was suddenly up.

"About time," Gondry said.

"And in fact we've been working on them all along," Passerini said. "Now that you've decided to commit to action, we can move some additional forces into place that you, uh … blocked when last we spoke." Passerini wasn't above taking a little shot to remind the president exactly how much their positions had flipped.

Graves was shaking his head, and Passerini skipped his next statement, the one he'd been preparing to volley back. Cooler heads needed to prevail, and what he'd planned to say was … well, it probably was akin to firing an AMRAAM up the president's ass. Or at least at Gondry's manhood.

"However, sir," Passerini said, and he didn't even have to try particularly hard to keep his cool, now that he'd seen Graves shaking his head, "any response we bring to bear carries the possibility of escalating this situation. In a normal war with a smaller country, like, say, just for comparison's sake, Estonia, they have no ability to raise the stakes beyond a conventional fight. We invade, they attack back on their own homeland. We hold the high ground, and they can't do anything but battle us there. With Revelen, though—"

"Yes, I understand what's at stake here," Gondry snapped back.

"Sir, I'd be derelict in my duty of bringing you war plans if I didn't inform you of this," Passerini said, and that shut him up for a second. "They have twelve ICBMs, sir. Stiletto-19's. Each of those has six multiple independent reentry vehicles."

"I don't give a damn—" Gondry started to say.

"That means every one of those missiles has six smaller missiles that break off once they reach striking distance of our country," Passerini said, not letting the president cut him off. Graves was nodding along. "Every one of those MIRVs has at least a five-megaton warhead. That's a city-killer. That means they can target our seventy biggest cities … and obliterate them. And that's just Revelen's capability, not counting Russia."

"I damned well know what we're dealing with," Gondry said. "I have read everything you've sent me. And we will not take this war nuclear, damn you, do you understand me? I want to invade them, though. I want them pacified. We will not have this threat hanging over our heads, do you hear me? This—this—second Hitler—out on the frontier … well, I won't leave him or his damned lunatic granddaughter to threaten us. You hear me, Mr. Secretary?"

Passerini did hear him. He didn't like anything about the situation, but he heard the president loud and clear. "I'll have you options in a matter of hours, sir," Passerini said, then made the throat-cutting gesture to the operator. The click was definite at the other end, beating him to the punch. He gave a quick glance around the map table, to the host of dour faces waiting there. Graves might have been the only exception, a strange twinkle in the colonel's eye. He was an odd one, even for the army. "You heard the president. He wants a war. Let's figure out what we need to do in order to win it for him."

38.

Sienna

"Wolfe knew, damn him," I said. Lethe looked at me funny. "He knew you were here. Told me so, in his dying words. 'Become Death,' he told me." I shook my head. "I thought he just wanted me to be more like you, but no … he knew I was coming here."

Hades loomed in front of me. "This was always to be your fate." He stood tall, almost incredibly so, while I sat on the bed next to Lethe. She was just off to the side, looking into my eyes, as though she could see the damage the Apollo had inflicted on them. "You were always bound to take up the mantle of Death. You are well suited to it, yes?"

"Is that so?" I asked, looking pointedly at Lethe.

She dodged my question by going back one. "Of course Wolfe knew," Lethe said, letting her hand fall off my shoulder. "You and I met before, remember? He knew me on sight. And I may have mentioned Revelen, so … I'm sure he put it all together. Me being supposedly dead, now living here. Some fearsome man in charge of the country. It's not a very big leap."

"Harmon also knew," Hades said. "I suspect, anyway. He was a mind-reader, after all. It would not have been impossible for him to sift through the minds of some who might have known me in the past, put it together with what he knew of me." Hades smiled. "We did, after all have dealings with him."

"And neither of them told me," I said. "Liars in my own head."

"You can't blame them," Lethe said, standing up. "They wouldn't have wanted you to come here. Wolfe served us for a time, and it didn't end well for him." That was an understatement. He'd ended up bent to the service of Omega, at least somewhat unwittingly.

"And Harmon had his own obligations to us," Hades said. "We provided him material support for his plans. Helped him—"

"With the serum," I said.

Hades shrugged. "We didn't know what he had planned for it until very late. Once we did, obviously I prepared to act. We believed he had more traditional villainy in mind."

"Well, way to screw up on that one," I said. My head definitely hurt, though whether it was from the blinding flash or these new revelations. "It's all starting to make some sense. But only some. You couldn't bring me here until now, because until you had the cover of nukes …"

"You would not have been safe," Hades said.

"And we would have rhetorically raised the stakes against all metahumans in the process of giving you that shelter," Lethe said. "They'd bomb us to nothing and use the justification that we're Weapons of Mass Destruction. And once that line of reasoning was applied once …"

"Would it be a far hike to believe it could be used again against our people?" Hades asked. "Pogroms have been started with less justification."

"Seems like a big leap," I said. "But … no, not utterly unreasonable. I still don't know if I believe you haven't worked against me some, too, though." I eyed the serum, which he still held in his hand. "And I really don't know how to feel about that."

"Feel strongly about it," Hades said, "as in feel how strong it will make you, having the power of my type, to rip out a soul at a distance, boosted to extremes never before seen in human history." He clenched the serums in his hand before me. "Imagine being able to reach across the planet and take the very soul out of President Gondry if need be." His eyes flashed. "And I have a very bad feeling … it may come to just that."

39.

Why was power such a tricky thing for me to take up?

I didn't have an answer for Hades, at least not immediately. He'd accepted that relatively graciously, and so had Lethe, and with a nod and a "Think about it" from him and a "Call me if you need anything" from her, they'd left me alone in my room to recuperate from my recent bout of blindness.

Alone in my castle room, with the sun going down outside my tiny window, darkness falling outside over the city of Bredoccia in the distance, alone, kind of afraid to go out for fear General Krall would spider-monkey jiu jitsu squeeze me to death if I wandered too far afield.

There were still spots in my eyes, and I was still getting used to the stale, somewhat stuffy smell of the castle. I eyed the window, wishing I could open it, but there was no sign of latches or hinges. It was for viewing only, and I wasn't in the mood for a view.

I settled back on the bed, and eventually, sick of my own thoughts, the disorienting whirling of my mind circling the fact that my great-grandfather Hades and my grandmother Lethe were still alive, running a country, and now raising all manner of hell on the geopolitical scene.

And now they wanted me … little old me … to truly embrace the power of death and become a Hades.

I blew air through my lips, and they made a spluttering noise in the darkening room, shadows lengthening across my bed.

Me.

With the power to rip a soul out of a human at ten feet. A hundred feet. Hell, a mile, for all I knew.

That'd trivialize the hell out of any fight I ever got in. I moved my hand, picturing ripping the life out of a person with but a flick of my fingers.

That'd beat the hell out of … well … beating the hell out of them.

It'd be like a Star Wars force choke, but with one little drawback that everyone seemed to lose sight of in their mad rush for power. And oh, boy, did the average person feel a mad rush for power. How many times had I been seated next to someone on a plane, had someone come up to me in a restaurant, or on the street … always with the same look on their face, of disguised awe and faint curiosity … always with the same damned question, every time. I could almost pick them out before they asked at this point.

"Why don't you just absorb every meta with powers?" they asked, this endless chorus of (mostly) well-meaning people. "Why not just take … *all* the powers?"

Like Rose, they mean, but of course they've never heard of Rose.

I always answer them in the same way. First, I plaster on a smile, one I've practiced in the mirror for … probably days of cumulative time. "That's a great question," I say, patronizingly if I'm tired and drained. Patiently, if I'm not. Then I explain.

In order to drain a metahuman … I have to *drain* that metahuman. Kill them.

"But so many of the people you fight deserve it!" they say.

How can I argue that? Because why I else would I be kicking their ass if they didn't deserve it? This is the chief reason why—despite whatever the press is reporting about me today—I'm not out just draining some random old lady off the street:

The people I kill are hardened killers, in most cases. Their souls are calloused by their deeds. I know what that feels like; it took me a while to work up to killing, and I still hesitate before going that last mile and ending someone. At least, I do when I have a moment to hesitate.

But see, after I drain this person, they don't just go away like a person I've killed. The coroner comes and gets the body, sure, but the person, the essence of them …

Well, if I take their power … I'm stuck with their soul essentially forever.

Eight souls. That was how many I'd drained in my time. Seven with powers. One without.

Six of them had been stuck in my head for five years. One for a year or so. One for about sixty seconds before he got sucked out. RIP Frankie, little did I know ye.

Those others, though? Wolfe, Gavrikov, Bjorn, Zack, Eve, Bastian and Harmon?

Shit, man. Wolfe and Gavrikov had killed tens of thousands between them. Gavrikov had killed thousands in one thirty-second period. Bjorn was a serial rapist and murderer. Eve and Bastian had done some pretty questionable things. Harmon had killed has his own wife. Even Zack had done a thing or two that made my skin crawl, including being coerced into dating me by our old boss.

Having someone stuck in your head was like a marriage you couldn't get out of, I wanted to say to those people on the streets. Like being married to someone who'd murdered, who'd raped, who'd slaughtered, who'd maimed, who'd drunk deep of the suffering of others—because that's who we were talking about, people worthy of being killed for their deeds. It was asking me to be totally cool with sticking a superpowered version of Richard Starkweather or Douglas Clark or Whitey Bulger or Jeffrey Dahmer in my head for the possibly thousands of years I potentially had in front of me. Together, forever, till death or a Scottish succubus did us part.

Forever, united with the worst scum I could imagine.

Yeah. It was a real mystery why I didn't absorb every evil bastard I encountered just "for the powers."

Or not, since I'd use their powers on average once a week, maybe, but hear their voice in my frigging head *always,* unless I pulled a Mom and locked them away when not in use. Which tended to make them not so much want to cooperate when I actually did need their powers.

Or I could torture them into buckling and rendering themselves utterly into my service. That's what Rose had done. And, y'know, I was definitely aspiring to be like the flame-tressed hellbeast who'd salted the earth of my already ruined life.

Did I want the power that came with the serum? The Hades abilities? The souls I could drain and put to use?

Sure. I wasn't stupid. I was always fighting, and it'd have been really nice to pull out a Thor-type's electrical bolts when someone came at me with eye lasers, or do a Wolfe and rapid heal when someone carved my guts out with fingernail claws. Or just have Achilles abilities and not even get hurt in the first place.

That would be awesome. I would love that.

The voices in my head it'd take to get there?

Well, power has its price.

"I don't want it," I muttered under my breath, lying on the bed, staring at the blank TV in front of me. I'd been doing that since Hades and Lethe had left, and finally, I'd had enough. Fumbling at the nightstand, I came up with the remote for the TV and clicked it on.

"Oh, man," I groaned as the screen resolved into a cable news show with an anchor solemnly droning to his audience as he stared into the camera as a chyron below him blared BREAKING NEWS.

"Sienna Nealon, the most dangerous woman on the planet, has escaped federal custody to the eastern European country of Revelen …"

"Yeah, I already knew that," I said. "That's not breaking news to me."

"To analyze this situation, we have Russ Bilson, a former aide to the Harmon administration—"

A smug man appeared on a split-screen to the anchor's left. I rolled my eyes and let out another groan. I'd seen him before, many times. Russ Bilson seemed like he was a paid, professional Sienna Nealon critic. Which probably paid better than being the actual Sienna Nealon these days, though I was curious as to who exactly was paying him.

"—and a former associate of Ms. Nealon's—"

I groaned yet again. The people that the news claimed were my associates were seldom actually associated with me. I mean, they'd claimed that Owen Traverton, the guy who posed as my dog, was an "associate" of mine. When I hadn't even known he was human, for crying out loud. If being a dog and spying on me for my enemies counted as being my associate, then, uh … well … he was probably my only associate.

But they'd taken to picking random former employees of my agency and calling them "former associates." A lot of them I couldn't have picked out of a crowd. But they showed up on TV regularly, and boy did they seem to have a lot to say about me for people who I couldn't recall meeting even once.

"—and joining us from his hometown of Nashville, Tennessee, former senator and presidential nominee—"

I sat up in bed.

"—Robb Foreman. Senator, welcome to the program."

Robb Foreman's dark face appeared in a split-screen to the anchor's right, his eyes twinkling with amusement. "Thanks for having me, Chris."

Huh. For once, they'd actually found a genuine "former associate" of mine. Weird. I shrugged. Even a blind squirrel found an acorn every now and then, though, I supposed.

"What we have here," Chris, the anchor/talking head said, whiffling a sheet of paper self-importantly in front of him, "is a very unique situation. We have public enemy number one, in the form of Sienna Nealon, who has escaped from a federal prison designed specifically to incarcerate people with her type of abilities, and she's fled all the way to an Eastern European country none of us had heard of until today—"

"I'd heard of Revelen before today," Robb Foreman said, eyes still twinkling.

"Well, fine," Chris the anchor-head said, recovering quickly, "a place those of us who haven't spent time on the Senate Foreign Relations Committee hadn't heard of before today."

"I was never on the Senate Committee on Foreign Relations," Foreman said, showing his deep amusement as Chris's face fell a little.

"The point is, Senator," Chris said, "it's a unique situation. A murderer has escaped custody, she's run to a country that, according to the State Department website," and here he glanced at the paper he'd been waving, "we have no extradition treaty with. This is unprecedented."

Foreman raised an eyebrow. "No, it's not unprecedented. You haven't ever heard of Joanne Chesimard?"

"I don't know who this Chesimard person is—" Chris started to say.

"Look, Joanne Chesimard didn't kill over two hundred people," Bilson said, talking right past Chris Anchor-head. "It's an issue of scale, Senator. Sienna Nealon is often referred to as the most dangerous person on the planet. We should take that threat seriously, especially when—"

"Sienna Nealon has the *potential* to be dangerous," Foreman talked over him, "but I object to the idea that she's the most dangerous person on the planet. She's only dangerous to the criminal threats. To the rest of us, just going about our lives, she's no more hazardous than a Chihuahua."

"Uh … thanks?" I said. "I guess?"

"Chihuahuas are a very dangerous animal," Chris said. "I've lost the heels of more than a few pairs of socks to my wife's Chihuahua. They're mean, intemperate—"

"I think I see where Chris is going with this," Bilson stepped in again, probably trying to save Chris from making himself look even stupider than he already had. "And he's right—Sienna Nealon has proven herself to be a very dangerous person. And not just to the 'criminal threats' as the Senator asserts. She's hurt and killed innocent people—"

"Prove it," Foreman said.

Bilson looked like a brick wall had just leapt in front of him as he was bicycling toward it full force. "Uh, well …" he countered with a fake, plastered-on grin. "… I'm not in charge of proving it, and the people who are have already held a trial—"

"Whoa, wait a second," Chris said, comically large brow now evidencing a hint of a furrow through layers of Botox. "Sienna Nealon has already been tried? We haven't heard anything about that."

Bilson looked momentarily dumbstruck. "Well … I can't confirm that—"

"I've heard the same," Foreman said, "through some old government sources I'm still in contact with." The twinkle in his eyes was turned down a notch, but I knew the man, and he was evincing more than a hint of triumph. If he hadn't just used his empath powers to steer Bilson into this particular wall, and then given him an extra shove to keep him from backpedaling … well, I'd eat the comforter I was lying on. "Nice to hear it confirmed by others."

"I'm … not confirming," Bilson said, and there was a hint of panic forming on his plain face. "It's not confirmed, it's just—"

"Has Sienna Nealon actually been through a trial?" Chris asked, leaning in. All three of them, while talking to each other, were facing the camera and staring at me, which was a totally normal thing when you're just watching the news and they're chattering about any old subject, but which felt strangely intense when the people on the screen were talking about you. "She was captured less than a week ago."

"Four days ago, in fact," Foreman said, taking the opportunity to drive the knife a little deeper. Now he was wearing his concerned face. "Four days, and she's already been tried and sentenced." His brow was lined, and his mood dark. "There was no plea, according to my sources. Which means that she was tried for any number of capital crimes and sentenced in a matter of days."

Chris was blinking, trying to take in this new information. "Well … she is subject to the metahuman criminal justice system—"

"Which is a shadow criminal justice system," Foreman said, and he was like a dog with a bone, not letting up at all. "Completely unaccountable, utterly lacking transparency. Think about it, Chris. If you were accused of a crime falsely—or even accurately—how would you like it if not a word of it was spoken aloud outside of a secret courtroom, with no chance to prepare a defense, no counsel even offered?"

"We don't know that any of that happened—" Chris said.

"Oh, it happened," Foreman said, and his voice was rising.

"She was railroaded into a sham trial, given no opportunity to defend herself, not allowed to consult with her attorney or even offered a court-appointed one, in a complete violation of the Fifth Amendment—and all in the name of this 'separate but supposedly equal' metahuman criminal justice system."

"Those are loaded terms and that's … that's a bit of a reach—" Bilson started to say.

"No, it's not, and I think of the three of us, I'm the most qualified to say so," Foreman said, not even breaking stride as he verbally rapped Bilson across the nose. Bilson blanched, paling a little under his fake tan.

I balled a fist and pumped it. Foreman had dunked on him in my name, and it was beautiful.

"This metahuman justice system is a complete perversion of everything our Constitution was intended to protect against. You may not like Sienna Nealon, you may even believe her guilty of terrible crimes—which I don't, by the way—" Foreman said.

"This is ridiculous," Bilson said, throwing up his hands very theatrically. "She is a criminal. I understand if maybe she's on your good side because she killed your opponent from the last election—"

"That's a pretty vicious accusation," Foreman said, calm as a still lake at sunrise. "I'd like to see you prove it, though I suspect that much like the rest of your rigmarole about Ms. Nealon, you can't."

Bilson just smirked. "Everyone knows she did it."

"'Everyone knows' that if you swallow gum, it stays in your digestive tract for seven years, too," Foreman shot back. "It's still false, no matter how many people believe it."

"That gum thing is totally true," Chris said.

"But regardless of what you believe about her guilt or innocence," Foreman said, "mere accusation, in our system, is not supposed to result in punishment. That was the lesson of Salem, in case you skipped class the day they read *The Crucible*. Sienna Nealon is entitled to her day in court, an attorney to represent her, a chance to prepare a defense and examine the evidence and witnesses against her. These are the systemic safeguards against us bringing the force of the government against the innocent, against locking up or executing an innocent person based solely on popular sentiment and mass hysteria, and you cannot tell me that she had those opportunities to defend herself in less than three days."

"We don't know whether she did or didn't," Bilson said. "She—I mean—this is all very speculative—"

"I was briefed on the construction of the Cube," Foreman said, and I saw the anvil coming, and knew that Bilson had no chance of dodging. "Do you know the layout of that particular facility?"

"Uh, no—" Bilson said.

"We need to go to commercial break," Chris said. "We—"

"It's very simple, and I'll leave you with this," Foreman said. "Up top are the holding facilities—jail facilities—for accused criminals who have not yet been convicted of a crime and are awaiting trial. Beneath are the long-term prison facilities. Sienna Nealon, four days after arriving at the Cube, according to the official story that's being shouted out on every channel right now, including yours, Chris—four days after arriving at the Cube, Sienna Nealon started a riot in the prison facilities." Foreman leaned in. "Tell me … if she hadn't been convicted … what was she doing in the long-term prison section of the Cube?"

"And we're going to have to leave it there for now," Chris said, smiling weakly. "Thank you, Mr. Bilson, Senator … for an … informative segment. Up next …"

"Thank you, Senator," I muttered as the screen faded to a commercial. It was nice to know that at least one person back home, other than my brother and my friends, still thought I was innocent. And worth … well, at least the basic human considerations.

The phone on the desk chirped. "Sienna," came Hades's clipped voice. "Report the Situation Room immediately." His voice was tight. "We have another situation." He paused. "That … came out lamer than I intended. But we do have a problem."

"What now?" I asked, rolling off the bed and counting on

the speakerphone to catch my words as I got up.

"Our border radar stations have detected a drone inbound from the west," Hades said. "It would appear that your enemies in America have failed to heed our first warning."

40.

When I walked into the Situation Room, General Krall was already speaking to Hades and Lethe, everyone grouped around the map table as she talked low in the guttural local language.

As soon as he saw me approach, Hades snapped his fingers. "In English, please, General Krall. For the benefit of the crown princess."

"Not getting used to that title anytime soon," I said as I stepped next to Lethe at the table. Her shoulders moved slightly as she let out a small snort.

"You have earned it," Hades said, giving me a nod, then turning back to the table. "General Krall ... please. Go on."

Krall's eyes found me with a predatory look that I didn't much care for. "The Americans have some small forces in Poland, not significant enough in combat strength by themselves to do anything. Heavier reinforcements await in Germany. Almost 35,000 US troops are stationed there. Air wings, full armored cavalry battalions ... everything a conventional US invading force might need is there. But they will not be able to stage a full invasion of this sort for several weeks."

"Why not?" Hades asked.

"Logistics," Lethe murmured.

"Correct. For this reason, a full-scale invasion is impossible in the short term," Krall said. "In general, the Americans prefer a more limited war these days, leaning heavily on special forces to attack key points, and keep from engaging well-matched forces on the field." She snapped her back straight and clicked her heels together. "And our tanks are a closer match to theirs than any they faced in the War on Terror. Furthermore, should they wish to prosecute an air war, they will find our new defenses more than equal to the task."

"Excellent," Hades said, putting his hands behind him. "Speaking of." And he nodded to the table.

Krall must have taken that as a sign and interpreted it accordingly. "Our radar stations have picked up an MQ-9A Reaper Drone. We believe it launched from Poland," and she traced her finger along a route marked by a line that rolled across Belarusian territory toward us. "Now … we may deal with it as you so choose."

"Decisions, decisions," Hades said. "Shall we make it a show of conventional force? Or truly display the power we have at our fingertips?"

"We should show them everything we have," Lethe said, a bit archly. "Leave them in no doubt how much hell we can bring to bear if we so desire."

"Restraint seems the more prudent course," Krall said, still at attention. "Conventional means would show them, clearly, that they cannot operate their air power over our territory, and it will cost them only the lesson of a drone. Then, should they come at us with more force, we will have a surprise waiting."

"Better to cut the problem off before it starts," Lethe said.

"Better to have something in reserve that they cannot counter," Krall said.

Hades put a hand on his chin, and looked at me. "Well?"

I blinked at him. "Well … what?"

"Surely you have an opinion, Your Highness?" Hades asked, a smile curling his lips.

"Uh, well … I don't know Gondry that well," I said, "but Harmon suggested he was what you'd call smart-dumb. Academically brilliant in his area of expertise. Crazy articulate, able to work a crowd, connect with people. But probably well out of his depth in this military stuff since he pretty much hates the military." I shrugged. "I'm not sure how he's going to react here. You bat his drone out of the sky with a missile? I guess that's business as usual. Or a little unusual, but still within normal parameters. You do something else? Something he doesn't expect? Something that escalates things …?" I blew air out slowly. "If he's in over his head already … I don't imagine he's going to react favorably to that."

"Your reasoning is sound," Hades said. "And Gondry is perhaps unpredictable. A more measured approach to his attempts to escalate seem prudent." He nodded at Krall. "Use a missile to take down his drone. We will keep Aleksy's powers in reserve should Gondry decide to … up the stakes."

I cocked an eyebrow at that. Suddenly it was a lot clearer to me what Hades had in mind—deploying Aleksy's metal-controlling powers to …

"Holy hell," I said.

Lethe nodded, once, stiffly. "Holy hell, indeed, if it comes to that."

"Can he …?" I asked.

"Should it be necessary," Hades said, with a glint of triumph in his eye, "Aleksy could clear the skies all the way to our borders, at least. The United States Navy and Air Force will find no comfort here. Anything the size of a drone or larger will be easily swept from the air."

I didn't quite gulp, but I felt like it. The US relied on air power in its missions, probably more heavily than anyone else. Air support for ground forces, missiles to soften targets and take out troublemakers from hundreds or even thousands of miles away.

With that option off the table … the US response was going to be considerably narrowed.

"Wait a second," I said, a troubling thought occurring. "If Aleksy can sweep the skies of all planes and drones and … ICBMs …" I threw that last one in there because intercontinental ballistic missiles were waaaay bigger than drones.

Lethe's face was like stone, but her eyes …

Man.

Her eyes gave away the game, and she turned away from me.

"Yes?" Hades asked. He didn't realize what I'd just figured out.

"What the hell do you need nukes for if you can sweep theirs out of the sky?" I asked.

"A precaution, only," Hades said, a little too quickly. "A feint, if you will. One that Gondry and the Americans can see. Unlike Aleksy."

"Dude, Grandpa," I said, "you knock a couple planes out of the sky with Aleksy's skills, it's going to become rapidly obvious what you have on offer. You pull their nukes down, it's even more obvious. Why—"

"Not now," Hades said, waving a hand in front of me.

"What the—do you think that's going to mute me or something?" I asked. "Because, ask anybody who knows, the mute button did not come factory installed on me."

"I believe I could find it if you want me to, Your Majesty," General Krall said, slipping back over to the table and watching me closely.

"That will not be necessary," Hades said, looking rather pointedly at Krall. "The drone—"

"The missile is already on its way," Krall said, then went right back to looking at me like a snake at a mouse.

I looked down at the table. Sure enough, there was a radar contact winging its way across the map toward the place where the drone was lazily moving over the Revelen landscape. I tried to imagine its operator, wherever they were—some air force base stateside—thinking their drone was pretty much invisible.

The missile met the drone a moment later on the screen, and with a circular rippling on the digital display, both vanished.

"Explosion," Krall said, glancing at the table. "Drone destroyed."

"Was it over an inhabited area?" Lethe asked.

"No," Krall said with a shake of her head. "We took it over the mountains. I have already sent a recovery team to retrieve it for study."

"Excellent," Hades said. "Now … what is their next move?"

"Best guess? More drones or a plane," Krall said.

"Depending on how cautious they wish to be in proceeding."

"We will shoot these down conventionally as well," Hades said. "Hold Aleksy in reserve as long as possible." He held a finger up. "We must make them realize that they are in for no easy fight, and after a time, Gondry will retreat to save face rather than lose thousands in a war."

"I hope you are right, my liege," Krall said, and snapped her heels together again as she bowed.

"Apprise me of any further developments," Hades said, moving a hand to his chest and rubbing at his scar. "I will be in my quarters." He looked at me, then Lethe. "Would you ladies care to join me? I should like to clear the air about a thing or two."

"Sure," I said, as Hades turned to leave, Lethe only a few steps behind. With one look back at General Krall, I followed, exiting through the thick steel double doors to the Situation Room, wondering what my great-grandfather would have to tell me now.

41.

Reed

"We'll be reaching Revelen airspace in a few hours," Greg Vansen's voice crackled over the speakers wired through the shrunken house that rested beneath the seat of his modified SR-71. It was a pretty neat way to travel supersonic, nearly invisible to radar under normal means and even more invisible when Greg took the plane to smaller sizes.

The air smelled funny, though, probably because the shrunken house required its own atmospheric system to maintain pressure in the face of an unpressurized cabin. There were no windows, and the door was sealed with a heavy steel and rubberized pressure skirt. It didn't exactly comply with safety FAA regulations, a fact I was sure was not lost on a smart guy like Greg.

"Does traveling like this get to you, too?" Scott Byerly asked, quiet voice punctuating the silence of the upstairs lounge. The miniature house was pretty large, lots of living room style spaces on the "ground" floor, a dozen or so bedrooms upstairs. "The lack of windows, I mean?" Scott asked, nodding at the blank wall.

"It's safer," I said, jarred out of my own thoughts enough to realize that Scott must have joined me in here a while ago. I'd probably noticed him at the time, but I'd gotten caught up in … well, worrying about Sienna … and hadn't so much as said a word to him. "Windows are the weakest point on a plane. Much less chance of emergency depressurization in a uniform, sealed hull design. One of the major manufacturers was looking at that a few years ago, switching to digital windows, screens on the walls instead of actual ones."

"But …?" Scott asked. "Why didn't they do it?"

"'Yet,'" I said. "Why didn't they do it *yet*. Because structural integrity isn't the only safety concern. They were afraid people would go nuts without windows. That's the short answer. I'm sure they're still trying to figure out a way to make it happen, though."

Scott looked around at the blank walls. Greg hadn't even bothered to hang a poster, which was … par for Greg, actually. "Is it driving you nuts, too?" he asked.

"Not seeing the sky? Yeah," I said. "Remember what my power is?"

Scott smiled. "I suppose it must be annoying to let someone else carry you through the air. I know it would be for me if I was traveling by submarine."

"Yeah, it's … vexing," I said. The thought of Isabella leaning over to kiss me before I'd parted ways with her sprang to mind, unbidden. "Hardly the worst thing we're dealing with right now, though."

Scott looked toward the archway that separated our little beige-walled lounge from a hallway lined with doors to bedrooms, most of which were unoccupied. Not seeing anyone lingering there, he turned back to me. "I'd never have said it in front of the others, but … Gravity kinda had a point, you know."

"No, she didn't," I said. And when he started to open his mouth to object, I said, "No. She didn't have a point … at least not for everybody. She had a point for her, which was that being involved in Sienna's problems all the time was messing with her life. That isn't true for everyone."

Scott raised an eyebrow. "You don't think our lives got a little messed up when Rose came after us and we had to go into hiding?"

How could I argue with that? "I'm not saying our lives didn't take a hit from the Rose thing. I'm saying that saving Sienna hasn't been an 'all the time' proposition for us, Scott. Remember back in January when she came and fought the guy in Minneapolis who kicked all of our asses? At a pretty decent amount of personal risk to her, I might add. Or how she literally ended up in prison to help Angel and Miranda not a week ago?" I had clenched a fist without even realizing it. "You make sacrifices for the people you care about."

"Okay," Scott said. "But what about people like Chase and Veronika? You can't tell me you're going to keep dragging them into these kinds of things." He leaned across the table toward me. "They're not like us. They've got a casual relationship to Sienna. We've been there since the beginning. They haven't."

"Where's this coming from, man?" I asked. "Are you getting sick of sallying forth to save the day?"

"Please, don't ever accuse me of sallying again," Scott said with a smile, "but … no. I'm trying to think of our co-workers here. You've got everyone on this, ignoring the fact that there's a metahuman prison riot that took place not twenty minutes from our office that some of us could be working—"

"This is the single biggest injustice—"

"Facing someone we care about right now," Scott said. "Hey, man … you and I both got caught up in Harmon's net. We know what happened to Sienna. How she got screwed in all this. And it sucks. No doubt. But you can't keep dragging your entire agency into trying to make up for your guilt at getting brainwashed into the same op that screwed up her life."

"Watch me," I whispered.

Scott settled back. "Well. Maybe that makes two of us, then."

I raised an eyebrow at him. "But you just argued—"

"That you shouldn't be using everyone for it," Scott said, settling back in his seat. "I'm in this for the long haul. Sienna and I? We settled our, uh … issues … a while ago. All that's left now is the loyalty between two people who have been through the foothills of hell together more times than I can count."

"When have you been through the foothills of hell with her?"

I almost smiled.

"This one time we fell out of a plane in Iowa," Scott said with a smile. "I saved her, and she had to kinda help me over to the road. That was like the foothills of hell."

"Iowa doesn't have hills."

"What are you boys going on about in here?" Kat appeared at the stairs, sliding in under the archway. Her ever-present phone was … not present, which meant, presumably, we had no Wi-Fi. "I could hear the arguing down the stairs."

"Then you oughta know what we were going on about," I said.

"Something about hell and Iowa, or maybe that was the same thing," Kat said, sliding in next to Scott, her green eyes bright.

"We were talking about old loyalties," Scott said, staring across the table at me. "How ours to Sienna are thicker than some of the new folks. How maybe we should stop dragging everybody else into these things and just settle 'em ourselves."

"Still don't agree," I said.

Scott's eyes wavered. "Lose one of these people in a fight to save her and you'll change your tune."

"If you decide to cull things down," Kat said, her tone … so different from usual Kat, "you let me know."

"So you can bail with the rest?" I asked.

Her perfectly sculpted eyebrows arched in a harsh right angle above her nose. "No, dumbass. Because I'd still be in. We've been with her since the start. Remember, outside Eagle River?"

"That Omega facility?" I felt the trace of a smile. "Where we rescued Andromeda."

"And I got bushwhacked by Sierra," Kat said, putting her head back against the diner-style headrest. "Good times. Not." She put her hands on the table, and I noticed her nails were not as perfectly manicured as they usually were. "Seriously, though … I'd still be in."

"So would I," Scott said.

"Well, I'm in for infinity more times," I said. "Hell, infinity plus one. She's the only family I have left. And …" I lowered my gaze to the table. "… She's alone in all this."

"No, she's not," Kat said, and she sounded so certain. When

we both looked at her, she shrugged. "She's got Harry."

"Graves?" Scott asked, frowning. "You think?"

"I don't think their relationship survived the prison thing," I said.

"Oh, no." Kat shook her head. "Trust me. I saw it in his eyes. He's with her all the way."

I traded a look with Scott, both of us looking at the other out of the corner of our eyes. "I guess that makes four of us, then," I said, trying to bury my skepticism about that idea.

"I think Augustus and Jamal would follow her into hell, too," Scott said. "Each for different reasons."

"That's good." I settled my gaze on Scott. "Where's this sudden concern springing up from, huh?"

"Reed …" Kat said.

"No, come on, Scott," I said, leaning in, "I know this isn't just out of the blue, and it's not because Gravity decided to bail. What are you thinking, man?"

Scott pursed his lips thinly, then did a lean-in of his own. "I talked to Miranda about the company accounts."

"Geez," I said, letting out a hard breath. "That's not your worry—"

"It's a little my worry, since I work here," Scott said, not taking his eyes off me. "I figured after everything we went through in Scotland, and how much you paid in overtime and bonuses for that—"

"Oh my goodness," Kat said, and I could that she was getting it now, too, the point he'd driven us to. "We're going to make a mint here, all of us who are on this little jaunt. I never even thought about—"

"How Reed's bankrupting the agency to keep pulling Sienna's ass out of the fire?" Scott asked, and now he settled back in his seat again. "I didn't either, at first." He tapped the side of his head. "The problem with growing up in a wealthy family is you don't necessarily think about money first thing. But I got to it eventually, just like checking on dad's business to make sure the golden goose is still laying eggs."

"Your concern is touching—" I said.

"Cut the shit, Reed," Scott said. "I don't care for my own

sake, okay? Obviously. Kat and I will be fine."

"I dunno about that," Kat said. "I have expensive tastes, and reality TV doesn't pay as much as you might think. It's the licensing deals where the real money is—"

"Okay, well, I'll be fine," Scott said, "but what I'm worried about is what happens to the agency if you end up busting us flat. Come on, man. We do good work."

"And we'll continue to," I said. "Just … maybe not with as big a roster."

"Shit," Kat said under her breath. "Reed …"

"Look, I don't know what to tell you," I said. "Sienna needs help, I go to help her. That means that the half or more of our number who expect to get paid—who show up for that specific reason? I have to pay them. More, in this case, because this isn't the up job they signed up for."

"How bad is it?" Kat asked.

We both looked at Scott. "Miranda didn't give me a number or anything," he said, folding his arms in front of him, "but you could tell by the look on her face it isn't good. Between Scotland and this …" He shrugged. "You're paying through the nose, and we aren't working during the times when you've got us all in the field for Sienna saving. It's a huge net negative time. We may get paid decently by local and state law enforcement agencies, but it ain't exactly a huge bounty, y'know? Which makes it tough to refill the coffers."

"Yeah," I said. "And with Sienna's accounts being tied up and hamstrung since Rose yanked them during the Scotland business …" I forced a smile. "Look … we don't need to talk about this right now. We have a job in front of us. And whether you wanted it to happen this way or not, we've got a nice little army behind us with all these people I've paid. So we're not in it with just the five of us who most care, all right? That's … it's worth it, if it saves Sienna."

Scott did not look so sure. "I'm all about saving Sienna. But, Reed, this agency does things that no one else does. Not even the FBI sends their task force out to deal with state problems the way we do. Especially to the states that don't always have it in their budget to pay a ton. We go out there, we get it done, because *somebody has to.* And if we end up running out of money …"

He didn't need to say it. Kat did, anyway. "It'll just be the five or so of us anyway," her green eyes flashed sadly.

"It's not going to come to that," I said, as the plane hit a little bump of turbulence. I tried not to take it as an omen. "We'll make it through." I forced a smile, but they'd known me too long to believe I was doing anything other than telling them what they—and I—wanted to hear. "We'll find a way to make it work. Somehow."

42.

Sienna

"Have I told you lately I really love what you've done to the place?" I asked as we filtered into Hades's quarters, sun shining in through the giant pane of glass. "I mean, really, most soul suckers would content themselves to embrace the darkness, but look at you—opening your world like this. It shows real growth of character. Or something."

"You are ceaselessly amusing, my child," Hades said, shutting the door behind us as Lethe walked over to the window and stood there, back to us, silent sentinel once more. "It seems it is a joke a minute with you. Have you considered writing a book of all-purpose retorts? You know, if this metahuman law enforcement thing or crown princess-ing doesn't work out for you? The advertising synergy would be, as you kids say these days, 'epic.'"

"Maybe we could all do a team-up on it," Lethe muttered. "It seems quips are our stock-in-trade around here. We could crank it up, make them Revelen's chief export."

"It'd beat the hell out of sending superpowered mercenaries the world over," I said. "Which … it surprises me that's not our chief export, given how many of the garden-variety I've run into that come from here."

"They don't come from here," Hades said, rubbing his overlarge forehead with his thin fingers as if to dissolve a growing headache. His eyes were squinted shut, and I wondered if he was actually suffering from photosensitivity from the window. "They pass through on their way to whatever destination job they're on." He looked up and his eyes met mine, the bright flashing. "Yes. We traffic in mercenaries. It's a poor country, we need to raise money somehow."

"Have you considered implementing a lottery?" I asked. "It's what all good first world nations do. It's a great way to pay for schools and gambling addiction rehab programs."

Hades snorted. "As you say … 'you are not wrong.'" He looked away for a moment, as though marshaling his thoughts for the inevitable confrontation. "So, Sienna … what is your favorite season?"

"I … huh?" I'd been ready to respond to pretty much any reprimand he was going to unleash—for fighting with him in the war room, for being a general pain in the ass. Favorite season, though?

That I didn't have an immediate answer for.

"I prefer autumn," Hades said, taking slow steps to stand next to Lethe by the window. "Hardly a surprise, I imagine. Death, enjoying the season where we claim our victory for the year. The leaves all dying and falling off … the grim march of winter setting in as life flees to more … hospitable climes or hunkers down to endure the march of cold." He looked up. "Cliché, I'm sure. But I'm also a sucker for a good apple cider. And Halloween. I'm just a little bitch for children dressing in costumes and getting candy."

"Ahhhhh … okay," I said, not sure what to say to … any of that, actually.

"So, what is your favorite season?" Hades asked again, taking his fingers away from kneading his brow.

"Well, there's only two in Minnesota," I said. "Winter and road construction. So I guess I pick … road construction?"

"Ah, a local joke," he said. "I am sure it is very amusing."

"Having lived in Michigan, where the climate is very similar," Lethe said, "I can vouch for this. It's funny." Yet she didn't laugh.

"Yeah, you look like it's taking everything in you to keep down the giggles," I said, causing her to frown, just slightly. "What's with the season question? Cuz I'd really prefer that if you want to chew my ass, you just get to it and skip the fluff."

"Just trying to get to know you a little better," Hades said. His shoulders drooped, like he was so tired he might keel over. "I have no interest in 'chewing your ass.' I would rather … 'chew the fat.'"

"Well, my ass is still a little fat," I said. "It's the cupcakes. I'm doing better, but y'know … like Kevin Hart in *Jumanji 2*, cake is my weakness, though the exploding effect is much less pronounced and more limited to little bits of cellulite—"

"Okay, perhaps I will just move to chewing your ass," Hades said. "We need to be united in our rule. United behind one person, when we are exercising command over this country—"

"Yeah, here we go," I said. "Don't sugarcoat it."

"I wouldn't worry about that," Lethe said.

"You are both so very frustrating," Hades said, hands back to his forehead. "I know you have your own ideas what should be done, and I am perfectly happy to hear them. Someday, this will all be yours, and under your dominion, but for now—can we try and keep the discord private? Rather than in places where everyone can see?"

"You're planning ahead for lots of future fights?" I asked.

Hades smiled thinly, looking right at me. "Well, I know your grandmother well enough at this point to assume everyone in your line is a similar sort of pain in the ass." He caught a glare from Lethe and shrugged. "Would you care to argue that point?"

"No," she said, but still glared.

"There is plenty of room for strategic disagreement," Hades said. "I am hardly infallible." His fingers ran lightly across the front of his suit, and again I could vividly see the scars beneath in my head, as though he were touching the signs of his own past failures. "But command of a country requires harmony, not disharmony. We must be united, a front when among our people, especially the military leaders. It can be a facade. You can despise my decisions in private if you wish—I will listen all day to you telling me what a fool I am. In private. Though I would hope you would restrict your attacks to my ideas rather than my person."

"I don't really want to attack your person," I said. "But … this 'united front' business? I don't think we are united."

"I wouldn't expect us to be," he said. "I am not Harmon. I do not control minds. I am merely suggesting we keep the enmity to a minimum and the argument well below the levels we just experienced."

"You don't like conflict?" I asked.

Hades's eyes flashed. "It depends on the circumstances. It has its place."

"I figured you had some use for it," I said, "or I wouldn't be here."

"What do you mean?" Lethe asked. Hades did not ask, nor do anything but stand there, his eyes glimmering slightly. Because he knew what I was talking about right off.

"Can we … cut some of the crap?" I asked, staring him down. "You helped power Rose."

"I told you—" he said.

"Yeah, I heard you the first time," I said. "I still don't believe you, though."

"What possible reason would I have for supplying her with … what you suggest?" he asked. His hands remained at his sides.

"I'm not entirely sure," I said, smacking my lips together. "But I think it has to do with what you just said … conflict."

His eyes glimmered again. "Interesting. Go on."

"I fought her," I said. "She pushed me to … well, to within inches of death. Real death. Not you, not me. It took everything I had to get out of that fight alive. And she, obviously, didn't make it out. Conflict. I fight her, she dies."

A little tug at the corner of his mouth. "And you are all the stronger for it."

"Yeah, except I lost my superpowers of flight and fire and all else."

"A smokescreen," he said, waving them off. "Powers are not

necessarily the same as being powerful. Look at the current president, Gondry. He has more destructive firepower at his fingertips than any meta besides …" Now he smiled. "Well … besides me."

"So you powered Rose," I said, "another of your so-called progeny, in order to fuel … conflict."

"In order to fuel our plans," Hades said, and I could see by the dark certainty he held in his eyes that, yes, he was admitting it. Finally. "This is a game, you see. We require pawns. Like Harmon. Though we were hardly alone in our interest in Rose."

I looked at Lethe. She didn't look back, but her lips were sealed in a surly, thin line. "So …" I said, "… now that I won … you're all … happy to see me? Welcome me into the fold?" I shook my head. "Man. I knew there was more to this sudden offer of asylum than just nukes and good timing."

"You have failed to ask yourself the right questions," Hades said. "You have embraced the role of Death when it suits you, contemplated the nobler associations of it." He stepped forward. "But you do not consider the less kindly role it fills—culling weakness and ensuring the survival of the fittest. You were stronger than Rose. That is why you yet live and she does not."

"So you *have* been throwing misery my way," I said.

"I have thrown trials your way," he said, eyes almost glowing now. Not with malice, but interest. "And you have risen to the occasion with every one. You have succeeded where no other has." He raised a hand to me. "Sienna … you have made your own name in this world. Created your own legacy, not ridden on my coattails or hidden in the shadows, afraid of what you can do—"

"Abandoned," I said quietly. "Alone. No help from you." I looked at Lethe. She did not look back at me. "From either of you."

"You did it all on your own," Hades said, taking another step toward me. "Your strength is known. It is legend, independent of mine or hers—" He waved a hand at Lethe. "That makes you … worthy. Worthy to take up the mantle." He reached into his jacket, pulling out the vials. "No one has been ready for this singular honor. No one has been worthy of the power that could await you if you but—"

The door creaked and opened behind me. I turned to look, stepping sideways out of the direct reach of Hades. He froze in place, brow thunderously arched at the interruption as General Krall stepped in, followed by ArcheGrey and Yvonne, both of whom spread out in a little triangle with her at the spear point as soon as they were in.

"What is this?" Hades asked, and his voice crackled with enough anger that I realized he'd been seriously holding back in our conversations. I would not have wanted to be on the receiving end of that.

Krall seemed unfazed, though, smiling. "My liege, I have brought news."

"You could at least knock next time, general," Hades said, hands still clenched at his sides. "It would be the courteous thing to do."

"I apologize," Krall said, slightly inclining her head, but never taking her eyes off me. "I thought you would want to know immediately."

"Yes?" Hades asked, a little hiss creeping into his question.

Krall looked at Arche, who took a step forward, lifting a tablet computer. "We've detected evidence of a cyber intrusion into our systems," Arche said. Nothing but what looked like computer code was on the screen and scrolling at a rapid rate. "It is constant, probing. I believe it has made it through my safeguards at least three times." She looked pointedly at me. So did Krall, and Yvonne.

"Oh, shit," I muttered under my breath.

Hades looked at me, and so did Lethe, coming a step away from the window to do so. "What is this about?" Hades asked. Now everyone was looking at me. Oh, goodie.

"This penetration seems to be very localized," Arche said, the computer code still scrolling across the tablet on its black background. "It has but a single target, and I have detected communication attempts, all aimed at a single person."

"Hold on," I said, "I can explain."

"So can I," Krall said, taking a step toward me, Yvonne and ArcheGrey moving to flank me. I was a little too close to the wall for comfort, stuck with them between me and any convenient exit. "It would seem we have a traitor in our midst."

And she smiled.

43.

"Well, this trip sure went to shit in a hurry," I said, taking another step back against the wall. It thumped against my butt, confirming that I was hemmed in on my right by the wall that led to the hallway (probably stone under the plaster and paint), a bed to my left, then Hades, then a window with a hundreds-foot drop below …

And in front of me, cutting off my other avenues of retreat, was General Krall, flanked by ArcheGrey and Yvonne.

Of the three, only Yvonne was looking at me with anything approaching trepidation, but then, she'd seen me in action back in the Cube and probably had some inkling of how things would go if I was cornered. Which I was.

"Let's … just everybody calm down a little," Lethe said, taking a step toward General Krall and her minions. "There's no need for this to get ridiculous."

"Oh, I dunno," I said, "like I said before, I kinda figured we were going to get to this a lot sooner."

"Stop," Hades said, holding up his hands.

"Make me," I said, focusing on Krall. I'd have to contend with Arche, too, and her lightning powers, but if I dodged just right, maybe Krall would sponge that up for me, and I could kick that tiny boy-bander into Arche. That'd just leave Yvonne …

Out of these three, at least. I'd still have Hades and my grandmother to contend with, whatever the hell that entailed. They'd certainly proven they weren't averse to causing me all manner of damage, given that they'd set Rose and Harmon against me, not to mention any number of lesser troubles.

"I will make you," Krall said, grinning. She shucked out of uniform jacket in an instant, and I got a little unpleasant rumble in my stomach as she stepped toward me, cutting the distance between us to mere feet.

"General …" Hades said, and his tone was not one for trifling.

"I serve you, my liege," Krall said, not taking her eyes off me, "but this one needs a lesson in humility."

"Good luck with that," I said. "I've gotten my ass kicked by waaaaaay more impressive specimens than you, General Crawls-like-a-snake."

"Snakes slither," Yvonne said, after her eyes flicked skyward for a moment in thought.

"There you go, wrecking my insults, Owens," I said, looking to my right, where sat a desk and a chair, and that was it. Well, it wasn't nothing. I set my feet in a shoulder-width stance, my right foot about six inches from the chair's nearest leg. I had a plan for it, and if Krall took one more step—

She did.

I hooked my foot around the chair leg and heaved it forward as Krall committed herself to coming at me.

Quite a few things happened at once.

Hades shouted, "No!"

Arche summoned up some Thor power, electricity arcing out of a nearby socket and into her hands. The fact that she didn't think she had enough on her without drawing more set off a couple alarm bells in my brain. The brightness of the light made me internally upgrade my threat assessment for her to a lot higher level.

Lethe moved, too, grabbing Yvonne by the shoulder. Yvonne let her and didn't do anything but stand there, looking at me, warily, as everything went right to hell.

I slammed the chair into Krall's path and she bulldozed into it, shattering it into firewood and sending the pieces in all directions. It didn't stop her, but it surely sent her off balance a step, and I clipped her in the side of the head with a short punch and then kicked her away as a follow-up.

Krall didn't take much damage, but my aim was good and she tried to seize my foot since I did a little more of a shove than an effective, damaging kick. I managed to yank my foot away just as she tried to clamp down on it, and she tumbled back into—

Arche.

It was like lightning in a bottle, or maybe the Emperor zapping Luke Skywalker. I was pretty sure I saw Krall's skeleton between the flashes, and that was just fine by me. Arche didn't exactly catch her effectively, and they both tumbled over.

They both came up a second later, too, and neither looked particularly happy with me, least of all Krall, who was literally steaming, smoke wafting off and seeping out of her collar.

"General, I demand you cease this at once!" Hades said, and his face was red like he'd been the one to take the stray voltage.

"She is betraying you," Krall said, a couple of black smudges on her cheek where the electricity had burned through. Other than that, she didn't look much affected, and I damned sure didn't want to close on her. "She is spying on us."

"That's just Cassidy trying to talk to me," I said, leaping onto the bed as Krall made a lunge for me. She was a hair slower than she'd been before, allowing me to dodge over it and down the other side. Hades reached out for me, but I knocked his hand away and he flashed an annoyed look at being shoved off, but did not try again. "She's a little miffed because you guys used her boyfriend to destroy the USS *Enterprise*." A little bolt out of the blue struck me as well, but of the thought variety, not electricity. "You did that to hamstring the US defenses in a war scenario."

"Their carriers are their most effective way to project power," Hades said. I'd left him behind, opening the gap between us to about ten feet, and now my back was to the window and everyone was still looking at me, and blocking the door.

Not exactly an improvement in my circumstances.

"You've been planning this showdown for a while," I said.

"How long? Years?"

Hades shrugged. "Power is a funny thing. It accumulates, usually more slowly than you would care for. Sudden moves make people nervous. Best not to be too obvious until you are ready." He smiled thinly. "But give them enough other things to worry about, and they can't spare the time or interest to pay attention to the little blade until it is at their neck."

"You got nukes, Grandpappy," I said. "That's not a little knife."

"I have a country filled with metahumans as well," Hades said. "It was just a metaphor. We have distracted them enough, though—now the balance of power in this world will tip in our direction." He traded a look with Krall, who had spider-monkeyed her way over the bed and was back to leering at me, too close for comfort. "You can be part of that, child." He lifted his hand, the vials still clutched in it. "You should be. You have earned your place here."

I eyed the serums. "Those … are not as easy a choice as you might think." I remembered Wolfe, how many times he'd flashed disgusting, horrific things unasked into my mind. He was guilty, evil, and a burden I had to carry, and did, in order to try and do some good in the world.

But whoever I hoovered up next in my quest for power? They might not be as evil, but I'd be just as stuck with them.

"It is the easiest choice," Hades said. "A choice I have made." His glare hardened. "One you have made in the past as well, but now, I see, like the decision to kill that Erich Winter forced you into … you have decided to soften yourself. Perhaps you need … a reminder."

My skin tingled, cold chills running down my whole body.

"Oh, shit," Lethe muttered. She still had one hand on Yvonne's arm, seemingly holding her back, though Yvonne didn't appear eager to step up to confront me the way Krall had. Even ArcheGrey was hanging back, leaving the bed between us.

My fist shook, my hand trembling. "What did you say?" I asked. My voice broke just slightly.

Hades smiled, and there was a hint of triumph. "Yes. You see it now, don't you? Power has ever been at your fingertips. But you must be persuaded to reach out and take it. Winter saw that. He knew what was necessary, and he—"

"Oh, my God," Lethe said. "Tell me you didn't just say—"

"You don't understand anything, daughter," Hades said, holding up a hand like that'd shut her up. "She is blind, she is a child, she—"

"You can't think this is the way—" Lethe said.

"I will subdue her for you, my liege," Krall said, slithering forward another step. "I will deliver her to—"

"Only strength matters, in the end," Hades said, his face a pale, ghostly facade over a grinning skull. "You will see that, Sienna, before we are done. And you will thank me for—"

I lashed out behind me, and everyone froze as I struck the plate-glass window that stretched the length of Hades's quarters. It shattered, shards the size of a hubcap falling as I yanked my hand free so as to avoid being sliced all to hell.

Hades's eyes widened. "What are you doing? Come away from the window."

"Can you pick out the thing you just said to me … that you never fucking should have let slip out?" I asked. My voice was scratchy, hoarse, deeper and huskier than I'd ever heard it.

"What?" Hades took a step forward. "Don't do anything foolish. This is—"

"The end," I whispered, swaying, taking a step of my own so that I teetered on the edge of the broken window, my right foot half off. The wind howled around the cliff. "Erich Winter used me. Killed people I cared about so he could use me …" I glared at my great-grandfather. "And you empowered my enemies to destroy me. Set them at me. Gave them aid and comfort. And now … now you want me to become … what?" I let out a thin, raking laugh. "Be your defender? Help stand between you and the whirlwind you're so damned intent on reaping?" My voice became abruptly serious. "Well, go shaft yourself with a redwood, Grandpa. Because the whirlwind you just set loose? It's not a nuclear war with the US of A.

"It's me," I said, staring him down, fire burning through my veins. "I'm going to level your kingdom. I'm going to annihilate you from the face of the earth. And I'm going to salt your corpse to make sure it shrivels up and never, ever gets brought back to life."

Hades just stood there, unblinking. I doubted it was the first time in his life he'd ever been threatened in that way. "You are, perhaps, not ready for the gift that we have for you. But that is … fine. All good things come in time. And in that time, you will learn … humility." He looked at Krall. "General." He glanced back at me. "Subdue her."

"I'm going to kill you," I whispered, as Krall took another step toward me.

Then I took a final step back.

And fell out the window.

44.

The trick to surviving an enormous fall is to not take an enormous fall. Even with Wolfe powers of near-invulnerability, there were limits to how much damage I could take from a leap. I'd once jumped out of a plane as it was crashing, landing flat and absorbing the shock in a superhero landing. It probably would have looked cool, if anyone had seen it. But unfortunately, it was pretty dark out when it had happened, and there wasn't really anyone around at the time.

Those carefree, damage-sponging days were gone, though, and with them my ability to free fall hundreds of feet without shattering my knees and ankles and dislocating every joint and probably sending my spine launching out my ass on impact like a javelin. The moment after I stepped out the window I sorely missed Gavrikov and his flight powers, because I tumbled, twice, end over end before I reached out with a hand and started trying to turn my giant fall down the cliff face of the Revelen castle into something less … fatal.

Naturally, as all my best plans did these days, it hurt. A lot.

I caught a ledge in the cliff before I made it more than about forty feet, but that was more than enough to tear some skin. No bones broke, so yay for that. I snagged, I stopped flipping, knees hammering into the stone cliff face, and all the breath went out of me.

Ouch. That was one.

The hit caused me to lose my grip, though, and the next fall was a vertical slide some twenty feet until I hit another cliff's edge, this time with one foot. It was an uneven surface, a little ledge of inches, and it cracked my ankle a little. Nothing broke, again, fortunately, but I damned sure felt it, and scrambled for a grip.

There was, unfortunately, nothing to grip. That was two stops.

This time I went sideways, doing my best not to shriek because the feeling of falling is one so universally awful that it tends to inspire fear no matter how close to invulnerable you are. Even when I'd had Wolfe's and Gavrikov's powers, falls had always scared me for a few seconds, before I'd remembered I could fly and shrug off anything that happened if I did land hard. It was instinct.

I tumbled into what felt like an endless void, clawing at the wall for any purchase. I caught something and lost it just as quickly, but the momentary grip had reversed my momentum so that I swung my feet back down to lead the way.

Three. Three stops.

The next section of the cliff was sheer, everything moving so fast that I barely had a chance to react. I gripped at a ledge about a foot wide, a natural break where water sloughed off. I caught it, my shoulders screaming at the sudden impact of all my weight catching, yanking down on them.

But I held.

Four stops.

A quick look down confirmed two things—one, I shouldn't have looked, because yikes. Two, it I let go now, there was still plenty of falling room for me to die in the landing.

Then the stone clutched in my fingertips cracked and broke loose, the long weathering process of rain sped up by my sudden and dramatic application of weight.

I fell backward, and my legs impacted on a ledge below, heels hitting hard through my shoes. This, by itself, would have been annoying, but luck was apparently on my side because it sent me, once more, end over end, and I tumbled until I was upright again, where I managed to catch yet another natural ledge.

Five.

Breathing heavily, I looked down. There was about fifty feet of fall remaining below me, I estimated, and it was completely ledge-free. There was, in fact, nothing below me save for tarmac and a giant, open door built into the cliff face.

The damned garage.

The shouts of men below, completely unaware that I was dangling above them, sounded almost comical to my ears as I hung there, heart hammering like someone's fists trapped inside me, struggling to get out. If I dropped now, best case, I'd break both ankles. Worst case, I'd die.

"Shit," I breathed.

And then the alarm siren started wailing.

It was loud and fierce and it assaulted my senses in none of the ways I would have preferred. Why couldn't people just stick to trying to punch me? Now we were getting into the territory of nukes and lightning and spider-monkeys. Why was nothing simple anymore?

A truck rumbled beneath me, one of the army types with a canvas roof stretched over it. It moved directly below my feet at about five miles an hour, taking it easy on its way out of the hangar.

It was a split decision, but a simple one—I wasn't going to get a softer landing than this unless I hung here and just waited for Hades and Krall and whoever else to park a trampoline beneath me or something. And even that was kinda iffy, assuming Krall was in charge. She'd probably just wait for me to get tired and drop, then squeeze me to death once I crashed down. Assuming she didn't have ArcheGrey zap me first.

It felt like a long drop, and I exhaled just before I hit the canvas truck top. Tearing through took about a half second of uncertainty, and I counted myself fortunate I didn't hit any of the metal spines that stretched across the top to hold the canvas in place.

I landed on something soft, and a scream told me it was a person. It hurt, sending a surge of pain up my back, but not an unmanageable amount. I managed it quickly, in fact, leaping off the canvas as quickly as I could, with only a minor struggle.

Six.

I'd landed on the last section of the truck canvas and came crashing down to the tarmac, shoes clinking into a field of broken glass I'd sent tumbling down moments earlier.

Seven falls. Ouch.

"That would have made Butch and Sundance proud," I muttered as the truck squealed to a stop. I didn't have time to wait and see if soldiers poured out. I wobbled, getting my balance, and hurried back into the hangar as shouts started all around me, confusion setting in with the wail of the alarm.

"What is going on?" a young soldier called as I hobbled my way across the hangar, trying to look casual but move quickly.

I did a double take. It was Aleksy, and he was looking at me with complete confusion, an AK-74 slung over his shoulder.

"Oh, the Americans are prepping another attack," I said, keeping it cool. "Aren't you supposed to be in the Situation Room? On missile duty or whatever?"

Aleksy's eyes followed me as I kept going, heading for the row of Hades's parked vehicles. Get a car and get gone, that was as far as my planning extended. It seemed like a good idea.

"I can track things from the console down here if need be," he said, moving closer to me, his weapon still slung behind him. "What happened to you?"

"What, this?" I stopped and held up my right hand, which was slicked with blood. "Window got me."

He stepped closer, peering at it in the dark. He was about two steps away now, moving fast, oblivious to the danger. "We need to get you to medical, that looks serious—"

I knocked him into oblivion, just cold-cocked him with my wounded hand. It wasn't a pretty punch, or a fun one, my knuckles meeting solid forehead. It was the sort of thing that breaks bones, and not his. I heard the crack, felt the crack, felt the pain, but didn't care. I was strong enough to both press through it and also know that it was the best way to get done what I needed to without killing him.

Aleksy's eyes fluttered and I caught him, looking around. No one had seen, no one was looking at us. They were all running to duty stations, jumping in trucks and buzzing off, or standing around the one I'd landed on, wondering what the hell had happened.

I dragged Aleksy's insensate form with me about twenty steps behind the cover of Hades's car collection. "Sorry," I said, but he didn't so much as stir from my sucker punch, "but I don't need you reaching out with your powers and dragging me back." I left him crumpled behind a Bugatti and looked around, trying to decide what my best bet was here.

"Damn," I said. A sports car was bound to draw attention of the wrong kind. But that wasn't all Hades had on offer …

I slipped up to a Humvee with military coloring. I'd seen a few of them moving around in the hangar and slipped behind the wheel. This one was a touch sleeker, a civilian model; must have been Great-Grandpa's personal Humvee. The keys were just hanging in the ignition.

I started it up and slid it into gear. It purred, smoothly, as I put my foot on the gas pedal and gave it a push. "Okay," I said, "off we go," and guided it out of the lineup toward the hangar door.

Nobody noticed or cared, and I kept the speed low as I drove out of the hangar and into the daylight beyond, tracing the path I'd come to this place on, uncertain of where I was going other than the bold, high skyline of Bredoccia, which waited for me in the distance with a promise that there, at least, I might stand a chance of hiding from the hell that was sure to follow behind me.

45.

Dave Kory

"Whoa," Dave said, little slickness of sweat forming across his palm, his hand slipping on his cell phone as he read the words on the screen, head down in his cubicle, acutely aware that anyone could peer over the wall at him at any time.

CHALKE: FBI Meta team was ambushed in Revelen, no survivors.

BILSON: Wow. This isn't going to play well.

CHALKE: It'll play fine. We just need to push the public in the right direction, get them whipped up and ready for what's coming—war.

Dave blinked at that. What?

CHAPMAN: Are we sure that's the direction we want to be heading? Revelen is best buddies with Russia, after all. And a nuclear power now, right?

CHALKE: That hasn't broken yet. Better to keep both those under wraps—for now.

JOHANNSEN: Better to present it as a small war, something akin to Desert Storm. The public can handle a small-scale intervention, after all. Then, if need be, we scale it up, once they're emotionally committed.

Dave stared at the screen. "Johannsen" was Morris Johannsen, public editor for one of the largest, most prestigious legacy newspapers in the US, one of arguably three that everyone in the journalism world looked to for guidance. It was the *New York Times*, the *Washington Post*, and Johannsen's *Washington Free Press*. That he was all in on this …

Well, Dave wasn't going to bring up the rear in this one, was he? Hell no.

KORY: This should be an easy lift. The public hates Nealon right now anyway. We just do a little push here, a shove there, and they'll hate Revelen by association. The stage is set. We shape the narrative a little, and boom, everyone will be clamoring for this war.

CHALKE: Perfect. We need to get Nealon out of the way and this is the perfect means to move the ball forward on everything. This Revelen group is looking to pose a problem in Eastern Europe, in general, and have exported trouble to our shores in the past. Getting them out of the way, however we have to do it, is a net good.

Dave nodded along. That was true. Where was the bad in getting rid of a group as destabilizing as whoever was running Revelen? That seemed like an overall positive for the world, eliminating a little chaos.

CHALKE: To that end, here's another scoop we need to get out there—Revelen is being run by Sienna Nealon's family. Specifically Hades, God of Death.

Dave blinked, not sure he read that right.

JOHANNSEN: Beg pardon?

Beat him to the punch. It burned Dave that the *Free Press* editor might scoop him. He started to type even as he awaited a reply.

CHALKE: Hades, the Greek God of Death, is alive and running a small Eastern European country. You heard it here first. Attribute to a "senior administration official" on deep background. Use previous suggestion of Berenger at DoJ to corroborate. Condition: make sure you tie this to Nealon heavily in your writing. Use phrases like "in cooperation with" or "cahoots" or something similar, but more sinister if you can. Furthermore, try and reflect nicely on the Gondry administration? Our man is doing all he can to deal with the situation, but this is obviously a heavy lift, what with Russia being involved and the general intransigence of the DoD.

Dave translated DoD automatically—Department of Defense. Which he took to mean SecDef Passerini being a pain in the ass, the fossil. Didn't he see what was at stake here? Maybe the next SecDef would be a little more willing to get with the program.

JOHANNSEN: What's the plan for dealing with Russia?

The gap of time it took Chalke to respond would have been troubling if Dave hadn't been busy formulating his story.

CHALKE: We're working on it. DoD has been readying for war with Russia for seventy years. They have drawers of plans.

Dave blinked at that. That was probably true. This was what they did, after all, planned wars that they hoped they could get started, right? Right. This time, though, it was a worthy cause.

BILSON: Okay, this should be an easy thing to set up. Let's just make sure we all stay on the same page as we start stoking this fire. The war is going to kick off fairly quickly, as soon as DoD gets its pieces in place, which they're already doing. The public needs to be ready for this fast, because they're going to get their fill just as quickly.

Taking that all in took a moment. Dave got the basics; when you were shaping public opinion, it was best to give them the news fast, the bitter part swiftly, then follow-up with a success within twenty-four hours, before they had much time to stew. Instant gratification warfare, a quick victory that could be sold as, "We're winning!" and which would offset any small losses that accumulated in the first week. It was a lot like his strategy of content delivery, and since they synergized so well …

Man. This war could be really good for Flashforce. That thought warmed Dave as he sat there, pondering the possibilities. Especially if he was one of two exclusive outlets getting the biggest news from the conflict first.

It was all he could do not to rub his hands together.

CHALKE: One suggestion, Russ. Maybe keep away from Senator Foreman from now on? I'm pretty sure the only damage he took in your last round was to his shirt when he got your blood all over it.

Dave chuckled. He'd seen the playback of the

Foreman/Bilson segment. It was brutal. He wouldn't have wanted to be the one tasked with facing off with Foreman. The man had pounded the hell out of Harmon in a debate, and no one did that. Ever.

BILSON: Oh, ha ha. Let me worry about former Senator Foreman and his thwarted ambitions. He's a has-been, and out of the game. His influence is minimal.

Dave wasn't so sure about that. Foreman had received sixty million votes. That wasn't nothing, and it certainly didn't suggest his influence was nada.

CHAPMAN: Strongly disagree. That segment is going viral right now, rocketing around social media and being shared with alarming frequency. We're moving to quash, trying to keep the focus on Revelen and Nealon.

CHALKE: Good. We don't need any distractions from the narrative. Not right now.

CHAPMAN: There's something else we should discuss at some point. A certain video that's now online.

Dave stared, trying to suss out what that meant. What video was he talking about?

CHALKE: Later. Right now we have more important things to deal with. Is the video under control?

CHAPMAN: Almost zero traction.

BILSON: Why haven't you taken it down?

CHAPMAN: Because that'd be a quick way to make sure it *got* traction. Leave it alone, let it get lost in the noise, and it'll die. Take it down, it becomes a martyr and a cause célèbre. Let it drown without signal boost. Don't give it oxygen. We're monitoring it carefully. Will apprise if anything changes, but for now, we're just burying it quietly.

BILSON: Well, you know best. Do what you have to.

Dave felt like he was hearing grudging agreement from Bilson on that, but tone was difficult with just the text to go by.

CHAPMAN: Five by five.

CHALKE: All right, you know what to do. Let's make this thing happen.

And the little flicker of a dozen people logging off kicked

Dave back to the real world.

Whew. A war. Crazy business behind the scenes. He felt little chills running up and down his forearms, and through the fine hair on his skin, he could see the goose bumps standing up. Was this how a war correspondent felt just before a big invasion? It probably was. He spun once around his chair, then bolted to his feet. He had marching orders to give.

"Everybody huddle up!" he shouted across the room. It was time to get this thing really moving.

46.

Sienna

The road to Bredoccia hadn't seemed this long when I'd driven it with Vlad—Hades—and company. It wound down from the high plateau where the castle overlooked the city, atop its rock like a fat toad perched in the sun. There wasn't a ton of traffic, and what there was seemed to be mostly military in nature.

I drove with the window down, wind blowing through my hair as I tried to get a handle on the shit that was happening around me. I was no stranger to things going severely sideways, but this might have been a personal best for even me.

I was wanted in the USA, and they were sending metahuman SWAT teams to retrieve me.

I'd just escaped prison.

I was in a country run by my long-thought-dead great-grandfather, aided by my slightly-less-long-thought-dead grandmother.

And now I was on the run. Again.

"Everywhere I go, people are always after me," I muttered as I leaned the Humvee into an S curve down a hill. It wasn't quite a hairpin turn, but it was close, and I gave the handling a good workout along with the tread on the tires. "Oh, to be unpopular for a little while." I blinked. "Oh, wait, I am unpopular. Well, to be ignominious, then." Wait. That wasn't the right word. "Anonymous? To be less well-known and less well-hated. That's what I'm aiming for, here. Do you think I've got a shot?"

"Given your steady appetite for causing chaos? No," came a voice from the speakers.

I let out a little shriek and almost wrecked the car into a steep cliff wall, regaining control only through my meta reflexes. "Damn you, Cassidy," I said once I was back in my lane, the squeal of tires and a cloud of rubber behind me. "Can't I even vent in private anymore?"

"Just be glad I'm locking your new friends out of your car's systems," Cassidy said, "because they're desperately trying to track you and kill the engine right now. You should have stolen one of the army trucks. They're dumb; no GPS, no LoJack, no smart integrated systems."

"Well, they're also not as pretty," I said, running a hand over the smooth leather that was stitched over the Hummer's steering wheel. "What the hell do you want from me?" I regretted the question as soon as I asked.

"What you promised me," she said. "Revenge."

"Right," I said under my breath. "One-track mind. Okay, so complication—Vlad is actually—"

"Your great-grandfather. Yes, I know."

I frowned. "Then why are you still trying to enlist me in killing him?"

There wasn't even a pause, and I wondered how much caffeine Cassidy was operating on right now. "Because you basically want to kill everybody, especially the people who piss you off, and Vlad?" Another beat. "I'm guessing he pissed you off if you had to jump out a high castle window to get away from him."

"It was less Vlad and more one of his lackeys on that one," I said, "but I take your point. Look, I was supposed to be the crown princess here, but let's just say I'm already starting to question my patriotism for Revelen thanks to the general in charge of the armed forces. That does not translate into desire to kill Hades, but—hell, I don't know where it actually lands me. Other than up shit creek again."

"You do have a talent for pissing people off," Cassidy said.

"I would advise you to avoid turning that talent in my direction, at least right now."

"Look, I'm trying to be square with you," I said, taking another turn, "I'm obviously in a jam right now. I know you want your revenge, but I don't want to kill my great-grandfather or my grandmother."

"Then I think we're about to have a problem," Cassidy said, as the car engine died suddenly. "Because I want them dead. Immediately, if not sooner."

I coasted the Humvee to the side of the road. "Don't do this, Cassidy. Please. They didn't kill Simmons. Stepane did, and he did it because he wanted to prove he was the best."

"But they empowered him to do so." Cassidy's voice was cold and emotionless in spite of the lightning-fast whip of her words. Caffeinated, frigid, focused on her goal above all else. "Gave him the abilities. Tormented him until he became obsessed with the Darwinian model of being strongest … And they were the ones who captured my Eric."

"I'm not denying any of that," I said as the Humvee came to a stop and I shifted it into park. "I'm just …" My head sagged, lurching forward, my neck muscles just tired of holding up the weight of my head, let alone everything else that was on my shoulders. "Don't push me in this, Cassidy. I might have to kill Hades just because the course of events seems headed that way … don't try and apply any more torsion to me right now."

"Why not?" She sounded pretty serious.

I lifted my head, suddenly empowered by a hot rage that flooded through me. "Because I am getting dangerously close to my limit with everyone on the damned planet right now, and on the planet is where you live, unless you've relocated to outer space."

"Not yet, no," Cassidy said, and there was a hint of give in her voice. "All right. Fine. I have a deep suspicion that whether you like it or not, you're going to come in direct conflict with Vlad himself by the time this is all over. I can afford to be patient, let events play out. It seems you're going to be thrust into a battle with the forces of Revelen in the meantime anyway. Escalation is inevitable."

"Why …?" I croaked. "Why can I not just … catch a break? An honest-to-goodness break? Why couldn't I come to a peaceful Eastern European country, with beaches and a friendly president who was like, 'I dig your style, Sienna'? One that everybody loved—like a male Grace Kelly, who had such good relations with everyone that nobody wanted to even bother coming after me. And I could have spent like a hundred years working on my tan and keeping my nose out of trouble and—who knows, maybe being a queen, but not because of hereditary reasons—"

"If you're queen, there's usually some heredity involved—"

"Shut the hell up and let me indulge in a moment of fantasy that might help see me through the shit that is about to go down here, Cassidy," I said. "Because I am at my limit, okay? *Years* of this shit. I have been through years of this shit, and I am—so tired." I thumped my hand against the steering wheel and it creaked a little, underneath the leather. "I just want—a—break."

"Well, you're not getting one now, so suck it up, buttercup," Cassidy said, and the engine roared to life again. "You might want to get into Bredoccia before they get their own drone force up. Ditch the car before they start scouring for you."

My shoulders sagged as I placed my hands back on the wheel. "Cassidy … I'm not going to kill them, okay? Just get that out of your head now." I put my foot on the pedal and goosed it gently. It spat gravel, and I was back on the road, fishtailing lightly.

"We'll see," Cassidy said, and she was back to being way too happy. If she had any more to say on it, though, she kept it to herself, and I followed the winding road down the rest of the mountain as it flattened out, running straight into the old-town section of Bredoccia.

47.

I slid into the quiet streets of Bredoccia sleek as a … well, a Hummer doing about fifty along quiet avenues. It was an interesting town, reminding me again of Edinburgh. Bredoccia touched the mountain only at the edge, and it looked to me like Vlad had done some work with the local zoning board to keep anyone from encroaching on his castle. As a result, Bredoccia stretched in the other three directions like mad, but downtown stayed pretty close to the cliff face below the castle rock.

The biggest skyscraper downtown, the Dauntless Tower, was just ahead, the mix of old and new buildings heading into downtown lending the city an eclectic air. The tall buildings breaking out of the mostly four- and five-story European apartment blocks gave Bredoccia a quality of old clashing hard with new. I'd have found it ugly but I had more pressing problems than aesthetics.

"They're tightening the net around you," Cassidy's voice piped up from the radio. "They know what you're driving, and there are troops on the streets. They're going to have eyes on you shortly, because I can't keep ArcheGrey out of her own grid for long."

"Maybe I'll hit the freeway and burn out of town before they get their shit together," I said, gunning my engine as the lights ahead started to go red.

"There's not really a convenient freeway to anywhere but Canta Morgana and the port there," Cassidy said. "And even that doesn't stack up to that road we took from Florida through Alabama. Which interstate was that?"

"I don't know and I don't care," I said, looking ahead. Every light had gone red. It looked to me like Arche was taking some action to slow me down. Too bad she didn't realize I didn't give a fig about traffic laws.

"You're not going to make it out of this country if they don't want you to," Cassidy said. "They're going to force a confrontation."

"My whole life is confrontations," I said, looking ahead, then checking my mirrors. No cars, no trucks in sight—yet. "I'm getting a little sick of them."

"Who do you think you're kidding? You love confrontations," Cassidy said. "The only reason you're flinching at this one is because it's your family."

"Yes, feelings are a complicating thing," I said. "Not that you'd know, what with being on a mission to avenge the boyfriend who constantly cheated on you while you were together."

"You don't know that much about me." Cassidy's voice was clipped.

"But I do know that."

"Well, where's your boyfriend?" Cassidy fired back. "Huh? Ditched you back in the Dakotas, didn't he? When you started to do things he didn't agree with?"

"In fairness to him, I can be kind of disagreeable," I said, keeping my voice even. Hell if I knew where Harry was now. Somewhere safe, hopefully, and well out of trouble. "I'm a handful. Maybe two handfuls."

"Stop bragging about your bra size and take a left ahead. There's a military truck two blocks up about to turn onto your street."

Whatever my grievances with Cassidy, in this I took her advice, taking a left onto a smaller avenue, a one way heading … hell if I knew which direction I was going.

"I like that you unquestioningly did what I asked there," she said. "If you could just get in the habit of that—"

"I'm not your slave," I said. "I'm following your directions of out pure self-interest. When they cease to be in my interest, I'll stop following them."

"Hm. Fascinating. Why would you assume I'm not steering you into trouble to precipitate a confrontation that benefits my interests?"

"I assume you are, actually," I said, looking either way. "But I've ruled out getting out of town without confrontation. Now I'm just looking for a way to make it … survivable."

"Another left. There's an alley."

I turned into the alley. It dead-ended, and the brick wall of a three-story apartment building waited in front of me.

I sighed. "So … confrontation now?"

"Probably shortly," Cassidy said. "I estimate only a five percent chance this Humvee survives, and they're less than a block away, so I'll make this quick. There's a gas main three feet under the street, an electric box to your right on the wall, a fire escape a story up on your left, and a dumpster you could probably lift in a pinch against the far wall. The soldiers in the truck have powers, of course, but I don't know what kind. Bet on a mix of the classics—Gavrikovs, Hercules, maybe some unique ones in there. They also have guns."

"Of course."

"There's a manhole in the middle of the alley, twenty feet from the back wall. If you can get the soldiers dealt with, that's your easiest exit. Good luck."

Then she was gone.

I stepped out of the Humvee just as a truck pulled into the alleyway, blocking that exit. It rumbled to a stop and I heard shouts as men cleared out from the back.

Ducking behind my Hummer in a crouch, I heard them hustling forward. Taking a peek, I saw what they were doing.

Forming a firing line. Pointed at me.

Yay.

48.

Dave Kory

"Focus up, everybody!" Dave clapped his hands once, trying to get everyone on point. "I've got exciting news." He could practically feel the glow of the information coming out of his body, and it was almost like it was lighting up the Brooklyn night. "I've got a couple sources on deep background saying that the Gondry administration is not going to sit back and let Sienna Nealon get away. They're going in after her."

A round of cheers and applause greeted his announcement. He didn't need to work very hard to take the temperature of this room regarding Sienna Nealon. She'd damned near killed a hundred reporters in the Eden Prairie incident. Everyone in this room knew, or was a degree or two removed from, someone who'd been there. Nealon was never going to win a popularity contest in any press bullpen in the US.

"Are you serious?" Mike Darnell asked. His brow was furrowed, making him look his age.

"Oh, yeah," Dave said, smile not fading a bit. "They've already sent in one team—"

"I heard," Mike said. "How'd that turn out?"

Now Dave had to work to keep the smile on, looking at one of the TV screens that encircled the bullpen. It was tuned to a cable news network and—hey, there was Bilson, doing another TV hit. "Not well. It seems like Nealon has the full backing of the Revelen government."

"Then if we're going in after her," Mike said, "won't that mean war?"

"It's looking that way," Dave said coolly. "But come on—things like this are why we pay more than anyone else in the world, by far, to have a top-notch military. So we can exert influence in the moments when it really counts."

A couple people clapped. Dave smiled; he wasn't usually a fan of military intervention, but dammit, this was a perfect pairing if ever he'd seen one. Dangerous criminal in a far-off place? A likely threat to the US in the future? She was like another Osama Bin Laden, given all that she'd done.

"What do we do, Dave?" Steve Fills asked. He had a little hum in his voice, excitement bleeding through.

"This is going to be pure dynamite, we're talking lit as—well, you know," Dave said, grinning. "Everything I've heard suggests the Gondry administration is going in hard and fast, trying to wrap this up quick. But they need to make sure they've got public support, and that they deliver on this unspoken promise and finish the war swiftly. That's the marching orders on their end. Now for us—this is nothing but opportunity. People are naturally curious and questioning in time of war. They're going to be looking for explainers, so I need someone to put together a brief history of the conflict, really playing up the elements of discord."

"You want us to do a research piece on Revelen?" Holly Weber asked.

"Yes," Dave snapped his finger and Holly started typing furiously into her laptop, taking notes. "But don't just go up the middle with it. You need an angle." He smiled. "Look to their history. Find the skeletons in the closet, and bring 'em out for everyone to see. There's gotta be some dark stuff in there. Let's shine some sunlight on it."

"Can I write a counterpoint?" Mike asked, hand partially raised.

Dave frowned. "To what? The Revelen history piece?"

Mike's look was deepest concentration. "To all of it. To any pieces you're going to run on the war, on Revelen … I'll finish my research, and I'll have something ready to go in two hours. I've got some sources in the State Department that have given me some stuff, along with Department of Justice … it'll be a nice counterpoint to what you're talking about here."

"No," Dave said, frown deepening. "Look, Mike … this is the narrative, okay? Sienna Nealon is a bad, bad, person." He paused for applause, because the whole damned bullpen except for Mike clapped for that. "Going to war to stop her, to bring her back to custody, is an unvarnished good."

"I'm not so sure," Mike said. "The data I'm getting is starting to suggest she might not even be guilty of the things we think she is. There's a video floating around of the Eden Prairie thing—"

"I don't care," Dave said, waving a hand furiously in front of his face as if he could banish Mike the hell out of here with a flick of his wrist. "We all know what happened there, okay? She tried to kill honest reporters doing their jobs. Just like in LA, when she nuked that Latino neighborhood—"

"It was one Mexican restaurant," Mike said, "and the government never even formally accused her of it, mainly because as far as we know, she has no power to create a nuclear event."

"Everybody knows Sienna Nealon explodes," Constance Shriver said, her small face pinched. She stared at Mike as though he were an idiot.

"There's a difference between an explosion and a nuclear explosion," Mike said. "LA was a nuclear event, it set off radiological sensors across the Western US. Sienna Nealon definitely had explosive powers, but not nuclear ones. LA was something different; my sources suggest it may have been an assassination attempt against her, not anything she directly caused."

"Bullshit," Caden Chambers said.

Mike gave him a glance. "I'm starting to think the people in this room might be a little too emotionally involved in this story to cover it dispassionately."

"Good," Dave said. "They're people. They have a perspective on things. That lets them write about it in an interesting way, with passion."

Mike just stared back for a moment. "It's not … strictly speaking … good when your objectivity is blown all to hell."

"Objectivity is a myth and a stupid one," Dave said, pacing a little, taking in the Brooklyn skyline, and Manhattan beyond. "The only people who don't have a point of view on something are dead. How can you not have watched what Sienna Nealon has done over the last two years and—I mean, anyone with a pulse can see she's a threat to human life." He spun on Mike. "I mean, seriously … what you're talking about … it's like going back to the 1930s and doing a soft-focus puff piece on Hitler."

"That's an extreme analogy, and an overused one at that," Mike said. "I don't think she's doing any ethnic cleansing, or even endorsing it."

"It's just an example," Dave said. "But it holds. You don't make apologies for terrible people. You don't film them in soft focus. You show the world. Boldly. You take a stand, you don't write a puff piece about how—I don't know—something went wrong in their past that made them broken like they are—"

"A human interest angle?" Mike asked. "Like her mother locking her in a metal coffin every time she misbehaved as a child?"

"See, that's sugarcoating it," Dave said, pointing at him. "You want to make her look sympathetic?"

"You want to completely dehumanize her?" Mike tossed back, still calm as anything. His lack of emotion was damned unnerving.

"Oh, I've doubted her basic lack of humanity forever," Dave said. "That's long decided. Now I'm starting to question yours."

That sent one of Mike's eyebrows up. "You're questioning whether I'm human?"

"Look at you, man," Dave said, taking a step closer to him. The crowd was quiet save for an occasional, "Mmhmm." "You're sitting here arguing for Sienna Nealon. Mass murderer. About to start a war—"

"I don't think she possesses the capability to start a war all on her own."

"—and you're like a Hitler apologist over here." Dave could feel the rage rising. "You can just sit there and think about the shit she's done, vaporizing that neighborhood—man, people lived there. Had their homes there—"

"No one died," Mike said. "It was one restaurant."

"That's callous as hell," Dave said. "That was their lives. And you don't give a shit."

"Well, I care more about human life than stuff, yeah," Mike said. "And I'm trying to see to the truth of the matter, because it seems to me that few people are right now. I hear a lot of rage about her, about the things she's done, but I don't hear a lot of cold, hard facts. Looking over the Eden Prairie casualty reports, I don't see a single reporter among the dead. Just the so-called protestors—"

"They were activists protesting that she'd taken away their freedom," Caden said, rising to his feet, face purple with outrage. "Without trial. Without evidence."

"I think there was some evidence, but I'm not unsympathetic to the 'no trial' part of it," Mike said. "That was wrong. And it was a story worthy of being covered, as a human rights abuse—"

"She's a sick murderer," Constance said. "A serial killer who's killed more people than anyone since Hitler. Which is why we call her Hitler."

"I don't think that's factually accurate," Mike said calmly.

"Screw you, man," Dave said, and shit, he was over this whole discussion. "She's serious. You want to write a fact-check piece on something we already know? Let me help you with a fundamental truth: Sienna Nealon is a heinous, murderous person. Boom. Fact-check?" He turned to Caden, the resident fact-checker.

"I rate it as 'Absolutely True,'" Caden said.

"Without doubt," Constance said. She was standing now, too, as one did in these situations. Others were coming to their feet, the anger in the room almost palpable.

Mike took a slow look around, arms folded in front of him. "Remember what I said before about lacking the objectivity to cover the subject in question? I want you all to think real hard about how you feel at the moment. And what you'd do if evidence suddenly came out that Sienna did not do the things you think she did."

"Man, to hell with you," Caden said. "And to hell with her, too." That spurred a round of applause. "She's guilty as shit."

"What if she wasn't?" Mike asked, still irritatingly calm. "What if you all had decided she was guilty, though, and weren't even open to discussion about it?"

"Because she's guilty and we're not stupid," Constance said, and everybody broke into applause again.

Dave was just smiling. Somebody threw something, a balled-up piece of paper, and it bounced off Mike's back.

"But what if she wasn't?" Mike asked, damn him, again. "And what if you've been wrong all this time?"

That produced a moment of silence. "Then she's still a heinous person and deserves everything she gets," Constance finally said, and boy did that get a chorus of agreement.

"Hm," Mike said. God, he was like a stone. "Have you ever heard of 'Two Minutes of Hate'?"

"Sounds like what your mother gives you every night," someone shouted from the back. That was good for a long laugh.

Mike just smiled tightly. "It's a concept from Orwell. *1984*. The idea being that you direct your anger toward a target that's considered acceptable. Someone like Sienna Nealon. And you just … hate her, yell at her, scream at her, freak out in her general direction. It gives you catharsis for the things that maybe have gone wrong in your life. Keeps you from thinking about your problems in terms of what you could do to solve them and instead lets you transfer that anger to someone else."

"That's beautiful, man," Dave said. Yeah, he was over this shit, and over Mike in general. "Have I told you lately that—"

"DO NOT ADJUST YOUR TELEVISION SETS," came a loud, mechanical voice from every TV in the place. Dave flinched, turning his head to look. It had cut him off just before he was going to say, "You're fired," to Mike. That would have been sweet, but it could wait a minute or two.

The nearest TV had lost the live feed from the news network, and instead there was a strange pattern and static. The picture took a moment, then resolved into something—it was like security camera footage from high up on a wall, and there, standing in the middle of an alleyway—

Was Sienna Nealon.

"Whoa," Caden said. "Weird. We were just talking about her, and here—"

"Look," Constance said. "Soldiers."

And there were, pouring out of an army truck, pointing guns at Nealon. The word LIVE was scrolling across the bottom of the screen in a very basic text pattern, definitely not the network feed.

"It's on every channel," Caden said, flipping the remote of one of the TVs. "Even this one," and he pointed at one in the far corner that Dave would have sworn was not on a minute ago.

"DO NOT ADJUST YOUR TELEVISION SETS," the voice said again, mechanical, like someone was using a scrambler. "What you are about to see is actually happening right now."

"This doesn't look good for Nealon," Dave said, peering at the screen. "Caden—start writing something up about this. Live updates, stream of consciousness. We need to be on this before anyone else is."

"But we don't know anything," Caden said.

"We know Sienna Nealon is on every screen in the office," Dave said, "including the one that wasn't even turned on a minute ago," and he waved at the screen in the far corner of the bullpen. "Start with that. If this is happening everywhere—and I bet it is, at least in New York—people are going to be wondering what's going on. Let's get those clicks."

He didn't wait for Caden to answer. He heard the tapping of keys seconds later anyway.

No, Dave settled in to watch with the rest, as the live feed showed the soldiers edging ever closer to Nealon, who stooped behind the Humvee, and he watched with his breath just slightly held.

49.

Sienna

"Sienna Nealon, in the name of the general, you will surrender to us!" The lead guy was shouting in English, voice echoing down the alleyway. His point was obvious and made still plainer by the military rifles he and his teammates had pointing at me, too.

The summer heat of the evening sent a cool trickle of sweat down the small of my back, rolling beneath my new blouse, which was, tragically, already a victim of being a piece of Sienna Nealon's wardrobe. Long tears in the fabric from the fall had left my arms exposed, the sleeves shredded, and a little section of my midriff showing.

"What if I don't want to surrender?" I shouted back. "What if I just want to huddle here behind my fancy Humvee and stroke the hood lovingly until I fall asleep?"

That prompted silence as the man in charge tried to figure what the hell he could say to that. "You will surrender now, and come with us. Or else."

"Oh, I don't like that 'or else,'" I said. I had the seeds of a plan, but it was not one I particularly liked. "It makes me feel unsafe."

"It . . . is not our job to make you feel safe," the head guy said a moment later, like he was spluttering to come up with a response. Couldn't tell if he realized I was just dicking around with him to buy time. It didn't seem like he did.

I took a long, deep breath, then another, sliding my hands under the front of the Hummer. The undercarriage was warm, but fortunately, I wasn't grabbing it directly under the engine, which I was sure would be hot enough to burn me. "Hey, man, you're talking to the crown princess of Revelen here. If it's not your job to make me feel safe, whose is it? What's your name, soldier?"

"I—what?" he asked. Confusion was definitely setting in. Time to act.

"I asked your name," I said, taking up some of the Hummer's weight, a little at a time. There was no easy way to do what I was about to do, but I wanted to keep my foes off balance until things busted loose, so … I continued to bullshit as I prepared to lift the damned Humvee. "You know, so I can report it to my great-grandfather, who runs this country."

"What is she talking about?" one of the other soldiers asked—in English, conveniently. A muttered reply in their own tongue illuminated nothing for me.

The lead guy brushed him off in their language, and I could mentally hear, in his tone, his closure of the conversational portion of our confrontation. "You will obey my commands and come out from behind the car with your hands raised or—"

"You want the Hummer back, right?" I asked. "Whole? In one piece?"

"That … was not our orders," the lead soldier said, once again dazzled by my bullshit and taking his eye off the ball briefly. "We are to bring you in, immediately, and—"

"Well, you can have the Humvee back anyway," I said and heaved, lifting that sucker high. It strained some of the muscles in my back, but only because I was practicing improper lift posture. I had to; it was a damned SUV, it extended at least fifteen feet past my grip on it. I levered it upright, then deadlifted with my legs, pushing it into the air from my waist on up.

This was the tricky part. Gasps came from the soldiers, and I had only a second to act before they started shooting, I estimated. So I got the balance as right as I could given the time I had—

And I walked the Humvee toward them.

"What are you doing?" Shouts and gasps of surprise greeted my gambit. They were all gathered around the army truck, which was taking up most of the mouth of the alley, a tight fit between the two brick buildings that surrounded us on either side. I just walked it forward, bumper about knee high, the tail of the Hummer extending way above my head, the engine shielding me from fire. And a couple of them did fire, which was not smart. A couple just stood there, gawking, which was arguably even less smart.

"You boys might want to move, because I'm not sure how long I can carry it like this," I said, weight really straining at my fingertips. "It's not exactly a Captain America shield, if you know what I mean, but having the engine block in front of my face makes me feel a lot safer than anything you guys could do."

"We are not here to make you feel safe!" the lead guy shouted again, from somewhere behind the Humvee.

"Same," I said, and walked a little sideways, tilted the Humvee, and sent it crashing down across the mouth of the alley longways.

It was almost a perfect fit, bumpers just about touching the brick on either side. They'd have a hell of a time squeezing between it and the alley walls.

"Oh, boys?" I called. "None of you are standing between this Hummer and the front of your truck, are you?" I asked sweetly.

"No, why—" their captain started to ask.

I buried my shoulder in the roof and shoved, hard, skidding the Humvee forward. After a few seconds of pushing I crashed into the front of the army truck, and man, did it make a nasty sound. Metal bending, glass shattering.

"No reason," I said, gasping from the exertion, looking back toward the dead-end alley behind me. This wouldn't keep them off me for long at all. The manhole cover waited, a black circle in the dimness, and I needed to get out of here before the next wave of soldiers arrived and made everything so much worse.

50.

The manhole led into the storm drains, which, fortunately, were not the sewers, but nonetheless they had a stench that felt like a metahuman punching me in the nose.

The stink of mildew and stagnant water took my breath away and made me wonder if there was something more than storm water going through down here. The piping was pretty decently large, I reflected as I slid the manhole cover back on. Not quite as big as you see in the movies, but high enough that I could walk while stooped over without worrying too much about bumping my head.

Into these concrete tunnels I went, hauling ass into the dark with only the occasional storm drain overhead to light my way. Daylight slipped in through these grates and fell over corrugated metal side tunnels that were more like pipes, ones that I couldn't possibly squeeze into given my hips, so I stuck to the main tunnel and hoped it would run somewhere useful.

The silence was a little unnerving, broken only occasionally as I passed a curbside drain that led back up to the world above. Once I happened to pass one as a big army truck rattled by overhead. I froze and sat in the semi-darkness with only my thundering heartbeat as company until I was sure by the sound of the rumble that they'd gone by. I gave a quick look up after it was gone and saw that the sun was getting low in the sky.

"'Come to Revelen,'" I said, aping one of the countless tourist advertisements that had popped up on billboards around the US the last few years, 'where the vistas command and the skies are endless.'" I looked up at the concrete ceiling that fenced me in from the so-called endless skies. "Hell of a vista, guys." They were definitely not getting the crown princess's endorsement for their next ad, not after this bullshit.

I needed a plan beyond 'run,' having learned the lack of utility of that one during my sojourn in Scotland last year. "I am so sick of getting chased around European countries," I muttered under my breath as another truck rattled by overhead and I clicked off my light and waited for it to go by. I could see nothing of the sky but a sliver of orange light through the slit of the storm drain, suggestions of the setting sun, but the last thing I needed was somebody to look out the back of the truck and see motion in a drain and decide to investigate. "Actually, I'm pretty sick of being chased everywhere. I want to go back to being the chaser. That would be fun, running people down for a change."

I sighed. Too bad I didn't see a way back to that from here. That part of my life seemed like a distant memory, something so far back in the recesses of time it might as well be my entirely forgotten childhood. Actually, I wondered if this was how most people felt about their childhoods, since I couldn't really remember mine at all until age six or so, once I was locked in my house. Just distant memories, things that felt like they emerged from the mists every now and again before sliding back under the surface and disappearing beneath the events of everyday life.

I mopped my brow, sweat trickling down into my eyes. How could it be hotter down here than it was above? I was not going to be able to navigate too much longer down here without a light, because the sun had apparently moved behind the buildings out in Bredoccia, the long shadows preventing the grates from casting much light. It had to be early evening by now. Once the sun set, I was going to be navigating these tunnels by whatever minimal light came from the street lamps into these drains, and while my night vision was good, it was not effective in total darkness.

"Manhole cover," I said under my breath. Cassidy had given

me only that guidance, plus some ideas about how to dispatch my pursuers. Well, I'd showed her. I hadn't even needed her stupid suggestions. Though I was beginning to wonder if maybe taking the high road and going up the fire escape would have been a better escape route than the storm drain.

Probably not. All it'd take was one flyer out of the castle and they'd be on me again. Or a helicopter, though I hadn't heard any of those buzzing around yet.

Another truck rattled by overhead, and I was left with the feeling that this moment of peace wasn't going to last. The guys back in the alley had probably gotten over the car by now, and even if they hadn't seen me go into the storm drains, they'd be narrowing my escape options down. Sooner or later, they'd be coming this way.

If they weren't already.

I listened for boots tromping along behind me. Didn't hear any, but my own footsteps were pretty loud, echoing off the walls as I hustled down the concrete passage bent nearly double. I was starting to become immune to the smell, which was good, because I couldn't really afford to stop off and toss my cookies. It'd leave a nice, fresh sign that someone had been this way.

The screech of tires in the distance was not a pleasant noise. It was far enough off, though, that I figured I was probably safe for the moment. I paused, stopping to listen, perched in the darkness about ten feet off the nearest drain. If someone shone a light down, I was far enough back they wouldn't see me, but I could hear—very quietly—a little of what was going on up there.

It sounded like a few voices, some shouting. An engine idling on a big diesel truck. Someone was being told to do something, in clipped, loud tones. A crackle of radio static as someone—Krall—spoke, giving someone their marching orders.

"Do it," I heard, a bare snatch of English, and then …

… A hiss?

No. It wasn't quite a hiss. It was a familiar noise, but one I couldn't place right off. It sounded like something moving down the passageway, rushing this direction.

Something touched my boots and I barely held in a gasp. Something wet and cool, shockingly so in the damned heat. It splashed as it touched me, and I sniffed, worried it was something terrible or toxic. It washed past my ankles and kept running down the pipe, into the light coming down from outside.

I reached down to touch it, though I already had a sinking feeling I knew exactly what it was. Bringing my wetted fingers to my nose, I sniffed.

Water. Running past me, already to my ankles.

"Shit," I muttered, and hustled forward. It was rising, and ahead I saw a little rippling wave as another rush of it came from the opposite direction, colliding with the flow that had just run past me. Near instantly it went to mid-calf on me, soaking my pants legs as it continued to rise, now feeding in from both directions. "Shit, shit, shit."

They'd turned loose their Poseidons to flood the storm drains to flush me out. It seemed incredibly obvious as a strategy now that I was almost up to my knees in running water, the flow washing from both directions and getting heavier by the minute.

This was going to force me to either get my ass back to the surface where they could more easily track me, or else risk my drowning as the water continued to rise.

I swore again under my breath, deciding quickly that this situation was not going to be a tenable one for me. The flow was already strong enough that it was threatening my footing; another minute or two and the water would be over my head. I'd heard a foot of running water could float a two-thousand-pound car, and I definitely didn't weigh anywhere close to that, no matter what the assholes on the internet had said about my ass.

"Worst vacation ever," I said, trying to fight my way to the grate and reaching it just as the water passed my knee. "Worst family reunion ever—unless you count Rose as my family. And I don't, that ginger whore." I reached up and grabbed the grate, pulling myself up.

Now the water was at my waist, and I pushed my way up

against the storm drain. It had a metal cover designed to keep people from shoving their way down here, the kind of grate that had clearly been exposed to the elements for quite a while, the rust visible in the light of the nearest street lamp. I braced against the bottom of the drain, both hands on the bars, and readied myself. The current was getting incredibly intense, and I needed to get out of here before it got any worse.

I shoved, expecting the grate to pop off so I could drag myself out onto the Revelen street, but …

It didn't move. At all.

"Uhmm …" I braced myself, foot slipping in the rising strength of the current. What the hell? These things were only supposed to be normal metal, not—

Aw, shit.

It occurred to me, just a little too late, that in a country where everyone was a metahuman, including, presumably, the children, child- and idiot-proofing would necessarily have to be escalated a step or two.

In this case, in order to keep people from lifting off a storm drain grate with their meta strength and hopping down to do who-knows-what kind of mischief, they'd probably taken the extra step of bolting the damned things down. Being former Eastern bloc, they also probably lacked the rather exhaustive US regulations that made sure someone couldn't get stuck in a refrigerator, let alone a storm drain.

So when I shoved against the grate, braced even harder, water rushing at my waist, unsteadying me … it didn't move.

"Oh, man," I said, the current threatening to rip my legs from beneath me. There was a sort of S-curve of water washing around my body—heavy pull to the left coming around my waist, a strong one to the right dragging at my ankles as the currents of water coming from both directions met and created a washing machine effect about where I was standing.

The main problem as I saw it was that with this impromptu whirlpool, the current wasn't really going anywhere. It was just spinning in the close confines of the tunnel as the water pressure tried to equalize, filling every square inch of the tunnel, at which point it'd start welling out of the very drain hole I was trying to use as an escape route. Depending on how fast the Poseidons were pouring it in, it'd probably start geysering, pushing me up into the bars as the water sought to escape the pressurizing pipe.

That … was not going to be an optimal solution, because I'd end up like one of those lumps of Play-Doh forced into a grated press. Squish goes Sienna.

I didn't see any easy outs, but I couldn't stay here or I'd definitely die, so I lifted myself out of the water and pressed my face against the metal bars. I took three deep breaths through the grate …

And let go, splashing into the water, hoping one of the currents would win and carry me free of here before I got killed by the pressure of the rising water.

51.

Passerini

"That was live?" Bruno Passerini asked. The signal had now ceased, returning to a news program in studio, a confused anchor interviewing his panelist about the strange interruption to broadcast that they'd just experienced.

"We don't know, sir," a weathered colonel named Murdock said, most of his attention on the screen—and the lieutenant working at it—in front of him. "Preliminary report from the NSA suggests it was on all channels. Total interruption of cable and satellite service."

"It had to be live, sir, or near to it," Graves said, tapping away at a computer console. "In the background of the video, it looked like it was getting close to sunset, and it's that time right now in Revelen. The alleyway they were in—we might be able to find it on the satellite if we looked—ah, here."

Passerini moved closer to Graves and his console. He'd found himself standing during the video, watching the "fight" unfold and unable to keep his seat. Passerini had been in a scrap or two in his life, but seeing Sienna Nealon pick up a Humvee and use it as first a shield and then a battering ram to keep those Revelen soldiers off her?

Well, that was a hell of a thing to watch. It certainly wasn't the kind of fight Passerini would have liked to find himself in.

Graves zoomed the big screen down to show an alleyway in

Bredoccia, truck parked at the entrance, and a Humvee on its side crushed against it. Soldiers swarmed around it and over it like tiny ants, gathered around an open manhole in the depths of the alley. One, in particular, was leaning over it, a blur of something coming out of his hand—

"What is that, colonel?" Passerini asked. He squinted, trying to make it out. The resolution on the satellite feed was just not up to the task, though. Or else Passerini's eyes weren't. Hard to tell which, these days.

He looked back at Graves, but the colonel had paled a shade, staring at the screen. "It's, uh," Graves started, looking like he was trying real hard to compose himself for some reason. "I believe that's a metahuman with water powers, sir. A Poseidon, they call them."

"A what?" Passerini turned to look again. Sure enough, now that Graves had said it, it did look a little like the guy was spraying a fountain of water out of his hand and down into the manhole.

Graves zoomed the picture out, then back in a couple blocks away. Here was another soldier, this time standing over a grate built into the curb, same rippling effect coming from his hands—both of them, in this case, water rushing out into the storm drain.

"What does this look like to you, colonel?" Passerini asked, folding his arms in front of him. He glanced at Graves. Graves was still pale, eyes flitting around, like he was stuck in his own thoughts. "Graves?" Passerini asked.

"Sorry, sir," Graves said, shaking it off, his pallor not quite returning to normal. That was understandable; Graves had been present for quite a while now, and Passerini was certainly feeling the effects of this Revelen crisis dragging on. "Looks to me like they're either going to drown her or flush her into the open."

Passerini nodded. "Yeah, I got that. I meant on the broader scale. Does it seem to you like Revelen has turned on Sienna Nealon?"

Graves's voice sounded a little scratchy. "It certainly looks that way, sir."

"Well, I guess this isn't any of our business," Passerini said, thinking out loud. "Though it certainly does seem like a radical swing, given that not two hours ago Hades was vowing murder on us if we tried to get at his granddaughter." Passerini shook his head. "Now it looks like he's trying to do the job himself. Unless she's immune to drowning …?" He looked at Graves.

Graves shook his head. "No, sir. She is, uh …" He swallowed, obviously, again. "… Vulnerable to that."

"Well," Passerini shrugged, "nothing we can do from here except watch. Especially since we have our own tasks to be working on." He turned his attention to General Kelly, USAF, who was hunched over a planning table halfway across the room. "General, how goes it?"

"We'll have air options in play in the next hour, so," Kelly called back. He was a balding man with reddish-graying hair wrapped around the sides and back of his skull. Looked a little like a bulldog and fought like one, too.

"Keep me apprised, general," Passerini said, looking back at the screen. Water was starting to well out of one of the grates visible on the street. "The president is probably going to be calling again soon, wondering what we can bring to the party." A geyser was forming from the pressure, blasting out into the street like a flower blooming in the overhead shot of the satellite. He tossed a look back to Graves, who was still white as a sheet. Probably just needed a break after all the intensity of the night. Well, maybe he'd get one soon, once they got things rolling here. Passerini turned back to the screen, watching the water just spray, wondering how hard it was blowing out now. "Though it sure is starting to look like our job vis-à-vis Sienna Nealon might be done by the time we get anything in position. Right, colonel?"

Graves didn't answer, but Passerini didn't really expect him to. The colonel was focused on the screen, too, eyes moving like he was reading a page in front of him, hands white-knuckled as he balled them into fists above the keyboard. Passerini shrugged, and went back to watching the screen. He doubted he'd see anything noteworthy happen, but hey, there was nothing else to do unless he wanted to micromanage the planners, so he watched the water flow out into the streets of Bredoccia and wondered if his job was going to be done before he even got the forces in place to do it himself.

52.

Sienna

Drowning was always my least favorite way to die.

I'd contemplated death quite a bit. You can't be in my line of work, constantly throwing your life onto the table as the ante to get into the game, to raise the stakes, to end things out—without anticipating death. And not my great-grandfather Death, either, but the real deal, the one that had caught up to me in that subway tunnel in LA when I'd gotten zapped to death. Heart stop.

Game over.

Except it wasn't game over. Scott Byerly had brought me back from the icy jaws of death before it had barely gotten a taste of me. I couldn't shake the feeling that a taste just wasn't enough, though, especially given how many times since then it had come back for another nip.

Rose.

Rose had been Death, in her way, same as me, taking a lick here, a bite there, until it had felt like there were vast chunks hewn out of me, missing pieces I'd never get back. Dead, for all intents and purposes, an inch at a time. I was five feet, four inches tall; she'd probably killed off a solid foot or two of me, proportionally.

Cold water flooded around me as I swept down the tunnel. I was going feet-first, which was not optimal, and I couldn't see hardly anything. Street lamps washed in through the occasional grate. They didn't provide much but a view of rushing bubbles in the foot or so in front of my face, but it was better than nothing.

I curled up into a ball then unfurled myself, using my hands to catch the sides of the pipe. It stung my fingertips, and I realized I was traveling pretty darned fast. At least thirty miles an hour.

Using my fingertips, I slowed myself—ouch—just enough to flip so that I was going headfirst. If I came crashing into something in the tunnel, like a stick, this would prove to be a terrible, terrible decision.

It was, however, the only way I could control my direction and momentum. Lying back and letting the current carry me? That was a prescription for certain drowning and death, and I wasn't down with that solution to my problems.

Now, with my legs behind me and my head in front … I could swim.

And I did, scissoring my legs to propel me along just as the current started to reverse. It must have been hitting something ahead, maybe the end of the tunnel, and doubling back, water surging as a return in this direction. It was bound to create a sort of feedback action, a nasty loop of current for me to get caught in. A great place for me to drown, if I wasn't careful.

I had no time for drowning. Kicking against the current, I swam, using my meta strength to push through the angry wall of water pushing back at me. I held my breath tightly in my lungs, not daring to let so much as a molecule of my precious air escape out my nose—which was bubbled, water threatening to wash in through my nostrils but held at bay by the breaths I'd taken and exhaled as I'd submerged. I kept my lips sealed, my lungs churning, trying to extract oxygen from the lungful I'd taken in before I'd dropped into the water.

How long could I survive like this? I didn't know an exact number, but some strong metas had survived, albeit severely brain damaged, after considerable periods with no oxygen. But they were essentially vegetables, no higher brain functions to speak of. Having no desire to go through life with the approximate intelligence of a cast member of *Jersey Shore*, I hoped I wouldn't find the limits of my air supply.

But as I kicked my legs, trying to push through the current as it washed back at me with considerable force … it did not look good.

My lungs burned in my chest as though someone had set them on fire. It was a desperate strain, keeping the air in and the water out. It started to feel like someone had parked a semi-trailer on my chest, in my chest, somewhere in the vicinity beneath my rib cage.

The water rushed on around me, pushing me ahead now that I'd broken free of the double-back eddy. I broke left at a fork in the pipe. The only reason I knew that was because I'd seen the sharp divide at the Y intersection of the tunnel, missing catching the splitting edge of corrugated metal by bare inches. That would have hurt.

I surged down the rightward path, the force of the water increasing as it sought to find its exit, the pressure ratcheting up within the confinements of metal and concrete. I was starting to feel out of control, desperate for a breath even though I probably didn't need one to survive, at least not strictly speaking, for a little while yet. The urgency remained, the hunger, the desire to feel cool air on my face as I sucked in oxygen, well … it was growing in intensity.

But all I felt around me was the cold water, pushing me forward.

The street lamps still shone in from above, shedding their anemic glow as I rushed forward in the jaws of the current. I felt a strong push as it doubled back on me again, water rushing back in my direction. I made myself as narrow as possible, trying to slip past. Either I was running into another Poseidon pushing back against me along this path or—

The answer was revealed by a dim light from above, and it was not good.

A concrete cistern waited ahead, small enough that I could see every side. The water pushed in, shoving me into this confined space and swirling in an unending whirlpool, my head caught in the center of the vortex and my legs spinning around

me.

I looked up as I twirled, caught in the roiling current. Somewhere, far above, I could see a suggestion of lamplight. Water tried to force its way into my mouth as I spun in the current. It made its way in as I thumped against a wall, hit the back of my throat and I gagged, bubbles of water blinding me for a second as the current began to spin me harder.

It was like being trapped in an industrial washing machine, the current its own agitator. It was like a vortex running around me, up becoming down, down becoming up, all sense of direction lost in the swirling miasma. There was light from above, faint and obscured beneath a thousand gallons of water and the inky stain of night.

Something slammed into my ribs, and I was pushed against a hard surface. It had the strength of metal, a latticework of unbending steel pushing against the bones in my back.

My bones … were not winning.

The water pressure was forcing me up, trying to spin me, still, but the overriding direction of the current was to force me ever upward, against the resistance of the metal guard. The sound of spray was coming from somewhere beyond, dim, like a train in the distance.

It was the end I'd feared before I'd let go back in the tunnel.

I was trapped against a grate, forced face down against it, water doing its best to find its level—through me.

Water forced itself up my nose, the bubble of air in my nostrils no longer holding it at bay as the pressure increased to insane levels. I gagged and choked, my mouth opening without my intention, more water surging in and into the back of my throat.

I was trapped, pinned, squirming, unable to find my escape. Desperation flooded me like the water, and the drowning instinct kicked in, taking over my limbs and removing all conscious thought as I flailed against unyielding steel, unable to escape as my body began to fill with water—

And I started to drown.

53.

Reed

"We are thirty minutes from the Revelen border," Greg Vansen's voice announced over the loudspeaker, coming in clear over the rush of wind around the body of the SR-71. "Course holding steady."

I sat across the table from Kat and Scott, a comfortable silence enveloping us for the last twenty minutes or so. We'd been together long enough that sharing a silence wasn't the worst thing in the world, though it was a little uncommon for Kat until recently. Scott looked a little troubled, lost in thought. Hardly a surprising thing, given what we were going into—

"Hey," Jamal said, popping his head in through the archway. He was lingering at the stairwell, a tablet computer in hand. "Y'all got a minute?"

"Sure," I said, as Kat turned her attention to him as well. Scott was still staring off into space, concentrating on … something. "What's up?"

Jamal slid in next to me, tablet lit up. "I did a little editing to the video. Figured I'd take the advice and make the presentation a little snappier, you know?"

"How's the video doing?" I asked. "Oh, right. You don't have Wi-Fi, so—"

"No, I got internet," Jamal said, a sly smile appearing, showing a few teeth. "Managed to create a direct line to the towers here in Europe, do a little encryption work as I go to keep from being detected. I'll shut it down when we get closer to the border, but for now … I'm uploading." He balanced the tablet in one hand. "Almost done, too."

"How's the first video doing?" Kat asked, leaning forward to look at the screen.

"A couple hundred views," Jamal said with a light shrug. "It's not going to go viral like that, I'm pretty sure. Lot of the debate in the comments sections—"

"You should never read the comments," Kat said, shaking her head.

"—about what's actually happening in it," Jamal said. "So, in the re-edit—check this out—"

The video started playing, showing the security camera footage from Eden Prairie that I'd already watched a couple times. This time, though …

"Here we go," Jamal said with a little hint of pride.

The time and date stamp expanded, a little graphical work that made it extra obvious when this happened. As if that were not enough, the words "**SIENNA NEALON—THE EDEN PRAIRIE INCIDENT**" were written in bold letters across the screen during a freeze-frame. They disappeared as the footage resumed.

It sure looked like a discussion was going on. A circle of the prisoners from the Cube were gathered around her, glaring hate and death, that much obvious even through the cold security camera footage. Sienna didn't seem to be too pleased with anything going on, and I could tell she was smarting off. A whole corps of press was waiting ahead of her, but …

I blinked. I hadn't really seen this before, having watched the first couple times just trying to confirm that she hadn't done anything wrong. She certainly hadn't yet; it was all talk, but the press … they were just standing there.

Motionless. Not taking pictures, not shouting questions. That never happened. They were just staring like dumb animals.

"Weird," Scott murmured across the table, still staring into space.

"It is weird," I said, as the press corps surged forward, launching into a mob attack like a pack of wild dogs. "What power is that, even?"

"Some kind of mind control that reduces people to animals?" Kat asked, watching over my shoulder. "Look at that. They are really going at her. I mean, I've always thought the press, especially the tabloids, were bad, but not this bad—wow, that one went right for her ankles."

"I think that guy is biting her on the ass," Jamal said, pointing at a reporter for the *Washington Post* that was, sure enough, about waist high on Sienna as she backpedaled from the onrushing reporters. She didn't make but a step or two before some invisible force—wind, I could tell from experience—sent her flying.

"Hmm," Scott said.

"Yeah. Damn," I said, glancing away. It was a full-blown fight now. The words, "Peaceful Protest?" popped up on the screen as it freeze framed again. I looked away as someone fired a shot and Sienna went down in a roiling torrent of hell.

"Whoa," Kat said, rubbing her hands along her upper arms. "This is good. Chills."

"I don't know that I'd call it good," I said as I glanced back. Sienna was now missing an arm, and surrounded by the "peaceful protesters." "Ugh. That's … good editing work, though."

I strained to watch as the prisoners let loose on Sienna, and things got even uglier. It was a full-on stomp fest with my sister at the center of it, and it was tough to watch. They were beating the hell out of her and then arguing, and even at the zoomed-in distance of the camera's maximum range, it wasn't hard to follow what was going on. One of them had a rifle in hand and looked like she was about to open up on my sister—

"They're going to kill her," Scott murmured.

"Yeah," I said, little chills running up and down my arm as the words, **PEACEFUL PROTESTORS?** flashed again on the screen. "Look at this. She's got a gun pointed right at Sienna. It's amazing how close they got to actually—"

"No," Scott said, standing up, knees slamming into the table and making him wince as he rose. "They're going to kill her, right now. She's in the water, I can feel her!" His eyes were wild. "I can *feel* her. She's under the city, they're flooding it and—" His eyes met mine and it was like I could see the intensity of the ocean roiling beneath them.

I didn't need to ask who he was talking. "You're sure it's—"

"It's her," he said, and his voice dropped to whisper quiet, under the noise of the aircraft around us. "She's in the water, she's trapped and …" his face twisted, and he looked me right in the eye as a chill flooded through me. "She's drowning."

54.

Sienna

The water was in my face, in my lungs, everywhere, pushing me against the unyielding grate with such strength I could feel my bones starting to give. The cracking noise and strain was audible just under the rushing of water that had flooded my ears, the hammering of my heart a distant beat as I was flooded, drowning—

It was a choking feeling, desperate, all conscious thought and control gone from my limbs as I struggled, madly, without any ability to think or plan or act for myself. Panic had set in, full force. There was nothing for me to brace on, so I flailed against the grating, unable to move it so much as a millimeter.

There was nothing peaceful about drowning, just an overriding sense of panic that I hadn't felt even when I was being beaten to death, even when I was having parts of my soul carved off. Not when I was shot nor stabbed nor even being crushed under the weight of a container once at a port.

All I could do was fight it uselessly, to feel it flooding my body, filling up my lungs and killing my ability to concentrate and think. My limbs were getting heavy, but I moved them anyway, still fighting the suffocation that would have stopped a normal human. I was beyond normal, but also beyond thought—

My lips sprang open, forced wide as something pushed them

free. The water blew out of my lungs, out of my mouth, dragging itself from me with great force.

This … did not help matters, because oxygen and air did not replace the water that left, exiting out my nose and ears at the same time as though dragged from my body by some sort of aquatic magnet. It left me just as oxygen-starved, just as flailing, only without the water weighing me down that had been there a moment earlier.

Something pushed me back down, interposing itself between me and the grate. It felt like fingers, but as I twisted in the water, nothing was there. The grate began to rattle, as though it were somehow tethered to the vibration of my own body as I continued to gyrate, the drowning instinct making me its fool.

The grate burst free and I followed, shoved out of the water, propelled as though by strong hands hidden in the chill liquid. I shot up into the air and felt the warm breath of air reach my lungs as I gasped, leaping into the dark night.

I tumbled down on a rooftop, propelled out of the deathtrap I'd been caught in and launched forcefully sideways from out of the geyser. Somehow the water broke my fall, catching me on a cushion that deflated as soon as I was safely down, rolling out of my clothes as if commanded—

"Scott," I muttered, the last of the water escaping my blouse and leaving my hair completely dry, if a little stiff. I lay on a flat rooftop, and the water rolled a few feet away to rest in a sizable puddle, all the life it had seemed to take on gone now that its job was done. I rolled to my side, watching it for signs of motion.

There were none. The spray that had carried me up here had not come from the same source as the flood that had trapped me—that had been the work of relatively unsophisticated Poseidons.

But Scott … Scott was a freaking God of Water. And he'd just saved my life from … wherever the hell he was.

"Thank you," I whispered my gratitude to the puddle, as though it could carry my thoughts to him.

It rippled slightly, though whether it was from my words or because he could hear me, there was no way to tell.

I rolled to my back, needing just a minute to recover. I stared up at the darkening sky above Revelen, wondering what the hell I should do next, staring into the falling night and wishing—so desperately—that I had any kind of home I could go to.

55.

Reed

"I got her out," Scott said, sagging against the table, almost collapsing where he stood a moment earlier. Kat caught his arm and eased him back onto the bench. "And I got the water out of her." He was nodding, slowly, and finally, he looked at me. "She's … she'll be fine. She was moving and everything, so … she'll be fine."

I chewed my lip. "I'm not sure that's so. What the hell is going on there that they're trying to drown her?"

He blinked a few times. "I don't know, but there are a whole lot of Poseidon types working in Bredoccia right now. A hundred or more—"

"Guess they've been putting that serum to good use," Jamal said.

"That's how they did it," Scott said. His normally ruddy skin was pale, like he'd wrung himself out saving Sienna. He probably had, doing it at this distance. "Reed … if they've got a hundred Poseidons there …" He leaned forward. "That can't be all they've got on hand. Can you even imagine—"

"Yeah," I said, feeling a little choked. I looked at Kat. She looked a little paler than she'd been a moment earlier, too, but she was holding it in pretty well, though she seemed to be gripping Scott's bicep just a little harder than she had before.

If they had a hundred Poseidons, which were not that common a type of metahuman …

What the hell else did they have waiting for us in Revelen?

56.

Passerini

"What am I seeing here?" Passerini asked, reviewing the footage for the second time. It was satellite imagery, and Graves had played it back for him.

"That was Sienna Nealon getting blown out of a sewer by a calculated effort," Graves said, spooling it back and replaying the ten seconds or so of film. The scene repeated itself on the big screen, a vaguely human figure flipping in 2D, then getting blown sideways out of the sewer geyser to come to rest on a rooftop, where she'd stirred only after a moment's rest. "My guess? One of her superpowered friends just saved her from that kill attempt."

"Hm. Did they do that from across the damned world?" Passerini asked, leaning to put his knuckles on the table. "From … Minnesota, right? That's where they are?"

Graves shrugged, but there was a glittering in his eyes. "I doubt it."

Passerini frowned. That didn't seem like a full answer, but it got to the core of the question. "Where are they, then?"

"No idea, sir," Graves said. "But close, I'd assume."

Passerini eyed the screen. "You think she's got people in Revelen? Unrelated to her grandfather?"

"Great-grandfather," Graves said. "And it doesn't seem out of the question, based on what we know of her … associates."

"Sounded like you were about to call them something else," Passerini said, mulling that.

Colonel Graves shifted where he stood then smiled. "Well … you have to admit, between this and that Scotland business, which sounded … immensely hairy … they seem willing to follow her anywhere."

"Loyalty," Passerini said, nodding. "That's admirable. But lots of dangerous people have inspired loyalty, colonel. Seems like this Sienna Nealon is no exception."

"She's definitely dangerous," Graves said, a little too quickly. "But it would seem to me … on the surface anyway … there's more going on here than meets the eye. Unless you believe everything the FBI says about her?" The look he gave Passerini was full of significance.

Passerini stared at Graves. It was tough to tell whether the colonel had been briefed in on what had happened in January, when the FBI had appropriated the Department of Defense's top metahuman asset and tried to use him as a battering ram to crush Sienna Nealon. That had left Passerini in the unenviable position of trying to free Colonel Warren Quincy from police custody in Minneapolis after some sort of fracas at a computer server facility. "You seem to be quite the fisherman, Colonel Graves."

"Well, I always have my ear to the ground, sir," Graves said, turning his attention back to his console.

"Oh, yeah?" Passerini stood with his arms on the back of his chair, squeezing the faux leather. Pleather? Hard to say. Passerini wasn't much of an interior decorating guy. "What do you hear coming now, Graves?"

"Trouble," Graves said, pausing from his tapping at the keyboard. Damn, he was fast. "Lots and lots of trouble. The *Theodore Roosevelt* carrier group will be in position by tomorrow night, sir. And Ramstein is launching the last flight of Raptors now. They'll tank over Poland and be in position within hours."

"Spooling up," Passerini said, with a taut feeling in his stomach. This was the first war he'd ever quarterbacked, and it was moving way too fast for his liking. With a glance at his watch, he wondered how long it would be before the first contacts. Not long, if he gave the order. Soon, he'd have to call the president, which was not something he was looking forward to. Better to postpone that a few minutes, hope the situation changed. Because there was no part of what was coming that looked like an advantage to Passerini.

But then, if there was someone who did see an advantage in a brewing war … Passerini would not have wanted to know that grim, nasty son of a bitch.

57.

Dave Kory

"There's gonna be a war," Dave singsonged under his breath as he typed, readying the headline for his piece on the alleyway thing that they'd all just watched live. Sure, the whole country had apparently seen it, but now they needed context and a chance to revisit and reframe the experience. An explainer article was just the thing to help them emotionally process the event.

Plus flashforce.net would soak up the clicks in the process. If Dave could have made it a listicle, with its myriad clicks, he would have, but the "Thirteen Times Sienna Nealon Murdered the Hell Out of People," currently up on the home page would probably fill that quotient.

"Hey, boss," someone said, and Dave kept typing. "TVs are flickering again. I think we're about to get—"

"DO NOT ADJUST YOUR TELEVISION SETS. THE FOLLOWING IS BEING BROUGHT TO YOU LIVE FROM THE NATION OF REVELEN."

"Whoa," Dave said, spinning in his chair as the picture resolved, fuzzily, into something like a traffic camera shot. There were army trucks rolling by on the street, and Dave just stared. Why would they interrupt everything for this—

"Hey, look," Sylvia Hunt said, pointing at the screen. "On that rooftop."

Dave stared. There was definitely something moving on the roof. A human figure, kinda tiny, getting slowly to its feet—

"Ermagerd," Holly Weber said, "that's her."

A little buzz ran through the office, and Dave shook his head. "Okay, okay. Who's got the live feed updates on this?"

"Yo," Steve Fills said and dove into work on his laptop.

"We're looking for story ideas, people," Dave said, smiling, staring at the live feed. "Remember—clicks. Traffic. Get people in, addict them to the narrative because it fulfills some need in them, and they'll keep coming back." He snapped his fingers and focused all his attention on the TV. "Let's do this."

58.

Lethe

"You shouldn't have left this to Krall," Lethe said, arms folded in front of her. They were standing in the Situation Room, and the reports were flooding in.

Also flooding: the storm drains. Thanks to Krall.

"Yes, I should go out there myself and lead a manhunt while we ratchet up to war with the most powerful nation the world has ever known," Hades said, smarting off without thinking as he stared at the map table. He sent her a sly smile without moving much. "That would be the best use of my time, you think?"

"Well, you were never much of a strategic thinker, so … yeah, probably," Lethe said.

"We can't all claim as much battlefield experience as you, my daughter," Hades said. "Which reminds me—I finally saw *Wonder Woman* while you were gone."

"And?" Lethe asked, impatience gnawing at her to get back to the discussion at hand.

"She reminded me of you, with the World War I business," Hades said. "And the idealism."

"I lost my idealism a long time ago," Lethe said, arms wrapping more tightly around her ribcage.

"I am not so sure of that," Hades said, straightening his back and rising off the table to face her. "What is your objection to sending Krall to handle this business with Sienna?"

"Krall is going to do her level best to kill Sienna," Lethe said. "That is my objection."

Hades blinked a couple times. "Of course she is. You didn't think I knew this when I sent her? You think I am blind in my advancing age?"

Lethe did some blinking of her own. "You knew Krall was going out there to kill her … and you sent her anyway? After my only granddaughter? Nearly the last of your line?"

Hades just shrugged with one shoulder, as though this topic were not worthy of two shoulders of shrug. "Did you think the time of testing was over merely because she was here?"

"Yes," Lethe said, "I assumed that if you made her crown princess, the testing was over."

"Well, it is not," Hades said.

"That's damned cold."

"Why?" Hades asked, seeming genuinely perplexed. "I gave her every advantage. She refused the serum. Had she taken it, this would all be trivial, yes? Perhaps she will learn from this experience. Or … Krall will kill her." He turned back to the table and leaned down. "I think I am getting to the age where I might need reading glasses. Can you see what this says? I can't tell if it's a smudge or I'm actually going blind." He moved his finger over the table. "Oh. Hah. It's a smudge. Whew."

"I didn't want your serum, either," Lethe said. Rage was simmering behind her eyes, but she was very adept at keeping her feelings to herself by now.

"Yes, well, perhaps you, too, will regret that decision before the end," Hades said without giving her so much as a look. "She will be fine. Or she won't. Her loyalties are suspect." He flicked a glance at Lethe, then toward a monitor that showed a display of Bredoccia. "A night on the town … that's what young people like to do with their time, isn't it?" He grinned. "See the sights? Have adventures? Why, she's practically in her element now. Probably much less uncomfortable than she was hanging out up here with aging relatives. It's almost like home for her now, hm?"

Lethe ground her teeth and looked away. "You can be a real

bastard sometimes, Dad."

"Frequently, yes," Hades said. "I think a night in the doghouse, being hunted … it will be good for her." He waved a hand toward the Bredoccia skyline. "A tour of the city under her own power. Perhaps she will see the Dauntless Tower up close, hm? See the crowning jewel of what we have achieved here. And at dawn, we will see which of them returns. Her or Krall."

Lethe just stared at him for a long moment. "Are you still testing me? My loyalties?"

Hades cocked an eyebrow at her. "Do I need to?"

"You keep this shit up, you just might." She turned her back on him as he turned, seemingly without care for what had just transpired, and went back to studying his maps.

59.

Sienna

It was like being back home again, complete with being chased by people who wanted to kill me.

Ah, Revelen. This was how I'd always figured it would be coming here. So nice to have things play to my expectations.

Not.

I flexed everything as I got to my feet on the rooftop, taking my sweet time. My body was reading out damage reports with every ache and pain, and they were extensive if not heavy. Lots of minor things—a tweaked neck, a muscle pain in my right thigh and right butt cheek (from landing on them, I assumed).

Nothing major. Yay.

Downside: I didn't have any weapons. And an unarmed Sienna was an unhappy Sienna. Especially when she was being pursued by metas. I flexed my right hand. That hurt, too. Either I'd dragged it along the tunnel edge or landed on it, probably the latter because it felt more like bone pain or bruising and there was no evidence of scrapes or lacerations.

"Another exciting day in the life of Sienna Nealon," I said, looking around. The skyline of Revelen was everywhere around me, from the several-story apartment buildings that dotted what looked like the majority of the old town to the sprawling new high-rises that were starting to take over a significant chunk of the real estate in downtown. "Why doesn't anyone ever run a profile on me that talks about the glamorous life of a superhero?" I flexed my back, which was tight and achy, probably from the rough landing. "Oh, right. Because it sucks to be me."

I looked around a little more. Staying still wasn't going to do me any good, not for very long at least. With an entire army on my trail, I was pretty well destined to have to leave here soon.

The problem was, which way should I even go? Without some drive to go in a specific direction, I could just as easily lay down right here and what the hell difference would it make?

I cracked my back. Was this what getting old felt like? All these aches and pains?

Nah. This was just what being Sienna felt like.

A whine in the distance caused me to perk my ears up. It sounded strange, mechanical. I couldn't place the sound, though it was vaguely familiar. I frowned, concentrating. It was either quiet or distant, and I couldn't decide which.

The question was answered for me a moment later as a quad-copter drone popped up above the edge of the rooftop across the street, four rotors buzzing and a little camera glinting at me in the street lights.

"Aw, hell," I said, turning to make a break for it as it shot toward me. Not even a doubt if it had seen me; its unerring path in my direction made me certain it had.

I broke into a run, heading across the rooftop. I was in the old town, with its level rooftops spreading out in front of me for a mile or so. I could maybe out-deke this thing until I found something appropriately heavy to throw at it. Knock it out of the sky, then I'd be down to worrying about hiding again—

Another drone erupted from the alley ahead, and I halted my forward momentum with a slide that ended with me catching myself by the fingertips before going completely over the side.

Okay. That direction was out.

I looked right, set to surge that way. It also presented flat rooftops, with just a little variation. I could parkour, I could run, I could jump, maybe escape that way—

A few shapes appeared in the distance, over the rooftops, and for a second I mistook them for drones.

Nope.

They were flying soldiers with rifles.

"Sonofa," I said, all the air bursting out in a hopeless sigh. "I have had about enough of this Übermensch army shit."

Only one direction left to run. I turned my head and started to go that way, emitting another mental sigh as I did so.

Downtown.

I was heading downtown.

And the rooftops I could safely jump were going to run out in the not too distant future, leaving me with an unenviable choice.

Surrender, leaving myself to the tender mercies of General Krall and, perhaps, if I survived those, eventually, my grandmother and great-grandfather, and whatever that entailed.

Or maybe a leap somewhere ahead that there was no way I was going to be able to make, followed by a fall that I might not be able to survive.

"Yep," I muttered, leaping from the edge of my rooftop to the next, clearing it with ease in spite of a six-foot differential in heights—not in my favor. "This is why they don't make a glamorous 'day in the life' documentary on me." I pumped my arms and legs, taking my speed up to full as the sweat started to roll unasked down my forehead, sprinting through the warm, Revelen night. "I've never had a glamorous damned day in my life."

60.

"The only easy day was yesterday." That was the motto of the Navy SEALs, and I kept repeating that thought because damn if it didn't hold the ring of truth. Except yesterday wasn't so easy, either, because I'd gotten my ass handed to me by General Krall, the spider-monkey. And if we were looking to the day before, well, that had been one where I'd woken up in a prison hospital in America after a different ass-kicking—

Actually, looking back … yeah, there hadn't really been any easy days for a while.

I leapt another rooftop, the gradual rise as we got closer to downtown becoming a growing worry. The next roof ahead looked like it was across an avenue and at least a story higher. I gauged it at a ten-foot change in altitude after a fifty-foot jump. With a six-story drop if I missed it.

No pressure.

"I really, really miss you, Gavrikov," I said as I took a deep breath and leapt for my life, legs pinwheeling in empty air as though I could run without a surface.

I hit the side of the building like a bug on a windshield, fingers clawing at the lip that surrounded the rooftop. I managed to gain purchase, but the impact of my body against the wall jarred me. Thankfully not enough to make me relinquish my grip, but the second of falling panic definitely reminded me that a) I was alive and b) that whole alive thing? A very tenuous proposition.

Clamping my fingers down on the edge, I used my feet to do the heavy climbing, leaping in a flip as though the edge of the rooftop were a gymnastics bar. I came down in a roll and didn't stop to reflect on the terrible, terrible life choices that had led me to being chased across an Eastern European rooftop by drones and flying supermen with guns. Because it was self-evident that said choices were indeed terrible if they'd led me here.

I alighted my gaze on the rooftop ahead. It was a two-story hop up, at least a twenty-foot vertical climb from the one I was on. Getting closer, legs pumping as they carried me toward the growing chasm, it started to look as though whatever cross-street was below was some sort of freeway, the gulf of air between the buildings enormous.

I looked left, then right. The flyers were closing on me, rifles in hand. There had to be a good dozen of them just in view on those sides. A couple were smiling. They had the lay of the land before, had realized what I was running myself into.

A dead end. Or just me being dead, and thus, the end.

"Motherf—" I grunted, kicking my speed up to absolute maximum. My legs were pinwheeling with constant fury, and I didn't think that I could have run any faster if Death itself was nipping at my heels. Which … technically was now sort of true, if only by proxy, since his ass had likely stayed at the castle, the bastard. He could have at least had the basic courtesy to hunt me down and kill me himself.

No. Maybe he hadn't intended the killing part. I could believe—rather easily—that Krall was taking the initiative on this. The alternative was believing that the last family I had on this planet, other than Reed, was trying to murder the shit out of me.

Then again, given what my mother did when I was a kid … maybe that wasn't so hard of a leap. Unlike what waited ahead of me.

The gaping chasm loomed ahead, the next building rising high as if to taunt me. *You can't make it,* it seemed to say, adding in the *Neener neener neener!* that kids use to taunt when something was particularly vicious or out of reach. Okay, maybe it didn't do that, but I added it myself in my head because—this gap.

Yeah. There was no way in hell I was going to be able to make this jump. And even if I did, a building or two ahead was a fifteen- or twenty-story residential tower that was all glass surfaces. And me without my Spider-man powers. (No, I never had Spider-man powers, it's a joke, come on, keep up.)

Couldn't go left. Couldn't go right. Couldn't go back.

Forward and up was going to result in me going forward and down, hard, so …

Might as well go forward and down, but softly.

The flyers on my left and right were shouting at me to desist or something, and I did the full Sienna and just ignored the hell out of their intelligent, reasoned shouts to not leap off a building to certain death.

Mostly because I had plans to make sure it did not turn into certain death.

To my left, the flyer was waving me off, a slightly panicked look in his eyes. Maybe they did still want me alive, because he didn't have his rifle pointed at me. Or maybe he just personally objected to someone committing suicide in front of his eyes. A main thoroughfare ran beneath him, another nice long gap between my building and the one past him.

That was out.

The flyer to my right did have his rifle in hand, but he was a little farther out and less panicked than the left-most guy. These two were out in front of the pack, presumably to herd me, though a look over my shoulder confirmed there were more following after them. If they really wanted to end it, a storm of bullets from those rifles they were carrying would do it in a hot second.

Yeah. So I wasn't under death warrant—yet. Maybe Krall's orders didn't actually include murdering me.

Well, I still didn't intend to go gently into this not-so-awesome night. To my right, there was a much narrower gap between buildings, but the one beyond mine was taller, too. A story or so, a leap I could easily make, but …

I was so sick of the running and jumping thing.

Veering right, I charged toward the flyer, who did a dodge of his own, trying to maintain distance between us. I poured on the speed, my legs numbly pounding as I went at him. He soared backward, trying to cover me, drawing a bead—

And slammed into the building behind him, hard.

I grimaced as he hit; it was not the sort of hit you'd see someone survive without injury unless maybe they were in full football pads. He was not, and took the full brunt of the impact, thumping hard and going limp, dropping into the alley.

"Shit," I said as I reached the edge and leapt, but gently, heading down. I caught him with one hand, getting his sleeve as I kicked out, hitting the building's stonework with a foot and arresting my momentum—and his—freezing in mid-air for a split second.

Then I turned, kicked off and did a little drop about ten feet, the flyer's wrist clutched tightly in hand. It was a manageable drop, and I landed a foot on a windowsill, turning my ankle just a little in the process. I did another spin, a one-eighty to face the opposite wall, and pushed off, taking the next stage of the fall in a twenty-foot increment and bouncing off a section of solid brick.

It took me about five bounces before I landed in the alley, the flyer's arm clutched limply as I delivered him to the ground, unharmed except for what his dumb ass had done to himself in crashing into the building. "Sorry," I said to his insensate form as he stirred in response to making landfall on the alley floor. I started to rip his rifle off his shoulder but a round of gunfire peppered the ground around me and I was forced to break for it, cursing madly as I bolted for the mouth of the alley.

There was no cover in the alley, I realized as I burst out onto the main road ahead, and I must have subconsciously decided that going for cover by reaching the corner of the building was the best option. These were the decisions that ran through my head, so many years of training driven in and reinforced to the point where they were written into my programming.

A concrete and grass park waited ahead, spreading out over the block to my right, tall, old trees sticking out every fifty feet or so providing some cover. The other three corners of this intersection were all spanned by tall buildings, not a door in sight. The gunfire behind me had stopped, the army flyers apparently enforcing a dictate to keep me from becoming armed by shooting at me. Well, it had worked, but I was not exactly excited at being chased by them without any way to respond or get them off my back.

I needed a moment to breathe, a moment think, a moment to plan.

And then I saw it.

Past the park, rising up out of the ground, was the Dauntless Tower, lights within giving me a little sparkle of hope in what was otherwise a dark and hopeless night.

It wasn't the best cover I'd ever seen, but when the flyers overflew me, shouting, I realized I was running short of great options. Try and find an entrance to any of the residential-looking buildings on the other three corners, or make a break for the biggest building in town?

I headed for the tower, hauling ass across the empty road under the cover of the trees in the park as I headed for the tallest building around, not really sure what I'd do once I got there.

61.

Dave Kory

"Wow," Caden Chambers said, voice soft across the crowd. They'd all just watched the descend-off-the-walls drop of Sienna Nealon down the alleyway in Bredoccia, a couple of flying meta soldiers in hot pursuit. "Why don't they just shoot her?"

Dave stirred in his chair, glancing sideways at the click counter for the LIVE UPDATES post on the website. It was climbing steadily, people probably sitting on their couches and reading their phones as they watched this live, seeking context. "Add that question to the piece, Steve," Dave said, looking back to the screen. The shot had changed; now it was overlooking a city park, and Nealon disappeared between the boughs of some tall trees, running at a superhuman clip. "If you're asking it, our readers are asking it. What's the answer?" This he asked aloud, crowdsourcing it to those in attendance rather than bothering to divert his attention from the click counter and the Sienna Nealon livestream playing out on the TV.

"Well, you said it's her grandfather running the place—" Holly Weber said.

"Great-grandfather," Steve said.

"Whatever," Holly said. "So maybe he doesn't want her dead? Maybe she just ... snuck out of her room to hang out with a boy or something, and he's really hacked off at her." That prompted a wave of snickers.

"I've got a better question," Mike Darnell said. "What are they going to do when they catch her? Because they may have shot at her, but it doesn't like they're aiming to kill."

Dave shrugged. The click counter was still moving up, though a little less swiftly than before. It made sense; everyone was watching live rather than surfing the web. "Can we stream this on our site?" he asked, looking for assurance from someone in the technical side of things. "Pick up a live feed somehow?"

Caden blinked a couple times. "I'll see if whoever's doing this is putting it out on any of the major sites. If so … yeah, we can probably just jack it. It's a pirate feed onto these channels anyway, broadcast without their consent, though they'd obviously run it voluntarily if they could. We could probably get it going on flashforce."

"So this is definitely a pirate broadcast?" Dave asked.

"Oh, yeah." Caden pointed at the corner of the screen. "No network logo."

Dave frowned. How had he not noticed that? Too much on his mind. "Right. Well, get it up on the site, however you have to. We might as well get the traffic if people are going to watch it anyway. Probably a lot of cord-cutters out there that'd like to see it and can't, for now."

Caden nodded. "On it."

"So why aren't they shooting her?" Dave asked, turning back to the discussion that had been going on while he was working on the tech question. "Why not just end her once and for all? Bullet to the head, boom, no more Sienna Nealon problems, bye-bye world?"

"Gotta be that grandpa doesn't want her dead," Holly said.

"Great-grandpa," Steve said.

"Get laid, Steve, you incel prick," Holly said. "Great-grandpa. Whatever. The point remains."

"Hm," Dave said, rubbing his chin. He looked over the crew; everyone was kinda nodding along with what Holly had said. "Love, then? That's the angle we're pitching? He's not having his army kill her because he loves her, she's just pissed him off? Or is running and causing chaos in his capitol for the fun of it?" His gaze fell on Mike, who wasn't nodding, who was just … watching the screen. "What do you think, Mike?"

Mike stirred, hand on his chin moving. "Hard to say. But you wouldn't think a guy who was once called the God of Death would have a lot of warm spots in his heart, even for his own blood."

"Dude, it's his great-granddaughter," Steve said.

"Who he hasn't ever tried to talk to up to now, near as we can tell," Mike said. "He's apparently run his own country for a while, she's been on the lam for years, and just this week he decided to invite her over?" He shook his head. "Something's fishy here. Too much going on, lots of dirt to sift out to find the nuggets of truth in this mess."

"What do you mean?" Dave asked. Suddenly he was glad he hadn't fired Mike. That feeling probably wouldn't last, but for now … there it was.

"We've got a war that looks like it's about to kick off," Mike said, ticking off points on his finger, "we've got a prison break, we've got Sienna Nealon, we've got the return of Hades, we've got Revelen becoming a nuclear power. That's a confluence of an awful lot of stuff. There are things going on in the background we're not seeing. Have to be. So … there's a lot to sift through. Who's doing what and why?"

"At least we know the where and most of the how," Dave said, trace of a smile flaring up. Even a broken clock was right twice a day, and on this, Mike seemed right. "But you're spot on, man. We don't even know what we don't know. Someone should write a piece on that. You want to?"

Mike shook his head. "I've got some other stuff I'm working on. Waiting on a call."

"Suit yourself," Dave said, and nodded at one of the raised hands, someone volunteering. "Make it a listicle, will you?" He glanced at the click counter. "Our traffic is sagging with this going on. Need to take advantage of every click we can get until we've got it going live."

62.

Sienna

I sent a rock crashing through the glass doors of the Dauntless Tower and came following a second behind like soccer moms charging into a 50% off Lululemon yoga pants sale. The flyers were right on my trail, and my little maneuver had forced them to swoop low to follow me into the glass lobby of the crown jewel of my great-grandfather's burgeoning city. It was all done up in steel and chrome, the sort of thing that wouldn't have looked out of place in any major American city.

"No, no, no," I muttered as I charged forward, looking for a direction to go. The lobby was ten stories high, dominated by a set of elevator banks that spanned the entire height of the place and disappeared into the ceiling where the upper floors began. A flash of motion behind one of them told me that the army flyers were already circling the building, establishing a perimeter now that they'd bottled me up.

Which was fine. Not actually fine, but rather the kind of "fine" a girlfriend is when she's about to unleash hell on her boyfriend. Or so I'm told. I have totally never done that kind of thing to Harry.

"Well, okay," I muttered and broke for the elevator bank as someone flew into the lobby behind me. The squeal of tires outside heralded the arrival of the rest of the army, and that wasn't good, either. "This is like a metaphor for my last two years." I bolted for the nearest elevator and when I hit the button, it instantly dinged. "No Muzak, no Muzak, please don't have Muzak—"

The first strains of "The Girl From Ipanema" in Muzak form reached my ears as I dashed into the elevator. "Damn!" I hammered the button for the top floor, because—well, I didn't see any other viable alternatives. Then I hit the button for the floor three below the top. That was where I'd get out. And swiftly press the elevator close button as I did so.

Wait. No. Even better, I'd climb out of the elevator now and leap out in the shaft, then force my exit from one of the middle floors, then—

"Aw, shit," I said, and the real truth of my predicament came hammering down on me right then. Because this really was a metaphor for my last two years.

I'd run and run and run, mostly without thinking, and now here I was, in an elevator, heading to the top of the tallest building in Bredoccia, the entire Revelen army on my tail.

What the hell was I going to do from here? Leap off and hope to survive by dint of the legs of my capris ballooning out to save me? (They weren't that spacious, to be honest.)

I bumped against the back wall of the elevator as I tried to tune out the irritating sound of the Muzak. Man, everything had gotten so muddled. The elevator box was not dissimilar to the one my mom used to stick me in. The parallels to my life abounded. At least there was symmetry.

I needed a moment to think about what I really wanted. A moment to plan so that I could extract the best possible outcome from all this. A moment to just … breathe.

The elevator dinged on the third from top floor, and as the doors opened I saw three soldiers with guns standing out there, waiting, a shattered window looming behind them.

No time to breathe.

No time to think.

No time to plan.

As per usual, I wasn't going to get anything from my wish list. I rolled some of the tension out of my shoulders as I locked eyes with the lead one, and reloaded my fists Henry Cavill-style as I stepped out onto the floor. A moment later the elevator door slid closed behind me, and I let out a quick sigh.

Yeah. This whole thing was a metaphor for my life.

"So …" I asked, staring down the barrel of three rifles, "… who wants to go first?"

63.

Passerini

"What does that look like to you?" Passerini asked. They were watching the satellite imagery of the big building in downtown Revelen, the one Sienna Nealon had just disappeared into. A load of army trucks had pulled up just after her, and now the soldiers were swarming the place, disappearing into the lobby like ants into an anthill.

"Well, they're establishing a perimeter," Graves said, peering at the screen in concentration. He was still at his console, making minute adjustments to bring the satellite picture around a little here and there, switch the lenses to infrared for a second. All this, projected on the big screen so they could stare at it while Passerini waited for the army and air force to finish dickering about their part in the Joint Task Force. Navy, of course, was done.

"A pretty flexible one, but yes," Passerini said. He had his arms folded in front of him; he'd already decided what was likely to happen next based on what he was seeing. "You see that thin thread running from the truck on the east side to the building itself …? And the guys working around it?"

Graves stared at it for a second, then did a double take.

He must have seen it, Passerini figured. "That's detonating cord," Passerini said, enjoying the chance to spell things out for the younger man. He was army, he probably hadn't worked demolitions at any point. Passerini's family had a construction background, and he'd spent a little time hanging around the SEAL teams. As much as a pilot could get away with.

"They're wiring the building to blow," Graves said, almost a whisper.

"That's right," Passerini said, noting the sudden, dramatic paling on Graves's face. "You're not getting emotionally involved in this little chase drama, are you, son?"

"Maybe just a little," Graves said, and hell if he didn't sound like he was about to choke.

64.

Sienna

"I am going to kick the ever-loving asses off you and everyone else who comes at me," I said, talking a lot of shit but not really sure how I was going to back it up given I was pigeonholed on the top floor of a freaking tower, being held dead to rights by three guys with guns who could fly—

Oh. Duh. Obvious answer.

Kick the ass of a flyer and make him fly you away. Obvious, really. How did I not see that before?

Right. No time to think, breathe or plan. Running on minimal sleep and maximal beatings the last few days. Actually, had I gone to sleep naturally without being pounded into unconsciousness any time these last few days? The last time I could remember achieving natural sleep had been the night before my "trial." And that had followed a pretty brutal night in which I'd passed out sitting upright in Ariadne's kitchen for all of an hour or two before …

Whatever. Before I did what Sienna does. What I was about to do now.

Kick ass. Take names. Beat the shit out of a flying man and make him take me away from this horseshit country to a possibly slightly less horseshit country where I'd be welcome. There had to be an African republic somewhere that could find some use for a sarcastic, superpowered enforcer.

"Okay, boys," I said, raising my hands and stepping out of the elevator as they closed on me, rifles leveled, "looks like you got me."

The first of them did the stupid thing that I hoped one of them would and stepped closer to poke at me with the barrel, as though getting closer would somehow make the bullet kill me faster. I didn't have the heart to tell him that five feet of distance wouldn't make a difference in the velocity, but it would make a hell of a difference in what I could do to him.

One of his compatriots seemed to realize it, too, shouting just a little too late.

First rule of getting shot at: don't get shot at.

Second rule of getting shot at, to be used if you fail rule number one: get out of the way of the bullets, if possible.

Don't ask me for a third rule, because it's pretty dicey if you get to this stage.

My strategy was to work hard on rule number two, because I was forever failing rule one in my life. I'd just sort of accepted that I was going to be shot at, it was part of the "being Sienna" package, and I was just trying to cope with it in my own way. Which was to grab the barrel of the rifle and get "off-line" or "off-axis," meaning the hell out of the way of the bullets.

I locked my elbow and pushed, and shoved the gun barrel away as the soldier let loose with a few rounds from sheer panic at having someone grab his gun. He still had control over the trigger and stock, but he wasn't going to be able to shoot me, which was kind of a bonus for me since I really didn't want to get shot right now.

Carefully positioning myself between the soldier and his two comrades, I yanked him a step forward, always working to keep him as a shield so his buddies wouldn't riddle me with holes while I was disarming him. He lost his balance and staggered, loosing a few more rounds with a thundering series of gunshots. The barrel was hot in my hand, but I didn't dare let go.

I brought around an elbow and jacked the dude in the jaw, hearing a satisfying crack as he wobbled and started to lose consciousness. His knees failed him, and he began to sag down.

Uh oh. That was my shield. I was short and all, but even I couldn't hide behind him if he hit the ground.

So I kicked him in the gut and sent him flying into the dudes behind him by applying a little shove and spin at the point of my foot. I held onto his gun as he went sailing, and he let it go because he was fully out. By the time he smashed into his two buddies and they went tumbling across the floor in a conjoined pile of limbs, his eyes were closed and he was evidencing no reaction to the bump, boom, slam that his body was making as he rolled with them.

Not content to watch them roll, I ran after them, delivering a hard rifle butt to the jaw of one of the soldiers as he started to fight his way back to his feet. The other got his sling tangled in the mass of limbs and tried to raise his gun to shoot me but snagged it, discharging a burst into the ceiling.

I didn't want to chance getting shot, and I wasn't quite to the point where I was ready to start killing these Revelen soldiers, so I dove for cover behind a nearby end table. It was lousy cover, but honestly, I wasn't thinking super hard and I was probably just going to launch it at him anyway rather than risk killing him by shooting back.

Reaching the table, I sent it flying at him with a kick, and it clanged against his rifle, knocking it free and sending a few more shots in various directions. I heard the muffled thump of bullets burying themselves in the ceiling, in the wall past me, even a couple shattering the massive windows that looked out over Bredoccia. The crinkling glass panes fell out as though someone had tossed something through them, twinkling with the reflection of the city lights as they fell out of sight.

I rose as the soldier's rifle clattered, bringing my own to my shoulder. He had a pretty pissed-off look on his face, but his hands were squarely at his side.

"Don't," I said, eyeing the pistol he had on his belt. One of his hands was inches away—

He went for it.

"Dammit, I said don't!" I fired my rifle, aiming over the sights at his shoulder. It was not among the smartest ideas, shooting someone you didn't want to kill, because bullets had a way of ignoring your intent and just fulfilling their mission, which was to rip through whatever you pointed them at, to hell with the consequences. Fortunately for him, I missed. Aiming for the outside of your target in a life or death battle? Dumb move.

The soldier did a drop to his knees, spinning and pirouetting as he drew his pistol. It would have been a cool move if it had been in a John Woo movie.

Here, it just looked stupid, and while he was doing it, I took a couple steps closer and heaved my rifle at him, butt-first, like a javelin.

Yeah, throwing away your rifle is stupid, too, especially when your opponent is shooting at you. I was just full of idiocy today, trying to save the lives of these soldiers. It felt stupidly noble, with heavy emphasis on the "stupid" part. Trying not to kill people who were killing me … well, it was a good way to get dead, and I really struggled with why I was doing it.

Oh, right. Because they probably wouldn't have chosen, "Go after Sienna Nealon," from the mission list if they'd been given a choice. Orders were orders, though, and I could respect that. It was only when people voluntarily chose to come after me that I lost all respect for their intelligence.

As he came around and started to aim at me, my rifle crashed into his nose and broke it, doing some pretty severe damage to his face in the process. He dropped his pistol, because remembering to shoot someone when you've just had your maxilla broken is tough. Blood was squirting down his upper lip and down onto his chin, and he tipped his head back, apparently forgetting he was mid-fight.

I clocked him, finishing things up, then slid his insensate body across the floor once I was sure he didn't have any other guns secreted on his person. I sent his buddies after him once I'd checked them for weapons and consciousness and contented myself they had neither by the time I was through. They were out because I'd clobbered them before, and they were weaponless after I finished my search because I confiscated their pistols, gun belts, rifles and knives.

Taking a quick assessment, I found I had three rifles of the

German G-36 variety and three Glock 17 variant pistols. Which was fortunate, because I was well schooled with all of them. It wouldn't have been the worst thing in the world if Revelen's army had gone the Russian route, with Makarov pistols and the new AK-74M, but I was less fond of them, especially the Makarovs.

"You couldn't have been on the cutting edge, Hades, and upgraded to the new HK416," I muttered under my breath as I pondered the next part of my plan, which involved waking one of these yahoos up with gentle slaps to the cheek and forcing him to do my evil bidding. I played with the G-36 sling in my hands as I squatted, the rifle on the ground, adjusting the strap length, trying to decide whether I needed to tighten it to the point where if I got washed through the sewers, I wouldn't lose it. Not that I'd get washed through sewers again, but you just never knew what—

The explosion was loud and long, and shook the floor beneath my feet. I reached to stabilize myself as the ground beneath me shifted at a subtle angle, the G-36 I'd just been playing with sliding out of reach, along with the other two. The Glocks went, too, except for the one I'd put in a holster on my belt.

Balance shifted again, the floor dropping a few feet. I let out a little cry; I didn't have time to be self-conscious, because I realized what had happened—

That asshat General Krall had just blown up the tower.

The ground rumbled and pitched, and everything tilted sideways in a sick and sudden twisting of the world around me. The building was collapsing on itself, but it was also going sideways, and I started to slide toward the busted windows along with the three soldiers who had tried to clobber me. They were coming to in various states of panic as the building came down.

"Oh—" one of them said, spitting out an exclamation, probably some choice local profanity and grabbing his closest bud. They swept out the open window as the ground lurched into view outside, the entire structure toppling in that direction.

He disappeared, flying up and out of sight, leaving me behind with one guy who was just coming out of it, nothing to arrest my slide toward the busted windows. The ground was rushing up at us; the top of the tower where we were had apparently dropped off. We were gaining speed, hurtling toward a series of apartment buildings whose rooftops I could see with increasing clarity.

"SHIT!" the last remaining soldier said as we free-falled. My right hand was the last thing that had even a tentative grasp on anything, and it was basically just touching the slick, glass tile floor, no leverage or grip to amount to anything. I could maybe shove off, but that wasn't going to do me one lick of good.

"Hey, you mind—" I shouted, trying to be heard over the rumble of the building coming down around our ears.

He didn't hear me. If he saw me, it was with wide, panicked eyes as he came back to himself and realized he was about five seconds from slamming into the earth at terminal velocity, the kind of speed that guarantees even a metahuman is going to splatter like a bug under a boot on impact.

The last soldier—my last damned hope—shot up and out the window visible beyond the elevator corridor in which I'd been standing, bursting through the residual glass windows like they weren't even there. I caught a little glittering of shards as he shot through, thought maybe I heard a curse of pain, and then that sucker was gone, disappearing into the night.

"Well, shit," I said, turning my attention back down to the narrowing view of Bredoccia's rooftops as the top of the Dauntless Tower came rushing down to impact. It had to be a twenty-story fall, and not the sort of thing I could survive. Even still, I wrapped my arms around myself and tucked my legs in, going full into the fetal position as I plummeted the last few hundred feet, nothing but air surrounding me—

65.

Reed

"They've got Sienna cornered," Jamal said, frowning as he stared at his phone. "Pulling from a few reports here, but it's all being broadcast live. Some kind of pirate takeover of the networks. Someone's hijacking the feed and deciding which security vids to show." He frowned. "Hang on. It's delayed a little. I've got a finger on the source. Let me switch to live—"

The screen changed up, and suddenly I was looking at an office building, where Sienna was kneeling over some military rifles, a few crumpled soldiers about twenty feet from her in a pile. She looked like she was gun shopping or something, messing around with a sling—

"That's our girl," Kat said under her breath. "I shop designer handbags, she shops designer weapons."

"Tools of your respective trades," Scott said with a wistful smile. That got a short laugh out of Kat.

"What the hell happened that's got her on the run is my question," I said. "First we get Scott's drowning thing, now—"

"Uh oh," Jamal said, and the feed flickered out as the entire camera lurched, then went black.

It snapped back to the view of the tower, the exterior shot, and …

The tower was coming down. A cloud of dust and demolition waste was billowing out, and the building lurched at the bottom, the first ten stories collapsing in on themselves.

"Holy shit," Scott breathed.

The rest of the tower didn't follow that pattern, though. About halfway up, the supports snapped, and the top half started to tilt, radically, to the right. It broke away from the rest of the building, falling sideways like it was London Bridge, falling down.

"Dear God," Kat said.

I didn't even realize I was on my feet. "Where is she in there, Jamal?"

"I don't know," he said, finger flashing with electricity into the port of his phone. "Trying to narrow it—third floor from top!"

Scott was ashen, staring up at me with wide-eyes. "Can you feel her from here?"

I swallowed, ignoring him. I was going to really have to concentrate in order to even have a chance to—

66.

Dave Kory

"Wow," Caden said as the tower came crashing down in Bredoccia, the cloud of dusting billowing up on the screen as they watched through this pirate broadcast, "I guess that kinda kills the point of the, 'Sienna Nealon is Fighting Her Way Through Eastern Europe and People on the Internet Are Not Having It,'" article, huh?"

"No, keep going with it," Dave said, watching the dust cloud rise over the city. The broadcast had switched to a camera a mile or more away. They'd watched the top of the building come off and slam down, and Dave had gotten a vaguely sick feeling in his stomach seeing it. It was like a natural disaster, only one with an unnatural cause: Sienna Nealon. "I mean, we might as well run it since it's almost done. Just make sure you get at least six tweets pulled into the story to substantiate the 'people on the internet are not having it' part of the lede."

"Am I the only one that thinks this is kind of a shame?" Holly said, eyes glued to the TV. She had a face that was too small for her head. "I mean, I was just starting to respect the hell out of her. She was really fighting—"

Actual boos came from her co-workers, causing Dave to blink, then smile. Holly shrugged, but her face was beet red. Someone even hissed. "This is Sienna Nealon we're talking about," Dave said, still smiling. These reporters were mostly kids. A lot of them didn't know shit, and it often showed. "Don't go feeling sorry for her. Look at all the people she's done shit to. Oppressed. She's not worth your pity."

"Yeah, I guess," Holly said, looking around with genuine contrition. "Still … story over."

"That's the real shame in this," Dave said, taking a deep breath. The dust cloud was a little less pronounced over Bredoccia, spreading out from the point of impact. "Along with the civilian casualties, I guess. We should write something up about that at some point, since it looks like this is Sienna Nealon's fault. Add it to her total." He snapped his fingers. "We need a death tally for her. Someone get to work on that. I wish we'd had it live during the chase, that would have been great, add to it as she—"

"DO NOT ADJUST YOUR TELEVISION SETS," the mechanical voice came again. "STAY TUNED … FOR MORE."

"More?" Dave asked, leaning forward, his chair squeaking beneath him. "More what? Are they going to launch into funeral coverage now? Because no one could survive that shit right there, not even her." He just smiled, shook his head. This was what he was here for, to provide leadership, guidance, and occasionally call bullshit when he saw it. "She's dead. Write it up. I want it on the front page in ten minutes. No—five."

There was a stir at that, the spell of TV broken, as they started to get back to their jobs. Dave watched them go, and realized—they'd just seen a moment of history made.

And now they needed to explain what just happened to the world … because that was the job.

67.

Sienna

"Ouch."

Yeah.

Didn't die.

I came to in the middle of the fallen building's debris field, not hurting too bad considering the Dauntless Tower had come around my damned ears. And after a fifty-story plunge, too.

The answer to how I was alive seemed obvious, given what had happened to me tonight already:

"Reed," I breathed. "Thanks, bro."

The wind didn't whisper to me in answer, but I didn't need it to.

Still … ouch. My back had a little ache to it where I lay across a mound of shattered concrete and rebar. An enormous pillar lay to my right, crushed pieces of concrete and sections of torn-up carpet dotting the ruin. I lay in the middle of it all, not so much as a stray piece of rubble across me thanks to my brother.

I spared a thought for Reed, who must be somewhere relatively close if he'd just spared me a deadly fall. Scott, too, saving me from that drain trap the way he had.

They were coming for me.

Again.

I pushed a piece of rebar away from my leg and it clanged,

making a little more noise than I wanted it to. My ears were ringing, so I couldn't tell how loud it actually was, but I didn't really want to draw attention to myself. Shit.

"Did you hear something?" A voice came from not far off, and I froze, looking around with darting eyes to find some sort of cover. There was a pretty large section of concrete sticking up at a low angle about a dozen feet away and resting on a huge girder, creating a little pocket of open space. I rolled swiftly under it, moving a couple chunks of block and a piece of stray carpet out of my way. That done, I propped the carpet up so that I could look out of a little gap from beneath the concrete pillar.

A non-English response filtered down to me, followed by laughter.

"I'm never going to adapt to speaking your language," the first voice said, still positively shaking with mirth. He had an Aussie accent. Or maybe Kiwi. I had a hard time differentiating them but definitely one of the two. "I may have come here as a refugee during the war, mate, but I'm still not planning on staying." Okay, Aussie. "No need to beg, Kloskiewicz. I know you love me and all—"

A hard, local curse must have hit him, cuz the Aussie broke out laughing again. "I don't see anything, mate, do you?"

A man floated into my field of view. It wasn't the Aussie; it was his companion, and he said something under his breath in the guttural local language.

"I don't know," the Aussie said. Now he floated into view. Both flyers, both wearing the local army uniform. "Seems like we might have to start digging if we're going to need to find—"

"No need to dig," General Krall's voice came from somewhere behind my pillar. Now she was speaking English, lucky for me. Must have wanted to impress something upon the Aussie. "She's weak. She would not survive this."

The Aussie drifted around, and I could see he had a blond head of hair and a lantern jaw. "You sure? We could set some people to digging, confirm the kill?"

"No time for that," Krall said. "We have a war at our borders. She lacks her old invulnerability. The fall has killed her, and if not … the tower surely did. Come. We must pursue other tasks." She clapped her hands. "Leave her with the dead. The rescuers will turn her up … sooner or later."

I raised an eyebrow. I was going to take delirious joy in making Krall eat those damned words. And my fist.

Just … not right this second.

"You're the boss, boss," the Aussie said, and off he went, drifting out of my field of view, along with Krall and his companion, disappearing over top of my shelter.

So … Krall had dropped a building on the damned city just to kill me.

Whether she was acting on Hades and Lethe's orders or not, she'd just shown me exactly who she was.

"You're going to die for that," I whispered, hiding in the dark, plotting my next move. I didn't dare even crack my knuckles, but I knew I'd have to get out of here soon, probably as soon as I was sure she was gone.

Now I had a mission again. And woe betide General Krall when I got in front of her again.

Because if it was the last thing I did—and I didn't rule out that it might be—I was going to make her pay for what she'd done to the people of Bredoccia, dropping a building on them just to get to me. My face felt heated as I lay there in the darkness, steaming. Some old words came back to me, ones that fit the situation perfectly.

"As the great philosopher Bugs Bunny once said," I muttered under my breath, "'Of course you realize … *this means war.*'"

68.

Passerini

"What's the word, Graves?" Passerini asked, looking up from a hastily prepared force readiness assessment for the 2nd Dragoons in Vilseck, Germany. It wasn't great, at least not from what he could see, the cupboard looking pretty bare compared to what they could have mustered around 1989. *Toujours Prêt,* his navy ass. He flicked his gaze to the colonel. "Any sign of …?"

Graves was working diligently. He'd worn a kind of ghostly expression for a little bit after the tower fell—probably echoes of 9/11; that one still got to Passerini, even all these years later—but his color had returned, and he was tapping away, working on something or another. "Just checking some stuff out, sir."

"Please," Passerini said, putting down the assessment. "Indulge an old admiral and give me a break from bad news. What have you got?"

Graves hesitated. "Call for you from the White House, sir."

Passerini frowned. "Right now …?" He looked around. Nothing was ringing—

The phone in front of Passerini beeped, and he sighed, then hit the speakerphone. "This is Passerini."

"Mr. Secretary," President Gondry's clipped tones came over the speaker.

"What can I do for you, sir?" Passerini asked, straightening in his chair. He'd hoped, just a little, that it would be someone else—maybe the White House Chief of Staff calling to set up a chance to talk. No such luck.

"I'm calling about the Revelen situation, of course," Gondry said. "Looks to me like it's resolved itself. We should start walking down our readiness level."

Gondry felt like his eyes were about to pop out of his head. "Sir … Revelen is still in possession of nuclear weapons pointed at us, and run by a man who has threatened us. I'm all in favor of calming things some, but I think walking down the readiness level would be premature."

"I disagree," Gondry said, firm as granite. "You will remove us from our current DEFCON status, bringing us back to ROUND HOUSE status. Begin to return your forces to their duty stations and out of that theater of operations. Immediately. That is an order." And with that, he hung up.

"Good God," Passerini said, once he'd confirmed the hang-up by pushing the speaker button. "First he wants no part in worrying about this, then he's gung-ho for a war, now—" Passerini sank into his waiting fingers, propping up his head. "I'd say 'make up your mind, sir,' but the problem is that he's making it up every which way but the right way."

"It's because of what's moving him," Graves said, the colonel looking around. No one else was listening to them. "Gondry thinks way different than you."

"Oh?" Passerini felt the tilt of the corner of his mouth as a smile tugged at it. "How so?"

"You've spent your whole adult life in the service," Graves said, adopting a serious mien. "You pledged to defend your nation from all enemies, foreign and domestic, but … you really can't target the ones you see on the domestic side. It may be in your oath, but—"

"Son, the enemies I see on the domestic side of things can't hold a candle to a nuclear warhead pointed at our cities or foreign terrorists trying smuggle them in."

"Exactly," Graves said, coming around his console. "You see the threats out there, from beyond our borders." He waved a hand around. "It's what you look at all day, it's what you prepare for. Terrorists in caves, readying plans to destroy us. Nation-states with imperial ambitions, thinking to roll over their neighbors, destabilize the world. And the big powers of the day, looking to take by force what they don't want to win through diplomacy and commerce. You see the 'foreign' side of our enemies with incredible clarity. You take briefings on them daily."

"So does President Gondry, son," Passerini said with a smile. "It doesn't seem to be helping."

"Because Gondry is an academic," Graves said, sliding up closer to him, "and because Gondry's focus has always been here—domestic. He sees what he perceives as flaws in our system, in our people. He's mired in national politics. Whatever dark vision you have of the threats that lurk beyond our borders?" Graves brought his hand in close to him. "He sees them here, in his political opponents. We've had relative peace in this country—no foreign wars that came to our shores, with the exception of 9/11—since 1812, basically. We haven't felt the real kick of loss since Vietnam. And we haven't suffered true economic privation from a war since World War II. Gondry's a product of that. Even the Cold War didn't crack through, really—we made it past nuclear annihilation, and now it's so far in the rearview he doesn't even see it as a credible threat.

"His obstacles are all here." Graves tapped the table. "His agenda is mostly domestic. Look at the legislation he backs, the policies he favors. His enemies are political enemies, because the threats you see? He doesn't see them the same way. His enemy is his own countrymen—and at the very forefront, the biggest burr in his saddle right now—"

"Is Sienna Nealon." Passerini nodded. "That's an impressive analysis, Graves. I think you might be on to something."

Graves inclined his head slightly. "Well, I've given it some thought, sir."

"Indeed you have," Passerini looked at the screen. It was just rubble now, the ruin of that building in downtown Bredoccia, all still and quiet. "In a way, I guess it's sort of a blessing that

Sienna Nealon went down there. It's probably better for us if Gondry isn't externally focused." Graves cocked his head quizzically. "No one here in the States is looking to heave a nuke at him if he just overheats his political rhetoric while he's focused on whatever bugbear he's after this week."

"Well, first of all, that's not necessarily true anymore, is it?" Graves asked. "With the rise of metahuman powers, we're looking at people domestically who can *be* the nuke you're talking about. And if he wants to treat his own people like enemies … sooner or later, that's going to turn ugly in the worst possible way. You can't declare someone your enemy unilaterally for very long without them eventually declaring the same right back at you. But as to the other thing you alluded to …" He flicked a gaze to the screen. "Sienna Nealon? Ain't dead."

Passerini let out a subtle laugh, under his breath, a bark and a huff all in one. "Son, her grandaddy just dropped a building on her. How do you think she's going to make it out of that one?"

Graves smiled. Looked sidelong at the screen.

Passerini followed his gaze, and there, in the rubble … "Sonofa—"

"That's how," Graves said.

The long dark hair was obvious. The walk—a slight hobble evident until she got up to speed—looked like her gait. Passerini was no expert, but he'd seen enough Sienna Nealon footage to recognize her, even at this zoomed-out distance. She'd crawled right out from underneath a big piece of girder or something, and Graves—damn him—he'd zoomed right on it.

Passerini came to his feet. "How did you know she was there?" He pointed at the screen.

"Just a hunch," Graves shrugged.

"Does the White House have this yet?" Passerini watched. She was moving furtively, crawling around the wreckage, probably using pieces of it as cover, though he couldn't tell for sure by the 2D imagery.

"Nossir," Graves said, returning to his console. "They won't figure it out for an hour. And when they do …" He mimed an explosion with his hands. "The president will not react well."

Passerini stared at Graves, thoughts churning hard. "Your assessment, in this, sounds as dead-on as what you presented a few minutes ago. But that doesn't excuse us finding this out and not telling the president." He reached for the phone.

"If I may, sir …?" Graves harrumphed a little with his throat. "Perhaps you should assign a group of intelligence analysts to monitor the situation. Do a double check. Triple-check. Make sure it's her before you inform the White House. If you're afraid of the reaction."

Afraid of the reaction? Hell, yes, Bruno Passerini was afraid of the president's reaction. The man was fixated on Sienna Nealon, and not in a healthy way, like some gym rat obsessing over his deadlift. "I don't know about that, Graves. Trying to manage the president seems like a real good way to drive a wedge between us at a time when it looks to me like he's going to start stepping us up again toward war."

"Sir, he won't figure out that we knew for months," Graves said. "He doesn't have a single loyal soul in this room. If you want to keep him out of it, you can. He'll figure it out on his own, and he'll blame CIA for not putting it out sooner."

"You're asking me to substitute my judgment for the Commander-in-Chief's, Graves." Passerini ran hands through his thinning hair. "That's a dangerous road, and not one I really want to march down."

"Fair enough, sir," Graves said. "I just thought you might want independent, third-party confirmation that it's her before you … stir the hornet's nest." He smiled.

Passerini let out a tightly-held breath. Damn if that didn't sound appealing. Graves had a definite point, which was what made Passerini agonize over what should have been a simple choice: tell the Commander-in-Chief that his target was still active.

But … he was also right that the president had gone absolutely Ahab over Sienna Nealon. Whatever explicit danger he saw in her, Passerini must have missed it, absent her being some sort of avatar for everything Gondry hated in the world.

How else to explain him ditching his otherwise fairly peaceful worldview to suddenly agitate for war with not one but two nuclear powers?

If he informed the president right now … what would happen?

Gondry would probably step up the war plans again, contra his previous order. Wouldn't he? It seemed likely; the man had lost all reason where Sienna Nealon was concerned. After all, once she was out of play, he'd suddenly thought a peaceful resolution to this crisis was on the table.

Revelen was a threat now, no doubt. Wedded to Russia, they were doubly so, at least in Passerini's assessment. He dealt with threats like that every day, though, including Russia and China right at the top of that list.

"What's the status of Russia's missile arsenal?" Passerini called. "And Revelen's?"

"No open silos, sir," one of the intel lieutenants answered. "They haven't stepped up fueling any birds. Readiness is at normal levels."

This was a dangerous game. Passerini didn't want to make it any more dangerous, not right now. They were still planning for a war, one which he didn't really want to fight. "Can you get me SecState Ngo on the phone?" he turned to look at Graves. "And order that assessment of the … subject." He nodded at the screen. "Triple check. Just to be sure."

"Right away, sir," Graves said, not able to hide his smile. The colonel needed to work on that.

Passerini stayed standing, arms clasped behind him. An assessment seemed a good middle road. After all … he wasn't a highly trained intel analyst. He could easily have mistaken whoever was running down there for Sienna Nealon. Better to have a professional opinion weigh in. Surely the president would appreciate that.

Passerini almost chuckled at that. There was no way in hell the president would appreciate his "diligence," not in this. But delaying every possible second before letting Richard Gondry know that his personal Moby Dick was still walking around in a country that possessed nuclear weapons?

Well … it seemed like a smart move, and so Passerini bit down on his discontent, swallowed his conscience, and started practicing what he would say to the president when he finally did have to deliver the news and account for the response.

69.

Lethe

"I am … not pleased," Hades said, jaw tight as his asshole probably was right now, because the man was completely clenched. He was staring up at the main screen in the Situation Room, a live feed of the ruin of the Dauntless Tower in front of him, and thunderclouds boiling on his widow-peaked forehead.

"Well, when you send a wrecking ball after a varmint," Lethe said, trying to keep from gloating—she'd had long practice, "you can't be all that surprised when a building or two comes tumbling down."

Hades turned a hateful glare her way. "That building was the symbol of our ascendance. It was to herald our rise onto the world stage."

Lethe rolled her eyes. "If you need a giant phallic symbol to announce your greatness … I think your greatness might need some work."

"Hilarious." He did not smile. "Reducing the economic successes of our country to penis jokes."

"It was a state-sponsored venture," Lethe said, raising a hand toward the screen with the rubble on it. "If someone here had built it of their own volition, I could get behind the idea it represented 'economic success.' But we built it, out of our own treasury, and it wasn't even twenty percent leased. It was a vanity project. Just be glad it's insured." Lloyd's of London would be paying out on the nose on that one.

A flicker of aggravation twinged at Hades's jaw. "I doubt our insurance provider will be sanguine about covering destruction caused by our own army."

Lethe shrugged. "Maybe next time don't send Krall to nuke it from orbit."

A cold fire sprung up in Hades's eyes. "Even funnier, coming from you, Sigourney."

"Don't get passive-aggressive with me because your pet spider-monkey turned into a bull in your china shop," Lethe said, folding her arms in front of her. "I told you not to send her. You ignored me. I warned you not to test Sienna in this way. You ignored me. Your favorite building is in ruins, and it probably killed scores of your own people as it fell. Don't try and act like I don't have cause to be a little scornful of your planning, genius."

"I never said you shouldn't make your little attempts at humor," Hades said, and the chill flared as some of the fire went out. "I only say I don't find them that funny, given the cost to us." He had his hands clamped behind his back. "And I had reason to test her—she has failed to rise to my expectations. First she was hobbled in her battle with Rose, losing her power. That was 'strike one,' as the Americans say. Then she declined the serum—that was 'strike two.'" He raised a hand to indicate the ruins of the tower. "And now you see 'strike three.' She is out."

"Would you like to bet your throne on it?" Lethe asked with a raised eyebrow.

Hades let out a sigh of disappointment. "Truly? You wish to bet on her survival? She had a building dropped on her, daughter. I realize you are somewhat more attached to her, but …" He waved that hand around, flopping it. "What is it they say in the US? 'Come on, man.' She's dead."

"If you believe that, put your throne where your mouth is, Pops."

Hades narrowed his eyes. "You cannot be serious."

"I'm not you, with your ever-present irony," Lethe said. "I'm very serious, especially in this. Put your money where your mouth is or stop whining."

"My liege," Aleksy's voice from behind them, "a small American drone is crossing into our airspace."

Hades kept his gaze on her a moment too long, still staring at her with narrowed eyes. "I'm not taking your bet, but later we will discuss this peculiar faith you seem to have in her. I wish to know its provenance."

"The evidence of my own eyes," Lethe said, not lying, but definitely not telling the full truth. "That's where it comes from."

Hades shook his head and picked his way through the Situation Room's knotted series of consoles toward Aleksy to peer at the screen. "What do you see?"

"A blip," Aleksy said, squinting at the radar. "On the edge of the country. Small. Very small. It has to be a drone. It's not big enough to be a plane."

"Hmm," Hades said, and then he nodded, once. "Take care of it, and then … I think we need to discuss destroying the rest of those planes, as a precaution." He looked up at Lethe. "Since we seem to have abandoned the path of moderation here at home, perhaps it is best if we go big or go home, as they say."

"Sir …?" Aleksy's curiosity filled into his voice, and it came out a degree higher than usual. "Taking them down outside our borders … that is an act of war … sir."

"Ares was a nephew of mine," Hades said, straightening up. "There has never been anyone quite like him since he died. No one to take up his mantle, really, other than Sovereign." He smiled and put a hand on Aleksy's shoulder. "War and Death, they go hand in hand, don't they? Like … peanut butter and jelly." He patted the lieutenant's shoulder. "Start with that small drone. We will discuss what to do about the rest." He brought up his hand into a clenched fist, and something about the gesture caused Lethe's stomach to turn over. "Let us show the Americans … that we are not to be trifled with."

70.

Reed

"Ejecting!" Greg's voice boomed over the loudspeaker, and the world suddenly spun madly around us as the house lurched, as though it had been kicked by a giant. It probably hadn't, I reflected as I hit my knees and tumbled into a wall, Jamal landing atop me a second later.

What had probably happened, I realized as the world outside our little travel house was beset by roaring winds louder than a freight train passing underneath us, was that Greg had snatched us up and then ejected from the SR-71.

"Steady us, Reed!" came the booming voice of Greg over the rush of wind, and I shook off the sting of crashing into the house's drywall. The atmospheric turbulence outside was violent, and I reached out.

The winds felt a hell of a lot bigger than usual, presumably because I was presently Ant-Man sized, no larger than an insect. Still, for a man who had commanded hurricanes to knock their shit off …

"Steady," I breathed and took the winds in hand. It was like taking the reins of a wild horse, but one the size of a tractor trailer, and angry at that. An angry, bucking tractor trailer. With no steering wheel.

I created a pocket of calm, running the winds around us, then created an updraft powerful enough to keep us aloft. The last thing we needed was to plummet to our deaths—well, for everyone else to, anyway, I'd probably be fine, other than being invisible to anyone not using a microscope.

"Thanks," Greg said, appearing out of nowhere in our midst. Kat let out a yelp of surprise; she was holding onto the leg of the table, which was bolted to the ground, and seemed fine except for Greg's startling appearance. "The SR-71 was crushed from without."

"You mean someone fired a missile at us?" Jamal rubbed the top of his head as he picked himself up off the ground. He held up his tablet; the screen was shattered, and he shook his head, electricity flaring into the port. He probably didn't need the screen working anyway.

"No," Greg said in his clipped way. "The metal collapsed, as though we were being snatched out of the air by a giant."

"A Magneto, then," I said. "Metal-controlling meta."

"That would be my guess," Greg said.

"You guys okay up there?" Augustus called from somewhere below.

"Fine," I said. "Are you—"

"Anybody need a healing hand?" Kat asked, getting to her feet. She brushed a hand over my shoulder. "You've got this, right?"

"I'm fine," I said, lowering my hands from where I'd thrust them out while taking initial control over the winds. Once upon a time it would have taken a lot more will to manage it.

"We have some minor injuries, yeah," Augustus called up.

"On it," Kat said and disappeared down the stairs.

"This house isn't metal, is it?" Scott asked, rising to his feet and dusting himself off.

"Synthetics … mostly," Greg said. "And fortunately pressurized, so we can stay here for quite some time, if need be, though I'd suggest we get closer to the ground. The drain on the power system will be the first thing to cause a problem, but we likely have hours, and I do have backup equipment shrunk and stored in one of the cupboards that will allow us to continue without issue for months."

"What do you think happens if we move forward?" I asked,

straightening my lapel. My suit had taken a beating in the crash into the wall.

"Nothing good, I would think," Greg said. "There is a definite concentration of metals within this unit. I had the SR-71 shrunk to smaller than drone proportions. If this Magneto could detect it at that size ..."

"You think he'll be able to pick this place out," Jamal said, "even if we're just riding in on the wind."

Greg nodded. "The closer we get, the deeper into his sphere of control, the more likely detection becomes."

I let out a low breath. "So what you're saying is ... we can't get to her."

He shook his head. "Not like this. Not in this, or any of my other aircraft. I don't have any plastic planes on hand."

I closed my eyes. "They just dropped a building on her."

"And tried to drown her," Scott whispered.

"And yet ... we remain out of reach," Greg said, "unless you want to risk detection. All our lives versus—"

"I know the arithmetic, Greg," I said. "And ... no. I'm not going to throw us forward. Not like this. Not at these odds, not at the cost of everyone's lives." I opened my eyes.

We were out of the game.

71.

Sienna

Time to stew, time to think, time to breathe and time to plan.

That was what I finally had while I waited for the military presence around the ruin of the tower to dissipate.

When I really broke down what I was dealing with into its basic elements, I realized that things were not as bad as I'd originally thought. Every task was extra daunting when you viewed it as a whole thing, especially something as mind-blowingly crazy as keeping an entire country of superpowered people from crushing me under its collective boot.

But, when broken down into its component tasks, there were only a few things to actually deal with. 1) I had to beat the living hell out of the Revelen army, at least in Bredoccia. That was to clear the way to 2) Kill the shit out of Krall. Which would in turn allow me to 3) Storm the castle and face off with Arche, Yvonne, Lethe, and Hades. Some of them might not want to kill me, some of them might decide to back off and not fight, but just in case, I was including them all and planning for killing all of them, which led to step 4) Deal with the US government.

So, really, there were only four things I had to do at this point in my life. Easy peasy.

Okay, none of those things was especially easy, but if I let myself get hung up on little details like the local army in Revelen was probably hundreds of combat-ready metas, armed and able to kill me, I'd just curl up into a ball, become useless, and wait around to die like a coward.

To hell with that. I was no chickenshit. I was a mean, mo-fo'ing killer of men and women. Cuddling up with a piece of rock in the ruins of this tower and waiting to be found/killed?

That was for other people. Not Sienna Nealon.

"Four little things," I whispered to myself as I left my hiding place beneath the rubble, crawling across the ruin bent over, trying to keep a low profile in the literal sense of the word. The place was crawling with rescuers, but I was in the middle of a little crater of debris that shielded me from immediate view. They wouldn't go stomping through the wreckage like I was, nossir. They'd have to be careful. They'd need to follow safety protocols. I was, after all, walking on the ruin of one building that had come down on multiple other ones, smashing them. There was no part of this ruin that was particularly stable for me to put my weight on, at least for long.

Which was why I hustled, metahuman-speed, as I crossed it, keeping my head down to avoid being spotted and with a wary eye on the sky in case they'd deployed drones to assist with rescue efforts. Thus far, I saw nothing, but I still kept my eyes peeled for movement skyward—and earthward, though I didn't see anything around me.

Also notable by their absence? The flyers who'd so menaced me during my recent pursuit. I'd hoped that my hiding time had given them a chance to go get involved in something else, like protecting a perimeter somewhere, or going back to their base to get chow and hold a circle jerk while bragging about how they took me out. Or whatever they did to celebrate success.

Reaching the edge of this little crater, which I realized probably was a street, a little valley of rubble that had been formed when my super tall tower had come crashing down on the buildings on either side of the avenue, I climbed, taking great care in the selection of my footholds and handholds. A few gave way; I shifted quickly, using my meta speed to avoid taking a nasty tumble on at least five occasions.

When I reached the top of the nearest little mountain ridge,

I peered over into the next valley. The wreckage was a hell of a mess, and I had proven to be right. The tower had hit another building where I presently hung, and I was actually holding on to part of the exposed structure of said building. The facade had been partially ripped off in the collapse, but it was still mostly standing, and beyond it was a debris field that nearly took my breath away.

A nearby avenue was partially clogged, but a few army Humvees waited there, along with a couple of ambulances, about a hundred yards from my position. There weren't many searchers there and they were really paying attention to one of the standing buildings on that street, one that had taken an indirect hit during the collapse. People were still flowing in and out, mostly in the out direction, and injured in a lot of cases, paramedics and other first-responders taking them for care under the watchful eye of a few army guys with guns who were much more interested in what was going on in the rescue than keeping watch on the ruin.

Yay, me.

I skittered down across the field in front of me like spider-monkey Krall, on my hands and knees and trying to distribute my weight so that it wasn't resting on any one thing. It served me well as I made my way down the slope of the building in front of me, and I soon found myself at its edge, the back corner of the roof collapsed by a stray beam into the floor below.

With a careful peek around, I dropped down to the floor below. The rubble creaked, and one of my feet found a section of roof that crunched in, sucking up my foot to the knee.

I cringed. It hadn't hurt much, but the sound had been kinda loud. I waited, listening.

Nothing. Some moans in the distance, but that was it.

"Damn you, Krall," I said under my breath as I pulled my foot out. If anyone had been in this apartment when the tower came down, they'd gotten crushed under the collapse of the ceiling. There wasn't much I could do for them, but I listened anyway.

No sound. At least, not nearby. The shouts of the searchers

on the next street I could hear just fine.

Picking my way through the debris field, I made it to the edge of the floor, where a three-story drop waited for me. Again, I turned it into a couple of jumps, breaking up the fall so it didn't kill me. I landed on a rubble-strewn street a few seconds later, letting out a sharp breath from the impact that my knees, fortunately, soaked up as I hit pavement.

This avenue wasn't in very good shape. It looked like something out of a post-apocalyptic movie, a few cars smashed under the falling facade of the building behind me. There was rubble everywhere, and one major pillar of the tower had neatly bisected the building across the street. No one was moving inside; hopefully they'd gotten out. The fact that this street wasn't swarming with people suggested to me that the damage had been considerable in the buildings behind me, and that people had followed a logical path the hell away from the chaos long before now.

A sound down the street made me leap behind a car that had caught a giant block of rubble, the roof smashed down and all four tires rendered flat by the weight. There wasn't a body shop on the planet that could have fixed this one, and I doubted anyone would try as I ducked behind the bumper and slowly, slowly peeked out.

There was a soldier with a rifle about half a block away, looking around. He must have heard me, because he was keeping a very sharp lookout, and as he walked, he shouted in his native language, which was—

Russian?

I blinked. I definitely recognized the language, which was weird. They didn't speak Russian in Revelen. I'd been listening; they spoke a local pig Latin, some Slavic language that had no common roots with my English. Russian didn't exactly, either, but I knew it when I heard it, having had a native Russian speaker in my head for several years.

He called out again, picking up his pace. As he got closer, I took another look at his rifle—

It wasn't a G-36.

It was an AK-74M.

I frowned. Had the Revelen army actually switched to the Russian standard? I looked at his uniform, careful to keep still behind that bumper so as not to draw his eye with sudden movement.

He wasn't wearing the standard Revelen army uniform, exactly—or at least not the one I'd seen in the palace. I squinted at the uniform patches, and didn't recognize it. His BDU was an urban camo pattern. Definitely not Russian army, though …

The soldier drew closer, scanning around, calling out as he walked. He wasn't apprehensive about running into me; he was doing rescue op stuff, looking for survivors. As soon as his head was turned, I snaked mine back behind the bumper and closed my eyes, listening to his footfalls.

He wasn't being cautious. He was prioritizing covering ground over watching his ass, probably because he thought he was hunting for a survivor to help, not a Sienna Nealon, who was clearly dead. I drifted a little lower, looked under the car and caught sight of his boots. He was less than a foot from the vehicle, coming up the side at a brisk walk—

I held my breath, readied myself, focused on his footsteps, and as soon as I heard him get close enough—

I lunged out and caught the barrel of his rifle, yanking and twisting it off-line from my body. The sudden violence I applied to it shocked him, and he let out a small cry of surprise as I swung the grip around and took hold of it.

Following in the natural spin I'd created while disarming him, I whirled into a back-kick, aiming straight for his gut. I caught him flat-footed and drove all the air out of him before he could shout. He made an "OOF!" sound and flew across the street, crashing into a pile of concrete and rebar with enough force that a miniature cloud puffed out from his point of impact.

I ran after him, coming up on him just as he started to rise. Slinging the rifle over my body, I checked that it was safetied—it was, stupid on his part—and swung it out of my way as I dropped my knee onto his stomach, driving the air out of him a second time. He gasped, and before he could suck in a breath, I raised my fist—

And cold-cocked him. Once.

Twice.

Three times … not so much a lady.

Once I was sure he was out, I disarmed him of his belt, which included a pistol and some grenades. This time, I wasn't frigging losing mine, I was determined. The Glock I'd been carrying during the fall had pretty much been rendered inoperable by … well, the fall. Barrel bent, shooting anything out of it would have been an exercise in potential suicide.

But now I had—what the hell?

He was carrying the new-ish Russian Grach, which I gave a cursory glance to before strapping on his belt and buckling it around my waist. Grenades, pistol, some other stuff. Okay. All Russian equipment.

I looked at his face. I'd probably fractured his skull, which didn't trouble me all that much given he was a meta and would heal. Besides, I had a more pressing concern.

Cracking my knuckles, I sunk a palm onto his face and braced myself, counting the seconds as I looked left, then right down the street.

No one was there. Whew.

It didn't take long to feel the burn as my powers started to work. If my four-part (would that be considered quad-partite?) plan was to work, I had to start on phase one immediately and that meant getting some active intel on this army that was running around Bredoccia. I needed to know their numbers, their disposition, in order to hamstring them—because killing was probably right out—

Hang on.

I burst into the soldier's mind with all the grace of an unsupervised kid into a birthday cake that had been left out. His whole life was open to me, and while I usually operated with a modicum of control so as to avoid damaging the brains I jacked, something popped out at me that was so damned apparent after a second within that it obviated my need for caution.

This dude … this yelling, incautious mf'er …

Was a mercenary.

In fact, Revelen's entire 1st Division, the army group that was currently spread out through Bredoccia …

They were all mercenaries. Every last one of them.

These were not gentle citizen soldiers defending their homeland against the tyranny of the evil invader Sienna Nealon. These were mercenaries pulled from the four corners of the earth, drawn here by the fact that Revelen was becoming the capitol for merc activity in Europe, a bunch of swarming assholes seeking payment and willing to do murder in exchange for it.

Visions of what this man had done in his career, which had started at the age of eighteen in the Russian army and then continued in a variety of places around the globe, put to the lie any illusions I might have had about the nobility of the trade. I dipped into a few memories about what he'd done to locals, to villagers in other countries, his laughing joy as he perpetrated evil—

And I just drained what I needed and broke his neck. He twitched, once, as he died.

I rose, a few details of specialized knowledge gleaned from his career in the army added to my repertory. I'd picked him dry, getting all the juicy things I felt I could use, adding his experience to my own without bothering with his power, which was near useless, some kind of luminescence in the darkness, or his blackened soul. I didn't need that in my head. I barely wanted the small dip into his history that I'd taken.

"Mercenaries," I said under my breath, a little smile cracking my steely facade like it was a building on this street about two hours ago, when the tower came down. All Bredoccia was swimming in them. Not a local soldier to be found.

That changed the game.

A lot.

I looked at the body at my feet, and smiled as I turned, leaving him behind in the mess he and his brethren had made at General Krall's order.

Mercenaries … mercenaries I could kill without feeling a damned thing.

And it was time to go to work doing just that.

72.

If I had a calling in life, it seemed to be to be a purveyor of death to the deserving.

It was all part of the same grand game, the same purposeful end, which was to deal all manner of hell to those who were bringing their own hell down on the undeserving.

Like the people of Bredoccia. Not one of them had asked for General Spider-Monkey to drop a building on their heads as they went about their everyday lives.

It wasn't clear to me how many people had died. It wasn't clear to anyone yet, and probably wouldn't be for months.

I couldn't do anything about that, though. Trying to aid in rescue efforts would be a really good way to insure that the Revelen army's 1st Division would stop rescuing and move all their efforts into killing me again, to hell with the civilian consequences.

Well, to hell with that, and to hell with them. I was done letting them kill civilians in the name of wiping me out, of me running and keeping the kid gloves on rather than engaging them. I'd pulled my punches before because I thought I was facing the real army of Revelen, not a bunch of for-hire killers who were in the same trade as me, without the moral compass.

Now that I knew what they were?

The gloves were off. Literally, in my case.

Along with the basic knowledge I'd pulled from that soldier's mind had come some more useful nuggets—namely, his understanding of the troop deployments in the local area. I had the basic sketch of patrol routes, of where they were concentrating rescue efforts in their coordination with the civilian authorities.

If you know where your enemy is and isn't, you can avoid contact with them until you're ready.

And I … was about to get really ready. With some major league contact.

I crossed two streets to get away from where I'd killed the Russkie merc, only one of which was a patrol route. I'd stopped off a block away and scoured an apartment building that had been evacuated, changing my clothes and picking up a knee-length coat that probably looked a little out of place in summer, but it hid my gun belt and rifle in its depths, and I added a hat to change the shape of my head, then slipped out into the third street west of my little ambush.

The crowds were a little heavier here, and I kept my head down, easing through them. A few people were walking around with obvious injuries, blood rushing out of gashes on their faces, refugees from the streets closer to the disaster. They'd been pushed back from the crisis zone by the soldiers, and now they milled around, some rescue tents nearby filled with doctors and medical personnel providing first aid, local cops doing their best to triage the situation, cutting through the crowds in search of the most seriously wounded.

Others were clustered in groups, talking, trying to make sense of what had happened here. I wished them good luck with that. Dropping the tower had been the senseless act of a violent personality with zero compunction about hurting people to achieve a goal. It churned my guts, because while I occasionally had a lack of compunction about hurting people, it was always because they'd hurt others to deserve it.

Like Krall. Krall had hurt and killed people, and now I was going to hurt and kill Krall. How much hurting happened before the kill … well, I was flexible on that.

I worked my way through the crowd slowly, doing my best not to draw any attention. I wasn't the most inconspicuous figure, with my weird hat and overcoat, but in the middle of a disaster zone, I was hardly the most noteworthy. People were screaming everywhere, hysterical from their own wounds or from losing someone, being separated from loved ones, or simple shock.

A girl with a hat and an overcoat making her way calmly through the crowd, head down?

I blended in.

About a block later I finally laid eyes on my objective, sweeping a calm gaze over my target.

The military HQ for this sector. A temporary encampment, situated in the parking lot of a retail store, I saw a couple of command trailers, a few bivouacs, and about a dozen military trucks and Humvees, all ringed by a bevy of soldiers who were way too distracted by their own conversations and the crowds to be effective perimeter guards.

In fairness to them, this was probably a unique situation for most of them. Maybe they'd been deployed in a national guard emergency-like function in their native armies before they'd started selling their souls and trigger fingers for hire. But those days would have been long past, and now they watched the civilian population in front of them with a curiosity bordering on contempt, laughing at the occasional plea from an injured person and pointing them back down the street to the nearest civilian medical tent.

Lookiloos lined the street, crowds thronged the center of it. They would probably make way for a military convoy or a truck, but nothing was moving in the immediate area. My guess was that there was a central road open for the ambulances and military traffic, and this wasn't it. This was where they'd chosen to put the response HQ, the nominal place where they had planned to coordinate their manhunt for me.

You know … before it had been called off on account of my death.

I kept my head down as I cut against the crowd, whose attention was still on the wreckage behind me. There was a calm, somewhat still quality this far out from the disaster zone, a sort of quiet awe from the spectators, most of whom were uninvolved in the scene. Other than flecks of dust on some dark clothing, for the most part the people I saw here were almost certainly well clear of the scene of the tower fall.

Some had probably come to help.

Some had come to watch.

None had come looking for me. Which was fortunate, because I was right here.

I slowed as I approached the perimeter of soldiers around the HQ. They were just off the main road, the civilian traffic passing in front of them as they stood back, guarding the parking lot but not very attentively. It only took me a few seconds and a quick count of the active defenders to decide on a plan.

Here, I was operating from a truth I'd gleaned in my brain picking of the merc. A quick scan of the camp revealed the thing I was looking for, prompting me to smile for the first time since …

Well, since I'd killed that Russian merc. I guess I was finding some reasons to smile now.

I stepped up on the curb, leaving the street and closing on the perimeter of soldiers ringed around the temporary HQ. If I'd had Harry's powers, I might have been able to stealth this, slipping between them without worrying about getting caught. He could have timed it so that he would have caught them all looking the other way. Harry was subtle like that; the scalpel in our relationship.

Me? I wasn't the hammer. Hammers were positively muted compared to me. No, nor a pistol, nor a shotgun, not even a machine gun. Those were too quiet.

I was the Mother of All Bombs, the MOAB that would detonate and send every soul within reach scrambling for cover. If they didn't get vaporized instantly by sheer proximity to my badassitude.

I angled toward the nearest soldier, head down, trying to make it look like I was just coming up to ask him a question. I lulled him, kept my hands visible on my approach, and said, quietly, in English, "Pardon me, sir …"

"Da?" he asked, defaulting to his native Russian before switching to broken English. "What you want?"

"Do you have a moment to discuss our lordess and savioress, Sienna Nealon?" I asked, looking up at him with a purely evil smile.

His eyes widened, his hands were on his rifle. He started to raise it—

I caught it and stepped sideways; I'd picked the farthest man out in the perimeter line, the one with no one on his left. The soldier next down the way from him caught the movement of our scuffle, his cry, and started to raise his own gun—

But not in time. I whipped the soldier's rifle around in perfect line with the next soldier and the dumbass's failure to follow good trigger discipline did my work for me, blasting his buddy into kingdom come with a round of fire that stitched the poor bastard from gut to throat. He keeled over in a spasm, blood spurting from the line we'd just made in him.

I brought my elbow around and shattered the jaw of my foe, taking away his weapon as he staggered back. With it already mostly aimed, I blasted the next two guys in line as they tried to bring their guns around to deal with me. I was hip-firing, something I'd practiced to the point where I was almost as good as if I'd had it up to my shoulder, at least this range, which was about thirty feet.

That done, I ran a couple more rounds into the guy I'd been grappling with as I broke into a run past him. No point in leaving him behind to recover, so I emptied his brains into the parking lot as I went past, then chucked the near-empty rifle and pulled my own as I shed the overcoat.

I kept the hat on, though. Because it was jaunty.

Someone behind me opened up with their AK-74 as I reached the cover of their parked vehicles. I dodged behind an army truck. A soldier stuck his head out the driver's side window, wondering what was going on and I lit him up with my stolen AK. Crimson splattered his windshield as he tipped back in, and I broke into a run through the alley between his truck and the one next to it, keeping a careful watch for trouble ahead.

When I reached the end of the truck, I looked left, then right. There were more trucks parked ahead, about a ten-foot margin between the ones I'd just run past and the next row. No one was visible down the aisles, and soldiers were starting to shout behind me. To my left, about four vehicles down, the Humvees were lined up.

I smiled again. I'd find what I was looking for front and center there. Now I just needed to make a clean sweep of the vehicles here in order to make sure that when all hell broke loose in the next couple minutes, this wasn't a direction they could flank me from.

Easy peasy.

I walked past the gas valve on the nearest truck and pulled a grenade from my stolen utility belt as I did so. Pulling the pin, I jammed it in the fuel filler and let it rest there, then broke into a run, counting as I hauled ass away.

One …

Two …

Three …

Shouts behind me. Soldiers in pursuit had found the dead guy in the truck cab.

Four …

Man, they sounded mad. They were still after me, too, running now, caution lost in their mad dash to catch me.

Five!

The grenade went off, still wedged in the filler of the truck. It wasn't much of an explosion, at least not by itself. Grenades don't go off in real life like they do in the movies; it's not all flames and pyrotechnics designed to look awesome on camera. Grenades, in real life, are designed to explode with force, not fire, and to take the metal shell wrapped around the core explosive and turn it into about a thousand pieces of shrapnel, which are then driven outward by the strength of the *boom* (technical term) into the fleshy parts of anyone around it.

So it's less about the *boom* and more about turning the people in range into pincushions for the shrapnel.

Unless, of course, you were to add something really explosive to the situation, such as, say, the diesel fuel tank of an army truck.

That explosion … well …

That sucker went off like something out of the movies.

I ignored the *whump* that threatened to drive me to my knees, moving steadily toward my planned objective. I was already partially behind cover anyway, having hooked around the rear of the last army truck in the line as it went off. The grenade boom was pretty loud, but the afterboom of the fuel tanks cooking off and launching the truck into the air was way, way worse. A wave of heat washed over me that even the vehicles between us couldn't stave off, and by the time I reached the Humvee I'd been going for, it was pretty clear that the mess I'd just made …

Well … it was going to be a mess for a long time.

A big, flaming mess that extended across about twelve army trucks and thirty meters or so of open ground where the diesel had spread when the truck had launched off the ground.

Chaos, thy name is Sienna.

And I was just getting started.

The camp was coming alive now that I'd blown this section of it halfway to hell. To my right, a retail store's brick front provided a nice block against a flanking attack. It merged into the building behind it, no entries or exits for a few floors, just a mural wall with some nice spray paint design work.

My rear was secure for the moment. The raging inferno to my left meant unless they had a Gavrikov, I was safe from that direction—again, for a short time.

But a short time was all I planned to stay here.

I leapt up on the Humvee in front of me, climbing onto the roof and sliding easily into the turret on top. I checked to make sure there wasn't someone in the interior; there wasn't, and nor was anyone hanging out in the Humvees around me.

Popping back up out of the turret in the middle of the Humvee's roof, I smiled once more.

Because now … it was time to party.

Not all Humvees have turrets, but when they do, they almost always have something nice and bounteous on them. A lot of times it's the M2 Browning, affectionately known as "Ma Deuce." Those are pretty common. A fifty-caliber machine gun that had been around since World War I and could spray

500 rounds per minute of bullets the size of my thumb.

Slightly less common, especially when you got outside the realm of the US military, was the beauty in front of me. Known as the Mk 19, it didn't look all that different—to the untrained eye—from any other crew-served machine gun. A boxy assembly with two handles on the back, the barrel jutting out front and a big box for ammo hung off the side. Why, if you didn't know any better, you might even assume that it was a pretty standard shooty shooty bang bang gun.

But it was soooooooooo much more.

Because the Mk 19 …

Was a 40-millimeter belt-fed *grenade launcher.*

And it came with the bonus of a couple of giant metal flak shields to either side of the barrel to provide cover for the shooter in case someone decided to fire back. They wouldn't stop everything, but they'd hinder anyone who was shooting a rifle at me.

My smile was a thing of ugly horror, I was sure, suddenly thankful there was no one around to witness my glee as I brought the grenade launcher sight picture around and aimed at the army HQ in front of me. People were starting to flood out, a knot of them bunching up as they came out into the harsh light of day to find their camp in flames.

I adjusted my aim, dropping the sight on the army officer in front—his name was Arkadi and he'd come over from the Russian army at some point, after a long and horrific career that dated back to the Soviet invasion of Afghanistan. I felt my smile do nothing but grow as I squeezed the trigger …

73.

Dave Kory

"Holy shit."

The picture had gone live again after a brief interval, some flashing scenes showing … crowds. Streets. Bredoccia in all its chaotic glory, with people fleeing the disaster and watching the disaster and just generally living in the aftermath. The view had flipped a few times before a particularly eagle-eyed Holly had pointed to a figure in a coat, with a hat, moving through the crowd:

"That's her."

There had been some argument, sure, but that had ended when Sienna Nealon had pulled her coat off and wiped out a few guards from the Revelen army just as cool as you please. Then she'd blown up a truck and huddled in a Humvee turret before finally …

Well …

Blowing everything the eff up.

The view was pretty solid, the camera mounted on a wall not twenty feet from her, the picture clearly zoomed to show her face as she let loose on the army camp in front of her with …

"Wow," someone breathed. "That's not a normal machine gun." There was no sound to go with the picture, either fortunately or not.

"It's a 40mm grenade launcher," Mike Darnell said, because

of course he would know something like this. When Dave shot him a look, Mike gave him an unapologetic one back. "I was embedded for a while with Big Red One in Iraq. They ran with these."

"She's wiping out the whole freaking Revelen army," Holly breathed, watching this … massacre unfold in front of them. The whole damned camp was exploding as Sienna poured on fire.

"She's clearly psychotic," Dave said, feeling a sudden need to look away. "I mean … my God." He focused his attention on Caden. "Get that kill counter up on the main page, now. And somebody take the feed of this, go slow-mo, whatever you have to—make up numbers if you can't figure it out. I want it live yesterday, and ticking up as she does …" He waved at the screen, where she was still just … unloading on people. "… This."

"If I may …" Mike said, peering at the screen. "I don't think these are regular Revelen army soldiers." He took a few strides up to the screen. "Someone pause?" Someone did, and he pointed at a soldier who, in spite of standing upright, caught in the frame at a flat run, was already dead because there was a grenade freeze-framed about ten feet behind him. "Look at their weapons." He pointed at the rifles. Nobody spoke. "These are Russian army issue AK-74s. I looked it up, and the Revelen army uses German-made—"

"Who cares where these guys come from?" Dave asked, finally just losing the last thread of patience he had for this blame-shifting bullshit. "She's wiping them out, man. Like they're cockroaches."

"I think they're mercs," Mike said. "Former Russian Army, by my guess, but … mercs. Soldiers-for-hire. Brought their own guns."

"And that makes them less human?" Dave just stared him down.

"Russian mercs kill for money," Mike said, "so … yeah. I'd consider them less human than most people."

"Whatever," Dave said, feeling a little grey in the face, unwilling to have this argument. His phone beeped, and he looked down at it.

IT'S TIME TO PLAY!

"Excuse me for a minute," he said, turning his back on the TV as someone resumed the livestream. Dave didn't see the grenade hit its target, didn't want to, really. He just took his phone and headed for the bathroom, not wanting to watch Sienna Nealon wage her own personal war halfway around the world.

74.

Sienna

I was singing the music from "Ride of the Valkyries" at the top of my lungs, and I couldn't hear a damned thing over the grenade launcher running in my hands and the explosions I was ripping across the Revelen army camp. The recoil was a little intense, the noise even more so, but honestly …

I was having the time of my life. It was a beautiful thing, watching every shot blow shit up.

An army Humvee came skidding around the corner around a burning bivouac, and I caught it with a volley along the side and sent it crashing into a light pole, in flames, before walking my fire back to one of the army trailers I felt hadn't absorbed enough in the way of damage yet. It still had a couple spots where the metal panels hadn't completely bowed out from grenades blowing off on the inside, and by God, that just wasn't acceptable. "Not on my watch!" I shouted to deaf ears—mine—as I launched about six more grenades in through the trailer's sides. It distorted comically with the force of each detonation in the confined space, definitely killing anyone who was inside.

"La la la la LA LAAAAAA," I sang, belting the opening bars of the Star-Spangled Banner, probably horribly off key because I couldn't hear a damned thing at this point, then slipped back inside the Humvee. I don't know why, but I was feeling incredibly patriotic just then. Maybe because the Mk 19 was an American weapon, mounted on the Humvee, which was—once upon a time—the most American of cars ever made. The keys were in the ignition, and my work here was pretty much done, so I started her up and rolled forward, taking a gentle turn toward the street and checking the gas gauge.

Nearly full. Perfect. In a vehicle this size and with its gas mileage, that meant I'd be able to go about five miles or so before topping off the tank.

Kidding. Sort of.

I came to a rolling stop at the curb and honked the horn. People were fleeing madly in all directions, but they damned sure made a hole for the Humvee, and I signaled my turn (because if I can do it in the middle of a war zone in the second world, you assholes can do it in Philly, or whatever hell hole you're driving in) and then went right, alternately tapping the gas pedal and the brakes as I saw openings.

It took a block or two to break loose of the crowd, at which point normal traffic operations resumed. My hearing hadn't quite returned, though, and I was experiencing that water-in-the-ear sensation as I tooled along an avenue that was lined with shops and trees that looked like it had been torn right out of the VISIT REVELEN tourist brochures.

I probably looked like I was just ambling along, but as usual, I did have a plan. I was still operating on objective 1) destroy the Revelen Army's 1st Division, after all, and the next stage of doing that was in this direction. Driving like a normal person was intentional, because nothing would have stuck out in Bredoccia right now like a Humvee taking corners and ripping up the thoroughfares like a bat out of hell.

Wait. No. Never mind. The army was alerted, so driving like that was expected. I stepped on the gas and watched the speedometer go from 30 to 60 in seconds, and I even heard the engine rev a little through my near-total hearing loss. Good thing I had meta healing; it'd probably return to normal in a matter of hours.

"Ohhhhh say can you seeeee—because I can't hearrrrr—" I kept singing, trying to gauge the level of my current deafness.

It wasn't total, but it was significant.

"By the dawn's early lighhhhhht," a voice came back from the radio.

I nearly the put the Humvee through the front window of a lady's wear store in shock. Silver lining: I might have been able to find a bra that provided some support, because this prison one I had on didn't seem to have underwire and for some reason Hades had decided not to stock that particular garment type for me.

"Damn you, Cassidy!" I swerved back onto the road. "What the hell?"

"What?" Her voice sounded a little watery, probably from the hearing loss. My head was aching a little, too. "I've been watching you work. Figured I'd chime in now that you've decided to wage that war on the Revelen government I was longing for."

"Yeah, well, I'm waging a war on this mercenary army division and General Krall," I said, signaling my turn, again, because I'm not a savage. "The status of my familial relationship here is still TBD, okay? I'm not going after Hades." I white-knuckled the wheel. "Yet."

"I know, I know, but I can afford to be patient as you lay your vengeance upon these people," she said. "You'll come around. And then you'll devastate everything they care about. Because that's the Sienna way."

"What? No, it's n—oh, who am I kidding, that's totally my way." I sighed.

"There's a regimental HQ a block away," Cassidy said. "That where you're heading."

"Mmmmmaybe," I said, being a little coy. "Why?"

"What's your endgame here, Sienna? If you're not aiming to take out Hades?"

"Find Krall, drive this Humvee up her ass, and unload the grenade launcher until she's internally exploded into oblivion," I said. "It's a simple plan."

"Yeah, but she's not at the regimental HQ."

"I know this."

"Then why are you going there?" Cassidy asked. "There's

about a hundred soldiers there on high alert. And, oh by the way, Arche is searching for you using the city's camera system, and I'm having a hell of a time keeping her out. It won't last long, and pretty soon she'll be all over you like James Gunn on a pedophile joke."

"I have faith in your abilities to keep her off my back, Cassidy," I said. "You're smart like that."

"Flattery will not make my hacking skills level up to the point where I can defeat a concerted attack from someone who can literally manipulate digital information at its most basic level. Holding her back would be an impossibility. The best I can do is co-exist with her in this space—for a little while, and maybe keep her busy putting out fires elsewhere."

"I'm sure you'll do extra well at that," I said, taking my last turn. The regimental HQ was ahead in an empty block that had apparently been demolished some time back in anticipation of building some sort of governmental center that hadn't come to pass yet. I brought the Humvee to a stop in the middle of the road and unclicked my seat belt, hopping into the rear and opening up an ammo can. "Now if you'll excuse me … I need to reload."

"Why would I need to excuse you for that?"

"I don't know," I said. "I don't even know how you're hearing me right now, honestly." I pulled out a massive belt of 40mm grenade ammo and joined it to the one that was already fed into the Mk 19. With care, I started to re-stack it into the box mounted on the side of the launcher so it would feed easily. "Is there a microphone in here?"

"Someone left their cell phone under the seat," she said. "You might consider taking it with you so I can talk to you after you inevitably have to flee on foot."

"Pffffft," I scoffed. "What makes you think I'm going to have to flee on foot?"

"You're about to attack an army's regimental HQ with a vehicle-mounted grenade launcher. You're going to call down the thunder—all the thunder—on your damned head. They're going to blow up your Humvee, and if you hadn't shown a particular talent for avoiding certain death, I'd say don't bother taking the phone because—duh, dead. But since you seem to be well-nigh unkillable at the moment, take the damned phone, Sienna, so we can coordinate after your truck gets blown all to hell."

I was done loading the Mk 19, so I slid back into the driver's seat and slid my hand across the floor until I found it. "Yes, Big Sister." I dropped the cell phone into my front pocket. "You know, this is really validating all my fears about how cell phones are actually wiretaps designed to listen to everything we do."

"You'll be glad later, when you try to figure something out on your own and can't. Because I'll be there."

"Yeah, you're like Siri," I said, "except more annoying and judgy."

"You're the one about to attack an army camp head-on. Crazy much?"

"Crazy much," I agreed. "Crazy always. And in this case—crazy mad." I checked the AK-74 that was still slung at my side, hanging into the gap where a center console would be in a car.

"Just keep in mind that those soldiers are all metas, so they'll be moving a lot quicker than—"

"I just killed a whole boatload of them back there, did you not see?" I waved a hand in the rearview. "I know what I'm dealing with, okay? I get it. Everyone here's a meta. Their beyond-human powers are understood."

"It's called a level playing field, Sienna," Cassidy said, softening just a hair. "And there are over a hundred of them. I just wanted to make sure you know what you're getting into. Because a hundred metas with guns? It's a lot to deal with."

I stomped on the gas pedal. I could hear the squealing tires faintly, and off I went, peeling out as I headed for the army camp.

"So am I."

75.

Passerini

"… Not sure how it's going to turn out, but we've entered negotiations with the Russian president himself," SecState Ngo said, voice crackling over the secure phone line. "Preliminaries look good. He requested the meeting, which is a plus given they cut off all communication with us … what? Two, three days ago?" She laughed weakly at the other end of the line. "I'm starting to lose count of the days, Bruno."

"Copy that," Passerini said, rubbing his eyes. He held the phone to his ear, figuring that a conversation with the Secretary of State wasn't the sort of thing he wanted to broadcast to the whole Situation Room, if they were listening. Graves was the only one within earshot of his side of the conversation, and the colonel was looking down at his console, tinkering with the screens. Passerini shot a look up at the farthest right display; Graves had switched to some sort of security feed with a Humvee rolling across the screen.

"Sorry, I just realized I called you 'Bruno,'" Ngo said. "I—"

"It's fine, ma'am," Passerini said, shaking his head. She couldn't see it. "We're in the foxhole now. No point standing on formality."

"Well … you can call me Lisa, then."

"Yes, ma—Lisa." That did not come easily, but it felt like the appropriate thing to say in the moment.

"So, Russia." Ngo sounded like she wanted to change the subject away from this awkward moment as much as he did. "A couple of interesting details I already forwarded to CIA: President Fedorov has an American advisor now. The ambassador didn't catch the full name—African-American fellow, started with a Z, introduced himself as a doctor—"

"Doctor Zollers?" Graves asked, mumbling to himself just loud enough for Passerini to pick it up and frown. The colonel must have been talking to himself. No way could he hear the discussion on the phone, and certainly not Ngo's part of it.

"—but the ambassador forgot his name, he said. Just couldn't recall it. Anyhow, the Russians look ready to back away from their Revelen allies. They're already walking back their alert status and are standing down their military. I'm waiting on confirmation, but … if true … this is a good sign."

"Yeah, it is," Passerini said. "Not that I'd want to go to war with Revelen on their own, now that they're nuclear-armed, but having Russia in their back pocket was a lot more daunting."

"How many nukes does Revelen have?" Ngo asked.

"Twelve ICBMs," Passerini said. "Enough to do some significant damage if they were of a mind to. Each has six MIRVs that can detach and hit regional targets. Each MIRV has a city-killer bomb on it. So their maximum capability is to flatten the core of seventy-two American cities. Less if they decide to concentrate fire on one metro—"

"What … what does that mean?"

Passerini took a breath, then let it out slowly. This was not the sort of information he relished imparting. "Well, take New York for example. If they wanted to be thorough, they'd target each borough with at least a MIRV each. Which means an entire missile and probably two would be tasked just to New York and its outlying areas—Long Island, Greenwich, Westchester County. DC would warrant at least two, on the low end, because you'd want to nail hardened structures like the Pentagon with a direct hit, their own dedicated warhead." Passerini felt a little churn in his gut, and not just from describing his own annihilation.

Bruno Passerini had always hated nukes. They were a brutal, indiscriminate weapon that made the already savage nature of war just that much more wholly destructive. The thought of someone firing one …

Well, it made him sick to his stomach.

"My God," Ngo breathed.

"It's a real bear," Passerini said, mitigating his language somewhat for the benefit of the SecState. "In my perfect world, we'd destroy the damned things and never build another, but … I'm not a big fan of asymmetrical warfare when it's being deployed against me, so … they stay on the TO&E."

"Would we fire back?" Ngo asked. "If Revelen launched on us?"

Passerini thought about it. "My gut? I don't think the president would do it, no."

"Wow. That's … I don't know how to take that."

"I doubt that it would matter, in any case," Passerini said. "It looks like Revelen has a meta at their border that's keeping out our drones. If they can do that, it's not a stretch to imagine they could knock our warplanes and nukes out of the sky—or worse, turn them back on us."

"Can they … can they really do that?" Ngo asked. "The metahumans?"

"I don't know their capability," Passerini said, "which is a little vexing considering we've known metas have been around for a lot longer than the government previously admitted. It's straining my credulity to think that someone hasn't assembled a capabilities list somewhere. I mean, I've had my people do some preliminary work solely with what we know, but … we don't have much to work with."

"But you have metas on your staff, don't you?"

"We have one," Passerini said. *And Chalke damned near lost us that one*, he did not bother to say. It still burned him that the FBI Director had gone and co-opted his single metahuman asset and got him arrested and imprisoned.

"That's … not much," Ngo said.

"Well, he's useful if we can get him in position in time," Passerini said, checking his watch. They might just make it, assuming the president didn't land on him and try to reverse every move he was making. A sudden, uncomfortable silence had fallen over the Situation Room, and Passerini looked around. All eyes were on the monitors.

He looked up at the screens again, and—boy, that was a surprise.

That Humvee video Graves had put up had turned into something else entirely. There was no sound, but it was prompting an awful silence because of what was happening onscreen.

"That is … a hell of a thing," some lieutenant colonel opined from the planning table.

"I think that might just be the woman of my dreams," a brigadier general from the Marine Corps said, watching with some serious enthusiasm.

"Get in line, boys," Graves said, "she's mine."

Passerini laughed. He could respect the sentiment because on the screen …

Sienna Nealon was firing an Mk 19 Humvee mounted grenade launcher into a Revelen army camp, and …

Damn. That was a hell of a show. And a hell of a lady.

"Bruno? You there?" Ngo asked.

"Yeah, I'm here," Passerini said. "Just watching Ms. Nealon put the hurt on these Revelen bastards. Kinda having a hard time figuring out who to root for in this."

"Don't let the president hear you equivocate," Ngo said with a trill of amusement. "I doubt he'd be pleased to hear you cheering for public enemy number one."

"Well, I find it very difficult to back the side that's got a bunch of nukes pointed at us," Passerini said, "over the All-American girl that's ripping them about eighty new holes." She landed a shot on a fuel bunker and it went up with a glorious fireball. The whole Situation Room erupted in spontaneous applause.

"She's a criminal, Bruno."

"Well, it's like watching *The Dirty Dozen*," Passerini said, "except it's more like The Dirty One. I mean, she keeps this pace up, I might not have to send in a single soldier to resolve this mess. Which would be fine by me."

"I wouldn't go laying any money down on that," Ngo said.

"Sir … call incoming from the White House," Graves said.

"I gotta let you go," Passerini said, and sure enough, the phone chirped a second later. "It's the Commander-in-Chief."

"I'll be in touch," Ngo said, and then a click.

"Mr. Secretary," President Gondry's voice sounded sharp, like he'd gone and stuck his fingers—or something more delicate—in a bear trap.

"Mr. President," Passerini said, bracing himself.

"I want you to reverse my previous order," Gondry said, and boy did it sound like he was building to a full head of steam, "and bring us up to DEFCON 2. Move everything you have into position." There was a pause as Gondry sucked in a breath and Passerini couldn't bring himself to, "Sienna Nealon is alive, and we are going to war with Revelen."

76.

Sienna

I couldn't hear myself sing but I was belting out a rendition of Metallica's "Enter Sandman" as I blazed away with the Mk 19 on the army encampment, which was less an encampment and more like a day headquarters and staging ground for about a hundred of Revelen's least-fine merc dregs. I did not offer them any warning to speak of, instead rolling up into the middle of the T-intersection in front of their HQ and opening fire on their trailers, vehicles and tents.

The results were grim … and yet hilarious since I had deemed these men bastards worthy of death. Bodies were flying everywhere, limbs lay scattered on the ground. If I had a conscience for scum-sucking mercs, I would have maybe stopped and taken a real serious assessment of where I was in life that I was killing a hundred human lives from this earth without giving a single damn about it.

Hell, I was singing as I did it. "Like roaches with the lights coming on!" I shouted with perverse glee as I caught one of the mercs running and turned him into a splatter with my shot.

But then, I was also blessed with the knowledge that these particular men were of the rape-and-pillage variety, the kind who viewed military service as their path to personal glory. They served their own whims, and their whims were sick, because they were looking for a way to kill human beings within the bounds of law. Mostly.

Me? I was totally not like that, and definitely did not have any uncomfortable, belly-churning thoughts that I might be hating on these guys so hard because I saw something in them that I despised in myself.

No, definitely not.

I set my jaw and grenaded the bastards twice as hard because I definitely was not anything like these soulless killers. "Enter Sandman" faded out somewhere around the chorus, my enthusiasm for singing just sort of dropping off.

There were certainly plenty of targets for me to choose from. People were running madly around the HQ, trying in vain to find cover from the machine-gun rain of grenades on their position. They hadn't deployed sandbag barricades, which was turning out to be a really bad decision for them, because covering behind vehicles was not working out so well, and they hadn't even deployed any of those forward to cower behind. Pretty arrogant move, assuming someone wouldn't attack them just because they were in the middle of a civilian population center and part of the local army.

This day would have been a real learning experience for these guys. If any of them survived. Which I did not plan for them to.

I spotted a guy coming at me from behind a tent, at least a good two hundred feet away. I could tell he was trouble because he wasn't running for cover, he was running at me. Never a good sign when you're raining hell on people and someone decides to ignore it and cast angry eyes at you out in the open.

I swung the Mk 19 around, lining up the sights with him and let loose just as he chucked a blast of flame at me in return.

Damn. A Gavrikov.

My shells passed his flames in the air, and he exploded into a pattern of blood and bone, his days of chucking flames at an end. He managed to land a hit on the hood of my Humvee, though, a fire starting at the grill.

"That's probably not good," I said. Or thought. Couldn't hear myself say it. But there wasn't much I could do about the fire, so I just ignored it and kept plugging away at the camp. There was motion in the air, and I swung the launcher up, dusting the shit out of a flyer about twenty feet off the ground with a flawless shot that turned him into a rain of gore.

Turning my attention to an army truck that was not a completely burned-out shell, I pumped a few rounds into the canvas back. It blew, gas tanks going up, sending black smoke into the air along with a curtain of flames. I'd already set off one fuel bunker to spectacular effect, but I wasn't going to rest until I blew up all their diesel. Napoleon said an army marched on its stomachs, but modern armies moved on their fuel bunkers, and I meant to deprive them of as much of it as I could. Somewhat out of spite, mostly out of necessity in case I had to run later. It was always helpful to prop open a back door in case of emergency.

A flash of motion caught my attention beneath the wing of the left-side metal shield that covered me from enemy fire. I spun, not bothering to bring the Mk 19 around. Someone had flanked, and fast, too. I drew up my rifle from its sling and tracked the movement—

It was a damned Speedster. He paused, coming out of his blur status for just a second—

I plugged him with three shots, walking them from his guts up to his neck, and he toppled over. His hand was over head, open like he was flagging me down.

He'd never even raised his rifle.

Something solid and metal hit me in the hip, bouncing down onto the platform I was standing on, making a clunk that vibrated through my feet as it landed.

I didn't wait to do the careful mind work of figuring out what it was for sure. I already had a pretty good idea.

I bailed out of the turret, rolling off the back of the Humvee—

The grenade went off inside just as I hit the ground. I vaulted back to my feet and made a break for a car parked nearby, throwing myself behind it

As the Humvee exploded, gas tanks going up from some combo platter of the grenade the speedster had thrown and the fire that the Gavrikov had started. Flames roared up within, completely consuming my beloved Mk 19 and cutting me off from the only thing that had been keeping the army in the encampment at bay.

"Well, damnation," I said, peeking out from behind the car as soldiers started to flood out from behind—hell if I knew where they were all hiding, I thought I'd leveled the place pretty good—everywhere, it seemed. They were dirty, cut up, bleeding, disheveled—

And angry. Really, really angry.

Also? Converging on my position, rifles raised. They were marching down the street, heat of the Humvee fire deterring them not at all. They were coming around it, cautious, about thirty or so out, formed up in a disciplined rank that I wasn't going to be able to just shoot my way through. Not without taking hundreds of bullets for my troubles.

Yeah. Damn.

I looked down the street from whence I'd come. There was nothing in the way of cover there, nothing but a stray parked car for the hundred yards to the next corner. Sprint for it and I'd get riddled with bullets for my trouble.

Nowhere to run.

They were coming up the side of my hiding place now. Close-knit formation. Another few steps and they'd be at me.

Likelihood of mercy?

Zero.

Nowhere to hide.

I huddled against the bumper of the little European car, rifle in hand, readying myself to go out in a blaze of glory.

Because it looked like that was the only option I had left.

77.

Lethe

"I am growing quite tired of your granddaughter," Hades said, watching the screen with obvious irritation. It was playing the news livestream, the one that her friend, Cassidy, appeared to be broadcasting to all networks. Lethe watched it calmly; Hades somewhat less so, though he showed only traces of his growing aggravation.

"I like how she's mine now," Lethe said, hands neatly clamped behind her back, keeping her voice as level as she could given what she'd just seen. "Now that she's pissed you off, rejecting your overtures, surviving the tower collapse, running through your hired help like a pro running back through peewee-league third stringers."

"Spare me your American football analogies," Hades said. "They are lost on me in the best of times. And these are not, obviously, my best times." One of his eyebrows quivered, a measure of his irritation.

"You're watching Death come for the worthy," Lethe said. "Isn't that your 'bag,' as they say?"

"Nobody has said that since the seventies," Hades stared at the table in front of him. "Get with the times, will you?" He moved a map of Bredoccia in front of him. "She is wiping out our army's 1st Division." His gaze flicked up to the screen; the surveillance footage showed her pinned behind a car, her

Humvee destroyed, clutching a rifle as the mercenaries approached. "Finally. At last, perhaps I will be rid of this nuisance before she destroys the entirety of our forces in the capitol."

"I wouldn't go counting on it," Lethe said, under her breath. As though he would miss it.

"I am unsure where from your loyalty to this obnoxious child springs." Hades stood up, not even bothering to mask his annoyance any longer, "but it clearly goes beyond blood or familiarity, since you have met her but once before we began this endeavor."

"Twice," Lethe said.

Hades's eyes narrowed. "What do you mean, 'twice'? When did you meet her before?"

"It was a long time ago," Lethe said, too airily. "And hardly worth mentioning."

"I somehow doubt that," Hades said, squaring his shoulders. "I am beginning to doubt your loyalty, daughter."

She shrugged. "Do you see me doing anything to help her along?"

A hint of mitigation cooled his anger. "No."

"Probably because she's got the situation well in hand," Lethe said. She held in the smile, but only just.

"This is fascinating to me that you sit back and let this play out while merely cheerleading her," Hades said, now draping his own hands behind his back. "You want her to beat us?"

Lethe shrugged again. "Perhaps I'm just enjoying watching her pull it off with nothing but a plucky attitude and a chip on her shoulder the size of a small moon."

"She takes after my brother in that regard," Hades said, shadow falling over his face. "Zeus never knew when to quit, either."

Lethe couldn't hold back the laugh at that. "Yes, blame your brother for her genetic predisposition to obnoxious arrogance. Or, conversely," and she took a step closer to him, "remember, perhaps, that time when, after one of your granddaughters was murdered by a mob, you actively ripped the soul out of nearly everyone in the region and would have done worse—except that Mother put a tree squarely through your heart, effectively staking you."

"I was trying to protect my family," Hades said, brow darkening. "To protect the garden, you must kill every weed that threatens to strangle it." He lifted a finger and shook it at her. "That is life, you see. A struggle, always, power matched against power wherever it sees an equal—a threat. It is much the same here, now." He turned away, looking at the monitor. Sienna did not have long before the soldiers would turn the corner on her, but there was some exchange going on, making them hesitate. "The Americans finally see us as a threat. They will need to respond. And their response will provoke another from us. And so it will go, until someone gains the upper hand."

Lethe watched the screen. "I wouldn't have figured you for the sort that would fall into the philosophical wilderness of thinking everything that happens is simply one power move after another."

Hades watched the screen. It certainly looked like an end was nigh. "Power … is all that matters, daughter. It always has been." His hands were clasped tightly behind his back as he concentrated on the chaos unfolding before him. "And I suspect … it always will."

78.

Sienna

"So, guys, I'm thinking … maybe we just call this one a draw?" I shouted as the soldiers kept creeping up on me. I couldn't hear their footfalls, but I could—just barely—feel them, with the knee I had braced against the ground. I was huddled against the back bumper of a tiny Euro car, my rifle clenched in my white-knuckle hands, steeling myself. The sun was beating down from overhead, the air still and quiet after the massacre. It was stifling out here on the street, summer in full force and sweltering, no wind at all to at least redistribute the heat.

"You will throw out your weapon and surrender!" came the reply, stiff and certain, apparently not hampered by the hearing loss I was dealing with, that fierce ringing like someone had installed a school bell in my brain and was trying to let me, personally, know that was I super late for class.

Options, options.

One, come out shooting. That would end in about a quarter second in a blaze of glory. I checked under the car, and, sure enough, there were enough pairs of boots walking my way that I had less than a snowball's chance in an angry Gavrikov's hand to last more than a second before my brains went airborne in molecular form from about a million bullets passing through my skull.

Two, run, die running. Self-explanatory, no more valid than

option one.

Three, throw out my rifle and surrender (call that 3A) or pretend to surrender (3B) and wait for something else to happen that might give me an advantage.

Four, wait. Die in a minute or so unless that something else happened to give me an advantage.

"Cassidy," I muttered, reaching into my front pocket and lifting the phone. "Suggestions?"

Shit. The phone was busted all to hell from my landing when I'd jumped off the Humvee. "Did you really think I could carry a phone through this mess and expect it to stay in one piece?" I muttered to no one in particular. "Do you even know me, Cassidy?"

"Come out now or we kill you!" the lead soldier shouted again.

"3B it is," I said and unslung my rifle, tossing it out. I raised my hands past the car's edge, waiting to see if anyone would fire at them.

They didn't, so a moment later, I stepped out myself to face the music. Or rather, the angry, soulless Russian mercs. Looking into the eyes of the nearest ones, I had a really bad feeling that my allotment of time for waiting for an advantage to present itself was going to be incredibly short, probably measured in seconds rather than minutes, because these bastards …

I could see from just looking them in the eyes that they were going to kill me. And it wasn't going to be the nice kind of killing, with a mercy bullet to the back of the head. No, it was going to be the French Revolution kind of killing, where they tore me apart after inflicting maximum pain and humiliation, and I had a sinking feeling that these boys …

They knew how to inflict maximum pain and humiliation.

"Come on, Cassidy," I said under my breath. "Gimme something."

The lead soldier flashed a malicious smile and motioned for a couple of his underlings to move up. They were all pointing their guns at me. There wasn't a chance in hell, short of getting a very concentrated bomb dropped on them, that I was going to walk out of this one with all my limbs.

"Shit," I said, as they started toward me. Cautious, of course, because they weren't stupid. Vicious and angry, but not stupid. They approached with an overabundance of care, the two he'd tasked to getting to me going extra slow.

"Take your pistol out of its holster with two fingers," the captain said. "Make a move out of turn, and we shoot you in the legs and arms and make a mess of you."

"I kinda get the feeling that's going to happen regardless," I said, lifting my right hand and slowly reaching with two fingers extended for the pistol in my belt.

I stopped halfway there when I saw something.

And then … I felt something.

A light breeze ruffled my hair, like a breath of cool autumn off the sea. It was a pleasant surprise after a long night and morning where the air had felt so close, so heavy. It blew gently at first, then began to whip the dark strands around my head as it got stronger.

I let out a little giggle as it blew all around, raising dust in the street, little eddies of dirt that swirled and moved like tiny tornadoes.

"What … what is this?" the captain asked, looking around, keeping his gun leveled at me.

"Is just the weather," one of the approaching soldiers said, still slow walking his way to me. "Now we skin her alive and see how she does without her powers—"

"You ain't gonna do shit to me," I said. The wind was pushing up to full force now, gale-force, in fact, and my attackers were losing their footing, their gun barrels swept aside by the fury of it. They spun and twisted as it lifted them off the ground in a mighty tornado, sweeping them up with the detritus of the camp I'd destroyed, the winds kicking up to churn in a curtain of pure, furious hell, the back ranks of them being swirled into a sudden tornado with metal debris in one giant, deadly blender.

"What—what is this?" the captain shouted as he, too, was swept away by the fury of the storm, wind dragging him off, unable to so much as point his rifle at me. He disappeared behind the black curtain wall now hanging over the enemy camp, and blood flew out in buckets as the entire remainder of the Revelen 1st Army Division was thrown into a man-made grinder.

"That …" I said as a figure dropped out of the sky, dirt puffing as he caught himself a foot above the ground then landed gently next to me, his long, dark hair not unlike mine as it swirled in the winds he controlled—

That he'd just killed my enemies with.

"That is my big brother," I said, staring at him for a long second—

Then I lurched forward on unsteady legs and hugged him tight, wrapping my arms around his neck.

"You missing me already?" Reed asked, the smartass. "It's only been a few days."

"What I am … is damned glad to see you," I said, as I buried my head on his shoulder in relief. "Just … damned glad to see you."

79.

Lethe

"Arghhhh!" Hades said, sweeping the maps off the table in front of him. "Damn her! Damn her straight to—to—to me."

"I'm sure that would be fun to watch," Lethe said. "Her in top form, fresh off of killing an army of metas, you a few thousand years past your prime—"

"If there is one of us who is past their prime," Hades whirled on her, finger up and extended in front of his face, "it is the girl who lost the souls that made her great."

"I think taking out a division of mercenaries is not too shabby on the greatness scale," Lethe said, "but maybe I'm missing something."

"Her brother did that," Hades said, dismissing the deed with a wave. "And he is empowered with the booster serum, or else he never would have been able to manage it." He shook his head. "No. She is still weak. Unable to make the hard decisions—"

"She just threw herself into the teeth of an army—"

"Foolishly," Hades said. "Stupidly, without any idea of how she could win that fight. She causes us damage, but little of it is fruitful. It is the tantrums of a spoiled child, angry that she was punished."

"I think you might be underestimating her emotional drive," Lethe said. "If she's furious, it seems very directed—and potent. Hardly an indiscriminate tantrum. You, on the other hand, seem to be exhibiting all the signs of losing it … Father."

"You think me on the edge, yet you missed all the fun, last time, when your mother stepped up and killed me," Hades said, turning a cool gaze on her. "Perhaps you wish to follow in her footsteps?"

"If I wanted you dead," Lethe said, "you'd know it because you'd be long dead by now. I've followed your lead. I haven't intervened in your insane attempts to kill my granddaughter by throwing everything including the kitchen sink and every dish at her. If I have any worries at the moment, it's for your state of mind."

"I have long had goals," Hades said, "to protect my family, my line. To build our future by embracing strength." He raised a clenched fist. "Every alliance I made was in service of this aim, every petty threat I supported from Cavanagh to Harmon to Nadine Griffin to the bastard who dwells in our basement even now, I did because I thought it would move me—move *us*—closer to the world I envisaged." His eyes were bulging. "I did it for me, and I did it for you, daughter. Because we were the strongest, the survivors. And I thought, perhaps, it might include her as well. But she has chosen her path, and with it, her fate."

"She chose to fight because you pushed her," Lethe said, throwing a little heat of her own. "You sent that little snake Krall after her, twisted the fact that she'd made preparations to fight before she even arrived here, before she learned the truth about us, into evidence of her treachery. Now she's demolishing your bought-and-paid-for army and surviving your idiot fearless leader's attempts to kill her, and rather than thrusting out an olive branch and realizing in this war of bulldozers, she's going to flatten everything you hold dear, your dumb ass is doubling down on pride. Well, I've had about enough of pride, Father," Lethe said, turning to leave. "I've—"

She didn't even realize General Krall had entered the room, let alone that the diminutive general had snuck up behind her and was waiting when she turned. Lethe flinched in surprise, but the general struck before she could react—

The first punch hit Lethe in the throat; the second in the side of the head. It was fierce, too, stars flashing in front of her eyes, causing her legs to buckle beneath her.

"I don't expect you to understand the things that I do for this family," Hades said, from somewhere out of the darkness that was swirling behind Lethe's eyes. Another blow flattened her, dropping her to her face, cold concrete floor touching her lips, the metallic taste of blood in her mouth. "Soon, you will see. Soon, the vision will become clear … you know, after the concussion passes. But until then, daughter … I think it best if you take a little nap …"

The last hit put her out, into sweet darkness, and Lethe let go of her worries about her father and her granddaughter, slipping into the embrace of unconsciousness without another word.

80.

Passerini

"... And we've got an AC-130 gunship, a flight of Raptors just past the border," Passerini said, reading from his prepared notes, "and a little farther out, B-1B Lancers, a couple B-2 Spirits close at hand, with their tanker support. I've got a front-rank element of F-35As, too, if we can get the damned things to fly long enough to pose an actual threat—"

"Enough of the mumbo-jumbo," President Gondry cut in, clear anger breaking through over the open line. "What does it all mean?"

"It means if we can get past that metal-bender at the Revelen border," Passerini said, "I can level a decent portion of the country in a matter of hours. But that's not all there is to winning a war."

"What the hell do you mean?" Gondry was starting to snap with impatience.

"Well, if you want a real war ... we need troops on the ground," Passerini said. Had Gondry completely ignored him during previous briefings? They'd covered all this logistics and planning stuff ad nauseam for multiple scenarios. "They'll have to come up from Germany through Poland, at which point they'll need to traverse Russian territory, and even assuming we get the nod from the Russians for that, we're not set up to do it effectively."

"What about invading through Canta Morgana?" Gondry asked. "Put troops on shore there, march them to the capitol."

Passerini let out a slow, careful breath, and saw Graves shaking his head out of the corner of his eye. "An amphibious assault through Canta Morgana is an option, sir … but it's going to take weeks. We'll need to get a Marine MEU into place and—"

"How long, Mr. Secretary?" Gondry asked, apparently just done with it all.

"For a real invasion … weeks, sir," Passerini said.

"You are truly useless," Gondry said. "We spend all this money on the damned military, and in our actual hour of need, where are you? Nowhere. Nowhere useful, anyway. I want that country taken over right the hell now. I want Sienna Nealon dragged out to face justice. Why the hell can't you deliver this? Send in your special forces, why don't you?"

"Well, sir, we do have special forces at the ready, within striking distance of the border," Passerini said, "but they're not going to be of absolute utility against the entire conventional forces structure of Revelen. They have two remaining divisions—"

"I don't understand," Gondry said, "she's at war with them now, too, yes? Maybe we can just bypass this war business entirely. Let's make a deal with Revelen and get her ass back here for trial. SecState? Where are you on this?"

"Here, sir," Ngo cut in. She was probably elsewhere, maybe Foggy Bottom, but definitely on the call. "We're attempting to make contact with Revelen through Russian channels at present. Our ambassador is meeting with the Russian president even now, and we're making considerable progress—they've even suspended their alliance with Revelen and are offering—"

"Wonderful, wonderful," Gondry said, "I don't give a damn. Nealon. She's the priority. How do we get her?"

"I'm not sure we can right now, sir," Passerini said, "because of the nuclear issue. We try and bust in the front door and go for Nealon, we're violating their sovereignty. It's an act of war, and with their missiles almost certainly pointed at us—well, you can surely connect the dots there, sir." *What do you want more*, Passerini thought without asking, *Nealon in your hands or the Revelen nukes to stay in their silos and out of the middle of American cities?*

"Don't be an absolute idiot," Gondry said. "Only an insane person would launch a nuclear weapon. This is not even a threat."

Passerini's eyes widened. "Sir … it's a threat. A very real one, in fact."

"The stability of the world has never been a question," Gondry said. "This Hades, whoever you think he is, he's a statesman. We can bargain with him in good faith, the same we've bargained with the Russian president. Look at the results we've gotten there in just hours."

"Sir, I would caution you not to be so optimistic," Ngo broke in, just in time to keep Passerini from experiencing a cerebral hemorrhage from holding in—well, a lot. "In our negotiations with the Russians, the president has been very clear in stating that Hades is dangerous. That he asked for and received from Russia some concessions we were not even aware of in the form of—apologies, Secretary Passerini, you're going to know more about this than I am—three Typhoon class missile subs and six Akulas—"

"Good God," Passerini said. The whole Situation Room had gone quiet again, everyone listening to—and stunned into silence—by that one. "Did the Typhoons have any missiles in them?"

"Yes," Ngo said.

Passerini put his face in his hands for a second. "Sir … if those Typhoons were fully loaded—and we have no reason to expect they weren't—Revelen has even more nuclear firepower than we previous realized, and with the Akulas, they have the capability to defend them against any attack by our submarine forces, which are moving into position right now but …" He shook his head. "Six Akulas and three Typhoons? Revelen's got a hell of a navy now." He waved for someone to bring up the satellite imaging, but Graves was already on it.

"No sign of them on the surface," Graves said and flipped the image to magnetic resonance. "Do we have any idea where they are?"

Ngo must have heard him. "The Russians say they were delivered to port in Canta Morgana yesterday but deliberately kept submerged. Revelen officers came aboard at the Russian ports before they sailed. They are in control, and most probably somewhere not too far from home, but ..."

"Shit," Passerini breathed. "The Baltic Sea is not a small place. If we're lucky, they're hanging out close by Canta Morgana, but ..." He let out another inaudible curse. That was another batch of nukes in play.

"Actually, sir," Graves pointed at the map, "I think they are close to the port."

Passerini looked to the map; Graves had zoomed it into the harbor at Canta Morgana. Sure enough, there were some mighty bright spots on the magnetic resonance imagery. "Why the hell would they park nine subs in their damned harbor when they have the whole Baltic to hide in? Or better still, get them out in the Atlantic or the Arctic Ocean?"

Graves shrugged. "I'm guessing Revelen's military planners are not experienced in running a sub navy. Probably thought to keep them close at hand."

"Well, it makes our job easier—if we can get our subs close in to hit them," Passerini said. "Where's the—?"

"Sir," Graves said, and suddenly he looked a little grey in the face. "There's activity in Bredoccia again."

"Again?" Gondry asked. "What is it now? Are she and her damned brother destroying the city? Because that'd turn old Hades against them in a hurry, I expect—"

"Sir," Graves said, and he swallowed visibly. "We are about to have a problem." And by the way he looked and the way he said it ...

Passerini knew exactly what he meant.

81.

Dave Kory

The chat was running fast and furious now, and Dave was just doing his best to absorb the mental flow of the best and the brightest as he sat, huddled, in the privacy stall, watching them bat ideas back and forth.

CHALKE: She's making a mess of everything. But maybe turning Revelen against her opens up the door for us to settle it with a careful peace—one that makes allies with them again. Negotiations are already ongoing with Russia.

BILSON: We have to spin this carefully. We already positioned things for war, and victory. If we're not going to have one, we should start pulling that narrative back now—Cooler heads prevailing, that kind of thing in its place.

CHAPMAN: The pace of change in this conversation is breathtaking. Maybe we should state the primary objective and work back from that into a coherent strategy.

JOHANNSEN: The strategy is to get Sienna Nealon the hell out of the way and have her die in disgrace before she can throw any more sabo into our well-oiled machine. She's an impediment to every kind of progress. Look what she did to Harmon. We need her off the board, now.

CHALKE: Working on it. ;)

BILSON: Agree. She's priority one. All this Revelen stuff was just a screen for getting her out of the way. She's proven way too much of a loose cannon. We didn't know half of what Harmon planned, but in this case the cure was almost worse than the disease. We have to keep the pressure up on her, regardless of what goes on with Revelen. We can find a satisfying resolution with them, but we CANNOT let Sienna Nealon walk out of this alive. She's way too dangerous.

Dave just stared at those words, almost snorted. Yeah, she was dangerous and all, but mostly to whoever she was pointing a gun at. He had more immediate concerns than some superpowered lunatic half the world away, no matter how much he disliked her. And he disliked her quite a bit.

He didn't feel the need to share any of that, though.

KORY: We'll keep the narrative heat on her. The video feed isn't helping, though. Any way that can get cut? Seeing everything live from the war zone is making people question things they shouldn't be questioning. She looks less like a criminal and more like a …

He didn't feel a need to use the word. Let 'em fill in the blank.

CHALKE: She's killing hundreds of people without any evident sign of remorse. I believe the term you're looking for is 'psychopath.' ;)

Dave rolled his eyes. Chalke and her stupid emojis. She texted like his mom. And he hated his mom. Hated both of them, actually. But at least Chalke had some power to draft off of.

BILSON: Has anyone seen this new video someone posted of her? Probably by her friends? It's the Eden Prairie thing, but spruced up by someone who knows what the hell they're doing.

CHAPMAN: Seen it. There's not much that can be done about it.

CHALKE: It's on your platform, isn't it? Can't you just make it, y'know, disappear?

CHAPMAN: We can take it down, sure—if you want to guarantee it will go viral.

Dave paused, nodding along. Jaime Chapman was a pretty sharp student of human nature, in his view. The quickest way to make something go big, true or not, was to try and squash it out. Hopefully everybody would get that one loud and clear.

CHAPMAN: Besides, if we take it down now for some stupid reason, it'll just appear on other platforms. Better to kill it with silence.

BILSON: It's not sitting in silence anymore. It's started to get views. This new version of the video is dangerous. We need to stomp it down, now. Deal with it somehow, before it ends up dovetailing with this Revelen mess and breaks out of the firewall we're forming around her.

Dave blew air between gritted teeth. That was a tall order.

JOHANNSEN: I agree. Just make the damned thing disappear. If it's not on the major sites, it's not going to get around. If you keep it out of the mainstream, it's a lot easier to ignore.

CHAPMAN: Mark my words, if you try and snuff it out, you're going to inadvertently give it more oxygen than you can possibly imagine. Virality is my business, and the more you try and blot these things out, the quicker they spread. If you ignore it, it's a lot more likely to go away than if you make a concerted effort to strangle it. People notice strangulation. They don't notice lack of coverage.

Should he weigh in? Probably not. If Chapman and Johannsen were going to argue over it, and Bilson and Chalke were going to land on Johannsen's side anyway … then it was going to happen, probably. No reason for him to trade swipes with anyone in the process. Not if he wanted the scoops to keep flowing. And he sure as shit did.

BILSON: Do it anyway. It's a distraction from the narrative. Let it come out after she's dead, then it won't matter, we can shout to the heavens that OHHH, SHE'S DEAD, SO SADZ and have an Irish wake or a Viking funeral or whatever. But we need her gone first. Priority one.

Dave just stared at that, frowning. Man, she had seriously pissed off the wrong people. He didn't care; he had his own reasons to dislike Sienna Nealon, but damn if Russ Bilson didn't absolutely despise the shit out of her for some reason. Chalke, too. Dave got the general idea about her being an impediment to their plans, and definitely got the worry about what she'd done to Harmon—though he wasn't a hundred percent clear on how that had exactly unfolded. He was on board with the program, because the smartest kids in the class, who were light-years ahead of everyone else, told him this was the direction to go. And kept throwing the raw meat of scoop after scoop in front of him.

He'd be a fool to go any other way. Flashforce's traffic was up double digits from the clicks their exclusives were bringing in.

KORY: I've got some stuff running to try and keep drumming up the hate on her. But if we're trying to get her dead—

He didn't even blink at typing that.

—then isn't it kinda up to either the Revelen army or our own military? Given where she is?

CHALKE: Yes. But we need the public support so we can continue to back that play.

Well, that seemed easy enough, Dave thought.

BILSON: What the hell is happening right now?

CHALKE: Oh, God. Gotta go.

Everyone else logged out in a hurry, the blips next to their names going offline quickly. Dave stared at the screen for a moment, then shrugged and put it away. His pulse quickened as he hurried out of the stall.

When he made it back into the bullpen, he found out exactly why everyone had logged off.

And then he really wished he hadn't.

82.

Sienna

"So ... you've been getting into a lot of trouble since last we saw each other," Reed said as I pulled my face off his shoulder. I wasn't crying, honest. It was just a little emotional release considering it had been a few hours since I'd last encountered anyone who wasn't trying to murder me, that's all. "I kinda figured after I handed you over to the cops that your trouble days were done for a little while, but no ... less than a week later and here we are, in a foreign country, and you've blown up ... everything." He surveyed the mess as his whirlwind came down and a whole crapload of body parts fell with it. And blood. Gallons of blood. "And I came along behind you and did this."

"Remember back when you were a baby innocent and flinched at the idea of killing anybody, let alone meat-grindering a bunch of Russian mercenaries into ... whatever the hell you want to call that?" I looked at the damage he'd done to those guys and ... well, there weren't a lot of cohesive body parts left anywhere around the remains of the camp. It looked like a fine slurry of red had been laid down, with dust mixed in for good measure. Kinda gross. I made a mental note to detour around.

"I call it my sister being herself," Reed said, surveying his work with a disapproving eye. "Russian mercs, you say?"

"Yep." I gave a nod. "Hired by ol' Hades himself to guard his lands. Not local patriots but hired hands, and some pretty murderous ones at that, so you can rest your head on the pillow with a clear conscience tonight knowing that you didn't kill anyone who didn't richly deserve it."

"Thanks," Reed said, turning away from his mess. "That's a real consolation." He fixed me with a serious stare. "What the hell is going on around here? Hades is alive? He's dropping buildings on you? The US government is about to start a war to get you back—I mean, seriously. Is there anywhere you go where you don't just leave a trail of absolute disaster behind you?"

"This is coming from the guy who literally made a Ninja blender out of air and tossed in an army."

"I was trying to save your life," Reed said, cocking his head in disappointment. He looked back. "I … was saving your life, right? Because it occurs to me that I kinda waltzed in right in the middle of this, and they might have been taking you prisoner or something—"

"They'd just talked about skinning me alive, and not in a metaphorical sense," I said. "You were on solid ground—also in the metaphorical sense—in doing what you did. Hell, another couple seconds and I was going to pull my pistol and turn this into a suicide-by-merc to avoid drawing things out the way they wanted to. So …" I drew a deep breath, and hugged him again. "Yeah. You totally just saved my life. Again."

"Well," he said, returning my embrace, strong arms wrapped around me, "I wish I could have been here sooner. And also that I could have brought the rest of the crew, because maybe we could have avoided, uh … making this level of mess with some help from the team." He frowned. "Seriously. Remind me not to do … that …" he gestured in the direction of the oozing slurry of a camp, "… ever again, if possible."

I managed a weak laugh. "I solemnly swear that if possible I will not entice you to use your powers to turn my foes into villain-shakes." I did a little frowning myself. "Mostly because that is super gross. Way more gross than anything I was doing with the grenade launcher."

He blinked. "You had a grenade launcher? Truly, this place is crazy, giving you a grenade launcher."

"Well, it wasn't like they *gave* it to me. I had to take it over some dead merc bodies."

"You do everything over dead merc bodies these days. Pretty soon you're going to be eating dinner on top of dead mercenaries, at the rate you're going."

"What kind of wine goes with dead mercenaries?" I asked. "Rosé, you think? I mean, not that I'm gonna break sobriety, I'm just thinking theoretically—"

A rumble interrupted our repartee and shut me up good and proper. I looked around, seeking the source.

"Where's that coming from?" Reed asked, already on guard.

"Better question—where's the team?" I asked, searching the skies myself.

"Stuck at the border," he said. "They've got a Magneto holding them back."

"Aleksy," I muttered.

"He blew up Greg's SR-71. I had to leave them behind in the house, and he's looking at bringing them across by land or something, but ..." His eyes glimmered. "I figured you needed help ASAP."

The rumbling was just getting worse. "You figured right," I said. "Now, figure out what the hell that noise is—oh."

Oh, indeed.

We figured it out.

A glow appeared in the southwestern sky, not far from where the castle loomed over Bredoccia from its mountaintop. This came from a field up in the high hills not far from the castle, nestled around it. It was a section of the countryside I hadn't toured, and yet, I knew what it contained by the rumble, by the glow in the sky as they rose, some twelve of them by my quick count, on pillars of fire—

"What ... the hell are those?" Reed asked. In his heart, I think he already knew.

"Well," I said, swallowing the mother of all gulps, "I don't think Hades has started a space program, and he definitely wouldn't be launching twelve rockets into orbit all at once, so

…" My hands shook, and not from the trauma of the battle I'd just been in, the peril I'd just experienced, but instead …

It was fear.

For what was to come.

"He just launched his nuclear missiles," I said in a voice of quiet awe. They were rising into the sky, a slow, steady climb, into the blue heavens. "Every last freaking one of them."

83.

Lethe

"Beautiful, aren't they?" Hades asked, watching the missiles climb on the monitor. "There is a sort of grace to them, yes? This technological descendant of the spear, the arrow? They have grown so far beyond their predecessors as to be nearly unrecognizable. Nearly … but still."

"Ugh," Lethe said, fighting off a hell of a headache. She tested her hands. Bound to a steel chair by handcuffs, bolted to the ground. "So … it's come to this."

Hades was standing a short distance away, looking at the screens in front of him. "I don't think you quite realize what it has actually come to, daughter." He half turned, and …

He was smiling.

"That's … not a good look for you," Lethe said, looking sideways at the figure that loomed out of the corner of her eye. Krall, of course, similarly smiling. "I take it the two of you have made plans of your own that you decided to exclude me from?"

"Yes," Krall said.

"Not exactly," Hades said. "The general and I are … close, shall we say."

"Ughhhh," Lethe said.

"Boffing, I think they call it?" Hades asked. "Hooking up?"

"Stop," Lethe said. "Just stop." She shivered with disgust. "So this is why you've given her so much leeway. I should have seen it, I suppose, but I figured you were a little too old to be a starry-eyed schoolboy."

"I have never been to school," Hades said, "I should like to try at some point, though I expect the near future to be somewhat too hectic. I doubt I will get a chance to enroll for a while, seeing as we are about to build a new world." His eyes flashed, and he looked at the screen. "An entirely new world, a fresh start for all us all."

"… Really?" Lethe looked around. "You're going full supervillain? Now?"

"But you see, every supervillain has a reason for their villainy, and I am no exception," Hades said. "I was God of Death in the old world, and it gave me an appreciation for death that so few ever get. My assigned role, my natural power, it forced to me contemplate death more deeply than any philosopher."

"If you're going to monologue, please have Krall choke me out first."

"You really are remarkably like her," Hades said, his patience clearly exhausted. "No wonder you chose her over me."

"I didn't choose her, idiot," Lethe said. "I just watched as she proved herself stronger than your army. And unless you kill me, I'm going to watch her and her brother rip your kingdom apart brick by brick, all while you impotently scream that you can't believe what she's doing against impossible odds."

"Mmmm," Hades said, pretending to think. "You know … I might agree with you, daughter, except I have given her much more pressing matters to think about." He smiled. "The end of the world, for instance."

"What are you doing?" Lethe asked, rattling the chains, a cold feeling of dread seeping into her as she watched the missiles climb on the monitor.

"Becoming Death once more," Hades said simply. "For I have let it take its natural course for long enough."

"Why?" Lethe muttered, rattling her handcuff chains again. "I didn't think you were this stupid."

"The Americans have their hands tied behind their backs," Hades said, looking at the screen and smiling. "Where is my disadvantage?"

"They're not just going to sit back and take that lying down—" Lethe said.

"What are they going to do?" Krall asked, and there was a maniacal light in her eyes. "Invade us? Try to bomb us? We will knock their planes and missiles out of the sky. We will annihilate their ground troops at the border."

"And we will vaporize their cities," Hades finished. "Get ready to feel it, daughter. Get ready to feel … Death," he whispered as the missiles launched, one by one, from their silos. "For Death … is, at last … again on his way."

84.

Passerini

"We have launch!"

Passerini's legs felt numb, but he was standing.

"Confirmed. We have launch. Twelve silos just outside Bredoccia, Revelen."

The voices around him did their jobs. Did the double-check, the triple-check. They'd be watching it out in Colorado at NORAD command, checking and checking again—

But there wasn't a lot of denying what he was seeing on the overhead shot. The flares at the silo locations—

"Mr. President," Passerini said in as firm a voice as he could muster, "Revelen has launched nuclear-tipped intercontinental ballistic missiles at us. Looks like … twelve," he did a quick count, didn't wait for anyone else to confirm. Count the empty silos and you get the number.

"What the hell," Gondry whispered, strain creeping into his voice. "What are you—"

There was a muffled hubbub on the other end of the line. One of the lieutenants looked sidelong at Passerini.

He held up his hand to stave off the man's concern. "That'll be the Secret Service, dragging the president to the bunker. I'm sure he'll be back on line in a few minutes. Until then …" He looked around, prepared to invoke his people to get back to work, but they already were. "I need target vectors."

"Missiles are still heading straight up sir," an operator called from across the room. "It'll take a few minutes before we have a clear—"

"Eastern seaboard," Graves said, "the Midwest, DC, LA—they're aiming for the big targets."

Passerini cocked an eyebrow. "Probably good guesses, Graves. But we'll have to wait a few minutes to find out how right you are—"

"Nossir," Graves said, shaking his head. "We won't."

Passerini frowned. The colonel was surprisingly calm considering he'd just watched the end of the world kick off. Oh, well. There wasn't much to do now but wait—

"Mr. Secretary," the president's voice broke back onto the line, harried and urgent.

"Welcome back, Mr. President," Passerini said.

"Mr. Secretary—Bruno," Gondry said, speaking directly into the line, coming out louder than he usually did when he wasn't shouting. "You have to fix this. This—these missiles—they're—we can't let them—I mean—my God, man, these are—they're coming to our cities and—" And he just stopped right there. "You have to do something," he said, when he finally managed to string his words together.

Passerini just looked at the screen. The rockets were in flight, but they'd yet to turn, to take their lazy arc west. There was a little hope in that, as they raced for the upper atmosphere and the lesser wind resistance they'd find there. There they'd make their turn, acquire their definite targets, and come homing in before releasing their MIRV payloads to seek and destroy the cities they were aimed at.

And all Bruno Passerini could do was watch. "I'm sorry, sir …" he said, and truly, he was, "… but there's not a damned thing we can do."

85.

Sienna

"Oh my God."

Reed's voice was quiet in the rising tide of oblivion, the missiles climbing up in the sky.

"This … is not an afternoon of delight," I said, watching them rise into the blue.

Something squawked in Reed's pocket and he reached for it, seemingly more out of annoyance at the noise than because he was consciously thinking. He came out with his phone, blinking at it in surprise.

"What the hell are you waiting for?" Cassidy's voice shrilled from the speaker. "An invitation? Get after them, idiot!"

I blinked. Too stunned, maybe, I hadn't even thought about—

Reed looked at me. It was a ghostly look, stricken and sick all at once. "I came here to help *you*," he said, almost a whisper.

"The world needs you more," I said, watching the pillars of fire rise into the sky. "Go. Go show the damned world what you are. *Go!*"

With my last shout, he blew into the air, pocketing his phone and reaching out. The winds howled for a second around me, and then he was gone, chasing the missiles.

And I was left alone, on the ground, in the middle of Revelen, with nothing but a shitload of anger.

"Krall," I said, almost growling, under my breath, as I retrieved my rifle and slung it over my shoulder. "Hades."

I used my elbow to break the window of the car I'd been covering behind not so long before. It only took a minute to hotwire it, and then I was off.

Back on mission.

86.

Passerini

"But why can't you just knock them down?" Gondry asked. Clearly in the "bargaining" stage. "We have a—we have something for that, don't we? Star Wars? Isn't that what they called it?"

Passerini cleared his throat, uncomfortably. "Sir … you helped cut the funding for that project back when you were in the Senate, and Harmon killed it shortly after taking the presidency. The residual assets—the missiles and launchers—aren't even in Europe anymore because last year you traded away our deployment of them to the Russians in exchange for diplomatic considerations—"

"Don't you dare try and lay the blame for this fiasco on me!" Gondry shouted into the phone.

"I'm not blaming you, sir," Passerini said. He didn't have much in the way of emotion left to add to his voice. "Just laying out what's happened and letting you know why the cupboard is bare."

"Can't you shoot them down with a plane? You have them right there at the border—"

"Nossir," Passerini said, and truly, he wished the president had been right about this. "That's not how it works. Our planes do not possess that capability. No plane does."

"Mr. Secretary … you're telling me those missiles are coming our way and there's nothing you can do about it …?" There was a thread of desperation. "That all this money we've funneled your way all these years—"

Which you cut at every opportunity, you prick. And that time Passerini did apportion some blame, at least in his head.

"—That it's all going to count for *nothing*? That it buys us nothing right now?"

"Well, sir," Passerini said, still calm, "you funded our troops, who have a specific mission. You funded our planes, our aircraft carriers … they have specific missions and abilities. You did not fund the anti-ballistic missile platforms. Too experimental. Too prone to failure. These were the arguments. And so we do not have those. Because you did not choose to spend the money on them. Because, I believe you said, not an hour ago, that we had not experienced a nuclear launch and no one would be foolish enough to change that fact. Well, I'm sorry to inform you that they have, sir, and this is how. Hades just launched nukes at us because he knows there's not a damned thing we can do about it except watch—and pray they don't hit anything too vital."

"Sir," Graves said, "the trajectory of the missiles is changing."

"Are we getting final trajectory?" Passerini asked, turning his attention to the screen.

"I don't think so, sir," Graves said, and he actually started to smile. "I think this … is something else entirely."

87.

Reed

The wind blew by in all its fury, and I rode it wildly, high into the sky above the cloud layer that hung over Revelen like a white ceiling.

I was rising, but even with the full power of the wind at my command, catching a rocket myself was a thing that was simply outside my reach. I couldn't propel myself fast enough to catch them, not with wind.

But I was about to grab the hell out of them nonetheless.

"You need to get them soon!" Cassidy's voice shouted, all tinny and faint, muffled from inside my pocket. "When they hit the upper atmosphere you're not going to have much to work with!"

"Tell me something I don't know," I muttered, figuring it'd be lost to the wind.

"There are entire websites devoted to discussing how amazing your sister's ass is."

"I … actually did not know that," I said. "And I'm not sure I wanted to."

Focus. This was a game of catch, and my targets were ahead. Twelve missiles.

No waiting.

"If I snuff the flow of air to their engines, what happens?" I asked.

"They fall and detonate upon impact with the earth," Cassidy called back. "Probably don't do that."

"Yeah," I said. "No shit."

The roar of the wind was deafening, and I could feel the roll of the missiles cutting through the atmosphere ahead. They were rising by the moment, and I needed to buy time, so …

I pushed down on them with everything I had.

Wind roared against their flat surfaces, drag increasing by leaps and bounds as they tried to claw free of the atmosphere and the atmosphere fought back ten times as hard as it would have by default. They slowed, got sluggish, and I flew closer—

"You might not want to push too hard on the nuclear weapons," Cassidy said. "Just a thought. Because they could light up right there, and I doubt you want to experience a detonation, especially an upper-atmospheric one, with all its attendant EMP effects. Which you would be dead and unable to appreciate, but … still. It'd suck for those of us left behind."

"Well, what the hell am I supposed to do here, Cassidy?" I shouted, looking down, trying to make myself clear by shouting at my pocket. "I can't push down too hard, I can't let them go, I can't cut off their oxygen—what would you suggest? Riding them like Dr. Strangelove to their targets?"

"Maybe pick a different target? But probably not ride them, because you wouldn't survive it."

"I am not hooked into their targeting system, I cannot just choose another place for them to—oh." I blinked a couple times.

They were rockets. They had to steer, and it wasn't via those big explodey engines spitting fire out the back.

They had fins.

Which meant …

They used wind.

"Did you figure it out yet?" she asked.

"Well, for crying out loud, why didn't you just say it to begin with?" I asked, using the fast flow of air running along the rocket bodies to find the place where it hit resistance and slewed. I found it for each of them and then … ever so subtly … and then not so subtly … started to change the flow.

"Sorry," Cassidy said. "Sometimes I forget everyone but me is an idiot."

The rockets changed direction, almost instantly, angling sideways.

"Go northeast," Cassidy said. "Toward the arctic circle. We'll figure out what to do once you're in uninhabited regions."

"I'm not detonating twelve nukes in the ocean, if that's what you're suggesting! I'm not a damned eco-terrorist!"

"I'm not suggesting anything yet," Cassidy said, "except that you steer them away from your precious fellow humans and hang out for a little bit while I see if I can disarm them. Then you can just ride them to the ground or ice or whatever without fear of turning into a crispy critter. Still … maybe stay back a ways."

"I … will …" I felt a hard tug. The lead rocket was really resisting me, and I wasn't able to bring much to bear on it. Looking up, I saw it was a few miles ahead of the rest of the pack, which were responding to my wind commands and had made the turn as I'd requested. They were blazing ahead on a lateral line.

That lead, though … it was pulling further and further away by the second.

"Shit," I said, thrusting a hand out, as though that would help. I was pushing on it from above, redirecting the current around the fins, even jacking it around with the flow intake, but …

"Uh, Reed. One's getting away."

"I know that, thanks!"

With my mind half on the ones heading northeast and the other firmly on the one still climbing, I concentrated. I pulled at all the levers I had at my disposal, every single thing I could think of …

But it kept sailing upward.

Out of the effective reach of my winds.

"Cassidy …" I said, watching it blaze as it climbed, up to the heavens, "I … I can't follow this one any higher if I want to maintain control of the others."

"Simple choice, Reed. One or the other eleven." Man, she

sounded indifferent about it. "If you let the others go to pursue that one, they will course-correct and be out of your reach in about a minute. And they won't re-enter the atmosphere until they're over their targets, at which point they'll split off the six warheads, and suddenly you'll have seventy-two nukes to deal with instead of eleven, and spread out over—I'm guessing, here—the entire North American continent. The answer seems obvious, doesn't it?"

I watched that lone rocket sail higher into the sky, like an upside-down candle rising above me into the clear blue. "Obvious," I said, my voice a little husky, "but damned sure not easy."

"Well, if it was easy anyone could do it," Cassidy said, so matter-of-factly that I wished I could reach through the phone and slap her.

But instead, I concentrated on the eleven rockets in my control and steered them north, kept them low in spite of their struggling to return to the course path that would carry them into the upper atmosphere and out of my reach. "Cassidy … tell Sienna … tell her … I lost one." I swallowed, the wind blowing past my face as I rushed to keep up, to keep the flaming tails of the ones I had in my grip at least in sight. "Tell her … I don't know … tell her …" A cavalcade of potential appeals came to me, all some variant of me seeking absolution for the fact I'd just let a nuclear weapon escape me.

That I had just sealed the fate of millions.

And I didn't even have time to mourn, because I had to prevent the deaths of countless millions more.

"Tell her I screwed up," I managed to choke out. "Tell her … I failed."

88.

Lethe

Hades's face was getting pretty close to purple, or at least as close to it as he got. Rage suffused it, twisted it, his mouth a wavy line of anger as the rocket track showed eleven of the twelve veering off their intended course, fighting madly against the winds that were blowing them, somehow, off course.

"Curses," Lethe said mildly, "foiled again."

"I am hardly foiled," Hades said, face lightening but a shade as he turned and shared a look with Krall. "I am perhaps Saran-wrapped, but only temporarily." He smiled. "I have, after all, three Typhoon-class submarines on the coast, waiting to launch … and the Russians, with their entire arsenal, in my back pocket."

"Sir," one of the console operators stood. "The port, at Canta Morgana. They are reporting—" He was a wide-eyed, fresh-faced lad, but his eyes seemed especially wide now. "Elevated waves, sir. Something—something is happening on the coast—"

89.

Canta Morgana, Revelen

Valter Liisu had been a fisherman all his life. Had roamed the Baltic all his life. From Riga to Canta Morgana, he had made his trade in his boat, the *Kalju,* and plied his trade up and down the coast.

He had sailed in sun, he had sailed in rain. Even in winter, though only before the port of Canta Morgana froze. Even then, sometimes he would fish out on the ice, with nothing but a pole and an auger.

Valter had, in his sixty years, seen everything. Or so he thought.

Because now …

Now …

He saw fifty-foot waves coming in off the sea …

And there wasn't a cloud in the sky.

A shouted exclamation to brace was lost in the roar of the lead wave rising up past the bow. It seemed very small, a tiny profile, running only a couple hundred yards in length. But it had fury, churning across the surface of the Baltic—

And missing his boat by what felt like inches.

Valter held tight as it seemed to shrink upon the edge, the *Kalju* bobbing furiously, spinning in the power of the wave's wake.

Valter gawped; another wave followed, rising just as high, and within it—

What … what was *that*?

He pointed as it passed, and his crew saw it.

"Like a metal … fin?" Rain Koit asked, the wave rolling through, missing them, once again, by feet, but spinning the boat about and carrying them closer to shore.

"Look!" another of his crew shouted, and pointed toward the shore only a mile off now, where the first wave was rolling in on an empty stretch of beach and sand and trees—

The wave seemed to roll higher, rising up to a hundred feet, two hundred feet, a solid wall of water, a tsunami that would surely roll inland, past the coastal hills, hell, it might even reach Bredoccia, Valter thought as it crested, high, just above the beach—

And stopped, just as suddenly, before the shore.

Something … fell out of it, barely visible from their position riding the waves. It dropped the two hundred feet and crashed on the rocky beach, metal landing hard on sand and stone.

"Is that a … submarine?" Valter asked as the first wave dissolved into the second, and the sequence was repeated, another grinding, crashing noise as a second sub was deposited on top of the first, and the endlessly tall waves continued to roll past the *Kalju*—

"What the hell is that?" Rain asked, pointing at the next wave in line. It, too, showed signs of a tail fin popping out of the water, but that was not what Rain was pointing at.

No … what he was pointing at …

Was a man. A man riding the top of the wave. As though he were some sort of mad surfer.

"WHO DO?" the man shouted, and Valter could see his sandy blond hair flashing in the sunlight, the wind calm and the seas mad. He seemed to let the question echo over the wild sea for a moment, and then let fly the answer, cracking over the roar of the waves. "SCOTTY DOOOOOO!"

And then he was gone, riding the wave into shore, another deafening clang as another submarine crashed onto the others, slamming into the stony shore, the ventral surface and conning tower crashing into the earth as it came shattering onto the beach. Another followed.

"Who … is 'Scotty'?" Rain asked, watching with his brow furrowed.

"Him, I hope," Valter said, watching the last of the waves roll in from the sea. Another thunderous crash; another submarine wrenched from the loving embrace of the waters and smashed upon the shore. The raw tonnage of those things … the power it would take to drag not one but … ten? Valter had lost count. "Because if another one of these … people … is coming …" He just shook his head. "What kind of madness might they bring?"

90.

Passerini

Passerini watched the satellite view that Graves had pulled up of Canta Morgana. He'd seen a ship graveyard once or twice. Time was, though, they'd put them at the bottom of the sea, not on a perfectly good beach in Revelen.

But then, beggars couldn't be choosers, especially when you were beggaring for the lives of every American those sub-bound nuclear warheads might be targeting.

"Sir," Graves said, barely concealing a smile, "it would seem that Sienna Nealon and her friends are helping to defuse this situation."

The main screen flicked back to the radar tracking. Eleven of the missiles were veering off, gathered together like a herd, maintaining a steady altitude and being herded off course. That last one, though—

"Do we have a target yet?" Passerini asked.

"The Midwest, sir," Graves said, and his smile vanished. "Chicago. Detroit. Des Moines and … Minneapolis."

Passerini blinked. "That was the first one launched?"

Graves nodded. "And so probably the first targeted. The most … important."

Passerini looked sideways, thinking about it. "Sending a personal message, you think?"

"A personal message?" Gondry's voice crackled in. Passerini

had almost forgotten the president was on the line. "To who?"

"Sir," Passerini said, "if that's aimed at Minneapolis … I think you know who the message was for." *You just don't want to hear it over your hate. Sir.*

"Well … still," Gondry said, and yeah, he was clearly back in denial on this one, "we have almost all the missiles under control. Treston has those, Byerly has wrecked their subs—what do we do about that last one? There has to be a way to stop it." His voice cracked. "We have to stop it, Bruno."

Earlier today you told me I was on my way out the door. Now I'm 'Bruno' to you. Bastard. "Sir," Passerini said, "there might be one way." And here he looked at Graves, because … Passerini felt like he was finally starting to get something that had been in front of his face all this time, something he damned sure ought to have gotten a long time ago.

"How?" Gondry asked.

"I'm going to need a few minutes, sir," Passerini said. "To get an operational concept together and get back to you."

"Whatever it takes, Bruno," Gondry said, and there was an unusual urgency in his voice. He collected himself a moment and said, "I trust you to … to get this done. However you have to."

"Roger that." Passerini cut the line and looked right at Graves. "You've been playing me all this time."

"No. No, sir, I haven't," Graves said, unbuttoning his uniform. "I've been trying to defuse this situation before it blows up—like this."

Passerini stared back at him. He liked to consider himself a good poker player, and there was certainly an earnestness there. "We'll deal with your impersonating an officer later—'colonel,'" and he imparted a savagery to the title. "What type of—"

"I see the future," Graves said. "They call me a Cassandra."

"The girl who saw but was not believed," Passerini said.

"You're quite the classicist, sir."

"Eat shit, Graves—if that's your real name."

"It is."

"How are you tied into all this?" Passerini asked. He looked sideways toward the door. MPs were there, of course, on guard—

"You can arrest me once it's over, if you like," Graves said, drawing his attention back. "I won't fight it. Really. I just want to save the situation ..."

The trail-off was all the tell Passerini needed. "Bullroar," he said. "You're with Nealon."

"Yes," Graves answered, without hesitation. "But consider this: I knew you were going to find me out, but I came anyway. Stayed anyway. Let you figure it out. I could have left anytime. I've been trying to help you, because you're the only one who's powerful enough and open-minded enough to help *her*." He came out from behind the console and approached with open hands. "Sir ... she's not what Gondry thinks she is. She's not a danger. She's not this terrible criminal the public sees." His eyes were bright, open, and sincere. "She's a damned hero, sir—and she'll give everything to save us. If you let her."

Passerini just stared at him. Part of him wished he carried a sidearm here, like he did on his last deployment. "Lieutenant Kefler—"

"Don't," Graves said.

Passerini's eyes narrowed. "What was I about to say?"

"You were going to order an F-35 to test the border," Graves said. "It'll blow up. And not just because it's a shitty plane. The Magneto will get it."

"You know I have to try anyway," Passerini said, staring at him evenly. He could have guessed the order, though it seemed improbable.

"Use a drone," Graves said.

"Will the pilot survive the attempt?" Passerini asked.

Graves thought about it a second. "Yeah. He'll eject in time. No injuries."

"Then I'd rather use the F-35 than a drone," Passerini said, almost shrugging, as he prepared to give the order. "Those things just suck."

91.

Hades

"So … less foiled and more … Tupperwared?" Lethe asked, not even bothering to test the cuffs anymore. Even if she did break them … what then? Fight her way through everyone in the control room? Kill her father? Kill Krall?

Well, maybe Krall. That could be fun.

"So very amusing you are, my daughter," Hades said. Now his lips were a grim line, set, and his eyes thickly lidded into slits. "Where is the Russian president? I asked you to call him an hour ago. We still have their arsenal at our disposal—"

"Sir," another of the lieutenants said. "The Russian president has been declining our calls."

"Try again," Hades said. Straining.

"I have been trying for ten minutes," the lieutenant said. "His secretary says he is in a meeting." The lieutenant licked his lips. "With the Americans."

A vein popped out at Hades's temple. "Betrayed. Betrayed by one of our very own."

"That's the problem with puppets. You can't remove your hand from their ass and expect their mouth to continue moving in time with yours," Lethe said. At this point, the best thing she felt she could do was add to Hades's irritation. It wasn't as if sitting quietly was an option. At least not for her.

"Sir, they are testing our air defenses," Aleksy said, rising to his feet, eyes focused on the radar console in front of him. "It's a—"

92.

Passerini

"F-35 lost sir," Lieutenant Kefler said. "Clean eject. Chute is good."

Passerini stared at Graves, who lurked just a few steps away, waiting for an answer. He got one.

"Get her on the phone—if you can."

93.

Sienna

"Excuse me ..." I turned, about to pull away from the curb in my stolen car. I'd just been looking away where Reed had just flown up into the sky to go be a hero when I heard the voice and turned my head. It was soft, feminine and pleading, but I raised my rifle across my body in preparation just in case.

There was an older woman, wearing one of those scarves over her head and tied under her chin, and she was lingering just outside the broken driver's side window, like she was trying to keep her distance from me but still be heard.

"Yeah?" I asked, probably a little rougher than I should have, finger hanging out just off my trigger. So sue me. My brother had just gone off to do something brave and dangerous, and I was about to resume my current murder mission, which was now against my great-grandfather and his chief general, at least, and maybe included my grandmother, too. And this lady was likely about to badger me for stealing her ride. "What? Is this your car?"

"No, no, it's my neighbor's," she said, shaking her head. "He's a—how you say it? Prick? Take it. Totally fine." She shook her head again. "No. I am so sorry to bother you during ... this," she said, turning her gaze from the car I'd just stolen to the bloody slaughter just down the street. It probably looked terrible, because red liquid was oozing into the drain gutters already. I'd never seen anything quite like it. I was a little proud that my brother had done it. And a little repulsed. "Ahhh … uhm … phone call for you." She held up a cell phone in her hand.

I stared at the phone.

She stared back at me, grimacing like I was going to hit her or something.

"Sorry," I said, and gently took the phone. "You, uh … mind if I keep this for a while?"

"Take it. Is fine," she said, handing it over eagerly. "Am due for upgrade anyway. Has cracked screen. Is insured." She looked around. "Will tell them it was lost in … this." Her attention settled, again, on the mess at the former army camp. "Should not be problem."

"Yeah … I am deeply sorry for all … this," I said. "And I'm gonna make the bastards responsible pay for it. One way or another."

"You 'rock on with your bad self,'" she said, and then gave me a double thumbs up as she eased away. "But … maybe do so on other side of town? I have grandchildren that live with me …"

"Yeah, no, I'll totally get out of your way. Right now, in fact," and I put the pedal to the metal without hesitation, leaving the poor old lady behind in the mess of her street. Once I'd gotten past the wreckage of the camp and its blood-sluiced streets, I switched the phone to speaker. "Talk to me, Cassidy."

"That was a really touching scene. I almost threw up in my mouth watching it through the phone camera."

I flipped the phone the bird where it rested in the cup holder. "Tell me something good or get lost."

"I do have some good news," she said. "While you were busy stealing cars and bringing sweetness and light to the local grandmas, your brother roped together eleven of the twelve nukes and is riding them to the North Pole like some sort of long-haired, young Santa. Which I thought was pretty good, y'know, eleven out of twelve, but which he whined about like you wouldn't believe—"

"Wait, he missed one?" I asked, just about skidding into a

parked Mercedes. Wished I'd stolen that instead of … whatever brand this was. Definitely not German. "Where's it headed? Please say out to sea. Or somewhere terrible, like Matt Lauer's sex dungeon."

"Current vector has it tracking for the Midwest," she said, kind of airily. "Probably it'll split and hit Chicago, Minneapolis—oh. Hey. Do you think Hades did that—"

"On purpose?" I clenched the wheel, my mouth suddenly dry. "Yeah. Yeah. I think he did that on purpose."

Lobbing a missile at my hometown?

You betcha he did that on purpose.

"You better not be bullshitting me, Cassidy," I said, my brow hardening.

"Hey, I'm not the one launching nukes," she said. "I'm trying to help you against the person who is."

I slammed my fist into the steering wheel and a piece of it broke off. "All right. Fine. I'm ready to—"

"Hang on, who is this?" she asked.

I frowned. "It's … Sienna."

"Not you, dumbass," she said. "I'm talking about the person who just dialed me—yeah, how the hell did you get this—oh, of course. Because you just mentally dialed every number until you landed on mine, right?" She sighed. "Fine. I'll patch you through. Hang on."

A buzzing screech in my ear almost sent me into a haberdasher whose window was covered in a thick layer of dust from the tower collapse. "Damn, Cassidy, what the hell are you—"

"Sienna," an urgent—and incredibly familiar—voice broke into the line.

"Harry?" I asked, and almost ran off the road again. "How the hell did you—"

"No time," he said. "Listen, I've got the Secretary of Defense sitting next to me."

"What?" I asked.

"You have been a busy boy, Harrison," Cassidy said.

"You can hang up any time, Cassidy," he said.

"I'm not her secretary, Harry. I'll keep listening if I want."

"Ms. Nealon," came a deep voice, sounding a little pained. "This is Bruno Passerini. Do you know who I am?"

"Yeah," I said, thinking quickly. "Naval aviator turned admiral. Now Secretary of Defense. They called you … 'Hammer.' Because that was your callsign when you were a badass navy pilot. Something about dropping the hammer on people?"

"You've read my Wikipedia page," Passerini said. "I'm touched."

"Harry, what the hell are you doing with Hammer?" I asked.

"Trying to keep this little war you're at the center of from turning into a nuclear holocaust," Harry said. "Thanks for not making it easy."

I rolled my eyes. "You can't choose your family. You should know; look at your mom, after all."

Passerini cleared his throat. "I'm not sorry to interrupt, and I'm not going to pretend I am. We have a very serious problem. A nuclear warhead in play. Roughly fifty-minute flight time to target, which looks to be—"

"Minneapolis," I said. "Cassidy told me."

Passerini was quiet for a second. "Your secretary told you this?"

"I'm not her secretary," Cassidy said, irritation rising.

"How does one get a secretary fresh out of prison?"

"I'm not—"

"Anyway," Passerini said, "We're backed into a corner here. I've chosen to … trust … Harry."

"With a nuke flying for the homeland, what have you really got to lose?" Cassidy asked, not exactly selling me on this. "Especially since you can't hack it or otherwise use electronics to drive it off course, and your ABM countermeasures are for shit."

"Your secretary is pretty knowledgeable about the problem—"

"The next person who calls me a secretary, I'm disconnecting."

"Listen, Sienna," Harry jumped in, "Scott just came ashore in Canta Morgana and wrecked Hades's nuclear sub arsenal, so if you can disarm this last nuke … he's helpless. It's game over."

I tried to puzzle through all the mental calculations on my journey to how the hell I was going to get that done. "How am I supposed to stop this? They have an override switch or something?"

"It'd be the control console from which they launched the nuke," Cassidy said, oh-so-conveniently. "In the castle. It uses satellite uplink technology, and a real nasty encryption. It's a black vault, off the internet. I can't pierce it from this end, but if you can get me close with a phone, I can probably take care of it via local network access."

"That's fortunate," Passerini said, "because there's nothing we can do on this end. Not with that—Magneto, I think you call it?—keeping a wall up around their country. With him in play, I can't promise you any assistance. We're locked out."

I sighed, turning to look right as I went through an intersection. I thought back to the info I'd co-opted from that soldier I'd killed … uh, more specifically, the one whose memory I'd drained before killing, since I'd killed quite a lot of them by now. "Okay, so basically you're saying I have to storm the castle and get to the control room." I mentally visualized that. "Hmm. That … is going to be a hell of an undertaking. I mean, I was going to do it anyway, but maybe a little slower, a little more carefully … but I guess it's gatecrashing time."

"Beg pardon?" Passerini asked.

"Nothing," I said. "Basically, I'm modifying my plan cuz I need to get that 'Magneto' as you call him, out of the way before I can do shit about the rest of the hired help up there. If I try and go in there guns-a-blazing, he can rip them out of my hand and shoot me right in the head with them. So …" I swallowed. "I gotta kill Aleksy first."

That gave me a little twinge of sadness. I kinda liked Aleksy, but there were pretty good odds he was sitting up there in the control room right now in front of that radar console, using it to help maintain a no-fly zone over Revelen that was keeping out air support, keeping out my friends …

And that meant he'd been there when Hades had launched

the nukes.

And he'd done nothing.

"Okay, I'm on it," I said, decision made.

"Uh … do you need any additional guidance?" Passerini asked. He sounded tentative.

"Nah, I got this," I said. "Already got a plan and everything."

A long pause. "Any chance you'd like to share?" Passerini asked. "I have to brief the president and I'd like to give him something other than, 'I talked to Sienna Nealon and she says she's on it,' you know?"

So I told him what I had in mind.

When I was done, he let out a low whistle. "Well … that certainly exemplifies the level of batshit crazy I've come to expect from you, Ms. Nealon. No offense. I've been known to do a little 'batshit crazy' myself, in my time."

"None taken," I said, "Hammer."

"Before you go," Passerini said, "is there anything we can do … for you?"

"Just keep watch," I said, swallowing heavily, "because this shit right here …? This is maybe going to get me killed, if it goes wrong. And if it does …" I choked down a couple things I wanted to say, and more than a few things I felt. "… Harry?"

"Yeah, I'm here," he said, quiet.

"Just … look away if you see it coming, okay?" I tried not to sugarcoat it, but I didn't want to get all weepy, either. "Don't watch."

Harry didn't respond for a minute, and when he did, his voice sounded thick. "Understood."

"All right," I said, braking into a turn. The last one I needed to make before I got to my destination. "Then watch this shit, boys. Sienna Nealon—out." And I hung up the phone.

I always wanted to say that.

94.

Dave Kory

"SIENNA NEALON IS SAVING YOUR WORLD FROM DESTRUCTION," the voice blared out of the TV, electronically altered, a little crackle/hiss in it as it flashed to the scene and showed the streets of Revelen, Nealon in her car racing along them, dodging a pedestrian here, avoiding an abandoned car there.

Dave chewed his thumbnail, watching. The thumbnail was a big bastard, usually took a few days of working on it with his teeth to get it to start breaking loose, but if this Sienna Nealon situation carried on much longer, he was probably going to break it off today, dammit, because—

"Wow," Holly said, a little whisper that could be heard in the silence of the office. "She's really doing it."

"Come on," Dave scoffed. "You cannot actually believe that voice on the television."

"I don't know," Holly said, shifting around in her seat, probably remembering the reaction the last time she'd gone against the crowd. "She's kicking the ass of this Revelen army, and … I mean, Dave, they literally just launched nukes at the US." She pointed at the screen. "I mean, look."

The screen had switched again, as it tended to do, to a tracking picture that showed a world map. One giant blob was heading over the Arctic Ocean to the east, with a little white-letter **REED** next to it, oh so helpfully telling everyone watching where Nealon's brother was, while a single dot was still tracking forward.

The picture zoomed, showing the trajectory coming over the Arctic toward Canada, terminating in a split somewhere north of the border. From there, six different tracks proceeded to every major city in the Midwest, from Chicago to Minneapolis to Des Moines. Multiple warheads descended on Chicago and Minneapolis, while only one hit Iowa's foremost city. Dave thought that annoying; he liked Chicago and didn't care for Des Moines. Minneapolis he didn't really have an opinion on.

"It sure looks like her brother's saving us," Holly said, "getting eleven of those missiles, because you just know one was aimed at New York, and …" She turned back to the screen. "Now she's trying to stop the last one."

"Why?" Alyssa Brewer asked.

Holly just stared at the screen. Her answer was a whisper, again, but the TV was silent and everyone heard it. "Because that's what heroes do."

"'Heroes,'" Dave said, dripping scorn. "Listen to yourself. She's a killer. A murderer. There's your 'hero,' okay? There's no such thing. Next you'll be saying there are gods." He shook his head.

"Isn't … isn't the guy running the country Hades?" Alyssa asked. "You know, like God of Death? From *Percy Jackson*?"

"I thought he was in that really stupid movie, *Clash of the Titans*?" Mhairi said

"I heard about him in the God of War games," Caden said.

"Uh, yeah," Mike said, "that's because he's from the religion of ancient Greece. All that other stuff is based on … well, him."

"So … gods kinda do exist, then?" Holly asked. She glanced at Dave for just a second, a very brief challenge before pulling away.

Mike seemed to think about it for a second. "I guess. You could almost say they're the superhero legends of the old days."

"Whoa, what's she doing?" Caden asked, drawing everyone's attention back to the screen.

"Something completely insane, I expect," Dave mumbled under his breath. Every eye was riveted to the screen. He looked at the click traffic. They didn't have a live feed, so it was down—way down. And no one was writing anything anyway. He turned his attention back to the screen, though, unavoidably, because, like everyone else, he couldn't take his eyes off this unfolding spectacle, either.

95.

Sienna

"Hello, boys," I said, driving my stolen car into three gawking soldiers who lacked the brainpower to save their own lives by dodging the hell out of the way. "You didn't miss me." They disappeared under the bumper, bodies slamming against the road and the undercarriage, bounced like sacks of flesh and bone and spit out the back of my car as I skidded to a stop just past them. "Or, rather, I didn't miss you."

I backed up and ran them over again, just to be safe. This wasn't a moment to take chances. I made sure and planted a tire on each of them, and when I got out of the car, only one was moving, and barely, at that.

"Okay," I said and looked around. The castle was visible to the north, up on its high hill, the fortress walls gleaming in the midday sun. It was less than a mile away, but I couldn't quite tell the range from here.

This was going to require a little planning to get right.

I was standing in the middle of what was unhelpfully called a laager, a word used to describe a wagon fort in the days of old, back when wagons were the military mobility unit of choice. They'd updated the term since then, and this laager did not contain any actual wagons, and these were the only three soldiers on duty. The rest had presumably been called out to deal with the chaos I'd caused elsewhere in Bredoccia, which was fine by me.

Because the dumbasses had left their laager basically unguarded, and all their oh so valuable "equipment" behind.

"Clock's ticking," Cassidy piped up from my pocket.

"Right." I tossed the phone into the open car. Then I unslung my rifle, took off my belt, and tossed both into the vehicle. I'd move it out of the way last. Scouring the ground around me, I saw nothing but churned-up grass where they'd moved through on mighty treads, ripping up everything and unearthing—

Pebbles. Rocks. Tons of little rocks.

"Perfect," I muttered and stooped to get to work.

96.

Passerini

"What the hell is she doing?" Passerini asked as Sienna squatted down a few paces from her car, one of the dead soldiers still twitching in the foreground of the security camera shot.

"Preparing," Graves said a little, well, gravely. He was back to manning the console because Passerini really couldn't spare him. "Don't worry. She'll take care of it."

"I hope so," Passerini said, and the clutching, clawing feeling of being in way, way over his head settled in again. Revelen had effectively blocked their every attempt to strike back at this new threat, and that didn't sit well with Passerini. In the War on Terror, he'd learned to manage expectations about finding his foes and delivering the kill shot, because the bastards were such effective hiders, but here, with this?

His enemy was sitting in plain sight, high up on a hill in that forsaken country, and he couldn't even pump a Tomahawk missile through the bastard's window because of that magnetic barrier surrounding the country.

"President calling, sir," Graves said, and sure enough, five seconds later, the phone rang.

"Mr. President," Passerini said.

"Where are we with this … plan of yours?" Gondry asked.

"She's working on it, sir," Passerini said. And that didn't sit well with him, either. Because it required him to actually sit, not seize the initiative with the bombers and fighters and helos and support aircraft he had stacked up all around the invisible line surrounding the nation of Revelen.

Gondry was real quiet for a second. "And you're sure there's nothing else we can do?"

Passerini swallowed heavily. "They've destroyed everything we've sent across the border, sir. There's no reason to assume that's changed in the last ten minutes, but if she doesn't manage something in the next fifteen minutes, we can try again." *And steadily draw down our aircraft numbers in the process*, Passerini didn't say, because it was obvious.

Besides, there'd be nearing nothing to lose at that point. NORAD's missile tracking had the bearing of the ICBM closing in on the Midwest, and it continued to sail, unimpeded, across the skies.

"I hate that it's come down to this," Gondry said, and the man's prickishness had all evaporated. Was that the start of humility? If so, it had been hard won, coming in well under the president's guard. His academic lecturing, his intense smugness, it had all been washed away with the immediacy of a nuclear threat to the US homeland.

Well, there was nothing like having your every assumption washed away in a miscalculation so great it might cost the lives of millions of your own fellow citizens. Passerini didn't imagine Gondry would have an easy time explaining that one during the re-election campaign, especially if the truth about his seesaw behavior regarding the threat or his utter disregard of its seriousness in the buildup in favor of pursuing Sienna Nealon came out.

"I know exactly what you mean, sir," Passerini said, as the video feed fuzzed out and a *PLEASE STAND BY* came up on the screen with a funny circular symbol reminiscent of old 50's TV network symbology popped up. "What the hell is this, Graves?"

"Cassidy cut the feed so Hades and company wouldn't see what she's up to," Graves said, and he was wearing a ghost of a smile. "Don't worry. She'll pick it up again in a minute, once events are already in motion." Now he smiled wider. "And trust me … it's going to be a hell of a show."

97.

Sienna

"I've cut the feed." Cassidy's voice brayed as I slid into the seat. I jumped a little, startled. I wasn't in my car, after all, and had left my phone and all my guns behind when I had pulled over about a block away, getting it well clear of the laager where I was about to go to work.

"Who are you feeding?" I asked, drawing on the stock of knowledge I'd ripped out of that Russian merc's head earlier, flipping switches and moving around to get the machinery going. The satisfying rumble of a diesel engine starting up filled the air, and distantly I could smell the exhaust, a sharp, distinctive tang wafting in from the open hatch. "Did you open a buffet or something?"

"I've been livestreaming your adventures today," Cassidy said. "To the whole world."

I stood up so fast I almost cracked my skull on the steel ceiling. "You whatted my what?"

"Livestream. It's what all the cool kids are doing these days. Except I took over the entire satellite uplink system for the planet and just broadcast your shit live to everyone with a TV." There was a brief pause. "You're welcome."

I was pretty sure my face was a horrorstruck mess. How many people had I murdered today? And she'd shown the world this? "Why would you do that?"

"Because it's damned good television," she said, a little too chipper, clearly leaning a little hard on the uppers today. "Forty minutes to impact."

That cleared the mind. "Shit," I said, shaking my head. "Are people watching me right now?"

"No," she said. "I cut the feed so you could prepare, but I'm going live again after you—y'know. Kick things off."

I grabbed a couple heavy items off the rack, selecting them carefully to make sure I had the right ones, then piled a few into my arms. They weren't light; they weighed in excess of twenty pounds each, and I loaded up and brought them to the front of the cabin, feeding them carefully into the autoloading mechanism.

Drawing on that Russian's experience, I prepped one, then slid into the turret control of the Russian-made T-72 main battle tank. "Great," I said. "I can't wait for the world to see me do *this.*" Pure sarcasm. If public opinion of Sienna Nealon was a gauge, we were already well into the red-line section of HATE, and me firing a Russian tank cannon into Hades's castle was unlikely to change things up much.

Dropping the reticle, I lined up my shot against the wall of the castle.

"Third window from the right," Cassidy's voice came through. "Aim two feet below it. Just above the 'waterline' of the castle rock."

"Thanks," I muttered and adjusted the reticle accordingly. Who was I to argue with the genius who was broadcasting my crazy misadventure to the entire planet, so they could see what a miscreant I actually was as I did horrible things, live? "At least she knows physics," I muttered.

"What was that?"

"Nothing," I said, and steadied my hand on the firing control. I readied myself and then shouted, "Fire in the hole!"

98.

Lethe

"I have let Death slip lazily along without my guiding hand for many thousands of years," Hades said, watching the single missile track with furious eyes. "I thought perhaps the world could manage without me, but look—things are worse than ever. Sovereign nearly ruined us all. Harmon almost brainwashed the planet. The United States and the Soviet Union nearly destroyed us all with these very weapons—and where was I?" He turned to Lethe. "Content to sit on the sidelines, abdicating my responsibility."

"I don't know what sort of ego pump she's attached to you," Lethe said, trying her best not to roll her eyes and failing, looking at Krall, "but you need to lance that infection immediately. It's going to be the death of you."

Hades merely arched an eyebrow at her. "I am Death himself. I cannot be killed."

"That scar on your chest says otherwise," Lethe said. "And if my mother was here … she'd show you otherwise. Again." Her eyes flicked to the screen. "But I believe her great-granddaughter is going to take up her part."

"You still don't understand the grander purpose," Hades said, shaking his head as he took a step toward her. "*Our* purpose. All these conflicting forces, all these petty human disputes, but at the core of it all, still lies the fundamental, overriding truth—Death conquers all. Inevitable, it is the fate of all men. But now it is wild, untamed, like a forest grown out of control and filled with dead wood, ripe for a wildfire. Sovereign was a wildfire. Harmon was a wildfire. They were prevented only by careful, and judicious effort—"

"*Her* effort," Lethe said. "Not yours."

"Because I have stood aside for too long," Hades said, squeezing his fist closed. "We require … control. Careful, judicious, exercise of power. The strong hand of Death steering things along toward a more productive course—"

"You've lost your damned mind," Lethe said. "You're not even powerful enough to feel it when those souls vaporize."

"I don't need to feel it," Hades said, smiling. "I need but to help it along. We must begin again, and the scourging, nuclear fires will be the instrument. This tragedy will awaken the world to the great dangers awaiting. It has been too long since they have seen loosed the power which they casually hoard. This will move the planet toward decision—they will start to work together to eliminate—"

"You," Lethe said.

"Nuclear weapons," Hades said. "And we will sit, secure in our fortress, and watch, and wait, and plan … as the world adopts a better way forward. A safer one."

"I don't think that's how it's going to go," Lethe said.

"It is the only way it can go," Krall said. She stood at the planning table, still smiling, snakelike, hands behind her, "They cannot reach us here. They cannot touch us—"

"Did you hear … something?" Hades asked. He was frowning, concentrating, perked up and listening.

"No," Krall said. "What do you m—"

The entire castle shook, and a six-foot hole blew in the wall behind them, stone block shattering and filling the air in a path before them with shards and stone. It echoed like a bomb had gone off somewhere nearby, which … it probably had.

Hades had hit his knees and now sprang back up, his suit coat covered in dust. "What was that?" He stared, wide-eyed, at the hole in his fortress. Daylight streamed in from outside. A half-dozen consoles were wrecked, their operators dead or moaning. Motes of dust floated in the beam of sunlight.

Lethe worked her jaw, popping her ears. The explosion had dramatically changed the atmospheric pressure in the room. "I believe that's your great-granddaughter." She wasn't bothering to hide her smile. "You know. The one I'm rooting for in this."

Hades's face darkened as though the sun had just set in front of him, and the castle rocked again as another shell hit somewhere nearby, beyond the front of the Situation Room. He spun. "Aleksy!"

The timid lieutenant rose on shaky legs from where he was crouched behind a surviving console. "Yes?"

"I want you to go out there and kill my great-granddaughter," Hades said.

Aleksy stared at him for a moment, then nodded. "Yes, sir." With a wave of his hand, he pulled metallic components, glittering in the sunlight, out of the wreckage, and they floated under his feet. Once there, he waved his hands, and they lifted him into the air, carrying him out of the hole in the side of the fortress as he disappeared into the daylight.

"You just sent him to die, you know," Lethe said, watching him go.

Hades stood there, back to her. He did not speak for a long moment, and when he did, he was so quiet she couldn't be sure of what he said.

But it sounded like: "Perhaps so."

99.

Sienna

"Magneto boy incoming!" Cassidy's voice crackled over the speakers, breaking through my umpteenth hearing loss of the day. I fired the HEAT (High Explosive Anti-Tank) shell that had just loaded and didn't even bother to watch it hit, because I was pretty sure it wouldn't.

I leapt up the ladder and out of the cupola in one good jump, hopping from the turret to the ground in a roll. The sound of something cutting through the atmosphere came just a second later—

The T-72 tank exploded as my round was returned to sender, and I ducked under the gutter edge of the road that went around the laager to try and manage some minimal cover as it blew.

It sorta worked. I caught some shrapnel on my left elbow and let out a scream that was drowned out in the fury of the tank blowing up with all its ammo. It went big, the turret lifting off in the blast, crashing back down as it burned, waves of heat so intense that I was afraid my clothing might catch fire even fifty feet away.

As expected, Aleksy had turned my last shell around and sent it back to me. I'd planned for this, even wanted it to happen, but as usual, I couldn't anticipate every consequence, ever, and the nice gash on my arm proved that.

"Ow, ow, *ow!*" I said, watching the blood roll down my forearm, making the usually invisible fine hairs stand out in the little tide of crimson. It looked mostly superficial, the shard of metal that had caused it striking and moving on, not sticking in the flesh, fortunately. But it was bleeding nicely, and I had to hope there wasn't enough iron content in my blood for Aleksy to do something terrible with. Because that was something I hadn't planned for.

"Your grandfather has sent me to kill you," Aleksy announced as he drifted down beside the pillar of flame that rose out of the burning tank. He had a bunch of metal shards under his feet and was using them to levitate. I'd expected that, too, or at least something similar. It would have been the fastest way for him to get down to me, after all, and stop me from continuing with my pain-in-the-ass schtick.

"He's doing that with his servants a lot lately," I said. "Not sure if you've noticed, being cooped up in the war room, but it's not been working out so well for them."

"It will work out differently for me," Aleksy said, now only about ten feet off the ground.

"That's what they all think," I said, rising up, a little unsteadily. My head was swimming from the explosion and maybe the loss of blood. It dripped down my arm, sliding down my wrist and onto my palm. Sticky, warm … I didn't love the feel of it draining out of me, added to the volume of sweat beading out of my skin. "I hate to spoil the end of the story for you, but it never does."

"This time … it will," Aleksy said, and he raised his hand—

And with the motion, the rifles and pistols of the three soldiers I'd run over with my car came up, barrels pointed right at me. He brought them in front of his face, lined up in a row, as if three invisible shooters were taking aim.

My own personal firing line.

"You sat in that control room and watched as Hades launched nuclear weapons at cities filled with innocent people," I said, looking up at him, clutching at the dripping wound on my arm. "You as good as sentenced those people to die, Aleksy."

His expression wavered, but he shook it off. "It is for the best. Lord Hades says so."

"And if Lord Hades told you to jump out of a castle wall and go kill yourself by picking a fight with me—well, I guess we know you would," I said, shaking my head. "I thought maybe you were smarter than that. I thought maybe you had a moral compass. But you're as lost as he is."

"But not as lost as you," Aleksy said, and now there was anger. "You have killed my friends."

"Your friends were scum," I said. "Hired killers. Sadists in their free time. The dregs of humanity."

"You didn't know them!" he snapped.

"I knew them better than you." I stared him down.

He stared back, over the barrel of six guns. "You don't know me." He straightened, his decision made. "So long, Sienna—" He waved his hand—

The guns, their barrels pointed right at me, fired all at once—

100.

Dave Kory

"Ohmigod," Holly whispered as the guns fired as one.

Dave looked at the clicks. They were way down. "Sienna Nealon dies live," he whispered. It would have been good to have the stream going on the site so everyone could see it here.

"Oh. My. Goddess," Holly said, and Dave turned to look. There was smoke on the screen, and movement—

101.

Sienna

"How stupid do you think I am?" I asked as I hurled myself into the cloud of smoke swirling around Aleksy. He was staggering, every single one of the pistols and rifles having blown up right in his face from the rocks I'd shoved down their barrels before I'd fired the first round out of the tank. Dumbass didn't even check them before shooting. As though I'd just leave functional weapons lying around for him to turn on me with his powers.

I jacked him in the jaw with a hard punch, knocking him off his metal supports. He collapsed, hitting the ground and rolling, kicking up a cloud of dust in the landing. He was bleeding heavily from a nasty gash on his forehead that looked superficial, and a piece of plastic rifle stock was sticking out of his chest.

He tried to get up, but I bashed him behind the ear with a closed fist, cracking a knuckle in the process. "I warned you," I said, hammering him again. "I tried to show you mercy, because I thought maybe you were a good guy in a bad place. But you're not. You're just another—"

Movement out of the corner of my eye. I leapt without looking, a high flip as a car flew from across the street, right through the place where I'd been standing a moment earlier. It kept going, crashing into the flaming tank, and I came down in a three-point superhero landing, my fist finding Aleksy's face on impact.

"—overinflated douchebag death cultist," I said, picking up right where I left off. Aleksy was crawling now, trying to get away from me. He moved his hand again, and I did another leap, twisting as little shards of metal—the remains of the guns which had exploded thanks to my blocking the barrels—shot at me in a minefield of pieces. One scraped past my shoulder, tearing my shirt and opening a scratch, another caught me at the hip in a graze. I was like a gymnast, tilting and twisting in midair, trying to keep him from tagging me too hard.

I came down again, this time getting him solidly in the back of the head. He went limp, stunned beyond the ability to concentrate, and the metal shards he'd been bringing back around at me for another pass fell, glittering.

Lucky thing I'd knocked him silly, because he'd put a little more distance between them on this pass. I'd have had a hell of a time not taking a direct hit from one or more of them, and it'd have been like getting shot by a tumbling, twisted piece of shrapnel. Worse than any bullet in terms of the damage it would do.

"Okay," I said, placing a hand on the back of Aleksy's neck. "Give me the lay of the land, and also …" I waited a few seconds, counting it out, as my power kicked in, "… Let's see if you can—"

I jumped into his head, that bluish haze filtering his important memories to the surface. I could feel his whole mind; it was right at my fingertips. I took a quick peek around the most recent ones, saw what was going on at the castle—

Ewww. Hades and Krall? Gross.

And Lethe in chains. Huh. That was interesting.

I also saw the disposition of forces around the castle, at least to the best of Aleksy's knowledge, and …

Shit.

It was worse than I thought it would be.

"One last thing," I said, and reached into Aleksy's mind, trying to tap into his powers. If I could reach that last nuke from here, with his abilities …

But I hit a wall a couple hundred miles out, unable to get past it. That was his limit, and the nuke heading for Minneapolis was beyond it.

I let go of the back of Aleksy's neck, his skin still warm against my palm. "Damn," I said. Killing the nuke from here would have simplified everything.

"What … what happened?" Aleksy asked, raising his head, sounding like he'd just woken up from a long nap.

I glanced to my right. Before he'd shown up, as part of my preparations, I'd scattered some bricks from a nearby construction site around the laager, figuring that sooner or later I'd be in a situation where Aleksy was vulnerable. Sure, with enough effort, I might be able to knock him silly, but applying my fist to him? Maybe that'd work in time, maybe it wouldn't.

"You told me everything I needed to know," I said, and I reached, slowly, for the brick.

"I … I did?" He couldn't see me, since I was on his back, holding him down, but he was sounding less hazy by the second. I could have scooped all his memories, maybe. Taken out all the reasons why he was loyal to Hades, left him a blank slate again, and just let him wander off from here.

But … not even a year ago, Rose had done that very thing to me, and I was still dealing with it. I hated it, hated the thought of it, hated every bit of it, and I didn't think it was merciful, not at all.

So I let him keep his memories, his loyalties, and everything that made Aleksy … Aleksy. Bad decisions and all. "You did," I said. He was getting stronger by the second. His hand was already extended, and he was reaching for the burning tank. He could control it, easily.

"You took it from me, then," Aleksy said, and he squeezed his hand tight. "Took it from me and—" The tank started to move.

I snatched the brick and raised it high, bringing it down behind his ear with all my force—

And caved his damned head in.

I raised it up.

Brought it down again.

The tank squealed as though the flames were bending the metals within.

But they weren't. I knew.

Aleksy had just relinquished his hold. His hand was limp, flat on the ground. A little tremor shook it, residual nerves causing a muscle spasm.

"Yeah," I said, rising to my feet, a little unsteadily. "I did."

I looked down at him. His head was good and smashed. The blood on me was not just my own now.

I let go of the brick and it thudded to the earth. Scarlet dripped off of it.

"I'm sorry," I said, and for some reason, I truly was.

Then I turned my back on Aleksy's body and walked away.

102.

Passerini

"That was impressive," Passerini said, watching her walk away from the fallen soldier. "Brutal … but impressive."

"She's a very impressive lady," Graves said, a little hoarse.

Passerini leaned over. "General Kelly … send 'em in."

"Aye, sir," General Kelly said from over by the planning table. "They're on the way. Everything is. It's a small country. Transit time is short."

Passerini nodded. "Now she just has to hang on until we get some support in position."

Graves just stared at the screen as it flicked to a different camera angle, this one following Nealon as she broke into a run, heading for her car. "I don't think she's going to hang around and wait, sir." A subtle beep highlighted something changing, and Graves looked down at it. "Thirty minutes to impact."

"Gonna be tight," Passerini said, watching. This was the tough part. What he would have given to be in one of those planes—not an F-35, but maybe F/A-18E, heading in hot over the Revelen border right now. Hopefully they'd make it in time to give her a hand, though by his watch … it was going to be awfully damned close

103.

Sienna

I didn't have time to take one of the surviving Russian T-72s and navigate it through the streets of Bredoccia. It was an old European city, one that predated the invention of the automobile by centuries, and that meant narrow roads, especially in the old town, where I was heading. Tightly packed buildings blew by at sixty miles an hour outside my latest car's open window as the air rushed in, rifle sling cinched around my shoulders and my belt squarely back around my waist.

I slewed around a corner and popped the e-brake, mimicking something I'd seen Angel do … when? Last week? When we were outrunning cartel thugs. Man, I lived an eventful life. My tires caught the cobblestone street, and I was off again, back up to sixty down a main thoroughfare, the castle rock rising ahead as the buildings in old town got shorter and shorter.

"You know you're going to hit resistance soon," Cassidy's voice piped from my belt, where I'd strapped in the old lady's stolen phone after I retrieved it and my guns. It was not a question.

"I assume so," I said. "You mind giving me a heads up when I get close to real trouble?"

"Heads up," she said, about a second before the tank shell went whizzing over my hood and into the building to my right.

It exploded the storefront; brick and glass showered the

sidewalk and into the street, fragments pelting the side of my car and spider-webbing my front window. I brought the car into a slide and looked right.

A T-72 was parked in an alley and had fired as soon as they'd seen me. Meta reflexes had forced the shot to go off a little prematurely, like they hadn't practiced aiming and firing since gaining powers. I jerked the car into a one-eighty spin that ended with my driver side colliding with the building just past the alley mouth, my hood exposed by a couple feet.

"Oh shit, oh shit!" I lunged over the center console and out the open window just as I heard the boom of another round being fired. Quick reloading.

The front of the car exploded as I was leaping out the window, and the shock of the detonation sent me tumbling. I hit the ground rolling and the frame of the car flew into me, sending me to the ground as it bounced and went airborne, rolling over me. It missed crushing my body and head by about ten inches or less. It still stung like hell, slamming into me like that, at least bruising my ribs, if not breaking them outright.

I had zero time to think about any of that and hurriedly pulled myself to my feet as the tank rolled free of the alleyway, turret swinging toward me. I had a couple seconds before it could fire again. At the top hatch, the cupola, manning the anti-personnel machine gun, the soldier swung it toward me with meta speed—

My hand was already on my AK-74 pistol grip, and I whipped it up, catching the foregrip with my left, settling the sight picture on the soldier just as he brought it to bear on me.

I fired first.

He fired not at all, his brains exploding out the back of his head and painting the alley wall behind him.

Like he was slipping beneath the waves on stormy seas, he disappeared back into the tank, falling into the top hatch as the big turret gun zeroed in on me. They'd missed with one shot, but if this one hit, it'd kill me a hell of a lot quicker than a machine gun.

I leapt for it, rolling as the air broke with the thunder of the main turret firing. A building across the street exploded, and I cursed into the ringing in my ears, agonizingly loud. Tears stung my eyes, partly from the pain of the loudness and my injuries, partly from the sheer indignation at these bastards for killing civilians all willy-nilly with every shot they took.

My patience for these senseless, evil, mercenary bastards? Zero.

I scrambled across the ground between me and the T-72, swearing up a storm the whole way. It halted in its tracks, the turret swerving to try and track me while the main gun reloaded. I leapt the last ten feet as I swiped at my belt, grabbing one of the frag grenades there, yanking the pin out, and cooking it as I moved.

It reached the four count as I crested the cupola, and I threw it into the open hatch, heard it thud on the body of their dead gunner, then ducked behind the lip of the hatch.

Boom.

The screams were fierce, and the surge of heat that bled out of there was hotter than any fire my grenade could have started. It was enough to convince me that I needed to get the hell out of there, so I did, leaping off the tank and hauling ass up the block.

The T-72 exploded, their ammo cooking off and annihilating the facade of the buildings on either side of the alley. It didn't take a genius to figure out what had happened, just someone familiar with pain and meta powers. One of the mercs inside had been a Gavrikov, a new one, and when he'd been filled with fragments from my grenade, he'd done a perfectly normal Gavrikov thing and lit off, which had in turn ignited the tank's magazine of ammo.

Bing, bang, boom. Finally, some luck had gone my way.

Except … now I didn't have a car, and it was still a mile to the castle.

"Shit," I said, and looked at the road wending up the mountainside. Even at meta speed, a one-mile uphill run was going to take more time than I had. I shook my head, cursing again at the delay, and started looking around for another car to steal.

104.

Dave Kory

TIME TO PLAY! Dave's phone declared, and he looked around, subtly, to see if anyone was paying any attention to him.

They weren't. Everyone was riveted to the action on the screen, the tank vs. Sienna Nealon battle that had just occurred. "I want that livestream up, Caden," Dave said, sparing a glance at him.

"Five more minutes," Caden said, moving his attention rapidly between the TV and his computer. "I've almost got the source—"

"I don't care how you do it, just do it," Dave snapped. "Our traffic is dying." *Like Sienna Nealon should have the grace to do*, he thought as he slid open his app.

Funny. He would have said that out loud a half hour ago without fear.

Now? He found himself holding it back. And he was the boss. He could say anything he damned well pleased, couldn't he?

Apparently not, he realized dimly as the app sprung to the chat screen. How had the world changed that fast?

CHAPMAN: The video is starting to go viral.

BILSON: The Eden Prairie video?

CHAPMAN: The new one, yes. The more interpretative one.

Kat Forrest seems to have shared it on social media. Gave it a signal boost.

CHALKE: You said it would die if we left it alone. You swore it would sink beneath the waves of the internet if we didn't pull it down.

CHAPMAN: I can't control everything. Yet.

BILSON: Then what the hell is the point of you?

Whoa. That was … strong.

BILSON: Sorry. Just … salty. This is bad.

CHAPMAN: It's not that widespread yet. Just letting you know … it's starting to break out.

CHALKE: Can you kill it now?

CHAPMAN: No.

Dave drew a sharp breath. Wow. Stunning admission from the head of the largest social network on the planet.

CHALKE: She's still in the middle of a hell of a firefight. Maybe this problem will solve itself. If she dies a hero … she still dies. That would serve our purposes just fine.

BILSON: True.

KORY: And it'd be a hell of a windfall for those of us in the business.

Dave smiled, thinking about that. The clicks would be amazing. He looked up from the phone. "Caden, I want that livestream up."

"Working on it. Two more minutes."

Everybody else logged off, probably to watch what happened next. Dave turned his attention back to the screen, too, rapping a finger against the hard surface of his desk as his millennial office staff set the temperature for him, exemplifying this weird shift in energy in the room, staring in silence at the incredible feats that were going on just in front of them—and half a world away.

105.

Sienna

I opened up the throttle on the sporty little yellow hatchback I'd jacked off the street, tearing up the mountain as quick as I could make it go. Gravity made it shudder as I hit a tight S curve, hoping a tank wasn't waiting to open up on me the moment I rounded it.

Nothing waited, thankfully, and I rolled around the curving switchback, preparing myself for the last turn. It would go hard left up ahead, and then I'd find myself faced with the wide tarmac that led to the big doors into the castle hangar. They definitely had tanks up there, but from Aleksy's mind I knew they had deployed them down in the town, that the laager I had hit had contained at least half of them, and I'd run into another on the way here. I had to hope that his info was up to date, because my yellow hatchback could take a tank shell about as well as Reed could take an insult to his hair—not well.

The engine got sluggish on the last of the slope, and I found myself wishing I had one of Hades's sports cars for this particular suicide mission. At least if I caught a round and blew up, I'd be going out in style, not in a European shoe car.

Ahead, the last curve waited, the rock's edge approaching closer and closer to even with the rising plane of the road. They could have put a firing squad along that edge and just blasted me straight to hell on approach from the high ground, and the fact that they hadn't gave me hope that maybe, just maybe, in spite of what Aleksey thought, they actually had deployed the majority of the castle's defensive troops down into Bredoccia.

Then I crested the ridge and turned onto the long tarmac leading up to the hangar, and all my beautiful dreams of rolling up and walking in were shot to shit.

Along with my sporty car.

It was a terrible sound, a host of 5.45x39mm bullets tearing into the front window, the side mirrors, the roof, the engine. It was like the scariest horde of mosquitos possible, the sound of gunshots distant enough to strip some of the menace from them, but the unmistakable impacts ripping the hell out of my vehicle as I stomped the gas and leaned over, driving blind and using my engine block as a shield against incoming fire. It would probably work.

Probably.

I looked up and out the side window to make sure I hadn't accidentally taken a dramatic turn to the left and headed back for the edge, but no, the castle continued to loom as a fixed point out there, which meant I was thundering ahead at all cylinders. Hopefully across a clear tarmac, because otherwise—

Boom.

Whoops.

The airbag deployed and caught me—mostly—before I could slam into the dash, but it whipped me around against the seats as though I were a pinball in a particularly aggressive set of bumpers. It hurt, and it realigned my spine in a not-so-therapeutic way as the hatchback did a flip and crashed down on its side, lurching as I came to rest with my left arm hanging out the driver's side window against pavement.

"Uhm … ow," I said, feeling it over every square inch of my body, but especially the square inches that had hit seatbelt, airbag and now the ground. The car was sideways, the bottom pointed toward the open hangar, presumably, because the castle was visible plainly out the shattered windshield. Little pebbles of safety glass were in my hair and clothing, and my rifle lay slung across my chest. Fortunately.

I did a quick inventory of pain and decided that if anything was broken, it was nothing crucial, though my left arm was bleeding profusely again from that cut Aleksy had given me. I clicked my seatbelt and it reluctantly let me go. I landed on that left arm, which let me know through a blaze of pain that it was not happy with me, no sir, and then I crawled through the pebbles of glass out the front windshield and crouched behind the hood, which had … oh so many bullet holes in it.

An abandoned Humvee sat on its side a little behind me, not a soul in sight, engine smoking and no one moving within the cab. Bastards had just left it parked there, and I'd blindly run right into it, wrecking myself nicely. And the Humvee, too.

The staccato sound of gunshots peppering the undercarriage of my car was alarming in its volume and … other volume. Because it was loud and there were a lot of them. The sound of bullets pinging into the vital parts of the car was worrisome, but less worrisome than if I'd landed with the roof facing them and been subjected to a firing gallery as I climbed out of my car. Pretty sure that would have been the end of my mission, actually. I was burning all my luck today. Maybe this was why I couldn't catch a break in life? Because I wasted all my luck not dying in moments like this.

I shook out the pain in my left arm, which felt numb at the fingertips. I needed to return some fire soon, because the gunshots were getting louder and closer, bullets spanging off the concrete and car, soldiers closing in on me. If I didn't shoot back, they'd continue pressing forward, flanking around the sides of the car to pincer me, riddling me with bullets. It was an ironclad law of the battlefield—shoot back or you let them build momentum enough to steamroll you.

Me? I wasn't a fan of getting steamrolled, so I crept up to the front of the car, took a deep breath, and sliced the pie—braced my rifle barrel on the bumper, using the car as cover and inched out until I saw a couple soldiers and they saw me. They shot at me and hit the car.

I shot at them, and they joined the legions of dead I'd already sent to hell today. Later, bitches.

That slowed their roll. I could practically feel the hesitation in the temporary cessation of fire as the soldiers who'd been eagerly pressing ahead a moment earlier took stock of the fact that two of their number had just gotten wiped out.

While they were reassessing their plan of attack, I sprinted the length of the car and squatted down at the hatchback. Another deep breath. Braced the barrel. Cut the pie and shot out of this side of the hatchback.

Got another one. The incoming fire on that side ramped up for a second and then paused as they realized they were no longer unopposed. I waited a sec, readied myself, repeated. Got two more soldiers before they started unloading on me and I had to scramble to get the hell out of there. The back of the car was nowhere near as good a cover as the front, lacking an engine to shelter behind.

"Congratulations," Cassidy's voice piped out of my belt. "You killed five. Out of hundreds."

"I'm not hearing any brilliant ideas out of you, genius," I said, moving quickly back to the front bumper. The volume of fire had died down here, and they were probably expecting me to do the same damned thing again, peek around the bumper and fire. I'd have to, if I didn't want to be overrun, but I'd need to be more careful about it. All it would take was a sniper with a .50 cal anticipating my position and they'd pump a round the size of my middle finger into me, which would really put a kink in my plans to storm the castle and save the day.

I raised my weapon up above my head to maximum extension like I was military pressing it. It would be hella awkward to shoot like this, but I'd pretty much have to if I didn't want to be pegged in the head. I sliced the pie again, careful not to expose my pretty face more than I had to …

The moment I saw a soldier with my left eye, I lined it up and shot, pegging him three times in the body. I caught a little motion just past him as a few more soldier scattered hard left, and then I bolted for the trunk as a .50 cal round blasted through where my body would have been had I been standing that last time.

Whew. A .50 round would put a severe hurting on me.

"They're coming at you from the trunk," Cassidy said, a little sing-songy, like she was having a great time watching this mess unfold. "Only like three hundred or so to go. At this rate, you'll get them about the time that the ruins of Chicago start to reach safe radiation levels again."

"Not helping!" I shouted, blind-firing a quick volley that hit no one from the trunk, then rolling back as another .50 round blasted through the transaxle, making the entire car squeal in protest. It also hurt my ears, because it was loud.

"Ms. Nealon?" came a voice over the speaker. Passerini, I thought, though it was tough to tell over the persistent ringing in my ears and that steady feeling of being underwater that was becoming the new normal for my head.

"Yeah?" I asked, deciding how long I had before I needed to risk another defense to my left and right. This was just going to get more dangerous as I went.

"Throw out your weapons and come out with your hands up," came a voice from somewhere near the hangar.

"I already tried that one once today," I muttered as another .50 round ripped through the center of the car, about three feet shy of where I was crouching. "If you've got any ideas, SecDef, I would be open to hearing them."

"We have planes stacked up in your vicinity," Passerini said, and I straightened a little. "They're closing in now."

"Music to my ears," I said, "because I could really use an angel on my shoulder."

"Well," he said, "there's just one problem."

"Of course there's a problem," I muttered. "There's always a problem. Because I use all my luck surviving and leave none for coasting on easy street."

"... What?"

"Never mind," I said. "What's the problem?" I went to the left and crouched, blind-firing around the bumper. Then I ejected the mag as—

A .50 round blew out of the engine about six inches from my head, a piece of shrapnel catching me across the cheek and throwing me to the ground, the rifle clanking as I landed on it, pinning it beneath me.

"Fire," I gasped, the wind knocked out of me. "Get these

bastards off me."

"Can't," Passerini's voice came over the open channel. "We're tasking the F-22s to hit the Russian SAM sites at the south end of the city right now. The only other thing in range that would be of use is an AC-130, which is—"

"I know what an AC-130 is," I said, trying to get up. I was bleeding from the face, warm liquid dripping down my cheek. My left arm was refusing steadfastly to bear much weight, and I couldn't even get to my knees. I reached for the rifle grip and started to raise it. "I understand the risks. But I'm about to get overrun—"

A foot lashed out and stomped the barrel of my gun flat against the tarmac, bending it and shattering the furniture as a combat boot landed atop it.

A squad of infantry phalanxed out around me from either side of my ruined hatchback, guns at the rise around me. Twenty of them pointed right at my head.

"Professional courtesy—last words?" the squad leader asked, never taking his eye off my face in the sight picture. He was staring straight down the barrel at me, and the moment I got out of line, he'd paste my brains all over the tarmac. He said it clear, loud, and his finger was right on the trigger.

I swallowed.

I took a breath.

I looked down the yawning barrel of the AK-74U, and knew I had one chance—and a very thin one, at that—for survival.

"Hammer," I said, no louder than a whisper, "Danger close."

106.

Passerini

Graves was white as a sheet, apparently seeing the writing plainly on the walls.

"Did she just say …?" General Kelly asked from across the room. It was so quiet in the ops center, you could have heard a cockroach fart.

"She did," Passerini said, setting his jaw. "She knows what she's asking for." He took a deep, long breath. "SPIRIT … fire for effect."

107.

Dave Kory

"What … what does that mean?" Holly asked, the hush fallen over the bullpen. "'Hammer … Danger Close'?"

Mike Darnell answered, of course. "It's military slang. 'Hammer' is the callsign of the current Secretary of Defense, Passerini. And 'Danger Close' means she's calling in fire on her own position and she knows—damned well—it will probably kill her."

Some good news in all this after all, Dave thought. But didn't say it. Again. He frowned. This was getting bad, wasn't it? He could feel the atmospheric change in the room.

But it'd be over soon, wouldn't it?

"Livestream is up!" Caden said.

"Shoot it out to everyone on our mailing list, and post it on all our social media feeds!" Dave said, spinning around in his chair. "Get it to everyone! Let 'em know …" and here he did smile, because he couldn't help himself, "that if people want to see Sienna Nealon die live … we've got it right here on flashforce."

108.

Lethe

"Look at this …" Hades said, staring at the live feed from outside the hangar. "All along, someone has been watching her through our cameras. Hard to believe they could get away with that from our very own systems." He turned a pointed gaze toward the corner, where ArcheGrey was seemingly joined to a computer by one hand, her head down.

"She's been fighting with someone all day," Yvonne said, positioned a step behind Arche. As Lethe watched, Yvonne shot her a sideways look as she answered Hades. Interesting. "But you've been busy, and she's been trying to handle it. Someone has a botnet that's operating worldwide, sending out a massive amount of—"

"He doesn't have a clue what you're saying," Lethe said.

"I understand the basics," Hades said, looking at the screen, and the soldiers swarming around the overturned car. "This little drama, filmed live on location in our country, has been going out worldwide." He settled his fierce gaze on Arche, who took no notice of it. "Not exactly a boon to our burgeoning tourism industry."

"What do you think killing Sienna Nealon is going to do for your tourism industry?" Yvonne asked, staring at the screen.

Hades turned his head slightly away, as if to answer her. "Nothing good, but … I wouldn't bank on it yet, because …

as, it seems, is the standard, these idiots have decided to give her a moment to fight back."

"What do you think she's going to do against fifty guns?" Yvonne asked as the screen view flipped to a long shot from a camera mounted on the side of the castle. It showed Sienna with her gun trapped under a soldier's boot, getting swarmed. "I mean, she's good, don't get me wrong, but … I don't see how she dodges out of this one—"

A loud, thundering boom echoed in through the hole in the wall, rocking the castle as something impacted, heavily, explosively, just outside.

"I imagine that is how," Hades said dryly, as the castle shook again. He looked over his shoulder and his eyes met Lethe's. This time … she did smile.

109.

Sienna

Asking for an AC-130 to rain down fire at the guys surrounding you is basically asking to get shot by rounds big enough to punch holes in tanks, so you better believe that when the first rounds started landing, I did my level best to pretend I was much smaller and much thinner than I actually was by dropping to my knees and huddling into a ball, hoping that I wouldn't be completely blasted into chum.

The tarmac was exploding all around me, fragments of concrete and asphalt peppering my sides as I put my hands over the back of my head and dealt with world-endingly horrific noise raining down around me for the … sixth? Tenth? Eight-hundredth time today?

My head rang with vicious and unstoppable thunder as the AC-130 gunship rained down all hell upon the men ringing me. Someone screamed and it might have been me; warm and wet liquid splattered across my back, something hard thumped on my shoulder blade and rolled off as though a baseball covered in saline had bounced off me.

About a thousand angry stings peppered my forearms, my biceps, my shoulders, back and thighs, as though a really pissed-off swarm of mutant bees was determined to find all the available skin they could and stab the hell out of me.

On the pain scale, it was somewhere below getting a building dropped around you and just above being shot.

In moments that felt like hours, the shower of pain eventually came to a stop, and I was left with the dull sting of all those countless injuries.

I lifted my head up. Dust and smoke floated in the air around me, and when I cracked an eyelid … the scene wasn't pretty.

Men were moaning around me, some dead, some very much not, but with some significant pieces missing from them. The AC-130 had fired all around us, with big guns and little guns, and the five feet directly encircling my position looked a little messed up, concrete shrapnel covering it thoroughly, but …

The area past that?

There wasn't a five-foot square of space anywhere within a hundred yards that didn't look like it had had a jackhammer applied to the surface of the tarmac.

I turned, and the hatchback was a good fifty yards closer to the hangar door than I'd left it. And also in three pieces.

"Hang on," a distant, tinny voice said, and a missile shot down from above. It felt like it missed my head by a few feet, but it was probably closer to a hundred. It came to an end just inside the hangar, and I ducked as an explosion lit the place up, one of the big, movie explosions with orange and yellow fire shooting out of it.

The volume of fire that had been coming my way out of the hangar started to pick up a little as I snatched up the nearest rifle—not mine, but that of the lead guy who'd asked me for my last words. He wouldn't be needing it, judging by the hole in his head that was currently filled by a piece of concrete debris. I sprinted for the cover of the burning, shattered hatchback, firing as I went, putting shots into the darkness of the hangar and not worrying much about hitting anything.

I slid in behind a section of the hatchback's transaxle and took a breath. Still couldn't hear very much. If I hadn't had super healing, I would have started to fear for it ever coming back. As it was, it'd probably be a day or two before the ringing would stop. It was so damned intense, I had to close my eyes for a second to let the adrenaline kick back in to blot it out.

"Ten minutes," Cassidy's voice made it through the fog and

ringing in my ears, cutting the bullshit and restoring a certain amount of clarity. "If you're going to do something, you might want to get a move on."

"How many guys in the hangar?" I asked. "Do you have control of the cameras in there?"

"No, Arche is fighting me on that one," Cassidy said, "but judging from the external views I've got, it's still at least a hundred, and they're dug in, under cover."

I took a breath, then another. "I'm going to have to run for it," I decided. "That's the only way."

"Hold on just a second," Passerini's voice came through.

"Hammer, I appreciate your efforts to clear the way, but if you lob any more bombs in there, you might bring the place down," I said, sneaking another look at the hangar. They definitely had fire superiority in there.

"Understood," Passerini said. "Stand by." And then, in the background, a sign of my returning hearing, maybe, I heard him say, "Deliver the asset."

"Deliver my ass from evil, I think you mean." This was under my breath. I thought.

"Yeah, well, he'll do that, too," Passerini said as explosions in the distance heralded the probable end of Hades's SAM sites. Something else sounded, loud, clear—

The chop of rotors as a Black Hawk appeared from behind the top battlements of the castle, doors wide. A silhouette was hanging in the open bay door, and dropped, falling the three hundred or so feet, a distortion of light and energy forming around it—

The figure hit the tarmac and spun at the last, directing an energy burst like a wave into the hangar that expanded out like a blue forcefield, destroying a dozen crates and flipping more than a few of Hades's surviving car collection.

He stood there for only a second after that before I kicked my piece of the hatchback forward and it slid up next to him. He dove for the cover it provided, and I charged and baseball-skidded in next to him. His skin was an ebony tone, and this time, when he saw me—unlike the last exchanges we had—he grinned like we were old pals. "Ms. Nealon."

"Well if it isn't my old bud, the Terminator," I said, firing blind over the top of my cover. "Welcome to Revelen. I could use an unstoppable force on my side right about now."

110.

Passerini

"Who is that?" President Gondry asked over the open line. "That soldier you just sent in?"

Passerini leaned in, letting a small smile escape. "That's Warren Quincy, the military's only metahuman asset at present. You might recall that Ms. Chalke borrowed him from us with your permission back in January to deal with Ms. Nealon, and he proceeded to chase her halfway around the country while she was tangling with that clown that ripped up the Chesapeake Bay Bridge and Minneapolis."

"Hm," Gondry said. "Good to have our people on the scene."

Now, Passerini smiled a little wider. "And he's just the first." To General Marks, he turned, and got a nod. "Here they come," he told the president, and sure enough, on the screen—

111.

Sienna

Navy SEALs were parachuting in at the edges of the hangar, into defilade, or cover, and snugging their chutes back behind them as they got into position to return fire on Hades's remaining troops.

"That's a pretty heavily guarded door," the Terminator said in that husky voice of his. "You sure you want to go in that way?"

I blinked. "No. You got any better ideas?"

Warren Quincy, USMC (Ret), gave me that wide smile again. "Maybe one." And he looked across the surface of the castle toward the hole I'd opened up in the wall with the tank shell. It felt like hours, but it had really been less than thirty minutes ago.

Oh. Yeah.

"Hey, Hammer?" I asked. "You got anything on hand that can put a new door in my great-grandpa's castle?"

112.

Dave Kory

"This is like watching the most intense finale of *The Bachelor* ever," Constance Shriver said, "except like, a whole city is going to not get a rose." She paused. "By which I mean they're going to die."

"More than one city," Mike said, resting his chin on his fingers and stroking a day's stubble idly. The view switched from the cameras pointed on the runway to a shot of the missile trajectory, now over Canada, streaking its way down over the Hudson Bay. "That's the whole Midwest that's going to get it if she doesn't stop this."

The screen stayed split; the long-shot camera on the left with Sienna Nealon and her new military friend, as Dave thought of him scornfully, and on the right was the satellite view.

Losing Chicago would be a shame. Losing those other cities? Meh. Dave never visited there, didn't care to. Oh, he'd act like it was a tragedy. There were probably some decent people there.

But mostly, this was going to be a chance to write a shit-ton of clickbait about *HOW SHE FAILED* and *WHY DID WE TRUST HER?* The headlines practically wrote themselves, and he tapped a few of the best into an open Word file as he thought of them. A countdown timer was ticking in the bottom right-hand corner of the map screen as the missile came closer and closer to its target …

Something blew up in the camera frame on the live-action side, a blast detonating against the castle wall just across the tarmac where Sienna Nealon was huddling behind a segment of burnt-out car for cover.

"Whoa," Holly said. "You see that? It's gotta be a ten, twenty-foot jump—"

113.

Sienna

"Dammit, Passerini," I said, once the smoke had sort of cleared and I could see the hole he'd made in the side of Hades's castle. It was way, way off to the side, over the edge of the rock and a good thirty feet from the last ledge of tarmac. Crawling out there on that was not going to be an option. "You couldn't have put it any closer?" I traced my eyes to the edge of the hangar where the SEALs were setting up with heavy weapons, probably fifty feet from the impact site. "I suppose you couldn't."

"I thought you metas could jump," Passerini said. Was he taunting me?

"I'll show you how it's done," Quincy said, and he started to move, smoky effect drifting off his body as he broke into a run, blurring as he sped across the tarmac toward the cliff's edge.

I followed after, breaking cover into a sprint. "You had a secondary power you never used on me last time," I called after him, huffing as I ran, my rifle banging uselessly against my ass with every step.

"I was trying to bring you in alive," he said and flashed a look at that crater of destruction he'd made when he landed, and the churned-up trail of concrete he'd shot out into the hangar. "That wouldn't have done it. I did come close, though, the last time. In the data center."

"Huh," I said, smiling. Harry had known, of course. He'd told me that Quincy was holding another power in reserve, and here it was.

The thunder of gunfire increased, waves of vibrato from all the shooting seeming to quake my very bones. A spray of bullets, lit by tracers, walked across the tarmac in front of us and hit Quincy in the foot. He stumbled, staggered, less than ten feet from the edge of the jump.

"Holy hell," I said as he hit and rolled, skidding to the edge and catching himself by his fingertips.

"Go!" he shouted, catching the edge as the SEALs opened fire from their positions, suppressing the machine gun and cutting its steady blast off as it moved toward me. It disappeared about two feet before I crossed its stream, reaching the edge, bending as I stooped to jump—

I leapt like I'd never leapt before, flying through the air with my legs pistoning over empty space. The hole Passerini had made was small, less than five feet, but hey, so was I, if I could just stick my landing—

I slammed into the hole in the wall, the bottom catching me across the shins and causing me to shout in pain. I started to tumble, scratching with my hands to find a hold—

114.

Passerini

Everyone in the room gasped. No one dared breathe, watching make her the leap—easily fifty feet—Sienna Nealon hit the bottom of the door they'd knocked for her—

And started to fall.

"Oh, for Pete's sake—" Gondry said over the line, presumably watching the same thing they were here.

She caught herself. On the edge.

A collective breath was drawn. Not deeply, not until she pulled herself into the hole, a little turtle-like, clenching her knees to her chest.

"That looked like it hurt," Passerini said.

"Yeah," Graves said. The young man was watching intently, but he was still watching. That meant everything was going to turn out all right, didn't it? It was hard to tell, just looking at his face.

115.

Sienna

"You just broke the five-minute barrier," Cassidy said as I dragged myself up to my feet. I was in some store room or something, and bumped into the door, a little wobbly. "You might want to get a move on."

"Next time, you get to fight an entire army while I sit back in an air-conditioned café half a world away and boss you around through a headset," I said, throwing open the door and cutting the pie with my rifle to get out. Two soldiers. They saw me, I shot them. That probably wasn't good. Gunshots echoing in the halls and all that. Now they'd know trouble was coming.

"Oh, I'm not in a café," Cassidy said. "I'm down in Bredoccia. I Airbnb'd an apartment with broadband just for this."

"What?"

"I am speaking to you live from my little fish tank setup, right here in the city. I told you I needed to get close for this," she said. "And now … I'm close."

"You're crazy," I said. "You could have done this from anywhere in the world—"

"No, I couldn't have," she said. "You know how I've managed to keep the world's best hacker at bay all day? It's because I jacked into her actual telecom network hardline. And the only reason she hasn't found me is because I'm been whipping her ass with an external botnet attack all this time that's got her so damned flustered she hasn't bothered to look on the inside yet. I calculate she'll figure it out, though, in the next twelve minutes or less, so you might want to hurry and get me in position for the shutdown in case she's brighter than I think."

"Okay, okay," I said, trying to figure out where in the castle I was. I started to turn right—

"Other way," Cassidy said.

No point arguing. I went left.

"Faster, pussycat," Cassidy said as I broke into a shambling run. My shins were screaming murderously at me and I was oozing blood from more of my body surface than was clean.

"Oh, I'm gonna kill, kill, when I get there," I said.

"Excellent," Cassidy said. "Finally. This has been taking all day. Second door on your left. Guard just inside."

I stopped outside the door and jiggled the handle, flinging it wide. Once that was done, I thrust my rifle in and blind-fired, letting the AK rip off a few rounds as I stayed around the stone jamb. It clicked and I pulled it back to me, fishing for another mag.

"You're out of ammo, but you got him already," Cassidy said. "The rest of the soldiers in there are unarmed. Console jockeys."

"But they're metas," I said, throwing forward the bolt on the AK so it at least looked like it was loaded. I glanced at my pistol; hell if I was going to win this thing on bullets alone. Not against a room full of metahuman Revelen army officers and their superpowers.

"What are you going to do, then?" Cassidy asked. "Less than four minutes."

I took a deep breath, and threw the door open. "Dunno. Something, though." And in I went.

116.

Reed

The arctic winds—

Slipping—

I was so cold.

So.

Very.

Cold.

"Just keep going," Cassidy's voice piped out of my phone, tinny and hard. "Sienna's on it."

"Don't know … how much longer I can …" I was putting everything I had into driving the missiles in a circle around the Arctic. Usually I could have brought warmer winds to sap some of the chill out of the air, but here …

I was freezing.

To death.

And it wasn't quick, either.

"Just hang on," Cassidy said.

"Okay," I said, and I hung on, propelling the missiles forward, pushing them slightly to the side again, running the wide circle around the Arctic once again.

117.

Sienna

"Oh, good, you made it back," Hades said mildly, his hands tucked behind his back as I strolled in with my rifle raised. "I was beginning to worry."

"Aren't you supposed to be on a bridge somewhere, granting boons to the Peverell brothers for having outwitted you?" I asked, sweeping the AK from right to left, illustrating very clearly to a room filled with Revelen army officers manning consoles that I was in no mood for heroic bullshit from any of them.

They got the message.

"Well, I am the true master of Death, I suppose," Hades said, "though I don't have any hallows to unite. I should work on that."

"Try and go up against my Elder Wand here," I said, nodding at the AK. "I think you'll find it beats your impotent little soul grab power in a duel."

He smiled and shook his head. "I wouldn't try to kill you like that—and it wouldn't work on you in any case."

"Glad we're clear on that," I said, and turned my attention to Lethe, who was handcuffed to a steel chair a little ways from where Hades stood. "How are you doing, Grandma?"

"Just sitting here," she said, sounding almost bored, "waiting to see what happens."

"Here's what's going to happen," I said, easing into the room. "Your team is going to get lost," I jerked my head toward the door, "or I'm going to make a mess in here. A big damned mess, akin to the one I made in the army regimental HQ, except I'm not going to need a grenade launcher and you'll all wish I had one, by the end, to make the agony end. Now move, you mass murdering shits, before I single-handedly claw through every one of you for committing war crimes."

That got them moving. Chairborne rangers, most of them; they weren't grunts, and they didn't want to fight. They went for the door in defeated clusters of twos and threes, streaming out until the last.

I kicked the door shut behind them.

"Three minutes," Cassidy said, a little softer this time, like she didn't want to break the spell of the moment.

"I don't think you're going to make it," Hades said, still standing there, hands behind his back.

"You don't think so?" I glanced over the room; Arche and Owens/Yvonne were in the corner to my right, apparently undeterred by my suggestion to leave. Lethe was, of course, still chained to the chair. Hades was smirking.

And Krall was standing next to the map table, offering a little smile of her own. "I don't think so," she said. "I heard the click of your AK bolt outside the door. You're empty."

"Bold gamble," I said, looking down the sight picture at her. After a moment in which her smile never wavered, I tossed the AK aside. "Or good hearing."

"One of those, for certain," she said, cracking her neck, rolling around like she was loosening herself up for a fight. She looked to be in peak Krall condition, not a spot on her uniform, and she started to set her feet in a fighting stance, smiling at me the whole time, just knowing in her heart she was about to tear me limb from limb.

I cocked my head at her. I was bleeding approximately everywhere, my entire body hurt, my knees and shins were killing me from that landing trying to get into the castle. Krall had already kicked the hell out of my ass once, and she looked to be in perfect form.

Me? I'd been through a damned war.

"Fuck you, Krall," I said, and drew my pistol. I fired and fired and fired and fired and fired—

I don't know how many rounds I put through her, but it was all of them that were left in the Grach. When I was done, she took a staggering step back, then another—

And pitched, over, dead, her eyes rolling back in her head.

"Sorry-not-sorry about your girlfriend," I said, tossing down the pistol. I was out of ammo for it, too.

"Easy come, easy go," Hades said with a shrug, taking a step down from where he stood to my level.

"Your concern for the people close to you is breathtaking," I said, taking a limping step forward.

"Your worry for trifling insects is … sad," Hades stepped forward again, finally unclasping his hands and bringing them forward. It looked like he was about to adopt a fighting stance. "This is why you are unworthy of the mantle. You have refused the call, abdicated the responsibility. You have turned down power because you do not understand its worth."

"Let me tell you what you don't understand," I said, taking another limping step forward, blood just dripping off me, most of it my own.

"A lecture from a millennial who has lived millennia less than me," Hades said, cracking his knuckles. "This should be informative."

"I am *Death*," I said, looking him square in the eye. "Not like you; I'm Death to those who earn it, who deserve it, who call it down on their own heads because of their acts."

"You speak of it as though this is some meritocracy," Hades said, still smiling, "when but a week ago they threw you in jail for crimes you did not even commit. They hate you, the world does."

"Well, I don't hate them back," I said, looking at the screen behind him. The missile was still on target, crossing the Canadian border. "I love this world. And the people … well, I'm mostly okay with them. Some suck. Some are good. But I give the benefit of the doubt to the ones I don't know, and on I go. I will protect these people with my life. That's how I'm

Death—because I'm going to bring it to you for threatening them."

"You can barely stand," Hades said, taking a step closer to me.

"And you had to sleep with a four-foot-tall member of a boy band to get laid," I said, prompting him to frown. "Oh, sorry, I thought we were just slinging favorite flaws at each other."

"You have chosen the world over your own family," Hades said.

"This from the guy who's been trying all day to kill me," I said, taking a matching step forward. There was less than ten feet between us now. "Who has his daughter chained to a chair. How important is family to you, exactly?"

Hades took another step, and now he loomed over me. "There can be only one Death, my dear. And I—"

I leapt for him, leading with a hard right cross that caught him on the chin and sent his eyes spinning like slot machine reels. I greeted his belly with a knee and got a well-earned "OOF!" as I drove the air from him, hooked his legs and took him down to his back, driving any residual breath from him as I landed on his chest—

And beat the living piss out of the God of Death with punch after punch.

I stopped after I heard Lethe say, "I think you got him," a little dryly, and the red I'd been seeing sort of cleared out of my eyes. "You might want to work on that nuke," Lethe said when I locked eyes with her, and she tilted her head toward the screen.

"Oh," I said, wiping a smear of blood off my cheek. "Cassidy's been on that since before I even shot Krall. Say hi, Cassidy."

"Hi, Cassidy," came a voice from my belt. "Two minutes … and … never mind."

I was hoping for something really dramatic to indicate we'd done it, but all I got was a little white blip on the screen that … blipped out.

"Done and done," Cassidy said. "Disarming Reed's now so he can stop whining about how cold it is."

Hades let out a long, pained wheeze. "You know … all things considered … I think you'll do … just fine as Death. You're better known these days … anyway."

"Damned right," I said, cracking my bloody knuckles. His face looked like hamburger straight off a store shelf. "I'm going to do you this courtesy, maybe. But listen up, Pops … if I ever see you again, if you stick that pointy nose or widow's peak of yours into one speck of trouble … I'm going to do my job on you, bitchnuts. You get me?"

"Yes, of course," he said. He flopped over onto his belly, throwing one hand forward and dragging himself along, crawling away. "Sounds eminently … fair. Retirement will suit me … just fine … I think I will go to the Villages … in Florida. Lots of death there. And other amenities. Golf carts to ride around in. Buses to Orlando … regular outings …"

"Yeah, well, get lost on that," I said, "some of us still have work to do." I paused. "If this is … amenable to you, Cassidy?"

"I might be able to work something out," she said over the speaker. "To compensate me for my … rage at your little broken toy crashing into my life. I'll be in touch, Hades."

"I … so look forward to it," Hades said. He'd made it to the door and was struggling to open it.

"Oh, for crying out loud," Lethe said and snapped her handcuffs. She walked right over and opened it for him. She even gave him a little kick to push him out. "Do I even need to tell you that I don't want to see you again, either?"

"I think the message is loud and clear," Hades said, and she shut the door on his rump.

"You could have escaped any time?" I asked, blinking at her.

She shrugged. "Another minute … then I might have busted out to give you a hand. As it was …" She smiled, and it really reminded me of Mom, maybe even more for how rarely my mother had smiled. "You had it under control." The smile went a little wider, showing …

Pride?

"Just like you always do," she said, and she put a hand on my shoulder. "Just like you always do."

118.

Passerini

"Yes!" Passerini pumped his fist as the missile tracker showed the ICBM go down somewhere in northern Minnesota with no detonation. His cheer was matched then drowned out by the sound of every seasoned military man in the room losing their collective shit in a very undisciplined display that, had it been under any other circumstance save for a near-miss with a nuke on the continental US, might have made the SecDef extremely unhappy with his fellow officers.

As it was … to hell with it.

"Sir," General Floyd Marks said, "our SEALs are being reinforced, and the Revelen soldiers are starting to lay down arms. Our people are beginning to enter the facility."

"Excellent," Passerini said, turning to retake his seat. "Get them in there and give her some backup. Let's mop this thing up."

119.

Dave Kory

"WOOOOOOHOOOOOO!"

The shout rang across the bullpen. There was a festive, party atmosphere in the office. Someone had brought in beer, someone else had brought out aged whiskey. Probably that bastard Mike. Or one of the hipsters on staff. They had so many.

TIME TO PLAY.

Dave looked around. No one was going to notice him on his phone during this fracas, so he tapped in his code and the app sprang open.

CHAPMAN: It's officially going viral. Search traffic is picking up now. People are getting bored now that the nuke is gone, and guess what's coming up first when they search for 'Sienna Nealon'?

CHALKE: Suppress it, you idiot. You run the damned search engine.

CHAPMAN: We're way past that now. It's over.

BILSON: This wasn't the plan.

CHALKE: This was so far beyond the plan. The military is en route to her as we speak to collect her. What the hell are we supposed to do now? For years we've spun up everyone against her, rallied the troops. The truth is going to bust out. Fingers are going to get pointed, and they're going to get pointed at us.

Dave just stared at the phone. It was like watching a slow-motion disaster, some monster leaping out of the screen and coming right for him.

And then … the answer came.

KORY: We leak it ourselves … in the gentlest possible way. Provide our own explanations in the sourcing that explain every decision, every move. We get ahead of it before it has a chance to come out on his own.

A long pause. One that made him wonder if maybe, just maybe, Dave Kory had just cut his own head off in this little circle. Then:

BILSON: I think he's right. This is the only way to take the wind out of the story. Tell it our way first, before everyone else has a chance to deliver a steaming hot take and start pointing fingers that will lead back to us.

Agreement came quickly; there was no other way, after all. Dave just stared at the screen, already thinking … this was an exclusive … and he was going to write it …

How many clicks would this get?

120.

Sienna

"You know … I really didn't have any idea that coming to Revelen was going to turn out like this," I said, staring at the blank screen frizzing in front of me. Cassidy's feed had gone dead; presumably she'd hit the end of her broadcast after the nukes had gone down, and so here I was, my grandmother next to me, looking at electronic snow as I stood in the empty war room of the Revelen castle. "First I was gonna be a princess. Then I was going to die getting chased by an army. And finally, I bust back into the castle and kick the shit out of Vlad. Hades. Whatever." I looked sideways at my grandmother. "You think I'm going to end up regretting not killing him?"

She was back to be her inscrutable, Sigourney Weaver self. "Maybe. Maybe not. I think you made an impression on him. With your fist, I mean."

"That's the only kind of impression I make on people," I said, and cocked my head, looking back. "Arche. Yvonne. Get the hell out of here."

"Gimme a sec," Yvonne said, nudging Arche who was in some kind of machine coma, attached to a computer in the corner. She started to stir. "Hey, we gotta go," Yvonne said.

Arche blinked a few times, looking around the war room. "What happened here?"

"I happened," I said.

She looked at me, cocked her head, shrugged and said, "Well, that figures." She stood and adjusted her trenchcoat. "Did Hades survive?"

"Barely," I said. "But I wouldn't go taking any future work from him if you value your health."

She showed an almost imperceptible scowl at the corners of her mouth. "He owes me."

"Well, he's crawling around here somewhere," I said, "why don't you go collect? Take it out of his hide for all I care."

"I have no use for human leather," she said, adjusting her coat sleeve, the one she kept that retractable, telescoping metal arm up. "I want what he promised me."

"Yeah, well, I wanted him to be the stable father figure I always lacked growing up, but wishes aren't exactly turning to horses around here if you know what I mean," I said. "Stay out of trouble, Arche."

"How about I just stay out of your way instead?" she asked, shooting me a faint smirk as she disappeared out the door.

"Same difference," I said, turning my attention to Yvonne. "And you … 'Owens.' Same thing."

"Yeah, I'll just give up my life of lucrative crime because you threaten me," she said. "I have definitely learned the error of my ways and will see about carving out an honest living. Maybe minimum wage cashier at McDonald's? I'm all over it."

"But on the benefits side," I said, "you get to live a lot longer than if I catch you doing shit you shouldn't be."

Yvonne seemed to weigh this, head bobbing back and forth as she walked toward the door. "That's true. But on the downside … no money to speak of. Money. Life. You see the conflict here?"

I looked around and found a piece of rock that had apparently been blown in from the tank shell hole I'd in the side of the castle. Snatching it up, I threw it at her, overhand, and she ducked with a grin.

"I'll try and stay out of your way, too, Nealon. Assuming you're even out in the world after this." She winked at me, and then she, too, was gone.

"I'm just letting people walk away left and right today," I said, sighing.

Lethe nodded, standing next to me. "It's like you're developing the concept of mercy. I discovered that one myself a little later in life than you."

I started to collapse, the adrenaline giving out and my legs going with it. I wasn't bleeding anymore, but I'd lost a lot of blood. A great deal of which was still on my clothing and skin.

Lethe caught me and steered me down to a step. I sat down heavily and leaned the small of my back against the step above. "Just … leave me here," I said.

She made a face, a kind of tight, pinched face. "You sure?"

I listened in the distance. "Hear that?"

She listened. "… No?"

"Exactly," I said. "No gunfire outside." I pointed at the hall in the far wall. "That means the battle is over, and the US troops are storming the castle. You need to get out of here if you don't want to get tangled up with them." I sighed again, and it felt like it was the first step before I passed out. "And trust me … you do not want to get caught in their dragnet."

"What about you?" she asked, rising to her feet.

"Just leave me," I said, waving her off.

"All right," she said with a nod, and headed for the door. She paused beside it, turned and said, "I'll see you soon."

"Huh?" I asked.

But she was already gone.

121.

Reed

"Just let them go," Cassidy's voice came, soothing, over the howling wind. "They're disarmed, and there's already a flight of military planes on its way to you to retrieve the plutonium. Let them go."

I let them go. I was so sick of pushing them this far … my fingers were frozen to the bone …

"Where … where am I …?" I asked, teeth chattering as I came around in a cloud bank. The chill was endless … endless … the glare off the cloud tops blinding. I felt like my eyeballs were burning in my skull, and my skin was burning from the cold.

Cassidy's voice was like a whisper in the distance. "I'd tell you to chill out, but it seems kinda counterproductive. Just … hang in place for a second, will you?"

"For what?" I asked. I could almost feel the ice crawling up my skin. The vortex holding me aloft was starting to stutter and die.

I was freezing to death.

My breath was like a block of ice in my chest.

I—

—couldn't—

—breathe—

I started to fall, fall back, infinitely back, out of the sky—

Strong arms caught me as I fell. Warmth surrounded me.

"Hey, kiddo," Veronika Acheron said, a little frost on the tips of her hair, a light plasma fire alight on her fingers. "Hang on and I'll warm you up."

"Please don't set the plane on fire." Greg Vansen's precise, clipped voice was receding. He'd grabbed me somehow—

I lifted my head.

We were on the Concorde.

"Did Cassidy tell you where to find me?" I asked, looking around. I saw them all—even June Randall, though she'd apparently shed her bonds in favor of just chilling in a first-class seat, flipping through a magazine and giving me barely a cocked eyebrow as I spoke.

"Yeah," J.J. piped up from the second row. "She guided us right in, man. Just in time, too, judging by the … uh … ice. I mean, seriously, bro, you look like Old Man Winter gave you a big, sloppy kiss all over."

"Yuck," I said, looking around. Someone was missing, and it only took me a second to figure it out. "Where's Scott?"

"Had to drop him off the coast of Revelen to deal with some stuff," Augustus said. "Per Cassidy."

"So we're taking orders from Cassidy now?" I asked, propping up on my elbows as Veronika turned down the plasma heat a notch. I eyed her, then the plane, and she shrugged. Having flaming plasma aboard a plane probably wasn't the safest thing. She doused the flames without comment.

"Seemed like the thing to do, letting her quarterback," Jamal said, popping his head up from the second row. "She was working with Sienna the whole time, after all. Helped you get those missiles under control." He was staring at me, and my face must have taken a turn. "What?"

That was the question I'd forgotten in the cold. The most important one of all, and I took a breath of the warm, cabin air to ask:

"Where's Sienna?"

122.

Passerini

"Closing in, sir," General Marks said, as Passerini sat in his chair, watching the screen. They had a live feed of some of the SEAL headsets, and the castle corridors were passing at a pretty good clip. Not much in the way of resistance now. "We'll be to her soon."

"Good," Passerini said, and then looked at the phone on the table. "Mr. President … are you following along?"

"I'm following," Gondry's voice came over the line, surprisingly clear and strong, given the day they'd just had. "That … was some damned fine work, SecDef. I'm not too proud to admit … I was wrong. And you—you steered us through that one. I should have listened to you earlier."

Passerini tried to keep his eyebrows under control. He looked around to see if anyone had heard that; Graves was only one close at hand, and he smiled and nodded, as if to say, *Yep. Heard it, too.*

"Thank you, Mr. President," Passerini said. He took a long, slow breath. "But if it's all the same to you … I'll have my resignation letter on your desk tomorrow morning."

"Now?" Gondry asked. "You want to leave … now? After all that? Good God, man, the press is going to eat me alive for letting you go after—"

"I'll … tell them that we had agreed to it in advance, sir,"

Passerini said, putting his hands behind his head. He turned, looked at Graves, and made the *shoo!* sign with his hand. "I'll make sure to take it to the press in a way that doesn't reflect badly on you, Mr. President. I appreciate your recommendation, but I just don't think our goals are going to be compatible going forward. They weren't before, I don't think they're going to change just because of this, and I don't think it's fair to hamstring you with a SecDef who doesn't share your vision."

Graves caught Passerini's eye. He sketched a rough salute. "So long, Admiral," Graves whispered.

Passerini just waved at him as the younger man disappeared. The impersonating an officer thing still rankled him, but he couldn't deny Graves had probably just helped avert a nuclear war. Passerini was a hardass, but he wasn't hardass enough to stick a man in Leavenworth after something like that.

"That's very fair of you, Bruno," President Gondry said at last. "I'm sorry we haven't seen eye to eye. That's probably my fault more than yours. Harmon left me a hell of a mess, and I—I suppose I can get a little … ornery sometimes trying to figure out how to make this presidency my own. I missed some pretty big moves that you tried to point out to me, and … well … maybe you can recommend a replacement who's a middle ground between myself and you. Someone who could help me see things … a little closer to your way."

"I'd be honored to, sir," Passerini said. "You'll have my recommendation along with my letter."

"You're a good man, Passerini. I'm sorry to lose you." Gondry paused. "But … there is one more thing I need from you before you go. One last duty, I guess you could say, in this whole mess clean-up."

Passerini listened. "Yes sir?"

There was a long, long pause before Gondry spoke again. "It's about Sienna Nealon. We can't just let her go." Passerini could almost hear him leaning closer to the phone, all the light-hearted tone gone from his words. "She has to be brought back."

123.

Sienna

I collapsed against the step, unable to hold myself upright any longer. My muscles hurt, my skin hurt, my nerves hurt, and my head—

Yeah, my head was still ringing like one of those giant bells that somebody had gone crazy on with a gong.

"Nealon?" someone asked, kicking in the door. A tall, heavily built black man in military garb hauled himself in, limping along, a good-sized submachine gun clenched in his fists.

"Hey, Quincy," I said. "Or should I say, 'Hey, Terminator.' If you've come to kill me … do it quickly. I don't even think I can fight back right now." I slumped a little further, because I was totally spent.

More footsteps. Bootsteps. Whatever.

Quincy was standing over me a second later, extending a hand. "Can you walk?"

"Jury's out," I said. "Unlike my trial. Bah dum bum! I'm here all week, folks. Mostly because no, I don't think I can walk."

Quincy let out a low chuckle. "Let's get her some help over here." And some SEALs entered the edges of my vision, one of whom was carrying a portable stretcher and put it together right before my very eyes while another gave me a quick once-over.

"How many fingers am I holding up?" the corpsman asked

me.

"More than me," I said, extending my middle one right in his face.

Quincy flat-out laughed. "She'll be fine."

The corpsman didn't seem so sure. "Looks like a concussion and gallons of blood loss, based just on the scabbing I can see through the holes in her clothes. If she was normal person, she'd be dead."

"Let's get you out of here," Quincy said and took one end of the stretcher up all on his own. I felt my weight shift, and lay back. I really couldn't do much of anything at this point.

I'd actually fought myself to the point of collapse.

That was new. Sort of.

"Where am I going?" I asked as they made it to the door, dragging me along into the corridor. Everybody was being way, way too quiet. Like they were carrying my casket out or something.

"We'll start with Ramstein Air Base to get you looked at by the docs," the corpsman said. "After that …"

I saw looks traded. Not good ones.

"Yeah," I said, settling back. Might as well enjoy the ride, since it was likely to be my last for a while.

Home. They were taking me home to the US. And then …

Prison.

Again.

124.

Dave Kory

The party was over in the office, it had moved into one of the local bars here in Williamsburg. Dave had cajoled a few articles and listicles out of people before they departed, but his heart wasn't much in it.

Traffic was down because people were celebrating all over the country right now. Hell, all over the world.

But that was fine. Good, even. It gave him a chance to sharpen the scoop he was going to go live with shortly. He blinked, trying to get some of the tiredness out of his eyes as he re-read the same passage for the dozenth time.

Sources in the Gondry administration have confirmed that while rumors had been circulating about a security camera video proving Nealon's innocence, no one within the government had seen the video until it broke into widespread circulation online during the height of the Revelen crisis.

Dave took a breath, blotting at his eyes. Not his finest writing, but he was tired, and he'd just watched this drama play out on a global scale. But he needed to get this up, and fast. And into the hands of certain people of influence, who could spread the message across social media, and in front of enough eyeballs to make an impact.

He went back to editing.

And while there is little to recommend Nealon's guilt in the now-surfaced video, it is hardly a total exoneration of her for other crimes, a source in the Department of Justice pointed out. Other investigations are ongoing, linking Nealon to a variety of charges up to and including murder …

That was the money shot. Give a little with one hand, take with the other.

This would have to do. It was just the vanguard of their plan, after all. It'd get good clicks, get circulated. If the story ever blew big because of some future break in Nealon's story, he'd repost it to the home page, make sure it got some more eyeballs. That was the nice thing about writing a Cover Your Ass piece like this. If someone came along in a year and said something like, "Man, you guys really didn't cover Sienna Nealon's exoneration very well," he could just shoot them the link to this. Boom. Answered.

And if they pointed out that he'd run ten thousand pieces talking about what a garbage person she was to the one, little one that exonerated her?

Well, to hell with them. Dave hit publish and logged off. No one was even clicking tonight anyway.

125.

The Watcher

He sat in the darkness, staring at the flickering screen. It had been suspenseful, watching it all unfold, the cool air around him unbroken save for the occasional rumble in the distance.

And now … the click of a door.

"I have some bad news for you, my friend," came a voice from a silhouette in the doorway. It was him—and he dragged himself in quite haggardly, slumped of shoulder and with a limp. "You are going to have to move on now, I am afraid."

The Watcher rose. "You cannot compel me to leave. We have an arrangement."

Hades stepped in front of the television. His face was bloody. Beaten. Bruises dotted his cheeks and he looked to be missing at least one tooth. "If you do not leave now, via the tunnels," he pointed past the Watcher, "the United States government will likely be kicking down your door in minutes.

The Watcher stared at him coldly. "He is not ready yet." His gaze slid around to the cylinder wherein the Sleeper rested. "You are a fool. You have let your own blood vanquish you. Well, I am not so easily dissuaded. I will show her—"

Hades snapped a hand around his wrist. "You will do nothing of the sort. You will leave her be and gather your … cargo …" he looked at the cylinder, "and get the hell out of here before you cause yourself and me further problems. You will not fight her this day."

The Watcher pushed back. "You are weak, Hades. Too weak to stop me if I go up there. And you know I will not fail with her. I have never failed."

"So you mean to kill her?" Hades lifted a hand. "Test me, if you care to. See if I can't rip your withered soul out of your body before you step one more foot."

The Watcher stared at him. Wavered.

"Have it your way, then," the Watcher said. "We will go—for now. But when the Sleeper wakes—"

"Yes, yes," Hades said, waving a hand at him as he went past, bound for the tunnels that lay beyond, in the darkness. "You have regaled me with this particular tale over and over again. When you leave the dark, she will die, blah blah blah. You should really stop being so tiresome, my friend. Learn to live in the now." And he disappeared into the dark. "And don't try and go after her today. I will know, and I will rip your soul asunder."

"I will not," the Watcher said to the fading shadow of the God of Death. "Not today." And he turned to look back at the cylinder where the Sleeper waited. "For I must gather things together … and go." He took a step forward and put his hand on the cool side of the cylinder. "For now. But soon the wait will be over. And Sienna Nealon—"

"Will die, yes, yes," Hades's voice echoed back through the tunnels. "You are such a drama queen."

The Watcher narrowed his eyes and said no more. But she would die.

He would see to it.

Just a little longer.

Without another word, he set about his task, preparing the cylinder for transport, to take it somewhere that would be safe, would not be disturbed … until the awakening.

126.

Sienna

"Where are we?" I asked as I stirred to consciousness, the skies a bright orange shining through a nearby porthole window. I was on a military transport plane, lying on the deck, surrounded by military guys in jump seats, and to my right was Warren Quincy, watching over me with a careful eye. As one should, for a dangerous prisoner.

"Over Germany now," the corpsman asked, checking the IV that he'd strapped into my arm.

"Great," I said, and pulled the IV.

"Hey, you shouldn't—"

"I'm fine," I said, sitting upright. I felt a little lightheaded, but most of the pain was already fading. I had a pretty thick layer of blood over the whole of me, most of which (I thought) was mine, but none of which was going anywhere without a shower and some intense scrubbing.

I just hoped that whatever prison they tossed me in, they at least went easy on the firehose. Or my skin healed first. Whichever. Beggars can't be choosers and all that.

"Just ... take it easy," the corpsman said, and moved off to one of the jump seats that lined the interior of the plane's cargo bay. I gave it a look around; it looked like a C-130 Hercules, a plane I'd become intimately acquainted with back when I was in government service. The toilet was a curtain and a hole, and smelled like you'd expect an open latrine to smell.

Quincy nodded me over, and I took it as a sign of respect coupled with a reasonable attempt to keep danger close in his sights. I wandered his way, watching the SEALs watch me. Not a one of them didn't have a weapon close at hand, which, let's face it, was smart.

"You had quite a day," Quincy said. He was wearing a headset that was plugged into a jack behind him, but apparently could hear me just fine through it.

"Yeah, but I didn't get shot in the leg and nearly plummet off a cliff," I said, "so congrats to you for surviving, too."

He broke into a smile. Very definitely different than how he'd appeared when we'd squared off back in January. "Respect, Nealon." And he raised his hand.

I fist bumped him. "Don't worry. I'm not going to test you."

He raised an eyebrow. "Oh?"

I shook my head. "Nah. I'll go quietly."

He just stared. Nodded. "Good. Have a seat."

I drew a long breath, then sat down next to him. He fiddled with his headset, then handed it over to me.

"What?" I asked, looking at it. "I can hear fine. Ish. Still a slight ringing. Or maybe that's the engine noise—"

"Put it on."

I eyed the headset. "If there's N'Sync playing on this, all that stuff I said about going quietly is out the window—along with you."

He cackled. "Put it on."

I did.

"Nealon, are you online?" came the static, slightly crackling voice of Bruno Passerini.

"Hammer," I said, "uh, I mean—Mr. Secretary. Sir."

"I think you've earned the privilege of calling me 'Hammer' if you want," Passerini said. He had that same tired, been-through-a-war tone that I probably did. "How are you feeling?"

"Like hell."

"Lot of that going around," he said. "But at least you aren't feeling like you're in hell."

"Well, if you want to go by the somewhat literal definition,"

I said, "being that I did spend this last day in Hades's kingdom … I kind of have been through hell today."

Passerini chuckled. "You've got a way about you, Nealon. You going to be all right? Do I need to have the crew put in at Ramstein for medical care?"

I pondered what he meant by that. Was it, maybe, a veiled offer to get me on the ground, where I could escape to safety? I had a fleeting vision of disappearing over a barbed wire fence, of wearing my hood up as I wandered down the streets of Europe—

And I'd never see home again, not even for a minute.

I'd always be looking over my shoulder. For the rest of my life.

Ugh. Prison again. I could only hope the damned Cube had been utterly destroyed in that little riot I'd caused.

"No, I'll be fine," I said, letting go of that idea. I'd done the running thing. I'd done the fighting thing. Hell, I'd just done a shitload of the killing thing.

No more.

"I'm having them direct your flight to return to Joint Base Andrews straightaway, then. You'll refuel in mid-air."

"First class service," I said. "Except the toilets on these Herky-birds suck ass. You really ought to do something about that, you know, as SecDef."

He laughed again. "I don't think even I have power over that. But … I have been ordered to get you back to Washington ASAP."

"I figured as much," I said, feeling that slow creep of resignation run over my scalp. "And I told Quincy here—I won't fight. My running days are done."

"That's good," Passerini said, "because I need a hole in that plane like I need a hole in my budget for next year. And I'd hate for my last act as Secretary of Defense to be tainted by such an inauspicious end as that when it could be … a little more triumphant."

I tried to parse what he said, but gave up after a couple attempts. "No idea what you're talking about there."

"You really don't, do you?" Passerini asked. "Well, in that

case … let me spell it out. These are my orders," and his voice changed to a slightly more serious timbre. "'*Deliver Sienna Nealon to the White House, Washington, DC, with all haste for immediate commendation. Details of her clemency to be worked out later. Signed, Richard Gondry*,' and well … you know the rest."

"Wait," I said, "… what … what did you just say? Was that …" I couldn't hear right, could I? My ears had taken some pretty severe damage today, after all, hadn't they?

He hadn't said 'clemency.' Or 'commendation.' Those were just engine noise. Ringing in the ears.

Weren't they?

The man who'd gone most of his professional life being known as 'Hammer' laughed on the other end of the connection. "You heard it just fine." He turned serious again, but in a different way, one that was more … heartfelt. "Congratulations, Sienna.

"You're coming home a hero."

Sienna Nealon Will Return In

FLASHBACK

OUT OF THE BOX, BOOK 23

Coming December 4, 2018!

Author's Note

Thanks for reading! If you want to know immediately when future books become available, take sixty seconds and sign up for my NEW RELEASE EMAIL ALERTS by visiting my website. I don't sell your information and I only send out emails when I have a new book out. The reason you should sign up for this is because I don't always set release dates, and even if you're following me on Facebook (robertJcrane (Author)) or Twitter (@robertJcrane), it's easy to miss my book announcements because...well, because social media is an imprecise thing.

Come join the discussion on my website:
http://www.robertjcrane.com!

Cheers,
Robert J. Crane

ACKNOWLEDGMENTS

Editing was handled expertly by Sarah Barbour as per usual, with Jeff Bryan and Jo Evans batting cleanup. Many thanks to all of them.

Once again, the illustrious illustrator Karri Klawiter produced the cover. artbykarri.com is where you can find her amazing works.

Nick Bowman of nickbowman-editing.com provided the formatting that turned this into an actual book and ebook.

And thanks as always to my family – wife, parents, in-laws and occasionally my kids, for keeping a lid on the craziness so I can do this job.

Other Works by Robert J. Crane

The Girl in the Box *and* Out of the Box

Contemporary Urban Fantasy

Alone: The Girl in the Box, Book 1
Untouched: The Girl in the Box, Book 2
Soulless: The Girl in the Box, Book 3
Family: The Girl in the Box, Book 4
Omega: The Girl in the Box, Book 5
Broken: The Girl in the Box, Book 6
Enemies: The Girl in the Box, Book 7
Legacy: The Girl in the Box, Book 8
Destiny: The Girl in the Box, Book 9
Power: The Girl in the Box, Book 10

Limitless: Out of the Box, Book 1
In the Wind: Out of the Box, Book 2
Ruthless: Out of the Box, Book 3
Grounded: Out of the Box, Book 4
Tormented: Out of the Box, Book 5
Vengeful: Out of the Box, Book 6
Sea Change: Out of the Box, Book 7
Painkiller: Out of the Box, Book 8
Masks: Out of the Box, Book 9
Prisoners: Out of the Box, Book 10
Unyielding: Out of the Box, Book 11
Hollow: Out of the Box, Book 12
Toxicity: Out of the Box, Book 13
Small Things: Out of the Box, Book 14
Hunters: Out of the Box, Book 15
Badder: Out of the Box, Book 16
Apex: Out of the Box, Book 18
Time: Out of the Box, Book 19
Driven: Out of the Box, Book 20
Remember: Out of the Box, Book 21
Hero: Out of the Box, Book 22
Flashback: Out of the Box, Book 23* *(Coming November 6, 2018!)*
Walk Through Fire: Out of the Box, Book 24* *(Coming in 2019!)*

World of Sanctuary

Epic Fantasy

Defender: The Sanctuary Series, Volume One
Avenger: The Sanctuary Series, Volume Two
Champion: The Sanctuary Series, Volume Three
Crusader: The Sanctuary Series, Volume Four
Sanctuary Tales, Volume One - A Short Story Collection
Thy Father's Shadow: The Sanctuary Series, Volume 4.5
Master: The Sanctuary Series, Volume Five
Fated in Darkness: The Sanctuary Series, Volume 5.5
Warlord: The Sanctuary Series, Volume Six
Heretic: The Sanctuary Series, Volume Seven
Legend: The Sanctuary Series, Volume Eight
Ghosts of Sanctuary: The Sanctuary Series, Volume Nine
Call of the Hero: The Sanctuary Series, Volume Ten* *(Coming Late 2018!)*

A Haven in Ash: Ashes of Luukessia, Volume One *(with Michael Winstone)*
A Respite From Storms: Ashes of Luukessia, Volume Two *(with Michael Winstone)*
A Home in the Hills: Ashes of Luukessia, Volume Three* *(with Michael Winstone—Coming Mid to Late 2018!)*

Southern Watch

Contemporary Urban Fantasy

Called: Southern Watch, Book 1
Depths: Southern Watch, Book 2
Corrupted: Southern Watch, Book 3
Unearthed: Southern Watch, Book 4
Legion: Southern Watch, Book 5
Starling: Southern Watch, Book 6
Forsaken: Southern Watch, Book 7* *(Coming August 7, 2018!)*
Hallowed: Southern Watch, Book 8* *(Coming Late 2018/Early 2019!)*

The Shattered Dome Series

(with Nicholas J. Ambrose)
Sci-Fi

Voiceless: The Shattered Dome, Book 1
Unspeakable: The Shattered Dome, Book 2* *(Coming 2018!)*

The Mira Brand Adventures

Contemporary Urban Fantasy

The World Beneath: The Mira Brand Adventures, Book 1
The Tide of Ages: The Mira Brand Adventures, Book 2
The City of Lies: The Mira Brand Adventures, Book 3
The King of the Skies: The Mira Brand Adventures, Book 4
The Best of Us: The Mira Brand Adventures, Book 5
We Aimless Few: The Mira Brand Adventures, Book 6* *(Coming 2018!)*

Liars and Vampires

(with Lauren Harper)
Contemporary Urban Fantasy

No One Will Believe You: Liars and Vampires, Book 1
Someone Should Save Her: Liars and Vampires, Book 2
You Can't Go Home Again: Liars and Vampires, Book 3
In The Dark: Liars and Vampires, Book 4
Her Lying Days Are Done: Liars and Vampires, Book 5* *(Coming October 2018!)*
Heir of the Dog: Liars and Vampires, Book 6* *(Coming November 2018!)*
Hit You Where You Live: Liars and Vampires, Book 7* *(Coming December 2018!)*

* Forthcoming, Subject to Change

Made in the USA
Las Vegas, NV
15 October 2023